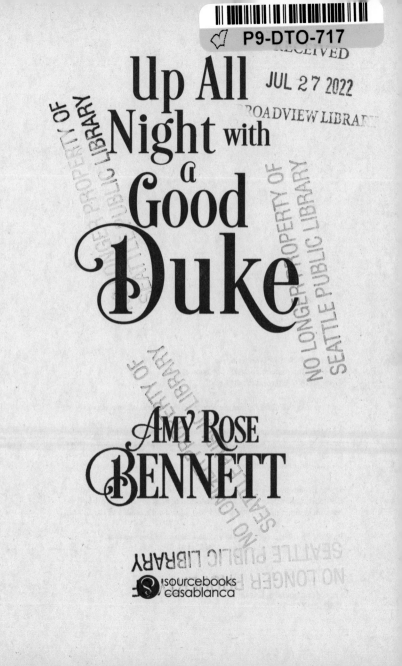

Up All Night with Good Duke

Amy Rose Bennett

sourcebooks
casablanca

Published by Sourcebooks Casablanca, an imprint of Sourcebooks
P.O. Box 4410, Naperville, Illinois 60567-4410
(630) 961-3900
sourcebooks.com

Printed and bound in Canada.
MBP 10 9 8 7 6 5 4 3 2 1

To my darling husband, Richard,
I love you now and always.

Chapter One

Somersetshire. Spring 1858

APPARENTLY, THERE ARE SOME THINGS A YOUNG WOMAN shouldn't say, especially if that woman is genteelly impoverished and must behave decorously at all times in order to maintain her teaching position at an exclusive young ladies' finishing school in Bath.

So when Mrs. Parsons, the exacting headmistress of the Avon Academy for Young Ladies of Quality, summoned Miss Artemis Jones to her private study and then accused her of corrupting her charges' minds by exposing them to an entirely frivolous, some might even say *dangerous* novel, Artemis really shouldn't have muttered "Beelzebub's ballocks" beneath her breath.

"I beg your pardon." Behind her wire-rimmed spectacles, Mrs. Parsons's pale eyes narrowed with dislike and suspicion. "What did you say, Miss Jones?"

Artemis attempted a look of innocence while she inwardly cursed her ill-advised slip of the tongue. "I said, 'Of course, Mrs. Parsons.' I do see your point. *Sense and Sensibility* is entirely frivolous. It teaches young women nothing at all about the value of exercising good judgment or that possessing an overly romantic nature can lead one into trouble. Or that it would be wise for women to develop the skills, and therefore the means, to support themselves considering the protection of a male—whether husband, or father, or another form of guardian—cannot always be relied upon in this life. I could go on, but heaven forfend, I fear that I might inadvertently corrupt your mind too."

Mrs. Parsons bristled like a cat set out in the rain. "Sarcasm does not become you." Raising her bony hand, she then held her thumb and index finger an inch apart. "You are skating this close to dismissal. Do I make myself clear?"

Artemis tried to look contrite, which was no mean feat considering she didn't think much of the headmistress or the curriculum of her finishing school. But needs must when the devil drives, so Artemis bowed her head. "Perfectly. Although, it was only one student who read—"

Mrs. Parsons slapped the leather blotter on her desk. "And that is one student too many," she snapped. "You know as well as I that these young girls have impressionable minds. Aside from that, I shouldn't need to remind you that reading novels for pleasure is *not* part of our curriculum. Parents and guardians do not pay me good money to have their daughters' time wasted or, worse, have their heads filled with utter nonsense. These girls need to acquire solid accomplishments. Aside from displaying good manners, excellent deportment, and impeccable grooming at all times, they should be adept musically and artistically and be able to dance with grace, speak French moderately well, and be skilled at needlework and balancing domestic accounts. They should also have mastered the art of maintaining polite conversation and to have a thorough understanding of etiquette."

"And a thorough knowledge of geography, literature, and history." Artemis felt compelled to remind her employer about the subjects *she* taught the school's pupils. If she were ever fortunate enough to realize her own dream of starting an academic college for women, there wouldn't be a dancing master or an etiquette manual in sight.

Mrs. Parsons sniffed, her manner as prickly as the black woolen gown she wore. "Our girls only need to know the rudiments. Just enough to enable them to converse without making fools of themselves. It wouldn't do for our young women to graduate here with *more* knowledge than the men who will court them." She shuddered dramatically. "No gentleman wishes to wed a woman with a masculine level of intelligence. It's entirely unnatural."

Artemis pressed her lips together to quell a derisive huff. Oh, the things she could say to counter that. Instead, she uttered the sort of unpalatable tripe Mrs. Parsons wished to hear. "Yes, you're quite right. As if a woman's intellect could ever match that of a man's. After all, we are the weaker sex."

The headmistress nodded her approval. "Exactly, Miss Jones. A woman must know her place in the world. And that is what the Avon Academy excels at. Showing each young woman that her *rightful* place is at her husband's side, managing his domestic affairs, bearing his children, keeping him entertained, and being an indispensable helpmeet." One talon-like finger tapped the cover of Volume I of *Sense and Sensibility*. "She won't learn any of those things in ridiculous novels like these."

"No, of course not," agreed Artemis. "I don't know what I was thinking lending an impressionable student such a terrible, perhaps even subversive book. It won't happen again."

"No. It won't." Mrs. Parsons lifted her chin. "Because I've confiscated the whole set. And indeed all the other novels in your private quarters."

"I beg your pardon?" Artemis couldn't hide the outrage in her voice. It shook with the force of it and momentarily masked her fear that the headmistress could have unearthed something even more damning than her treasured collection of novels by Jane Austen. For instance, the latest Gothic romance manuscript her alter ego, Lydia Lovelace, was presently penning. "You...you went through my belongings?"

"I did." Mrs. Parsons rose to her feet and, eyes flashing, looked down her beak of a nose at Artemis. "You've proven yourself to be untrustworthy, Miss Jones. And you shan't have your dreadful novels back until you leave this establishment. Which might be sooner rather than later. One more black mark against your name, and you'll be dismissed, do you understand? And do stop gaping at me like a landed carp. The look does not become you."

Sometime during the course of the headmistress's admonitory speech, it seemed Artemis's jaw had indeed become unhinged. She shut her mouth with a snap and somehow swallowed her pride along with her burning anger. "Yes, Mrs. Parsons. I understand."

Dropping her gaze lest it further betray the depth of her ire, she then dipped into a respectful curtsy, something she rarely did. As much as she loathed the Avon Academy—indeed how she'd endured working here for three years quite amazed her—she couldn't afford to lose this position. Because if she did, she'd end up living with her fearsome aunt Roberta, Lady Wagstaff, who would parade her like a prize heifer for sale through London's ballrooms. Her aunt's unrelenting but ultimately fruitless quest was to marry both Artemis and her younger sister, Phoebe, off to "gentlemen of means." That eventuality didn't bear thinking about. Phoebe was dying to marry, but at nine-and-twenty, Artemis was firmly on the spinster's shelf and there she meant to stay.

Artemis was about to take her leave—it was only four o'clock in the afternoon, and she still had mountains of work to do before she could retire to her room to alternately fume and lick her wounds in private—when Mrs. Parsons pushed an envelope across the desk. "Some correspondence for you, Miss Jones. See that you read it in your own time."

"Yes, of course. Thank you." Artemis picked up the letter, and after she'd ascertained the sender was her dear friend, Lucy Bertram, she slid it into the pocket of her cambric pinafore. "I shan't look at it until after supper and prayers when the girls are all settled for the night," she added for good measure, even though that was a lie.

Indeed, as soon as Artemis gained the corridor, she ducked into a nearby music room that was currently vacant. Lucy, a baronet's daughter and her oldest friend from childhood— they'd both grown up in the hamlet of Heathwick Green near Hampstead Heath—was only a year younger than Artemis and equally happy with her lot in life as a spinster. She did write, but not all that often, so it was decidedly odd that she'd sent *another* letter on the heels of her last one, which had arrived but a fortnight ago.

A peculiar mixture of anticipation, curiosity, and concern buzzed about inside Artemis as she cracked the envelope's seal, unfolded the parchment, and started to read.

Dearest Artemis…

Lucy began in her beautifully flowing handwriting.

I hope this letter finds you well. I'm afraid I'm not particularly "in the pink" at the present moment, even though I stated that I was so in my last letter. And no doubt you're wondering why...

Actually, to be perfectly honest, I'm all at sixes and sevens. In fact, my hand is quite literally shaking as I write these words, so please do forgive my poor penmanship and what might seem like my sudden, entirely out-of-character penchant for hyperbole. I do not mean to cause alarm. But you see, the news I'm about to impart is quite disconcerting, if not altogether terrifying—to me at least.

My papa has decreed that I should have a Season and absolutely must wed by summer's end. And I... Frankly, I can think of nothing worse. At all. I'm not sure what terrifies me the most: the thought of marriage to some man who doesn't give a jot about me or my ambitions in life, or the idea of actually having to venture into society to begin with. And the idea of courting... I'd rather eat nothing but chalk and charcoal for a year and a day than set foot in one of London's ballrooms.

What? Artemis's jaw dropped open for the second time that afternoon, and she sank onto the piano stool behind her. Her knees suddenly felt as insubstantial as a freshly unmolded flummery.

Poor sweet Lucy. Just like Artemis, her dear friend had no love for London with its crowded, noisy streets and hectic pace. Or its members of high society. Gatherings any larger than a small, intimate dinner party or an afternoon tea with close acquaintances were anathema to her. Indeed, on countless occasions, Artemis had witnessed how Lucy's tongue would tie itself into hopeless knots when trying to summon a response to the simplest of questions from a stranger, and how she would blush redder than a platter of roasted beets when even a smattering of attention was directed her way.

Her heart clenching with sympathy for her friend's plight, Artemis quickly perused the remaining paragraphs of the letter.

> I'm afraid there's no reasoning with Papa. He's absolutely determined that this will happen, despite my genuine trepidation and the fact that I'm surely too spinsterish and singular in my habits. Even though he will never admit it, I suspect he is terribly short of funds. No doubt his last expedition to Ceylon depleted the family coffers considerably. And then, my brother's tendency to live extravagantly has not helped. But of course, Monty is being as obstinate as an ox and will not even lift his little finger to win the hand of some biddable heiress. So apparently I am to be the sacrificial lamb who must save the family. Naturally, marrying me off to the highest bidder will certainly reduce Father's—or perhaps I should say our—financial difficulties. But I, for one, am not willing to pay the price. I cannot. I will not.
>
> Artemis, you know better than anyone that I am not equipped for any of this. Unlike you, I've never even had one Season. You, my fearless, indomitable friend, are definitely cut from a different cloth.

Oh, hell's blasted bells. Artemis closed her eyes. Dread coiled through her belly. She knew what was coming even before she read her friend's next words. Lucy went on:

*And so I had a slightly mad, but hopefully not alto-
gether unappealing idea. If you were by my side, my
dearest Artemis, helping me to navigate society's treacherous hunting grounds while fending off any potential
suitors—I'm sure they will all be objectionable with not a
Mr. Darcy or honorable version of Mr. Rochester amongst
them—I'd perhaps stand a fighting chance of surviving
unscathed this Season. I'd be forever grateful. Of course,
I know I'm putting you in a horribly difficult position—
asking you to give up your post at the Avon Academy to
be my companion for a few months. But I need you most
desperately, and I do so hope you will consider my request.*

*Who knows, perhaps you could even court a sponsor
for your own venture. Then you'd have your college and
never have to work at a place like Mrs. Parsons's horrid
finishing school ever again. And of course, we could reconvene our Byronic Book Club meetings with dear Jane at
her grandfather's bookstore. Just think of the fun we could
have, plotting and planning our futures while simultaneously swooning over our favorite book beaux. It would be
like the old days. The three of us—unconventional and
unrepentant—the heroines of our very own stories, forg-
ing our way through the world on our own terms. (Well,
it's a lovely dream anyway.)*

I await your reply with bated breath.

Ever your devoted friend,
Lucy

Artemis blew out a deep sigh as she rose to her feet and wandered over to a nearby window. For long moments, she stared

out of the rain-streaked mullion panes and contemplated her future. The options that might be open to her if she were brave enough to chart a course that was different from the plodding pedestrian path she'd been following for years. While she loved being an author of lurid Gothic romance novels—her publisher advertised them as "literary" penny bloods—it was, for obvious reasons, a clandestine career and indeed must remain so if she were to achieve her ultimate goal. Unfortunately, her book sales, while steady, were such that it would still take her a few more years to save sufficient funds to start her ladies' college. The same could be said for the wages she earned as a teacher. But if she could find a wealthy, forward-thinking patroness to support her project this Season while also coming to the aid of her closest friend…

If she did agree to Lucy's plan, she'd somehow have to manage both Aunt Roberta's and Phoebe's expectations. As soon as they learned Artemis would be in London for the Season, the cat really would be set amongst the pigeons. There'd be little respite from their nagging to "do her duty and find a husband." But she'd also have both Lucy and Jane to confide in when it all got too much to bear. Perhaps it *would* be like old times.

"Well," Artemis murmured at last as she pushed the letter back into her pocket, "nothing ventured, nothing gained." Her mind was made up. She couldn't abandon her darling friend to society's wolves. And she owed it to herself to at last pursue her own dream. Come what may.

Her heart tripping with anticipation, Artemis lifted her chin and marched straight back to the headmistress's office. After a cursory knock, she entered and announced with a wide smile and not one iota of regret, "Mrs. Parsons, I'd like my books back, please. I'm tendering my resignation, effective immediately."

Chapter Two

London

As Artemis stepped off the train onto Paddington Station's teeming Platform One, she squared her shoulders and pushed her way through the heaving fray of passengers and those there to greet or bid them farewell. Overhead, the enormous vaulted wrought-iron and glass roof revealed a leaden gray sky, while all around the platform swirled clouds of gritty steam that had been belched from the departing train on the adjacent track. The acrid odor of jostling bodies and burning coal filled the air.

Old Nick's nob. Artemis winced as a liveried footman accidentally elbowed her in the ribs. The hustle and bustle of city life was something she did not miss. At all. But it was too late to turn back now. She was actually here, in London, about to commence a brand-new chapter of her life. A *better* chapter. All going well…

Except things started to *not* go very well within a surprisingly short space of time. Within fifteen minutes, Artemis had ascertained that her two traveling trunks had gone missing and all she had in her possession besides her overstuffed carpetbag and coin purse was a great deal of simmering frustration.

After filing a "Missing Items" report at the Lost Property Office, she at last made her way toward the station's exit. Before she'd departed from Bath, she'd sent a telegram to Aunt Roberta and Phoebe where they resided at Wagstaff House in Cadogan Square, and one to Lucy, to let them all know she'd quit her post and would soon be arriving in London, but she hadn't mentioned precisely when.

While she wanted nothing more than to stay with Lucy, Artemis felt she owed it to her sister, Phoebe, to spend some time with her before the Season proper commenced in a fortnight. In any event, whether Artemis liked it or not, she was going to have to grin and bear it and stay with her difficult and overbearing aunt, at least for a little while.

Hefting her carpetbag from one gloved hand to the other, Artemis emerged onto Praed Street and scowled at the crowded pavement and traffic-congested road, then up at the sullen sky. It had begun to rain, and of course, she'd neglected to pack an umbrella. Thank goodness she had enough money to pay the cab fare to Cadogan Square. She'd rather not have to contend with a packed-to-the-gunwales omnibus.

Once she spied a gap in the sea of bodies and mushrooming umbrellas, she forged her way to the curb and for several frustrating minutes tried but failed to wave down a cab. The rain was growing heavier by the moment—the icy, needlelike drops pricked at her face and a sliver of her nape not protected by her bonnet and jacket's collar—and just when she thought she'd best look for an omnibus after all, a hackney splashed to a halt a few feet away. Artemis rushed toward the cab's door... and then crashed straight into an unyielding wall of masculine muscle that hadn't been there a moment ago.

What the devil?

As Artemis's shoulder connected with the wool-clad chest of the tall, solidly built stranger, she skidded and stumbled, and her full-to-bursting carpetbag flew out of her hand and onto the pavement. The battered clasp came undone, and several books fell out, skittering across the wet flagstones toward the gutter and the cab's wheels.

"Lucifer's love truncheon," Artemis muttered without thinking. And then her heart did an odd little tumble when she realized that the man had put out a hand to stop her from slipping. His fingers were curled about her elbow, and when she looked up, her gaze collided with his. Caught.

Lingered.

Lucifer's love truncheon indeed…

"I beg your pardon." The man's voice was a deep velvet stroke that Artemis felt all the way to her bones. From beneath the shadow of his top hat, storm-cloud gray eyes bore into hers and she was momentarily transfixed. Frozen.

It didn't seem to matter that her carpetbag was on the ground with her books, getting wetter by the moment.

Because this man. He was… Artemis's befogged brain struggled to function. To formulate a single thought. Retrieve a single word.

She had the oddest sensation of falling, plunging, as though this stranger's gaze was a turbulent ocean and she was being pulled into a maelstrom. Sucked below, sinking deeper and deeper. Or perhaps she'd been struck by lightning. Awareness shot through her body like a searing hot electrical charge, heating her blood and scalding her cheeks, despite the chill rain trickling down the back of her neck.

Artemis instinctively recognized this man was as formidable as a force of nature. And just as dangerous. Not only was he as handsome as sin—all austere good looks with his sharply cut jaw and jet-black hair save for a touch of silver at the temples— but he exuded an innate authority.

He was clearly an aristocrat. Wealthy, beautiful, and powerful beyond imagining.

Beneath the scent of damp wool and starched linen, even his cologne—clean and sharp like the sea—smelled powerful.

Somehow Artemis absorbed all of these impressions within a few seconds. Between the space of one wildly pounding heartbeat and the next.

Then the stranger spoke again, rousing her from her stupor. "My sincerest apologies. It seems we were both intent on securing the same cab."

Artemis swallowed. Drew a shaky breath. A shiver dashed down her spine, and she wondered how she could feel hot yet so cold at the same time. As though she'd suddenly been afflicted by a strange fever. "Yes…" she managed at last. "May I offer my apologies as well. I was in a rush and not paying attention to my surroundings."

"No harm done at all. Not to me at least." The gentleman at last released her arm. "But your books… Let me make amends for my own carelessness."

In the next instant, he'd crouched down to retrieve her scattered belongings. His expertly tailored black trousers pulled tight over his muscular thighs, and Artemis had to remind herself not to stare at his legs or any other distinctly masculine parts in their immediate vicinity. *Artemis Jones, stop gawking like an utter ninny*, she silently admonished herself as she dropped to the ground beside him. *He's not the first indecently handsome man you've ever met. You'd do well to remember that the road to ruin is paved with lustful thoughts.*

Reaching for Mary Wollstonecraft's *A Vindication of the Rights of Woman*, she began, "You really don't have to—" but then her breath caught as the stranger grasped the book at the very same moment. Their fingers brushed, and Artemis felt a spark for a second time. An electrical crackle that mysteriously penetrated the kid leather of her glove, then radiated up her arm, making her flesh burn and tingle. Thunder rumbled overhead.

The man withdrew his hand, but she sensed his gaze upon her, studying her face beneath the brim of her sodden bonnet. Had he felt that strange flicker of connection too?

"It's the least I can do," he said, handing over *Frankenstein; or, The Modern Prometheus* along with Artemis's own novel, *Lady Violetta and the Vengeful Vampyre*. One of his slashing black brows arched when he caught sight of the latter title. Or was it Mary Shelley's book that he looked upon with disdain? Or that of Mary Shelley's mother, Mary Wollstonecraft? The woman's reputation was much maligned in some circles.

His next observation made it clear. "I see you've a penchant for 'horrid' novels." His mouth twitched with a smile that bordered on sardonic. Even though his opinion shouldn't matter, his change in demeanor rankled Artemis more than she could say.

"The more horrid, the better," she rejoined, stuffing her books back into her bag and securing the clasp with jerky movements. Ignoring his proffered hand, she climbed to her feet, hoisting her carpetbag as she rose. "It might also shock you to know that I'm an outspoken bluestocking. And proud of it."

He stood too. "There's nothing wrong with being a bluestocking." His slightly amused manner seemed to belie his pronouncement though. Artemis bristled at the thought he might be laughing at her, but before she could mount any sort of defense, he reached for the hackney's door. "You take the cab. I insist." His good breeding required him to play the gen-tleman, despite the fact he clearly didn't think much of her taste in books.

Artemis's reply was stiff with grudging politeness. "Thank you."

She gave the driver her direction, then climbed into the dark confines of the carriage. It contained a musty odor, redolent of damp leather, tobacco smoke, horses, and stale sweat, and she wrinkled her nose. If it was the least bit socially acceptable— and the stranger hadn't mocked her reading choices—she would have invited him to share the hackney, just for the chance to smell his tempting cologne. She might be an uncon-ventional bluestocking who would never be a perfect model of gentility, but she wasn't foolish. She had to maintain a veneer of respectability.

Once she'd deposited her bag on the seat, she reached for the door handle and was surprised to see the stranger still standing there. Raindrops glanced off his hat and impossibly wide shoulders, but he seemed oblivious to the downpour. Even though his perfectly chiseled mouth had compressed into a hard line, the light in his storm-cloud eyes was almost wistful rather than disdainful as he regarded her. "I wish you good day, Miss Bluestocking," he said in that deep, dark velveteen voice of his. And then the door shut, and he was gone.

As the hackney pulled away, Artemis couldn't resist the urge to look back and follow the forbiddingly handsome stranger's progress. But he'd already been swallowed by the crowd.

What a particularly odd and altogether disconcerting inci-dent. In all of her twenty-nine years, Artemis had never been so singularly affected by a member of the opposite sex. Even the rake that had charmed and almost ruined her when she was a naive debutante a decade ago couldn't hold a candle to...well, whoever *that* enigmatic, mercurial man had been.

It was as though her imagination had conjured him up—the epitome of a darkly brooding, Byronic hero who'd stepped out of the pages of one of her own books. One thing was certain: A man like that—no matter how much he provoked her interest by a mere glance and a touch—was not of her world. Nor would he ever be. This had been a completely inconsequential, chance encounter, nothing more.

Chapter Three

"I HATE YOU!" THE DOOR TO THE LIBRARY SLAMMED SHUT, shaking the very foundations of Dartmoor House. The sound of light footfalls and distraught sobs in the hallway outside quickly receded.

Bloody, blazing, blistering ballocks. Dominic Winters, the fifth Duke of Dartmoor, dragged a hand through his rain-damp hair as he stared at the door's gleaming oak panels. He'd only arrived home ten minutes ago, and already he was regretting it. If he hadn't been so dog tired, he'd have gone straight from a meeting with the Great Western Railway board at Paddington Station to White's, and then he could have avoided all of this. Well, at least until the following day.

Flicking out his coattails, he deposited himself in the heavy oak chair behind his desk and huffed out an exasperated sigh. For years, he'd effectively negotiated with cutthroat industrialists and entrepreneurs looking to take advantage of him when striking a deal. He'd managed pernickety stewards and cantankerous tenants on his numerous estates. When the occasion called for it, he did his ducal duty and ruthlessly pushed through key parliamentary legislation that would not only earn him favor with the Queen but also benefit his own business interests in Britain and on the Continent.

But never, in all of his thirty-eight years, had he been so damn frustrated and lost for words.

And all because of a spiteful hellion. A virago in the making. His fifteen-year-old daughter, Celeste.

Miss Rosalind Sharp, Celeste's governess, stepped forward from the shadows of the curtained window embrasure. Her clear hazel eyes met his. "I'm so sorry about all of this, Your Grace," she said gravely. Her high, pale forehead was creased with a frown. "Perhaps I should go after her. With your permission, of course..."

Dominic gave a curt nod. "Yes. I think that would be wise. But before you go, Miss Sharp, I wanted to thank you again for bringing all of this"—he placed a hand upon the stack of slim, leather-bound volumes on the blotter—"to my attention. I know you had concerns about bothering me unnecessarily, but given the delicate nature of this particular matter, you did the right thing. This is indeed a situation I needed to deal with. You've exercised sound judgment in coming to me."

"Thank you, Your Grace." The governess sank into a neat curtsy. "I'm here to serve both you and Lady Celeste to the best of my ability."

With her head bowed, Dominic could see the straight line of the woman's precisely parted hair and the fact that the tips of her ears had turned a bright shade of pink. Good heavens, was the governess blushing because of his faint praise?

Dominic cleared his throat. "Before you go, tell me, how did Celeste manage to procure such 'horrid' novels?" His mind immediately darted to the attractive flame-haired bluestocking he'd bumped into outside Paddington Station and her fondness for Gothic literature. "Do you have any idea?"

"I..." The governess's blush deepened, marching its way across her entire face from neck to hairline. "I'm not entirely certain, Your Grace. She wouldn't tell me, but I can't imagine that reputable bookshops such as Hatchards would sell such titles. Not that I've been to Hatchards lately. It might have been Delaney's..."

"Delaney's?"

"Yes. I've heard that it's a store specializing in antique, rare, and unique books. Apparently, it's in Piccadilly, not far from Hatchards. But then, Lady Celeste could have picked up those"—the governess made a moue of distaste as she indicated the pile on the desk—"from a circulating library. I don't think a friend lent them to her."

"No..." Dominic wiped a hand down his face as guilt sliced. The sad fact was, Miss Sharp was right. Celeste *didn't* have any friends to speak of. It was through no fault of her own that no one wished to associate with the Dastardly Duke of Dartmoor's daughter.

"I'm sorry I don't have a better answer for you, Your Grace," the governess continued quietly. "I could attempt to question Lady Celeste further if you'd like."

"I wouldn't worry. And I suppose it's really neither here nor there at this point in time," Dominic said with a heavy sigh. "The important thing is, Lady Celeste won't be polluting her mind with such licentious content any longer. Content that, as you so rightly point out, is not suitable for a fifteen-year-old girl."

"Yes, Your Grace. Only..."

Dominic arched a brow. "What is it?"

"As you know, Lady Celeste is quite bright. And a voracious reader. So I did wonder if a trip to Hatchards might be in order. While the library here is extensive and has an excellent collection of classic literature"—Miss Sharp nodded at the towering mahogany bookcases surrounding them—"the actual number of titles that would particularly interest a young lady are limited. Indeed, anything that has appealed to Lady Celeste, she's already read. And more than once. The same could be said for the library at Ashburn Abbey."

"Ah, I see." Dominic cast his gaze over the multitude of leather-bound volumes. "You're telling me that she's bored and needs books that will entertain rather than merely educate."

"I…" A look of alarm flared in the governess's eyes. "I apologize, unreservedly, if I have come across as critical, Your Grace. It is not my place to do so. To criticize. And of course, it is my duty to engage Lady Celeste's mind. I will endeavor to do better."

"No offense taken, Miss Sharp. And I'll consider your request to visit Hatchards." He gave another curt nod. "You may go."

As soon as the governess quit the room, Dominic crossed to the sideboard where he kept a tray of spirits and splashed a large measure of brandy into a cut-crystal tumbler.

Of course, *he* could do better too. Who would have thought that bringing up an adolescent daughter would be such challenging and altogether frustrating work? Up until now, Celeste's antics had been all relatively innocuous, and he supposed it was only natural for a girl—no, young woman, he reminded himself—to be testing the limits of what she could or couldn't get away with.

Although, when he'd learned that Celeste had recently been trying out her fledgling feminine wiles on some of the household's male staff—Miss Sharp had reported that she'd been casting flirtatious glances at several younger footmen and one of the grooms—he'd taken his daughter aside to remind her about what was appropriate behavior for a young lady of her station and the importance of guarding her reputation. He supposed it was something his wife would have done, if she were still here. God rest her soul.

His mind returned to the fraught interview that had taken place only minutes ago. Celeste had rolled her eyes at him and muttered a string of unladylike curse words beneath her breath—something she'd never done before—when he'd sternly admonished her for reading such "frivolous, morally questionable books." At least that's how Miss Sharp had described them, and he had no reason to distrust the governess's summation. When he'd subsequently threatened to send Celeste back to Ashburn Abbey in Devonshire until she showed him respect and learned some manners, she'd burst into tears and declared that he didn't understand her, and that she hated him.

And she was right. Dominic didn't understand why she'd become so surly and insubordinate, practically overnight. Up until her fifteenth birthday last November, she'd always been a sweet-tempered, well-behaved girl. She was growing up too fast. Turning into a young woman before his eyes. With a young woman's interest in the opposite sex. And given the evidently far-too-graphic content of the "novels" she'd been reading, she now possibly knew far too much about sexual congress. A most disconcerting and thoroughly uncomfortable thought.

If he didn't do something to curb Celeste's wilder tendencies, he suspected it wouldn't be long before she did something completely disastrous like sneaking out of the house in search of some amorous adventure. Fortune hunters abounded in London, and the daughter of a wealthy duke—whether his own reputation was tattered or not—would still be the prime target of countless unscrupulous cads.

Egads, if he were Catholic, he'd consider packing Celeste off to a nunnery until her twenty-first birthday.

After Dominic replenished his brandy, he looked up and caught a glimpse of his reflection in the gilt-edged mirror above the sideboard. There were fine lines radiating from the corners of his eyes and a peppering of silver in the black hair at his temples. Dear God, his daughter was sending him gray.

What he *needed* to do was take Celeste in hand. And even though he was as busy as hell, he must endeavor to spend more time with her. He certainly didn't want to send her away to his country estate unless he absolutely had to. She'd already spent far too much time at that isolated place on the edge of desolate Dartmoor. She was crying out for attention, and it pained him to realize that his daughter wasn't simply bored.

She was lonely. And he was to blame.

Trying to ignore the canker of guilt and regret sitting uncomfortably in his belly, Dominic wandered over to his desk and picked up one of the books Miss Sharp had confiscated. *Lady Violetta and the Vengeful Vampyre.*

He released a derisive huff, and his thoughts immediately returned to the prickly but strangely beguiling bluestocking he'd bumped into. What was the dashed appeal of these books? Of course, he knew about Gothic horror novels. Why, he'd read Mary Shelley's *Frankenstein; or, the Modern Prometheus* and Polidori's *The Vampyre* years ago to see what all the fuss was about. While they weren't his cup of tea and he didn't regard them as literary classics, he respected that not everyone had the same reading preferences.

But the books Celeste—and apparently Miss Flame-haired Bluestocking—enjoyed reading appeared to belong to an entirely different category. On skimming through the pages earlier on, he'd been shocked to discover that these particular Gothic romances contained quite suggestive love scenes. Miss Sharp had actually likened the books to "cheap, poorly written penny-bloods that one could buy on any street corner" and not worthy of anyone's coin, let alone time. While Dominic didn't have a problem with someone Miss Bluestocking's age reading whatever she liked, these books were certainly not appropriate reading material for his daughter. And they were all penned by the same author using the pseudonym, Lydia Lovelace.

Lydia Lovelace. Ha! Dominic smirked. Miss Lovelace was probably some dissolute, crusty old hack of a writer who smoked a pipe and chuckled over his porter as he invented his ridiculous alliterative titles. Dominic picked up another slim volume. *Lady Fanny and the Fantastical Phantasm. Lady Wilhelmina and the Wicked Werewolf.*

And then there were the entirely outrageous euphemisms he'd spied in the thinly disguised lovemaking scenes. "His masculine rod." "His colossal column." "Her quivering bosom" and "vermilion velvet purse." Oh, and how would he ever be able to forget the term "Lucifer's love truncheon"? He recalled Miss Bluestocking had uttered something that was shockingly similar when she'd dropped her carpetbag.

While he was no prude and he couldn't deny part of him was both titillated and amused by the ribald language—so much so he was tempted to read more just for the entertainment value—it wasn't funny at all that Celeste had been reading such risqué material.

Dominic tossed the books aside and reclaimed his seat. While Miss Sharp appeared to be doing an adequate job—she'd been with Celeste for three years now—she also seemed… He frowned. A little too staid and serious perhaps? But then

Dominic had initially hired her because he'd felt Celeste needed someone who was no-nonsense and set clear boundaries. Miss Sharp wasn't paid to be Celeste's friend, and of course, she could never fill the shoes of a female relative. Let alone a mother.

Guilt shredded Dominic's gut, and he took a large swig of brandy to blunt a surge of pain. Celeste's mother—his wife, Juliet—had passed away nine years ago in the most tragic of circumstances. Rumors abounded that Dominic had had a hand in her demise, despite a coroner's clear ruling to the contrary.

Steadfastly locking away his bittersweet memories of Juliet and a tumultuous past he'd rather not revisit, he fell to contemplating what he could do to rectify the lack of a suitable female role model in Celeste's life. He could call upon Horatia, his sister, but Celeste had never really warmed to her aunt. His own mother had passed away many years ago, and any other female relatives on his side of the family were elderly and infirm.

Considering Juliet's family blamed Dominic for his wife's death—particularly Juliet's brother, Guy de Burgh, Lord Gascoyne—they wanted nothing to do with him. They'd made noises about taking Celeste away from Dominic when she was young, but he was a duke and there was no legal basis for them to do so. Besides, he loved Celeste beyond reason and there was no way in hell he'd let anyone else raise his child. Even though he seemed to be making a right royal hash of the job now…

Devil take him. Dominic tipped his head back and studied the plasterwork riot of rosettes and ribbons and cavorting cupids on the ceiling. The most obvious solution to his problem was the one he'd been avoiding for years. Even though he didn't want to, logic dictated that he needed to take another wife. But she had to be the *right* sort of wife. Someone who would take Celeste under her wing and guide her. Someone she could look up to and admire.

Someone with an impeccable lineage and reputation.

A woman he'd be happy to share his bed with to beget an heir. He certainly wasn't getting any younger, and he had a responsibility to the dukedom to ensure a smooth line of succession.

The problem was, any woman who was remotely respectable would probably avoid him like the plague. He was the Dastardly Duke of Dartmoor after all.

A knock at the door pulled him from his morose bout of brooding. It was his personal secretary, Morton. A large stack of papers was tucked beneath one arm and in his hand, he brandished several messages.

"Your Grace, I have a telegram from your man of business in Liverpool, which I'm sure you'll wish to see straightaway," he said, approaching the desk with sure, swift steps. "And there's a letter from your solicitor, with an attached contract for you to review. Oh, and Disraeli and the Prime Minister kindly request your presence at Westminster at noon tomorrow. They're keen for an update on the Great Western Railway's position on the line to Falmouth. Disraeli is considering the establishment of a joint committee of management, so the proposed bill for the line doesn't stumble in the House of Lords yet again."

Dominic accepted the missives, glanced through them, then issued a few instructions. But then he halted Morton as he prepared to leave. "Just one more thing."

The secretary tilted his lean frame into a small bow. "Of course, Your Grace."

"On top of everything else that you do for me, I don't suppose you keep abreast of the latest gossip about Town?"

Morton's already lined forehead crinkled farther. "I'm afraid I only know as much as the social pages in London's newspapers tell me, Your Grace. Although I'd be happy to keep my ears open. Is there anyone in particular you wish to glean intelligence on?"

"No, and that's half the problem." Dominic sighed. Since Juliet had died, he'd effectively placed himself in self-imposed social exile. Burying himself in work seemed far easier than having to face the unpleasant rumors constantly swirling around him every time he set foot in a ballroom. His presence might be tolerated in gentleman's clubs and the House of Lords—no one could deny him a seat that was his by birthright—but the Dastardly Duke was not the sort of man you'd invite to dinner to meet your wife and daughters.

Indeed, Dominic had been avoiding social events for so long, he had no idea who would make a suitable duchess these days. Any gossip going round White's tended to focus on the most salacious scandals involving wives and widows who were free with their favors, or which "prime articles" of recently debuted womanhood were worth ogling with a view to debauching or courting if the chit possessed a decent dowry.

He drummed his fingers on the blotter, annoyed that he was very much in the dark on this particular topic when he was aware of everything else of significance that was going on in the British Isles and even on the Continent.

There was nothing for it. He was going to have to swallow his cursed pride and seek his sister's counsel. Given the fact Horatia had been harping on for the past year that he should remarry, he could almost hear her crowing with delight.

He dashed off a quick note inviting Horatia and her husband, the Earl of Northam, to lunch or dinner sometime in the next week, handed it to Morton to deal with, then focused his attention on the documents his secretary had furnished.

Better that than continuing to dwell on the trials and tribulations of fatherhood and his imminent foray into the cutthroat marriage mart. If his head of mostly jet-black hair had turned completely gray by the end of the Season, Dominic wouldn't be the least bit surprised.

Chapter Four

"At last, my dear Artemis, you've finally come to your senses and given up all that teaching nonsense." Thus proclaimed Roberta, Lady Wagstaff, in her customary strident tones as Artemis entered her aunt's opulent drawing room. Seated upon a plumply cushioned damask armchair by the fire, the baroness was as regal as the Queen herself. Her bejeweled fingers stroked Bertie, her snow-white terrier, who was installed upon her lap. "Humph, although I see your dress sense hasn't improved," her aunt added with an imperious sniff. Through the lenses of her silver lorgnette, her cool gaze swept over Artemis's disheveled form. "Indeed, you look like you've been cavorting in mud puddles, my gel."

"One does what one can with a teacher's allowance," returned Artemis dryly. She was used to her aunt's critical, bordering-on-rude observations about her less-than-stylish appearance and wasn't the least bit offended. Indeed, needling each other had become somewhat of a perversely enjoyable pastime for both of them over the years. "And I got caught in the rain. So I should apologize in advance for dirtying your carpets."

"Oh, don't worry about the carpets," declared Phoebe, rushing forward and enveloping Artemis in the warmest of hugs. "Welcome back to London, dearest sister." She drew back and smiled, her doe-brown eyes aglow with unabashed delight. "Since your telegram arrived this morning, I've been abuzz with hope all day that you might turn up. And now, here you are! Just think of all the fun we're going to have together. I'm certain both of us will be engaged, if not wed, before the Season ends."

Artemis's stomach lurched, then fell to her aunt's now slightly soiled Axminster rug. She hated the fact that she was ostensibly here under false pretenses. That she'd really quit her post to support Lucy this Season, not Phoebe. Indeed, husband hunting—for herself or her sister—was the last thing on her mind. At some point, she'd have to set Phoebe and their aunt straight.

Aunt Roberta interrupted her troubled thoughts with a rather pointed "ahem" before continuing in a tone that brooked no argument. "I imagine you'll want to freshen up before dinner. As usual, it's at seven sharp."

"Ah, about that." Artemis winced. "I'm afraid my luggage has gone astray somewhere between Bath and London."

Aunt Roberta waved a dismissive hand that only narrowly missed the pointed tips of Bertie's ears. "I don't think it will matter all that much. If you have any hope of snaring a husband this Season, you'll need a new wardrobe anyway."

Despite the fact she was four-and-twenty, Phoebe clapped her hands together and bounced on the spot like a small child who'd been presented with a Christmas stocking stuffed full of oranges and sweets. "We must visit Aunt Roberta's French modiste. First thing tomorrow. Until then, you may borrow something of mine."

Guilt twisted through Artemis's belly once more as she followed Phoebe to the upper floors where the bedchambers lay. Her sister twittered away like a flock of chaffinches; she was clearly excited about the prospect of being released from domestic captivity. For several years now, Aunt Roberta, manipulative old tabby that she was, had insisted that she wouldn't sponsor a Season for Phoebe until Artemis was ready to give up her "stubborn bluestocking ways" and have another Season too. It was her way of coercing Artemis into accepting the shackles of matrimony.

Sometimes, Artemis felt like she'd been forced to adopt the role of Katherina in *Taming of the Shrew* and poor Phoebe was Bianca, the younger sister who couldn't wed until Katherina did. At any rate, Aunt Roberta wouldn't make her, Artemis, marry some beastly fortune hunter like Petruchio. Or a ruthless cad.

At least, she didn't think so.

———————

Wallowing. To wallow.

At this present moment, that would have to be one of Artemis's favorite words in the whole world. Because that's exactly what she was doing. Wallowing in an enormous copper bathtub before an equally enormous fire in a ridiculously sumptuous bedchamber.

Of course, such extravagances were *not* unexpected when one's aunt was literally wallowing in money.

She released a sigh of drowsy contentment and leaned back in the tub. The last time she'd had anything resembling a bath like this had been two Christmastides ago when she'd visited Lucy and her family. At the Avon Academy, she'd always had to make do with a cracked ewer of tepid water and a hard scrap of astringent-smelling soap.

Lathering. Now that's another lovely word. Artemis picked up a delicate cake of floral-scented soap, dipped it into the warm, sudsy water, then rubbed it along her arm, leaving a foamy trail in its wake. The bubbles caught the gleam of the firelight, illuminating the rainbows within.

Hmm, perhaps she could use that analogy in the Gothic romance she was currently penning, *Lady Mirabella and the Midnight Monk*. What if Count Bellugio, the "midnight monk" in question, came upon Lady Mirabella in her bath while a violent tempest raged outside the castle? He'd drop his cowl, revealing his rain-slick, black-as-midnight hair and dark hooded eyes—or perhaps storm-cloud gray eyes would be more enticing… His gaze would penetrate her very soul, and when he—

A knock on the door made Artemis jump, and the soap slipped into the water with a soft plop. "Who is it?" she called.

"It's only me. And Hetty." Phoebe and her lady's maid entered the room with armfuls of fresh garments for Artemis to try on. "Apologies for interrupting."

"No need to apologize." Artemis retrieved the soap and then picked up a sponge. "In fact, I should thank you for lending me something to wear tonight."

"I'm more than happy to." Phoebe smiled as she draped an embroidered corset, matching drawers, and fine silk stockings across the tester bed's brocade counterpane. "It's a good thing we're a similar size." She lifted Artemis's discarded jacket from the damp pile of clothes by the fire, and her expression shifted from pleasantly amiable to mildly disapproving. "I don't mean to sound like Aunt Roberta, but your clothes are a little careworn and out of fashion. You have such a lovely figure, yet anyone would think you're a—"

"Frumpy old spinster?" Artemis hooked one of her legs over the edge of the tub and slid the soapy sponge all the way to her toes.

"Well, no. I wouldn't put it quite like that." Phoebe passed the offending garments to Hetty to deal with before opening Artemis's equally threadbare carpetbag. "But clearly a trip to the modiste is long overdue."

Phoebe's observations were quite correct, but Artemis didn't wish to admit that she'd been neglecting her wardrobe so she could squirrel away most of her money to establish her college. She shrugged. "You know me. I'd rather have my nose in a novel or a philosophical text than the latest edition of the *New Monthly Belle Assemblée*. In any case, sedate rather than fashionable apparel was the order of the day at the Avon Academy. Mrs. Parsons preferred it that way."

"Mark my words, dearest Artemis, that's all about to change." Phoebe grinned. "The Jones sisters are about to be the talk of the Town. We'll be the belles of every London ball."

Oh, how was she to tell Phoebe that she'd be devoting most of her time to Lucy? That it was her friend's summons that had brought her to London? How was she to juggle their needs and her own? It suddenly seemed like all too much.

To hide her discomfiture, Artemis lathered soap into her hair. She'd almost finished rinsing away the suds when Phoebe shrieked, and Artemis jumped for the second time, dropping the water pitcher onto the floor.

Dicken's dick and dingleberries! Water splashed everywhere, soaking the indecently plush hearthrug. "What's wrong?" When Artemis pushed a curtain of dripping locks out of her eyes, she expected to see a herd of stampeding elephants invading the room or, at the very least, a mouse.

"What. On. Earth. Is. This?"

Artemis inwardly cursed. Phoebe was holding Mary Wollstonecraft's *A Vindication of the Rights of Woman* aloft as though it *were* actually something a cat had dragged in. "It's a book," Artemis replied matter-of-factly.

"Don't tell me you are a champion of this woman's outlandish beliefs." Phoebe shuddered. "I should cast her so-called book into the fire."

Good Lord. Was everyone in London set against Mary Wollstonecraft? The poor woman had been dead nigh on sixty years.

"There's nothing wrong with advocating for a woman's right to receive a decent education," returned Artemis with studied calmness. "I was a teacher after all. And please don't burn my book."

Phoebe huffed indignantly and tossed the tome onto the bed. "According to Aunt Roberta, Mary Wollstonecraft was godless and clearly not of sound mind. She had affairs with numerous men, bore children out of wedlock, and even attempted suicide several times according to her very own husband. She has no moral let alone intellectual standing whatsoever."

"Well, that's a matter of opinion," muttered Artemis, squeezing the water out of her hair with considerable vigor. "And while I appreciate your help, I'll unpack the rest of my carpetbag."

Rising from the bathwater, she reached for a towel from the washstand and wrapped it around herself. She didn't want Phoebe to dig deeper and discover her half-drunk bottle of sherry and Richard Carlile's *Every Woman's Book*, which was a manual detailing the ins and outs of sexual congress and methods to prevent conception. Or any of Lydia Lovelace's books, including her latest wicked manuscript. Lady Mirabella's amorous exploits with the midnight monk would surely give Phoebe a fit of the vapors. No one in her family knew of her second, scandalous occupation. And it must remain that way.

"As you wish. However…" Phoebe turned to face her, hands on hips, her expression uncharacteristically stern. "You must promise me that you won't espouse your controversial views on womanhood this Season. I won't have you bringing shame upon us and spoiling our chances at finding husbands, not when I've been waiting for this opportunity for so long. Besides, what would Aunt Roberta say if she knew you were a devotee of Mary Wollstonecraft?"

"What, you'd think she'd be surprised that her oldest niece is a rebellious bluestocking? A godless, amoral hussy?" Artemis stepped out of the bath and grabbed another towel to wrap about her wet hair. She understood Phoebe's concerns, but the idea that she was somehow "not quite right"—someone to be ashamed of—irritated her no end. "I can't change who I fundamentally am or what I believe in. There's nothing wrong with wanting to remain a spinster."

"Oh, Artemis, I'm sorry if I've offended you. But you've just left the Avon Academy, so I'd assumed your views on getting married had changed too." Phoebe sighed, then waved a hand around the luxurious room. "You probably think I have everything, but I don't. And despite the fact our parents were miserable, I know marriage doesn't *have* to be like that. I *do* want a loving husband. I want children. I want a full and happy life. I'm tired of feeling like a bird trapped inside a beautiful cage. It's as though I'm waiting for something to happen. And I thought it was about to because you've come back to London." Phoebe's eyes suddenly glimmered with tears. "Please don't ruin this chance for me."

Artemis donned one of her sister's satin robes, cinching the tie with jerky movements. She hated seeing Phoebe so upset. "Aunt Roberta is the one who's always set on ruining everything. For both of us," she said as gently as she could, given the remorse and anger and resentment bubbling around inside her. "But I won't be controlled by her and neither will you. Not anymore. Her tyranny must end. While I still don't want to marry, I'll do everything in my power to help you. We can outwit her. I promise."

Phoebe nodded, her expression pensive. "I have to ask… What precipitated your sudden change of heart? You've avoided having another Season for years, so I'm a bit perplexed." Her eyes widened and panic flared across her countenance. "Were you dismissed?"

"No. I wasn't. The truth is…" Artemis paused. Now was the time to tell her sister everything. Hetty had quit the bedroom, so Artemis inhaled a fortifying breath and continued. "I resigned because Lucy Bertram wrote to me. She urgently needs my help." Ignoring the uncomfortable knots in her belly, Artemis explained the substance of her friend's letter. "But upon reflection, I think I can make this situation work so that everyone will benefit. I'm sure we'll all be invited to the same society events. While I'm shooing suitors away from Lucy, I can send them in your direction. Actually, the more I think about it, the more feasible it sounds. As long as Aunt Roberta doesn't find out what I'm up to—that I'm not really looking for a husband—all will be well. Everyone will get what they want."

Phoebe gnawed at her lower lip. "And what about you, Artemis? If you really are set on remaining a spinster, what do *you* want? What will you do when the Season ends? Are you going to return to the Avon Academy?"

"No…" Artemis lowered herself onto the stool before the rosewood dressing table and reached for a comb. But instead of teasing the snarls from her wet hair, she fiddled with the ivory teeth. "Mrs. Parsons was not altogether happy with me, so I doubt she'd have me back." Considering she'd told the headmistress exactly what she thought of the academy's curriculum during their last encounter—that it belonged at the bottom of a dustheap—she was absolutely certain she wouldn't even get a reference.

"Not that I want to return anyway. I..." She met her sister's gaze directly in the mirror. "I want to start my own school. Not a finishing school but an academic ladies' college along the lines of the esteemed Queen's College or the Ladies' College in Bedford Square. And while you're hunting for a husband, I hope to discreetly find a sponsor. A benefactress."

Phoebe blinked. "Your own academic college? For women? You'll think me awful for saying this, but you sound a little mad. I really don't understand why anyone would want to attend. It's not as though women could then study at Oxford or Cambridge. Or become a doctor or solicitor. It's just not done."

"But what if we *could*, Phoebe? If women can meet the entry requirements of any university, why shouldn't we be able to study for a scientific or medical or law degree or whatever we want to? We are not intellectually inferior to men, and I'm determined to prove it. And instead of carefully scrimping and saving for years, I hope to attract the interest of a wealthy patroness."

"Artemis, I can see by the determined look in your eyes that you're quite set on this course," said Phoebe. "And while I don't understand your passion, I promise I won't say anything to Aunt Roberta. But please be careful. If she finds out what you're up to..." She shuddered.

"I know." Artemis grimaced. "There'll be hell to pay."

Phoebe quit the room to get ready for dinner, and Artemis turned back to the mirror. As she loosened the tangles from her unruly hair, she eyed her reflection and sighed. Perhaps she was a little mad but not in the way Phoebe meant it.

Try as she might, she couldn't seem to get Mr. Disapproving Byronic Hero out of her head. As soon as she found a spare moment, she'd return to Lady Mirabella's bath scene and use her handsome stranger as a muse. If she was going to be afflicted with a strange obsession, she may as well make use of it. She'd also compose messages for both Lucy and Jane to let them know they could reconvene their Byronic Book Club meetings.

Now that was something she could definitely look forward to.

Chapter Five

WITH ONE HAND ON HER LEGHORN BONNET AND THE other gripping her voluminous skirts, Artemis dashed down Piccadilly through the sheeting rain toward her destination just up ahead. The one place she truly loved in this whole chaotic, teeming city.

Delaney's Antiquarian Bookshop.

Despite the fact that Artemis's trunks had turned up at Cadogan Square shortly after breakfast—so Artemis wasn't without *some* kind of wardrobe—Aunt Roberta had declared her clothes were so dreadful, they were not even fit to tear into rags to clean the scullery. A baroness had standards to maintain, and a niece dressed like a guttersnipe was not to be borne.

Subsequently, from noon, Artemis had endured being measured and poked and prodded and tutted over by Aunt Roberta's French modiste, Madame Blanchard. All the while, Aunt Roberta and Phoebe had taken turns in disagreeing with Artemis whenever she'd attempted to politely point out that a ball gown or walking gown was not quite to her taste. Or that the color clashed with her auburn hair, or the garment was too expensive, or too tight, or just too much of everything.

After nearly three interminable hours, Artemis had staged a mutiny.

By Jupiter, she would not miss the reconvening of the Byronic Book Club. While Artemis wasn't ungrateful for Aunt Roberta's magnanimity, she'd made plans and simply *had* to see Lucy and Jane, so Aunt Roberta and Phoebe could jolly well deal with it. With a firm farewell and a promise she'd be home in time for dinner, she'd struck out on her own, determinedly striding down Bond Street. She certainly wasn't going to waste her coin on a hackney, not when the bookstore was only half a mile away.

However, before she reached the corner of Bond Street and Piccadilly, the heavens opened up and, of course, she'd neglected to bring an umbrella *again*. By the time she passed Burlington House and then dashed into Sackville Street where Delaney's was located, she was soaked to the skin.

Unfortunately, Artemis was a tad early for the book club meeting—Mr. Delaney, Jane's grandfather, informed her that Jane was out but due back soon and Lucy had not yet arrived. But he kindly invited her to browse even though she'd burst through the door in a flurry of wet russet wool, drooping ribbons, and waterlogged petticoats and no doubt resembled a drowned rat.

The first floor where the novel section was located was deserted—as far as Artemis could tell because there were so many nooks and crannies one could lose oneself in. She was removing her damp gloves to look through a nicely preserved first-edition copy of *The Mysteries of Udolpho* by Ann Radcliffe when she heard the front doorbell tinkle.

Glancing over the wooden balustrade to the floor below, Artemis expected to see Lucy or Jane. But no, it was a gentleman. Aside from the fact he was tall and broad across the shoulders, she couldn't see much of him beneath his black top hat and well-cut greatcoat.

But then he asked Mr. Delaney for directions to the novel section, and Artemis's skin prickled with awareness.

Oh no, it couldn't be... Artemis took a step back and her breath quickened. She was absolutely certain that her Mr. Mysterious Byronic Hero was coming this way, straight up to the first floor. And she had nowhere to go.

Although, perhaps she could duck down one of the narrower corridors between the tightly packed bookcases. It would be easy enough to disappear...

No. Artemis squared her shoulders. Even though her pulse was racing like a creature about to be cornered by a dangerously seductive predator, she wouldn't scurry away and hide in a corner. Mr. Bothersome Byronic Hero was encroaching on her territory, not the other way around. She would stay her ground.

Heavy-booted footsteps on the rickety winding staircase heralded his arrival. Upon spying Artemis, he hesitated on the top step, but only for the briefest of moments. He swept off his hat and approached with sure, smooth strides. His eyes gleamed with sardonic amusement rather than ill humor as he said, "It appears that fate keeps thrusting me into your path, Miss Bluestocking."

Thrusting. Was his choice of words calculated to throw her off? Irritation warred with reluctant attraction as Artemis replied as nonchalantly as she could. "So it would seem." As the stranger's gaze raked over her sodden form in a far too leisurely fashion, she suddenly felt uncharacteristically self-conscious. Which was also annoying because how she looked *shouldn't* matter.

Despite her determination not to betray her uneasiness by fidgeting, she tucked a rain-damp curl behind her ear and added without thinking, "As luck or misfortune would have it, it also appears that whenever we meet, I'm dripping wet."

Oh. Dear. God. Artemis barely resisted the urge to clap her hand over her mouth. Had she really just blurted that out? Heat scorched her cheeks.

To his credit, the gentleman barely reacted beyond a flicker of movement at the corner of his mouth. "Under the circumstances, I feel an introduction is in order." He removed his leather gloves, pushed them into a coat pocket, and then extended a hand. "Miss…"

Even though this man was beyond forward and she was also breaking a thousand rules of etiquette, Artemis threw caution—and any remaining remnants of her good sense—to the wind and placed her bare fingers in his. "Jones. Artemis Jones."

The enigmatic stranger bowed. "I'm very pleased to make your acquaintance, Artemis Jones."

The sound of her name on his lips, on his tongue, felt shockingly intimate, and Artemis was aware of tingles and warm flutters gathering in all sorts of secret feminine places beneath the confines of corsets and drawers. Then again, perhaps it was simply the way the man's lingering gaze dipped briefly to her mouth before returning to her eyes that had sparked such an inconvenient flurry of sensation. Or the fact his large hand still held hers captive.

However, within a moment, he straightened and released her from his warm grasp and his spell. Gesturing at the book she still held, he said, "I must confess, I'm intrigued by your taste in literature, Miss Jones. During our brief encounter yesterday, you professed you're a bluestocking. But from what I've heard about books penned by authors like Ann Radcliffe and Lydia Lovelace, one could hardly deem them works that would stimulate the intellect."

Oh, the gloves really *were* off then. Chiding herself for being so easily beguiled by a charming smile, Artemis raised her chin.

"And I would contend, good sir, that even the most scholarly among us likes to read for pleasure on occasion," she returned. "Unless you subscribe to the particularly draconian school of thought that novel reading will expose women to dangerous ideas that will provoke them into subverting overly rigid, and I would say unfair, societal rules. Or worse still, that we are so foolish that we cannot even distinguish fiction from fact. Fantasy from reality, so to speak. That reading novels like *The Mysteries of Udolpho* and *Lady Violetta and the Vengeful Vampyre* will fill our heads with ridiculous fancies, prompting us to run off in search of wild adventures featuring nefarious villains or, heaven forbid, sharply fanged suitors."

The stranger's wide mouth twitched with a wry smile. "You've obviously been challenged about your taste in books before, Miss Jones. Your arguments are well thought out."

Artemis stammered a thank-you while she mentally cursed him to Hades. Why did Mr. Nameless Byronic Hero have to deploy his smile again? And compliment her? Like yesterday, Artemis had the strangest sensation of being breathless and hot and shivery all over. Glancing away, she tried to shake herself free of the illusion. She really was becoming as fanciful as one of her hapless Gothic romance heroines who'd been caught in the wicked hero's thrall, and it just wouldn't do. This supremely confident man was clearly used to dispensing his charm to disarm the opposite sex whenever it suited him. Her first impression of him the day before had been correct. He was, indeed, dangerous.

"Actually," he continued after Artemis failed to think of anything else to say, "I'm keen to obtain a few novels for my daughter, and Hatchards doesn't have what I'm after. She's fifteen and she very much enjoys the works of Jane Austen.

Apparently, she's only read *Mansfield Park* and *Northanger Abbey*."

"Oh…" Artemis blinked, momentarily taken aback. This man had an adolescent daughter? And he cared for her so much that he was bothering to purchase her a book or two that she actually liked? She hadn't expected that. "I adore Miss Austen's books too," she managed after she'd somehow gathered her scattered wits. "And Delaney's usually has all of her works on hand." She indicated a nearby bookcase. "Just over there."

"Thank you." A fleeting look of uncertainty flickered in the man's eyes. "Forgive me if this sounds presumptuous, but as you're clearly familiar with Miss Austen's books, perhaps you could suggest a few that my daughter might enjoy."

"I'm sure your daughter will love anything that she's written, but…very well."

As Artemis perused Delaney's range of Jane Austen titles, she was acutely aware of the stranger's disconcerting presence behind her. Why she'd agreed to help him, she had no idea. If she had any sense at all, she'd turn and run as fast she could.

Because she was all too familiar with "gentlemen" like him. The confident, charismatic kind that turned your head and then broke your heart without so much as the bat of an eyelid. Even though she didn't know his name—and it was telling indeed that he hadn't offered his after he'd asked for hers—it was as clear as the aristocratic blade of a nose on his too-handsome face that he was a member of the upper class.

Ignoring the tripping of her heart, she reached for a copy of *Pride and Prejudice* and then *Emma*. "These two are my favorites," she said, carefully handing them over so that her fingers wouldn't accidentally come into contact with his again.

Mr. Aristocratic Byronic Hero took the volumes, but instead

of leafing through the pages, he caught her gaze. Mischief danced in his eyes. "I take it these don't contain references to Lucifer or any of his noteworthy anatomical features like Lydia Lovelace's books do. As I mentioned, my daughter *is* only fifteen."

Artemis winced with embarrassment. *Oh, dear.* The gentleman had obviously taken note of her unconventional way of cursing yesterday when she'd dropped her carpetbag. And then she narrowed her gaze. "Actually, now I'm intrigued. How do *you* know Miss Lovelace's books contain such references? It sounds as though you may have read a few yourself. If you'll pardon the pun, how novel."

Was it Artemis's imagination, or did the crests of the gentleman's carved cheekbones darken with a ruddy flush? "I've read…bits and pieces," he said.

Artemis couldn't resist casting him a knowing smile. "Trust a man to only focus on the salacious bits and pieces."

He cocked a brow in challenge. "So you're not denying her books are salacious?"

"Oh, yes. They are indeed," agreed Artemis. At the risk of blowing her own trumpet, she added, "But I also believe they're exciting and romantic and, quite frankly, just simply entertaining. However, I will concede that perhaps Miss Lovelace's books might not be suitable for a fifteen-year-old unless she's particularly mature for her age. Maybe in a year or two your daughter will be ready for such content."

"Hmmm." The stranger didn't look at all convinced. His gaze returned to the leather-bound volumes in his hand. "So, tell me why you like Miss Austen's books so much."

Artemis considered his request, and given his serious expression, it seemed he really did wish to know her opinion.

"Well, aside from her ability to create agreeable characters and an engaging narrative, I think she's particularly adept at formulating witty conversational exchanges. And her observations about the human condition are insightful. I also like the way she portrays women. As if we have minds of our own."

He smirked at that. "I've never met a woman who didn't. Or one who's afraid to tell me exactly what she thinks, for that matter. Especially if she believes she's right and I'm wrong."

Artemis arched a brow. "And I'm sure in your world, that's a rare occurrence. That you're wrong."

"Goodness, we've only just met and yet you know me so well."

"Not that well," she rejoined. "You have me at a decided disadvantage, sir, because all this time we've been conversing, you haven't shared your name."

"And that is an unforgivably rude oversight on my part." He performed an elegant bow. "Allow me to introduce myself, Miss Jones. Dominic Winters. At your service."

It was Artemis's turn to smirk. "*Mr.* Winters? Now why don't I believe you are just a garden-variety mister?"

Dominic Winters's eyebrows shot up. "Whatever do you mean? Are you accusing me of being dishonest?"

"I'm not easily taken in by flimflam, sir. White's and Brooks's are a mere stroll away, if I'm not mistaken. If you're not a member of the *bon ton*, I'll eat my soggy bonnet."

He laughed out loud at that. A rich, deep, throaty chuckle that seemed to curl around her, inviting her to smile openly too. "We can certainly agree on one thing, Miss Jones," he said. "Your bonnet has seen better days."

Gah! Why was this man so...likable? Perhaps her first impression of him had been completely wrong. But that didn't mean he was any less dangerous. Artemis had to shore up her crumbling defenses, and quickly. She tamped down her smile and narrowed her gaze. "By the way, how did you know that *I* wasn't married, Mr. Winters? When you first inquired after my name. That was a rather large assumption to make."

"You're not wearing a wedding ring."

"Perhaps I pawned it so I could buy my horrid books."

"So you're ruthless *and* clever."

"Flattery will get you nowhere."

"Well, I should hope not if you're married."

"And if *you* are married, *Mr.* Winters, I would hope that you wouldn't try to flirt with a strange woman you had bumped into at a train station, then a bookstore, regardless of her marital status."

He inclined his head. "*Touché.* I concede defeat. You are absolutely right. Married men shouldn't flirt with strange women, single or wed. So, it's a good thing I'm not married."

Oh... He had a daughter, but he wasn't married. As divorce was so rare, that probably meant... "I apologize if I've inadvertently raised a painful subject, sir."

Mr. Winters waved a hand. "It's quite all right, Miss Jones. How were you to know that I'm a widower? It *is* Miss Jones, isn't it?"

She inclined her head. "Yes. Yes it is."

"Well then, I'm very pleased to have made your acquaintance. However, while I've enjoyed our chat, and I thank you for taking the time to assist me"—he pulled a silver pocket watch from his dark-blue silk waistcoat and consulted it—"I'm afraid I must go now that I have what I came for." After pocketing the watch, he bowed once more. "Until we meet again."

Artemis eyed him with suspicion. "What makes you so sure that we will?"

His mouth tilted into a rakish smile that made Artemis's belly flutter in the most disconcerting *and* annoying way. "It's just a feeling I have. Farewell again. I'll leave you to continue your book browsing in peace."

In peace? Artemis felt anything *but* peaceful as she watched Mr. Dominic Winters's long strides carry him past the rows of shelves and then down the stairs. She felt giddy and flustered as though she'd been spun around, turned inside out and upside down. Not like herself at all.

If she ever *did* encounter the far-too-charming Dominic Winters again, she most certainly would have to be on her guard. She'd been taken in by a rake once before, and that was one story she *never* wished to repeat.

———

When Dominic reached the bottom of the stairs, Morton stepped forward from the shadows of a towering set of bookcases.

"Would you mind taking care of these?" Dominic handed over his peace offering for Celeste. She hadn't spoken to him since their altercation late yesterday, and it bothered him more than he could say. "I'm running late for an engagement at White's. Just begin an account here."

"Of course, Your Grace." Morton inclined his head. "Is there anything else you require?"

"Yes, actually." Dominic donned his top hat and lowered his voice. "There's presently a young woman upstairs. Tallish, slim, attractive, with auburn hair, and I'd place her age somewhere between five-and-twenty and thirty. She claims her name is Miss Artemis Jones, but I'd like to find out more about her background." He paused. When Miss Jones had given her direction to the hackney driver outside Paddington Station, she'd mentioned some square or other, but he hadn't quite caught which one because of the rumble of passing traffic and the drumming rain. It seemed he'd have to rely on others for additional information. "I suspect she's a regular customer here," he continued, nodding toward the shop attendant. "Make your inquiries discreet though. The last thing I want to do is alarm her."

"Yes, Your Grace."

"Excellent." Dominic pulled on his gloves, then accepted his umbrella from his secretary. "I shall see you anon."

As he strode out of the bookstore onto Piccadilly, heading in the direction of St. James's Street, Dominic took a brief moment to ponder why on earth he wanted to know more about Artemis Jones. While she was handsome in a physical sense—both her figure and face were most agreeable to the eye—he'd also found their exchange refreshing. It had been a long time since he'd engaged in such an entertaining bout of banter with a member of the opposite sex.

Indeed, he imagined most society women of marriageable age would eye the Dastardly Duke of Dartmoor with fear, as though he were some sort of vile monster—a sharply fanged suitor perhaps—who'd pounce and cart them off to his lair to commit perverse acts. Then there were the truly avaricious who saw nothing beyond his title and wealth. And then there were a rare few with decidedly odd inclinations, at least to Dominic's way of thinking—women who seemed to believe it would be thrilling to wed a man whose wife had disappeared under mysterious circumstances. It was as though Dominic's notoriety and his wife's tragic history had imbued him with some strange sort of glamour. Those individuals he didn't understand at all.

While Miss Jones hadn't known he was a duke, she'd been

perceptive enough to suspect he was a member of society's upper echelons. Yes, Miss Jones was whip smart and that was appealing. However, given her obvious intelligence, her taste in lowbrow Gothic novels on the lurid side was surprising. And if she were a proponent of someone like Mary Wollstonecraft, her views about society could be on the controversial side. She certainly wasn't the sort of woman he had in mind for a future duchess or a mother for Celeste.

But there'd been a wicked glint in her gaze and a knowing edge to her smile that Dominic found eminently appealing. No, it was more than that. If he were being perfectly honest with himself, the base male in him would admit he found them stimulating. And he was sure that she'd felt the spark of attraction flare between them too. He was...intrigued.

It had been such a long time since he'd had a casual affair or engaged a mistress. He supposed that would explain why Miss Jones had him in such a lather. The question was, would the sharp-witted Miss Artemis Jones with her flashing brown eyes and fiery hair be interested in getting to know *him* better? Until Dominic managed to find a suitable wife, he was certainly going to make it his business to find out.

Chapter Six

"ALAS," SAID ARTEMIS WITH A DEEP SIGH, "IT IS A TRUTH *never* universally acknowledged that a single woman—whether she is in possession of a good fortune or not—doesn't necessarily want or even need a husband. I like being a spinster. In fact, I relish spinsterhood almost as much as I relish your company"—she caught the gazes of her two childhood friends as she raised her chipped china teacup—"the books we love, and this fine Darjeeling tea."

Lucy, Jane, and Artemis were presently gathered in Mr. Delaney's cluttered parlor above the bookstore. Heavy curtains of claret velvet and blond lace obscured the view of Sackville Street below. On the scarred oak table in front of them sat their favorite novels—*Jane Eyre*, *Wuthering Heights*, and *North and South* topped the pile—along with the mismatched tea things and a delicious light-as-air sponge cake that Lucy had brought to celebrate their reunion.

"I so agree." Lucy's flaxen curls bobbed as she nodded. "Being a spinster has much to recommend it." Her smile lit her lavender-blue eyes as she added, "And that's why I'm so grateful you are here, Artemis, to help me maintain the status quo."

Artemis's mind immediately wandered to Dominic Winters…and then she gave herself the equivalent of a sharp mental pinch to the wrist. She certainly didn't want or need any man in her life—even a handsome one who dispensed charm as effortlessly as a cup of tea. Although, as she, Lucy, and Jane had revisited their favorite books this afternoon, she kept transplanting Mr. Winters into each scene they discussed. Which was ridiculous because he couldn't be Mr. Rochester, Heathcliff, *and* Mr. John Thornton. She really must keep her thoughts of him locked up safely inside a secret drawer labeled "Muse" that was only to be opened when she was writing her own books. If her friends knew she was harboring a ridiculous tendre for such a man, there would be no end to the ribbing she'd receive.

Jane put down her cup with studied grace. The weak gray light filtering in through the curtains highlighted the strands of bronze and copper in her brown hair but did little to obscure the jagged scar arcing across her left cheek from her ear to the corner of her mouth. Or the smudges of fatigue beneath her eyes. "It's so infernally frustrating, isn't it?" she said in her lovely, smoky voice that reminded Artemis of autumnal bonfires. "Why is it so hard for others to accept that women can be perfectly content if we are left to our own devices? That we do not wish be at the beck and call of some man or be subject to his capricious whims—whether that be husband or father or brother or guardian. My grandfather understands, but the rest of my family do not."

She caught Lucy's gaze, then Artemis's. "I don't have the same immediate pressure upon me to wed as you both do for obvious reasons"—she gestured at her ruined cheek—"but my mother, in particular, is profoundly disappointed that I'm no longer as marriageable as I once was. I'm seen as an embarrassing encumbrance despite the fact I tend to be the indispensable family drudge." She sighed. "But such is the life of a spinster when one is strapped for funds. If only some newspaper or periodical would take a chance on me and employ me as a columnist or editor on a regular basis."

"I'm so sorry they all take you for granted," said Artemis. When Jane wasn't acting as an unpaid personal-secretary-cum-companion for her mother, she was more often than not playing the part of a chaperone for several of her cousins who were "just out" and all looking for husbands. When she had any spare time for herself, she could be found here at Delaney's helping her grandfather appraise books or penning poorly paid literature reviews for a handful of London's newspapers, including the notorious society scandal rag, the *London Tatler*. "You know that as soon as I start my college, I'd love to have you on staff as a teacher if that's what you would like to do in the meantime."

Jane smiled warmly. "I would certainly consider it."

Lucy scowled into her cup of tea. "I wish my father thought that I was unmarriageable. If only society would permit us the freedom afforded bachelors. My brother, Monty, does whatever he likes, whenever he likes. I love him to the moon and back, but I don't see why he shouldn't do his bit for the family cause. He could marry well too."

"I don't blame you for feeling frustrated." Artemis offered her a sympathetic smile. Aside from being as knowledgeable as her father in the field of botany—despite the lack of a formal qualification—Lucy had dreams of traveling the world to conduct her own research on the medicinal properties of plants. While she was a member of the Botanical Society of London, and several of her own papers had been published in the society's quarterly journal, she would never receive the same degree of recognition as her father.

Lucy sighed. "I'm almost at the point of rubbing myself all

over with stinging nettles, wild parsnips, or hyacinth bulbs, so I develop some ghastly rash. No one in their right mind will want to court a spotty spinster with a tendency to constantly scratch."

"Oh, heavens no. Surely it won't come to that," said Artemis. "Even though I'm staying with my aunt and sister at the moment, just know that I'm here to help you, Lucy, in whatever way I can. The irony is," she added, "that while both you and I are actively trying to avoid getting married, my poor sister, Phoebe, wants to wed with her whole heart." Artemis filled Lucy and Jane in on her plan to divert Lucy's would-be suitors Phoebe's way, should they attend the same balls and soirees. "As Aunt Roberta has at last conceded that Phoebe may have a Season, I'm hoping she will give her blessing to any suitable offer for Phoebe's hand because I am not likely to receive—or accept—any proposals of marriage."

Lucy looked horrified. "Surely she won't stop Phoebe from marrying if she really wants to and if the gentleman in question is respectable and his offer genuine. She is of age."

Artemis shrugged. "The problem is that Aunt Roberta has a fierce, uncompromising grip on the purse strings of our not-insubstantial dowries. My real fear is that she won't let Phoebe wed until I do. She's effectively holding us both to ransom, and it's all so terribly unfair."

"And she's pitting you against each other." Jane's expression was thoughtful. "I'm sure you've tried umpteen tactics to make your aunt see reason."

"Oh, I have. Indeed, I've been racking my brain for years to come up with some sort of effective argument or method of persuasion that will change her mind. Unfortunately, Aunt Roberta is just as mulish and set in her ways as I am. Both of us are like the Rock of Gibraltar. We will not budge an inch, ever."

A sly look crossed Lucy's face. "Even though we've declared ourselves confirmed spinsters, if you were a little more mercenary, Artemis, you could find yourself a wealthy but malleable husband to fund your college rather than just a sponsor. A man who admires you for your intellect just as much as your fine brown eyes."

"Oh, I like your idea. A philanthropic-minded Mr. Darcy sounds quite delicious," said Jane with a twinkle in her gaze. "I'll keep an eye out for any suitable-sounding candidates that appear in the gossip columns of the *London Tatler*. Or next time I'm out and about chaperoning one of my cousins."

Artemis emitted a huff of laughter. "I don't think that such a man exists, my dear friends. But if I do happen to meet someone like that, I *might* be tempted to change my mind." *Especially if he has storm-cloud gray eyes, wears snugly fitting trousers, and cologne that smells like the ocean…*

Ugh. Her mind was straying to *him* again.

"Yes, but I'd warrant there are far more men resembling Mr. Collins or outright bounders like Rawdon Crawley from *Vanity Fair* out there," said Lucy glumly. "I daresay the sort of Byronic heroes we swoon over only exist in the books we read. And the books you write, Artemis."

"I think you're both right," agreed Jane with a sigh. "Unfortunately, life isn't like an Austen novel or a Gothic romance."

Artemis rallied a smile. "But at least we have each other. Along with plenty of books and dreams."

"And tea and cake," added Lucy. "What more do we need?"

"Nothing at all," said Jane, and with that, she proceeded to slice several more slices of jam and cream sponge, which Artemis and Lucy accepted with alacrity.

"Huzzah! It's about time you got married again." A bright smile broke across Horatia's face as she dispensed Dominic's coffee just the way he liked it. They were presently sequestered in Dartmoor House's drawing room, sharing a light luncheon. "However"—she paused to pass Dominic his cup—"I'm afraid I'm not inclined to compile a list of eligible women for you to court this Season."

Dominic raised a brow. "Whyever not? Considering most families with suitable daughters won't want to have anything to do with me, that should narrow down the field a bit. I can't imagine it will take you too long."

His sister gave him a flat look over the plates of savory pastries, cucumber sandwiches, and petit fours. "Oh, that should be easy, then, coming up with a list of well-connected, preferably titled women who are not too young or too old. Women who are paragons of propriety with a modicum of intelligence and possess the usual accomplishments, along with an even temper and physical attributes that you will find pleasing to the eye. And as you so rightly point out, they must also be willing to overlook your much maligned reputation. Am I correct?"

Dominic stirred his coffee. "More or less. Which is exactly my point. You'll know who will suit me and who won't. Who is duchess material and who isn't. Who is willing to look beyond all the calumny and accept my suit rather than run screaming from the room or collapse into a dead faint if I look her way. Even after all these years, there's still talk that the Dastardly Duke of Dartmoor murdered his wife. Society doesn't forget something like that."

Horatia snorted as she added a lump of sugar to her teacup. "There should be a special corner of hell set aside for scandalmongers and newspaper editors who spread such lies. But in all seriousness, I might be adept at picking a good brood mare for my stables, but I'm certainly not going to presume to know what sort of woman is going to appeal to you, dear brother. Matchmaking is not my forte. I'm afraid you're going to have to separate the wheat from the chaff yourself."

Dominic sipped his coffee, then grimaced. "You know how much I hate balls."

"As do I. All that false gaiety and gossip." Horatia shuddered. "Of course, I'm happy to look over anyone who catches your eye, but *you* have to do some of the groundwork first. And as for your other problem. With Celeste…" Horatia selected several sandwiches before settling back in her chair. "I can counsel her about her questionable reading choices and encourage her to behave in a manner befitting her station as a duke's daughter, but I doubt she'll listen. I'm the mother of four rumbustious boys, so have no experience with rearing female offspring to call upon. Aside from that, I'm far too 'horsey' for her."

"Horsey?" Dominic scoffed. "Whatever do you mean?"

Horatia rolled her eyes. "I thought it was quite obvious. I'd much rather be ensconced in the country, striding about with my dogs at my heels or riding hell for leather about the estate. In Celeste's eyes, I'm far too 'rustic.' We have barely anything in common, and I'm certain my opinion will hardly signify. So yes"—Horatia picked up her tea—"your daughter does need a mother to guide her, Dominic. And the sooner you find a suitable duchess, the better." Over the rim of her cup, her eyes twinkled wickedly. "I hear the Earl and Countess of Castledown are holding a ball next week. The first of the Season…"

Egads. Dominic gave a resigned sigh. "You really are determined to make me brave the marriage mart all on my own, aren't you? Given the fact most of polite society will eye me like I'm some pox-ridden, murderous monster, it's bound to be a futile exercise."

Horatia smirked. "Oh, the conceit of you, Dominic. Do you fear that you *won't* be swamped by hordes of women throwing themselves at you like they would have done once upon a time?"

"Well…yes. Ordinarily, a widowed duke in the possession of a decent fortune, all of his teeth, and most of his hair but no heir isn't likely to have an issue with finding a suitable wife. But in my case…" Dominic shrugged. "I'm going to need help to dispel the cloud of infamy hovering over me. Most of my peers tolerate my presence in the House of Lords and their clubs because they have to, but I'm not welcome in their homes. Nor do I want to be there if they think so ill of me. If *I* were to throw a ball—God, how does one even do that these days?—Lord knows who'd attend. I think it's fair to say I'm either going to get title-hunting, money-hungry chits or the morbidly curious turning up on my doorstep rather than anyone with a genuine interest in becoming my wife."

Horatia at last offered him a sympathetic smile. "I suppose you have a point. However, I doubt that having me by your side will do much to restore your reputation. I have a small circle of close friends, but I'm certainly not a social butterfly and would have negligible influence over the opinion of others. For the sake of the dukedom, and Celeste, you're just going to have to grin and bear it."

"True." Except for the moment, Dominic couldn't stop thinking about one particular woman. A certain enigmatic, redheaded bluestocking with a rebellious streak and a razor-sharp wit.

In the week since their encounter at Delaney's Bookshop, Morton hadn't been able to uncover any additional intelligence about Miss Artemis Jones. Which was most disappointing. To think that the only woman who'd caught his eye in a long time might never cross paths with him again was frustrating indeed.

He stared into his coffee, disgruntled yet intrigued that the rich, dark hue reminded him of Miss Jones's liquid brown eyes. "Very well," he said at last. "I'll reach out to Castledown and seek an invitation." He'd known the earl for years—they'd been firm friends at Oxford, and both of them were members of White's—so Dominic knew he wouldn't be snubbed. Not *everyone* believed the malicious falsehoods spread by Juliet's family—in particular, her brother, Lord Gascoyne.

"Good," replied Horatia with a satisfied smile. "And I'll expect a thorough accounting from you the following day at Northam House. Dinner is at seven. Don't be late."

Chapter Seven

THE EARL AND COUNTESS OF CASTLEDOWN'S SPRING BALL, one of the first major events of the Season, was a crush and the ballroom was simply dazzling. At least Artemis thought so. The gaslit chandeliers illuminated a massive, opulently appointed chamber. A profusion of bright spring blooms all but spilled from enormous porcelain vases, and the window embrasures and gilt-framed mirrors were festooned with cascading floral garlands.

The fact that Aunt Roberta had managed to secure invitations for all of them at short notice was apparently an absolute feat, according to Phoebe who was abuzz with nervous excitement as they hovered on the edge of the dance floor, watching as waltzing couples spun past, the silk and satin of skirts shimmering, and jewels at wrist and throat and ear sparkling.

"You don't think I'm overtrimmed? Like I'm trying too hard?" she asked, plucking at one of the silk roses on the buttercup-yellow bodice of her ball gown. "I hadn't expected Madame Blanchard to add quite so many embellishments. I don't want everyone to think I resemble a flower bed at Kew Gardens."

Given the veritable whirlpool of color in front of them, Artemis remarked she hardly thought so. Indeed, *she* didn't feel particularly flowerlike. More like a trussed Christmas goose, considering she was stuffed into a tightly cinched whalebone

corset and a suffocating ball gown constructed of acres of crimson silk skirts, frothy petticoats, and a wire-cage crinoline. And
then, of course, there were a million pins stuck into her head to
keep her cascading sausage curls in place.

Aunt Roberta gave her niece a reassuring pat on the arm.
"There's no need to be anxious, Phoebe. *Both* you and Artemis
look beautiful and are sure to attract the attention of quite a few
eligible gentlemen. You're both going to have such capital fun.
But not too much…" She directed this last comment straight at
Artemis. "Don't think I don't recall your troublesome habit of
sneaking off in pursuit of mischief during your first Season. The
last thing I need is for you to create a scandal that will besmirch
your reputation or your sister's."

Artemis bit back the retort dancing on the tip of her unruly
tongue. If she wanted a dalliance, she'd indulge in one, thank
you very much. She wasn't a naive girl anymore who'd lose her
heart *or* end up in the family way. She'd learned her lesson long
ago and knew how to guard against both eventualities if the
right opportunity for a bit of fun presented itself. But it would
have to be someone special indeed to convince her to risk all for
a few moments of fleeting passion. Someone like Mr. Dominic
Winters perhaps…

Although, she should focus on why she was really here. To
support Lucy—she was supposed to be at the Castledown's ball
tonight too—and to find a benefactress for her college. As if
her thoughts had conjured her up, Lucy suddenly materialized
out of the crowd along with her father, Sir Oswald, her dashing
brother, Monty, and a tiny silver-haired woman in black bom-
bazine who was introduced as Lucy's cousin and chaperone,
Miss Mabel Babbington.

Once the customary greetings and pleasantries had been

dispensed with, Lucy pulled Artemis aside. "I'm so happy to see you," she whispered. "I've been such a bundle of nerves all day. Actually, I almost cast up my accounts in the carriage just before we arrived." She gave a little shiver, then placed a trembling hand upon her belly. "If I had, maybe I wouldn't be here right now."

Compassion welled inside Artemis's heart, and she gave her friend's gloved hand a gentle squeeze. "You *can* do this. And I promise that I will stay by your side. You can count on me. I won't leave you to fend for yourself. And if I suspect any of the men are scoundrels, or you simply don't like them, I'll chase them off with my scorching she-devil stare." She narrowed her eyes, affecting a fulminating glare, and Lucy laughed.

"Oh, Artemis, you are too funny. And yes, that glare would burn them to a crisp. You always know how to make me feel better."

Artemis smiled. "I'm glad. All jokes aside, remember that when any gentlemen do wander your way, I shall encourage my aunt to introduce them to Phoebe. My sister is such a chatterbox, she should keep them busy. I mean, look..." She nodded in Phoebe's direction. "She's already making eyes at any bachelor within striking distance." Indeed, her sister's eyelashes were fluttering faster than her silk fan as she cast longing glances at a pair of handsome young bucks across the room.

Lucy was about to make another remark, but Sir Oswald politely interrupted. He wished to introduce his daughter and Miss Babbington to another middle-aged couple and their debutante daughter. Monty Bertram had apparently disappeared into the crowd. *Lucky sod.*

At loose ends, Artemis armed herself with a flute of champagne and surveyed the other guests in her immediate vicinity.

She had no idea how she could easily identify members of the upper ten thousand who possessed progressive views about women's education. She would need to tread carefully. Earning the reputation of a radical certainly wouldn't do, not this early in the piece. The problem was, even though Aunt Roberta was a relatively well-connected baroness, Artemis couldn't wheedle any useful intelligence out of her without giving her own scheme away.

An attractive dark-haired man on the other side of the dance floor caught her eye, and her mind immediately conjured up an image of Dominic Winters. It irked her no end that ever since their encounter at Delaney's two weeks ago, she hadn't been able to *stop* thinking about him at odd moments during the day or at night when she was alone in her bed. He wouldn't stay put in her drawer labeled "Muse" no matter how hard she tried.

Would he be here tonight? The way he spoke, dressed, and carried himself practically screamed monied nobleman. Given the fact that half the population of Belgravia and Mayfair seemed to be attending the ball, it wasn't outside the realm of possibility that he might be on the guest list. Artemis's stomach performed an odd little somersault at the mere thought of seeing him again. And then she chided herself for acting like the caper-witted debutante she used to be.

Aunt Roberta touched her arm, drawing her attention to a tall, bespectacled gentleman sporting a set of impressive muttonchop whiskers. "Artemis," she began, "I'd like to introduce you to Mr. Adam Whittaker—" But then she broke off as a collective gasp followed by a strange echoing silence descended upon the room. Conversations ceased. Dancers stilled. Even the orchestra ground to a screeching halt.

And then Artemis's gaze fell upon the commanding figure

framed in the ballroom's grand arched entrance. The gentleman that everyone else seemed to be momentarily transfixed by.

It was Mr. Byronic Hero himself. Dominic Winters.

But no, he wasn't just "Mr." Winters, because the Castledowns' footman was announcing him as "His Grace, the Duke of Dartmoor."

Ha! Artemis smiled to herself as she studied the duke's marble-hewn profile and the way his glittering, incisive gray gaze swept about the room like a wolf scanning his hunting ground for quarry. Or a general identifying a conquest before he entered the battlefield. She'd been right all along. Dominic Winters *was* a nobleman. And an exalted one at that.

The Duke of Dartmoor... Artemis frowned. Now why did that name sound vaguely familiar? For a fleeting moment, she thought the duke's gaze settled upon her, but then his attention moved on. Even so, her pulse began to race as though a chase was about to begin.

The orchestra and the buzz of excited voices filled the air again as the duke descended the short flight of stairs to the ballroom floor. His pace was unhurried, his manner unruffled, his expression inscrutable. Immaculately dressed in black-as-midnight evening attire, he cut a fine figure as Artemis tracked his progress—he was at least half a head taller than most gentlemen in the room—before she lost sight of him.

"Well, well, well, the Duke of Dartmoor has emerged from social exile. He must be looking for a new wife." Aunt Roberta snorted. "I doubt he'll have much luck though. Indeed, I can't believe the man has the temerity to set foot in polite society again." Her aunt's voice was stiff with disapproval as she added, "I thought Lord and Lady Castledown were quite particular about who they invited into their home."

"What's wrong with the Duke of Dartmoor?" returned Artemis, curiosity leaping inside her like sparking fireworks. Mr. Whittaker had faded away, so she didn't see the harm in gathering information about the man she'd hitherto known as Dominic Winters.

Aunt Roberta sniffed, her expression smug. "I keep forgetting you've been away from Town so long that you wouldn't know."

"I don't read the gossip columns either, so no, I wouldn't."

Her aunt shot her a narrow-eyed look. "Careful, my gel. I don't like your tone. In any event, it sometimes pays to keep abreast of who's who and what's what. One must do what one can to stay safe."

"Safe? Are you implying the Duke of Dartmoor is dangerous?"

Her aunt leaned in. "He hasn't earned the soubriquet of 'the Dastardly Duke' for nothing. So yes, I am."

"What on earth did he do? Murder someone?"

"Shhh. Keep your voice down. And yes, he may very well have killed his wife. I know he's entitled to sit in the House of Lords, but really, to hear that the Prime Minister himself seeks his counsel, and that on occasion the Queen still receives him, boggles the mind. In my opinion, he should be put on trial for murder and, when he's found guilty, stripped of his title."

Artemis raised a brow in skepticism. "Surely if he had committed such a terrible crime, he would have been."

Aunt Roberta huffed derisively. "He's a duke. Rumor has it that he bribed the coroner at the inquest into his wife's disappearance to let him off scot-free."

Artemis seriously doubted it. Nevertheless, her curiosity was piqued. "His wife disappeared?"

"Yes. In the most mysterious of circumstances. Nine years ago. You see, she'd apparently been unwell for some time after the birth of their first child, a daughter."

"Unwell?"

"Yes. You know, not quite right. Unstable." Aunt Roberta affected a dramatic whisper. "*Mad.*"

"Oh, how awful."

"Some—not many—say it's all a terrible tragedy. That the duke is completely innocent of any wrongdoing. But I don't think so, and neither does his late wife's poor family. You only have to look at His Grace and you can see that he's—"

"Rather handsome?" supplied Artemis.

Aunt Roberta fixed a gimlet-eyed stare upon her. "Don't let his good looks and charm fool you. He's also dishonorable and devious. And, as I said before, dangerous."

"Humph," said Artemis. "I'm not one to gossip, but you really must tell me more so I can judge for myself."

"Well, apparently the duke and his wife, Juliet, were a veritable love match and married quite young. But she only bore him a daughter, and then, as the years went by, failed to produce a son so…" Aunt Roberta shrugged. She might as well have run a thumb along her throat in a slashing motion.

Artemis sipped her champagne, then frowned into its sparkling depths. Why did the name Juliet also ring a bell? Something began to niggle at the back of her mind. A distant, hazy memory, but then it disappeared like one of the bubbles in her glass. Aloud she said, "I'm afraid I'm missing your point."

Aunt Roberta rolled her eyes. "It's obvious, isn't it? As I mentioned, it was rumored that Juliet went mad. And so that the duke could remarry and sire an heir, he murdered her and then disposed of her body in one of the bogs near Ashburn Abbey, his estate on the edge of Dartmoor. In fact, her remains have never been found. The coroner ruled it was all a terrible accident—a death by misadventure—at the inquest, but who in their right mind would believe that?"

Artemis arched a brow. "As opposed to the idea that a man would kill his wife because she couldn't beget a male heir? Are you seriously comparing the duke to a murderous tyrant like King Henry VIII?"

"Well"—Aunt Roberta lifted her lorgnette and gave her a pointed stare—"the duchess had only produced a useless daughter after seven years of marriage. And the duke is a man in his prime..."

Now it was Artemis who gave a derisive snort. "This isn't Tudor England. One would think we're living in more enlightened times. And daughters are *not* useless." She tossed back the rest of her champagne and handed the glass to a nearby footman. "Haven't you noticed that our present monarch is a woman?"

"Daughters *are* useless if you're a duke, and you need a son to ensure the continuation of the family line," replied her aunt dryly. "Suffice it to say, you need not worry that I'll allow that man to put his name down on your dance card, or Phoebe's. If he comes anywhere near you—"

"Lady Wagstaff? I hope you'll forgive the interruption."

Artemis looked up to see their hostess, Lady Castledown, standing right in front of them. And beside her was none other than the Dastardly Duke himself. His mouth twitched with the ghost of a smile as his gaze briefly touched Artemis's before returning to her aunt.

Aunt Roberta's mouth dropped open. "Lady Castledown.

I... Of course. I mean..." Her startled gaze darted to the duke, then back to the countess.

If Lady Castledown noticed Aunt Roberta's befuddlement, she didn't show any sign of it. She was the picture of practiced poise as she said, "His Grace, the Duke of Dartmoor, has asked for an introduction to you and your charming niece"— she inclined her head in Artemis's direction—"with a view to asking Miss Jones for the next dance."

The duke had been watching Artemis as Lady Castledown had spoken. "If your dance card isn't full of course, Miss Jones," he added smoothly.

Oh, how had she already forgotten that his deep voice reminded her of the powerful roll of a distant ocean?

"I..." Artemis swallowed, momentarily flummoxed. She'd never expected anything like this to happen tonight. She suddenly felt like the whole room was watching her and the duke. And like her, everyone was holding their breath. She was conscious that Phoebe was openly gaping and that Lucy's hands were pressed to her cheeks. Whether in horror or with excitement, Artemis had no idea.

Of course, Artemis could refuse the duke's invitation. No one would blame her. Many claimed he was a murderer. However, rumors weren't facts and Artemis's instincts told her that the duke was not a man to fear.

As if her aunt could hear her spinning thoughts, she leaned close and murmured, "You don't have to, you know."

And in that moment, Artemis decided. "I would love to, Your Grace," she said, dropping into a small curtsy because it seemed like the appropriate thing to do in the circumstances.

"Wonderful." The duke smiled widely and extended his gloved hand. "I believe it's a waltz."

She said yes…

Dominic had taken a chance, thrown the dice, and Miss Artemis Jones had accepted the challenge and was now quite willingly accompanying him onto the dance floor. As soon as he'd entered the ballroom and surveyed the assembled guests, he'd quite unexpectedly spotted her. In that moment, he'd felt a frisson. A thrill right down to his bones.

Artemis Jones might be a bluestocking, but it had been clear to him at first glance that she had elevated connections. She wouldn't be at the Castledowns' ball otherwise. Or attired in a haute couture gown of crimson silk that was the perfect foil for her dark auburn hair and deep brown eyes. Indeed, Artemis Jones stood out like a flame, beckoning him closer. She was, without a doubt, the most arresting woman in the room. Her boldness of character—her willingness to take a gamble—made her appealing as hell.

It had been no trouble to secure his hostess's help in engineering a formal introduction. Within no time at all, he'd learned that Miss Jones's aunt was a wealthy dowager baroness. Although he was certain Lady Wagstaff was none too pleased by the turn of events. The matron's eyes had fairly popped out of her head when her niece had agreed to dance with him.

Of course, he'd expected blatant stares and tongues to begin wagging as soon as he singled out Miss Jones. The entire room was presently agog, the crowd watching and whispering with an excitement that bordered upon frenzied as he slid one gloved hand about her corseted waist and his other hand enveloped hers.

He sought her gaze as the orchestra began to play the opening bars of a Viennese waltz. Something by Strauss no doubt.

"Thank you for accepting my invitation, Miss Jones. I must say, I admire your pluck."

Her eyes sparkled with amusement. "My pluck? What a curious compliment, Your Grace. And here I was about to say something terribly prosaic about how much I admired the sapphire pin nestled in the artful folds of your cravat."

Dominic pressed forward as the dance began. "You may jest all you like, Miss Jones, but I have no doubt that you'd already heard certain rumors about me even before Lady Castledown introduced us. It takes a considerable amount of courage to brave the stares and whispers at such a large gathering of exceedingly influential members of high society."

"Pfft." Miss Jones lifted her hand from Dominic's shoulder and waved it in the air as though she were shooing away a pesky gnat. "They might be talking about me now, but I'm really no one of consequence. I'll be forgotten about as soon as this waltz is over and you move on to another partner. Yes, I think it's safe to say it's *you* that everyone is interested in. Aside from that"— her lips quirked with a wry smile—"I thought it might irk my aunt if I agreed to dance with you."

He cocked a brow. "I'm flattered."

"Oh, you should be," she returned. "I don't dance with just anybody, Your Grace. In fact, I'd rather stick your cravat pin in my eye than waste my time dallying with most of the gentlemen here."

"Forgive me for being so frank, but you're not here to find a husband?"

She gave a small unladylike snort. "Hardly. No, I'm here to support a dear friend and my sister, Phoebe, who are both making their debuts. Although, my aunt would be most pleased if I did happen to catch an eligible gentleman's interest." Miss

Jones glanced over his shoulder in the direction of Lady Wagstaff. "Well, someone other than you, Your Grace. No offense intended, of course."

He couldn't suppress a sardonic smile. "Of course."

They danced in slightly strained silence for another minute or two, and then Dominic noticed that Miss Jones's lovely mouth, the color of crushed berries, had curved into a small, wicked smile.

"What is it?" he asked. "I know I haven't waltzed for some time, but I didn't think I was making a complete hash of things."

She laughed. "No, no, it's not that. You dance very well, Your Grace. It's just that we've passed my aunt again, and I can tell by her expression that she is fretting that you and I might become entangled in some sort of untoward way. Which amuses me no end. She's probably having conniptions imagining the headlines in tomorrow's scandal rags: *The Rebellious Bluestocking and the Dastardly Duke Waltz the Night Away.*" A becoming blush blossomed across Miss Jones's high cheekbones. "Oh, I'm so sorry. That was entirely thoughtless of me to say that."

"Do not worry. It's not as though I haven't been addressed by that name before," Dominic said as blithely as he could. "Too many times to count, in fact. But returning to something you said a moment ago…" He paused to deftly execute a tight turn at the end of the room before capturing her gaze and murmuring, "I rather like the word 'entangled.'"

The word lingered in the air between them, hovering like a possibility. An ember that could spark a blaze at any moment. Miss Jones's dark eyes widened, and he swore he caught the tiniest hitch in her breathing before she recovered her impressive composure and gave him a wry smile. "Really? 'Entangled' has all sorts of uncomfortable connotations in my opinion."

Her expression grew mischievous. "'Entwined.' Now that's a word I much prefer."

"Like this?" Dominic couldn't resist threading his fingers through hers. It was a shocking breach of etiquette, and she knew it. This time, there was no mistaking her sharp intake of breath and the flare of heat in her eyes as her gaze flew to his. "I also like the sound of 'enticed,'" he added in a low, soft voice by her ear.

He sensed that her mouth twitched. Whether it was with mirth or annoyance, he could not say.

"You have a way with words, Your Grace," she whispered huskily.

"'Enchanted' is another favorite of mine," Dominic continued. "Closely followed by 'enraptured' and 'entranced.'"

"The breadth of your vocabulary is impressive indeed," she returned. This time, her tone was clearly laced with dry amusement. "If you're not careful, I shall soon be reduced to a puddle of enthralled womanhood at your feet."

Dominic laughed. "Ah, I think I do recall some swooning in puddles the first time we met outside Paddington Station."

"There was no swooning," she countered. "You bumped into me and almost knocked me clean off my f—"

She got no further as at that moment the waltz ended, and Dominic spun her to a halt. Her crimson skirts billowed and swayed about her like an elegant flare of flame.

"Thank you, Miss Jones"—Dominic released her from his hold and tilted into a gentlemanly bow—"for the dance and the simple pleasure of your company. It's been most entertaining. For me at least."

"I trust that the rest of your evening will be equally enjoyable," replied Miss Jones. As Dominic studied her face, the color rose in her cheeks again. He shouldn't deliberately flirt with her like this. Not in such a public setting. But he couldn't seem to help himself. To say that he was enchanted wouldn't be a lie.

Reluctantly, he escorted her back to her waiting aunt.

One thing was certain: Artemis Jones was no shrinking wallflower. She was more like an arbor rose—beautiful and as beguiling as sin. And despite the fact he was an infamous duke, she was unafraid to aim a well-deserved barb or two his way. She was definitely a refreshing change from the usual fare on offer at society balls.

While furthering his acquaintance with Miss Jones might not help him solve his problem with finding a duchess—she'd clearly stated that she wasn't looking for a husband and her quip about being "a rebellious bluestocking" had a ring of truth to it that he couldn't ignore—Dominic decided he hadn't quite sampled enough of her just yet.

Chapter Eight

AFTER THE DUKE OF DARTMOOR BID HER ADIEU, ARTEMIS immediately helped herself to another glass of champagne. She was more than a tad shaken and not in the mood for her aunt's sniping, which went along the lines of "Artemis, how could you make such a shameless spectacle of yourself by making calf's eyes at such a notorious character, dukedom or no?"

The additional alcohol was definitely needed.

Phoebe, who was evidently still flabbergasted by the unexpected turn of events—her cheeks were marked with high color, and her fan was fluttering faster than the wings of a hummingbird—had little to say to Artemis other than, "You waltz very well for someone who hasn't done so in quite some time."

And dear Lucy...she was nowhere to be seen. According to Aunt Roberta, "the silly gel" had apparently torn her hem and, much to Sir Oswald's chagrin, had repaired to the ladies' retiring room. That would give Artemis a valid reason to quit the ballroom as well. She certainly needed to regroup after such an unsettling encounter with the Duke of Dartmoor. Yes, it *had* been unsettling because never, in all her life, had she enjoyed herself quite so much.

Curse Dominic Winters and his abundant charm.

She *had* actually been very close to swooning in his arms when he'd all but brazenly whispered in her ear. She'd *almost* believed he'd been enticed and entranced by her.

However, the cold, hard, habitual cynic in her believed that he'd merely approached her because she was a veritable nobody, who would find it hard to refuse his request to dance. Especially after Lady Castledown's formal introduction.

Yes, she'd been a convenient choice, and there was nothing more to it than that.

Artemis swiftly downed the rest of her champagne—she really should find Lucy—then handed her empty glass to a nearby footman...and when she looked up, she spotted someone else she hadn't expected to see at the Castledowns' ball.

At all.

It was the man who'd taken her virtue and all but ruined her a decade ago. A man who'd crushed her heart and thrown it into the gutter like it was one of yesterday's broadsheets.

The "Honorable" Guy de Burgh.

Or was he Viscount Gascoyne now?

Artemis didn't know and certainly didn't care, especially when he caught sight of her too. Turning away from a tight knot of guests that appeared to be hanging on his every word, he sketched a bow and then a mocking smile broke across his handsome, hateful face. Even though he was several yards away, that didn't matter. Gooseflesh prickled and spread beneath Artemis's gown; she felt as if Guy de Burgh were breathing down her neck, whispering all sorts of pretty lies and false promises in her ear. His dark gaze traveled over her, lingering in all the wrong places and evoking memories that were far too painful.

To think she'd once fancied herself in love with him.

Well, not anymore. Shock at seeing Guy merged with a wave of rising resentment. The last she'd heard, he was residing in New York with his shipping heiress wife, Evangeline, helping to manage the family's business empire. Artemis had reasoned that she'd never, ever have to see the loathsome rogue again.

But here he was, smirking at her. Dredging up emotions she'd rather keep buried. And she didn't like it. Not one little bit.

She touched Phoebe's arm. "Forgive me for leaving, but I need to visit the ladies' retiring room. To check on Lucy. I won't be long." Then she turned and pushed through the crowd, seeking an exit from the ballroom. As much as she wanted to pick up her skirts and flee, she didn't want to alarm anyone or create a scene. She wouldn't give Guy the satisfaction.

In the elegant but cramped parlor that served as a retiring room, Artemis found Lucy installed on a settee in a shadowy corner. A maid sat upon a footstool at her feet, fussing with the Bruges lace at the hem while Mabel Babbington was making good use of a nearby armchair and an ottoman as she drank a cup of tea. All about them, other ladies twittered away as their hair was repaired or their own genuinely soiled or damaged gowns were put to rights. Although, a few of them did turn to pointedly stare at Artemis as she entered the room.

Artemis ignored them.

"I'm so sorry I left before your dance ended," said Lucy when Artemis joined her. "But my father was trying to foist some American industrialist chap by the name of Whittaker onto me. Even though he had lovely blue eyes, he had the most fearsome muttonchops I've ever seen. They were so distracting I had to force myself to stop staring at them. And of course, we had nothing in common and I could not think of one word to say that wasn't 'quite' or 'capital' or 'jolly good.' I sounded like a complete imbecile, and the whole encounter was hideously wince inducing." She suddenly smiled and nudged Artemis's arm. "Unlike your waltz with that devilishly handsome duke. Now that was blush inducing. I swear his gaze was fairly smoldering as he looked at you. Everyone was riveted by the sight. And the fact that he picked you over anyone else…" Lucy's eyes filled with a wistful light. "You know, I'm quite the pragmatist when it comes to most things in life, but that was entirely romantical. You must have caught his eye, my gorgeous friend."

"Oh. Yes. Perhaps. Red hair does tend to stand out in a crowd." Artemis felt her cheeks heat with a scalding blush. She didn't want to confess that she'd already met the duke on two other occasions and sparks had flown—at least, she'd thought so—so she simply added, "And you're right. He is very handsome. But it was just one dance so it hardly signifies. And then there's all that scandal attached to his name. I'm sure that's the reason everyone was watching us." She briefly recounted what Aunt Roberta had told her. "I'm not inclined to believe any of the rumors about him though."

"Neither am I," said Lucy. "Of course, I only read about it in the newspapers last year, but the coroner's verdict was good enough for me. Society is far too cruel sometimes."

"Indeed, it is," agreed Artemis. *And so are so-called gentlemen like Guy de Burgh.*

After accepting a cup of tea from dear Miss Babbington, Artemis wondered again if she *had* seen something about the duke, and his poor late wife, in the paper so that was why their names sounded familiar.

But no, there was something else… She frowned as she sipped her tea.

Juliet… Dartmoor…

And then she remembered. It was as though someone had turned on a gaslight in her mind. During her debut Season, she'd heard whispers that Guy de Burgh's sister had been supremely well connected. A duchess.

The Duchess of Dartmoor.

Artemis deposited her teacup on its saucer with a clatter. How completely bizarre and disconcerting in the extreme. To think the Duke of Dartmoor's brother-in-law—a thoroughly coldhearted, cold-blooded scoundrel—had been Artemis's first lover. And his poor sister was now dead…

Despite the warmth of the room, an ice-cold shiver slithered through Artemis, and her cup rattled against the saucer again.

"Artemis, are you all right?" murmured Lucy. Concern filled her lavender-blue eyes. "You've spilled your tea."

"Oh, so I have." Artemis gratefully accepted a napkin from Miss Babbington. "I'm just tired. That's all." She'd never told anyone about Guy de Burgh—not even Lucy or Jane. At the time, she'd been too humiliated. And then, as the years had gone by, it hadn't seemed all that important anymore. There was no point in crying over spilt milk.

"Are you sure?" asked Lucy. "You've gone awfully pale. Perhaps you need some fresh air. It *is* terribly stuffy in here."

Artemis couldn't disagree. Perspiration prickled along her spine, and the tea and champagne she'd drunk earlier began to swirl uncomfortably in her belly. "I suppose I could take a quick turn about the Castledowns' terrace. I know it's probably not the 'done thing' at an event like this, but surely a spinster nearing thirty is able to exercise a small degree of autonomy."

"Exactly," said Lucy with a nod. She glanced at Miss Babbington, who appeared to be drifting off to sleep. "I'd come with you to keep you company, but I feel I should stay and look after Cousin Mabel."

"I understand," said Artemis. "When I'm feeling restored, I shall return."

As soon as Artemis emerged from the ladies' retiring room, she was immediately grateful for the fresher air in the hallway outside. The terrace couldn't be too far away. She'd just gained the gallery that led back to the main staircase when someone called her name. A man.

Guy de Burgh.

Curse him to the farthest reaches of hell. He'd clearly followed her.

Artemis halted, and after dragging in a steadying breath, she slowly turned around to face him. Perhaps it was better to have this out than to run away.

They weren't alone in the gallery. Another couple who seemed to be admiring a marble bust dallied at the far end, and surely at any moment, some of the women crowding the ladies' retiring room would emerge and make their way back to the ballroom. Or Phoebe and Aunt Roberta might even come looking for her. In any event, she wouldn't have to endure Guy's odious company for too long.

Lifting her chin, Artemis attempted to stare down her former paramour as he stalked across the polished parquetry floor toward her.

"Artemis," he said, his voice silky with a familiarity that made her skin crawl. "It's been such a long time."

"Not long enough, Mr. de Burgh," she returned frostily.

"Now, now. There's no need to be rude. Not when we used to be such good friends. And it's Lord Gascoyne now."

Artemis arched a brow in disdain. She wasn't going to verbally acknowledge his title. She certainly wouldn't curtsy either. "Friends?" she huffed. "I utterly dispute your characterization of our former relationship. Friendship is not based upon a bed of lies."

Oh, no. Why had she chosen to use the word *bed*?

Lord Gascoyne's smile was the epitome of sly. "If my memory serves me correctly, we managed quite well without a bed. But in any case, I suppose you're right." He took several steps closer. "We were far more than friends, weren't we, my dear?"

Artemis narrowed her eyes, but the viscount didn't retreat. Apparently, her scorching she-devil stare didn't work on the likes of Lord Gascoyne. "It doesn't matter what we were in the past," she said in the most glacial tone she could muster. "What matters is the present. And there is nothing between us at all. To that end, I would ask that you cease to address me by my first name. Or 'my dear.'"

He emitted a derisive bark of laughter. "Very well, *Miss* Jones. Although now that I'm a widower, I predict it won't be long before we're on familiar terms again."

Artemis couldn't suppress a gasp. "A widower? I had no idea your wife had passed away." Even though Guy had chosen Evangeline Gibbs over her, she'd never borne the woman any malice for what had happened. Her ill treatment, her betrayal, had been at the hands of Guy. "I'm...I'm sorry for your loss," she added with grave sincerity.

Gascoyne shrugged. In the golden glow of a nearby wall sconce, his dark gaze glittered. "Don't you read, Artemis? It was in all of the newspapers both here and in America. I wouldn't feel too sad for me though. It wasn't the most amicable of marriages in the end, and Evie's been gone over three years now. A case of typhlitis, the doctor said. Nothing could have been done. In any event, since I inherited the viscountcy, I'm back in London for good—"

"And on the prowl for another wealthy wife?" Artemis couldn't resist aiming a nettled barb his way.

"Just like you appear to be on the prowl for a rich, titled husband."

"Is that what you think I'm doing?"

"Well, clearly." His mouth twisted with a cruel smile. "Isn't that why you did what you did with me all of those years ago? Weren't you trying to tempt me into marriage with your Jezebel wiles? And isn't that why you just shamelessly threw yourself at the Duke of Dartmoor? In front of an entire room full of people?"

Oh...the things she could say to this detestable, despicable, contemptible *arse*. Anger shimmered like a heat haze in front of her vision as Artemis bit out, "I am *not* here to find a husband. Nor to use my supposed Jezebel wiles on anybody. Least of all, you."

Gascoyne snorted. "You can deny it all you like, but take it from me, you'd best stay away from Dartmoor. I don't care what the coroner decreed—I take it you read about *that* in the papers, didn't you?—I know the dog murdered my sister. He's a dangerous man—"

"Oh, and you're not?"

"Artemis"—Gascoyne stepped close and grasped her upper arm—"I know we didn't part on the best of terms all those years ago, but in all seriousness, you should heed—"

"Don't attempt to play the role of my knight in shining armor," she hissed. "I have no reason, at all, to trust a single word you say." She tried to shake Gascoyne off, but to her alarm, his grip only grew tighter. Even through the silk of her sleeve, his fingers pinched with bruising force. "Now remove your hand, or so help me—"

"Yes, remove your hand from Miss Jones's person before I remove it for you, Gascoyne."

Chapter Nine

Artemis glanced past the viscount's shoulder, and her mouth dropped open. The Duke of Dartmoor stood directly behind them, his expression thunderous. The air around them crackled with tension. Even the gaslights flickered.

Gascoyne's hand fell away as he turned to face her unexpected champion. "Dartmoor," he snarled. "This is none of your bus—"

"I beg to differ." The duke's cutting, steel-laced tone brooked no argument. It resonated with absolute authority. "Miss Jones clearly wants nothing to do with you. So I'd suggest you leave. Before things become…unpleasant."

A muscle twitched in Gascoyne's cheek. "Go on then. Have her," he snapped. His ire-filled gaze flicked to Artemis. "Remember, I did try to warn you about him. Don't blame me if—"

"It's a pity no one thought to warn me about you, *my lord*," returned Artemis coldly. "But there is something I can thank you for: I'm not as gullible as I used to be."

"Despite all evidence to the contrary," muttered Gascoyne through his teeth. Nevertheless, he turned on his heel and marched away from Artemis and the duke.

Well… Artemis attempted to inhale a bracing breath, but her corset restricted the movement of her ribs. Her heart was racing. Galloping. Whether her agitated state was a result of encountering Lord Gascoyne again, or the fact she was stand-ing face-to-face with the Duke of Dartmoor, she couldn't be certain.

She flicked open her fan and fluttered it as madly as Phoebe had been doing earlier. "Your Grace," she said, hoping she didn't sound as flustered as she felt. Indeed, her wits were so scattered by anger and now sheer relief that she was surprised she could speak at all. "I–I must thank you for your timely intervention. I am most grateful."

The duke smiled and tilted his head. "Think nothing of it, Miss Jones."

"Oh, but it isn't nothing." Artemis found herself smiling back, and some devil in her made her add, "Indeed, if you hadn't stepped in, I would have been forced to take drastic action myself."

"Such as?"

"Well, I would have had to whack Lord Gascoyne's knuckles with my fan." She snapped the silk leaves shut for emphasis.

The duke's eyes glinted with amusement. "A knuckle whack-ing. How positively brutal. Remind me never to get on your bad side, Miss Jones." He offered his arm. "May I escort you back to the ballroom?"

"I…" She smiled as she placed her gloved hand on his fore-arm. "Yes, of course. That would be most kind."

The duke led her toward the stairs. "I just wanted to reas-sure you that I only caught the end of your exchange with Lord Gascoyne," he said in a low voice. "I'm not one to eavesdrop. I only intervened when I heard your raised voice and noticed that he wouldn't release your arm."

"Lord Gascoyne…" Artemis pressed her lips together. She didn't really want to discuss such a personal, sensitive topic with a man she barely knew. But she also felt compelled to offer an explanation for the fraught scene the duke had stumbled upon. For some reason she'd rather not examine, the man's opinion of her mattered. "I met him during my first Season a decade ago," she said at last. "Not long before he proposed to Evangeline Gibbs. Of course, I haven't seen him in years. And quite frankly, I never wish to see him again. He... Suffice it to say, he is not my favorite person."

"I understand entirely." Apart from the flicker of a muscle in the duke's lean jaw, his expression was unreadable. "Actually, you might have heard that Gascoyne and I also have a testy relationship."

"I have." They'd reached the bottom of the staircase, and the hubbub of the ballroom surged toward them. "However, I should also add that I'm not the sort of person who listens to gossip eith—" Artemis got no further because all at once, she felt decidedly odd.

She clutched the duke's arm as black spots clouded her vision and her head spun as though she'd danced a wild mazurka.

"Are you all right?" he asked, concern filling his gaze.

"I'm...I'm not sure," she murmured. "Actually, I feel a little faint." Her chest was tight again, and perspiration trickled down her back.

"It's probably all these deuced gaslights." The duke nodded toward the enormous chandelier above them. "They suck all of the air from the room. If you can manage a few more steps toward those French doors, I recommend taking a therapeutic turn about the terrace."

Artemis hesitated, but only for a moment. Rightly or wrongly, she was inclined to believe the gossip about the Duke of Dartmoor was nothing more than a load of malicious rot.

She'd seen nothing to suggest he was a dangerous, perhaps even murderous man. If anything, aside from a handful of sardonic quips on the few occasions they'd met, he'd been nothing but chivalry personified. Tonight, he'd chased off Gascoyne for her. And even though he might not approve of her reading choices, that hadn't stopped him from helping her to collect her scattered books in the middle of the pouring rain. Not only had he saved her from falling over when they'd collided, he'd then insisted that she take the hackney.

He'd also sought out novels that would interest his daughter. Would a man who did something so thoughtful really be capable of doing away with his wife? Was he actually a cold-blooded murderer?

Artemis doubted it.

Mind made up, she acquiesced to his suggestion.

Once they stepped outside and the cool night air enveloped them, Artemis began to feel better; the dizziness faded, and she could breathe freely again. Several other couples, who only seemed to have eyes for each other, were dotted about the terrace. Nevertheless, it was a risk to linger out here with others for too long, so with Artemis's agreement, the duke led her down a short flight of stone steps into the garden.

"We'll find somewhere quieter for you to recover," he said.

Away from prying eyes… The inference, although unspoken, was clear, and Artemis appreciated that the duke understood the need for discretion. They'd already created a stir on the dance floor. If they were discovered out here alone together… Artemis shivered. The consequences, for her at least, could be catastrophic. As a confirmed spinster looking for a wealthy benefactress to invest in her college, *compromised* was a word she feared above all others.

Benefactress. Patroness… Or would a patron do? Could someone like the duke become a sponsor for her college? Artemis considered the idea, turning it over in her mind. She'd never actually thought about approaching a member of the opposite sex before because her school was for women, and it would take a progressive man indeed to embrace her radical philosophies. However, securing the support of a man with the moniker "the Dastardly Duke of Dartmoor" might not do her fledgling cause any favors either. Although, Aunt Roberta had mentioned the duke still retained the support of Queen Victoria…

And then she couldn't ignore the fact that she was currently engaging in less than ladylike behavior. How could she possibly court the favor of a nobleman like Dominic Winters when she'd quite readily accompanied him out here? She could hardly claim her own character was beyond reproach, could she?

Artemis sighed inwardly. Unfortunately, it seemed her true, passionate, reckless self—the part of her that she kept carefully pinned up and buttoned away most of the time—was also secretly thrilled that she was alone in a dark garden with someone like the Duke of Dartmoor.

The duke quickly located a stone bench in a secluded, shadowy corner near a towering box hedge and a tinkling fountain. The scent of roses from a nearby arbor drifted around them. If seduction *was* on the Duke of Dartmoor's mind, it was the perfect spot for a romantic encounter.

To dispel some of the gathering tension—just thinking about what might happen next made Artemis's stomach flutter wildly—she cast about for something to say as she sank onto the bench. Of course, she'd like to know more about Juliet, the duke's poor late wife, but that didn't seem like an appropriate topic at the present moment. Instead, she ventured into safer territory. "Your Grace, I've been wondering if your daughter likes the Jane Austen titles you purchased from Delaney's."

"Yes, I believe she does." He shrugged a wide shoulder, then winced. "At least, her governess tells me so. My daughter keeps to herself these days. Well, when she's not telling me I don't understand her or making some outrageous demand. To be honest, I had no idea adolescent girls could be so complicated. I hope it's a passing phase."

"It's been my experience—" Artemis broke off, not sure if she wanted to reveal too much about her past. But then, the duke was being surprisingly candid with her, so she added, "Until recently, I was a teacher at a finishing school in Bath. And yes, girls aged between fourteen and sixteen can behave like veritable she-devils on occasion. No doubt, that was why my own late father—he was a vicar—packed me off to boarding school when I was fifteen, and then he supported my aunt Roberta's wish to send me to a rather strict finishing school after that." A rueful laugh escaped her. "Like most fathers, I think he rather hoped that I would have grown out of my wicked, wayward ways by the time I graduated."

The duke flashed her a rakish grin. "And did you?"

She cast him an arch smile in return. "Considering I'm now alone in an isolated arbor with a nobleman I barely know…"

"Good God, I'm done for." Dartmoor groaned with mock drama and clutched at his chest. "My daughter will be the death of me. She's already turning me gray."

Artemis couldn't help but laugh at his theatrics. "You look healthy enough to me, Your Grace."

"I'm glad you think so." He smiled and her heart performed a strange little somersault.

Oh…oh, Beelzebub's ballocks, and Mephistopheles's member,

and Lucifer's love truncheon. Why did the Duke of Dartmoor have to be so damned attractive *and* charming with just the right dash of roguishness thrown into the mix? He could be the Prince of Darkness himself, sent to lead her astray. Yes, he was dangerous, but not in the sense everyone else meant. He was exactly the sort of dangerous that should be written in bloodred ink in bold capital letters as a warning to jaded spinsters like her. In fact, the word should be emblazoned upon the back of his practically painted-on evening jacket. Or better yet, tattooed in the middle of his high, noble forehead so it couldn't be missed.

She'd once been taken in by Guy de Burgh, but of course, this time she wouldn't be fooled by false declarations of love and lies about happily-ever-afters. She'd have her eyes wide open. Because men like the Duke of Dartmoor didn't wed women like her—the too-brazen-for-her-own-good bluestocking daughter of a lower-gentry clergyman. Her aunt might possess a title by marriage and considerable wealth, but that hardly signified. Artemis was still lowborn. Not of the right bloodline. Not suitable duchess material at all. She certainly wasn't stepmother material.

No, the Duke of Dartmoor would only want her for one thing. The only question that really mattered was: Would she be willing to risk everything if Dartmoor did indeed try to seduce her? Was she strong enough to resist her own libidinous impulses?

Of course, as she'd surmised before, simply being caught alone with Dartmoor would be an unmitigated disaster. Her reputation would be mud. Her plans to open a college would become dust.

She should go back inside.

At once.

But she didn't. It had been so long since she'd been with a man. Ten long years to be exact, and while Guy had burned her, she would be a hypocrite if she didn't acknowledge the fact that she'd enjoyed lovemaking even if love had little to do with it. Women had needs too, and it seemed like forever since hers had been met by anyone other than herself. Having a little amorous adventure with the Duke of Dartmoor was a tantalizing prospect, despite the danger.

She glanced at the duke who waited nearby at a respectful distance, hands clasped behind his back. He seemed to be engrossed in his own thoughts, his storm-cloud gaze cast downward. A pale wash of silvery moonlight and the ambient glow of garden lanterns revealed that his slashing black brows had dipped into a slight frown. His chiseled mouth was set in a serious line. In his evening attire, he was a study in male beauty—all sharp masculine angles and lean, elegant lines. In a word, breathtaking. Or as Aunt Roberta had stated earlier, a man in his prime.

Artemis flicked open her fan. Just imagining what was beneath the duke's clothing was making her all hot and bothered again. At least the shadows concealed the fact that her cheeks had probably turned the same rosy-red hue as her gown.

At her movement, the duke looked up and his mouth tilted into a smile that was pure sin. "Am I making you swoon again, Miss Jones?"

Artemis didn't want to give away how actually flustered she was, so she rolled her eyes. The man clearly knew he was attractive and didn't need any encouragement. "Oh, the conceit of you, Your Grace," she returned. "It's my tightly cinched corset and the layers of fabric I'm drowning in that are the problem."

Even though her last comment was more of a mutter to herself, it seemed Dartmoor had excellent hearing. "I could help you with that," he said with another wicked grin. "The cinching. Or should I say, uncinching?"

Artemis couldn't contain a huff of laughter. "I'm sure you could." Oh, but he was indeed a conceited coxcomb. And for some reason she couldn't fathom, she liked that about him too. The fact that his innate arrogance was appealing rather than off-putting should terrify her.

"That being said..." She snapped her fan shut and stood. It was time to put the duke in his place and put some distance between them before she did lose her head completely. "It would be remiss of me *not* to take you to task for making such an entirely improper suggestion. Which also begs the question: Do you say things like that to women often?" Even though she tried to maintain a reproving look, she failed utterly, because the corner of her mouth kept hitching into a smile. "It's not terribly gentlemanly. Or original."

With a few swift steps, Dartmoor was standing right in front of her. "But judging by your expression, you're amused, no? And you'd be surprised how infrequently I make such an offer to anyone, Miss Jones."

"Oh, so I'm one of the chosen few? I count myself fortunate indeed."

"Do you know what I *especially* like about you? The quality that marks you as different from most of the women I've encountered in the past?"

"I have not the slightest idea," she said. And she truly didn't.

"I like you, Miss Artemis Jones, for the simple reason that you *didn't* swoon when you learned that I'm a duke. Or that I have an infamous reputation. You have a mind of your own and are not easily swayed or intimidated."

Oh... Artemis hadn't expected such an admission, and she

was momentarily lost for words. "Well, I suppose some women would. Swoon, I mean. But"—she met his steady gaze—"I rather like it that *you* aren't impressed by women who are fawning or foolish or overly timid."

His perfect teeth flashed in a wolfish grin. "A point in my favor, then."

"If this is a game, I'm not keeping score, Your Grace."

"Oh, I am," he said. "And it's a game I hope to win."

"Win?" Artemis lifted her chin. "And what is the prize, pray tell?"

Oh, that was a silly question. Dartmoor drew closer. So close that his legs brushed her skirts. So close that the heat radiating from his large body seemed to warm every bit of Artemis's bare flesh that was on display—her cheeks, her throat, her shoulders, and her arms. The tops of her breasts that rose and fell with each quickened breath she took.

"I thought it was obvious, Miss Jones," he murmured in a voice as dark and hot and soft as smoke. A voice that curled around her and set her aflame. "I want you in my arms. The question is…do you feel the same way?"

Artemis bit her lip, intense want warring with her last shreds of common sense. She should be affronted that he was insulting her honor, but she wasn't. Their innuendo-laden verbal sparring had no doubt revealed she wasn't a virginal shrinking violet who'd run away at the first suggestion of a moonlit tryst.

And then of course, she couldn't deny she wanted this. This feeling of being alive. Of being desired. She knew what the risks were—all of them—and yes, she *was* willing to take them, right here, right now. To steal a few heady moments in the arms of someone like Dominic Winters who happened to be the most handsome, compelling man she'd ever met.

A Byronic hero in the flesh.

She glanced about. No one else lingered in this corner of the Castledowns' garden. Although the muted buzz of conversation, laughter, and music floated through the velvet darkness toward them, they were ostensibly alone. Of course, that might change at any moment…

Perhaps sensing her hesitation, and the reason for it, Dartmoor whispered, his voice as deliciously persuasive as a caress, "I understand the need to be careful, Miss Jones, and precisely what's at stake. What you're risking. If you prefer, we can return to the house—"

"No. That's not what I want. I want…" She swallowed and reached for one of his large hands. Entwined her gloved fingers through his. "I want this too." It wasn't a lie. One thing she'd learned in her twenty-nine years on this earth was that life, for many, could be unfair and far too short.

So yes, she'd take hold of this experience Dominic Winters was offering her, with both hands and with no regrets.

Capturing her gaze, Dartmoor lifted her hand, then pressed his lips to her knuckles. Even through the thin silk of her gloves, the light touch seared the skin beneath. "This? Is this what you want, Miss Jones?"

"I…" She licked her lips. Exquisite anticipation unfurled low in her belly. "Not exactly, Your Grace."

"Hmmm." He turned her hand and, with a deft flick, undid the pair of pearl buttons securing the top of her glove. "What about this?" he murmured before parting the fabric and brushing a whisper-soft kiss on the exposed tender flesh of her inner wrist. His warm breath teased even more than his intimate touch. "Is this any better?"

"A little." He was playing games again, but she didn't mind. Not in the least.

"Well, a *little* better isn't good enough. I certainly wouldn't want to disappoint." Dartmoor leaned in. The scent of aroused male and the expensive cologne he favored drifted around her, tantalizing her. Brushing aside her curls with gentle fingers, he placed his mouth upon her neck, just below her ear before grazing her jaw with another kiss.

A tiny moan tumbled from Artemis's lips. "I think you're getting closer to the mark, you cruel, cruel man," she whispered. Unfulfilled desire was burning her from the inside out. One of her hands came up to grip his arm. Through the layers of fine fabric, she felt his hard-as-marble biceps twitch and flex. It was all she could do not to wrap herself around him.

His warm breath gusted against her cheek as he emitted a low chuckle. "Cruel, am I?"

"Yes. Excessively so," she returned. She caught his sharply cut jaw with one hand and turned his head until their lips were almost touching. "You know exactly what I want, Dartmoor, so just do it. Kiss me before I expire with—"

She got no farther as Dartmoor at last relented, pressing his mouth to hers. The sinuous glide of his lips was commanding yet languid. The pressure firm yet as soft and voluptuous as satin. As he ever so gently cradled her face between his hands, she tangled her fingers in his thick silky hair. Dragged him closer. Kissed him harder. Oh, how she'd missed this glorious feeling. It would be far easier to live the life of a spinster if her body didn't crave this sort of contact. If she felt nothing at all for a man like Dominic Winters.

But she did, and God help her, Dartmoor was a masterful kisser. When his tongue caressed hers, the hot, slick strokes were long and deep and slow. And the taste of him… Her mouth was flooded with the flavor of warm brandy and the man himself.

He tasted like the perfect blend of heaven and sin. This kiss was so potent, so wickedly delicious, her head began to whirl. But the most intoxicating thing of all was the way Dartmoor continued to kiss her with determined, deliberate languor. As though he had all the time in the world to explore her mouth. To devour and savor. Give her untold pleasure.

One of his large hands slid to her shoulder, then lower. When he cupped her breast, she shamelessly pushed herself into his palm, striving to get closer, to increase the pressure. Lust raced through her veins, setting every part of her alight. If they were anywhere else right now, she'd—

"Artemis? Are you out here, gel?"

Oh God! Artemis ripped her mouth from Dartmoor's and jumped away as though she'd been struck by lightning. "It's my aunt," she whispered, breathless with panic and thwarted desire. "She cannot find us here together."

Dartmoor inhaled deeply and ran a hand through his already tousled hair. "I understand and I'll make myself scarce. Only…" He reached out and gently grasped her arm. His eyes locked with hers. "I must see you again. Tell me that you'll agree to another—"

"Artemis?"

Dartmoor swore softly. In a voice that was low and urgent, he murmured, "Send word to me." And then he seemed to meld into the deep shadows of the hedge behind them.

Artemis blinked. The duke wanted to see her again? She had no further opportunity to reflect on the matter as in the next instant, Aunt Roberta rounded the corner.

"Artemis! Thank heavens. I've been looking for you everywhere," her aunt declared. "Phoebe's frantic with worry. What on earth are you doing out here all by yourself?"

"I..." Artemis glanced nervously toward the shadows again. Thank goodness the duke *had* completely disappeared. There must be a convenient gap in the hedge that was impossible to discern in the darkness. "I'm sorry to have upset you and Phoebe," she continued as she bent to retrieve her fan and reticule from the stone bench. "I wasn't feeling well and needed a breath of fresh air."

Aunt Roberta examined her through her lorgnette with a critical eye. "Now, why don't I believe you?"

Artemis squared her shoulders. The best thing to do in a situation like this was to creatively embellish half-truths. And if that failed, she'd brazen it out. She couldn't have her aunt thinking she'd sneaked outside for a romantic rendezvous. "If you must know, I crossed paths with..." She paused—perhaps it was better not to mention Lord Gascoyne. "I learned that someone I used to know some time ago, a young woman who I debuted with, had passed away. I had no idea, and as you can imagine, such unexpected news was upsetting. I simply needed a few quiet minutes to regain my composure. Given the ladies' retiring room was terribly crowded, the garden seemed like the perfect place to escape to."

"Hmmm..." Aunt Roberta looked skeptical. "Is it anyone I know?"

"No. I shouldn't think so. In any event, I'm feeling much better now, so let's return to the ballroom and let Phoebe know I'm all right. And then I should check on Lucy." She'd only just realized that one of her gloves was still undone and she surreptitiously refastened the pearl buttons as she began to follow her aunt back toward the house. She should probably check if there was anything else amiss with her appearance in the ladies' retiring room.

Most of all, she needed to calm down. The duke's last words echoed in her mind: *I must see you again... Send word to me...* Artemis's cheeks burned at just the thought of meeting Dartmoor again, but she resisted the urge to fan herself in case her aunt remarked upon the fact she seemed so flustered.

But perhaps Aunt Roberta had noticed something was amiss. They'd almost regained the terrace when she said, "Artemis, I feel it is my duty to remind you, yet again, that you must not skulk away on your own at events like this. I know you see yourself as on the shelf, and you value your independence, but you'll only feed the gossipmongers. In the absence of facts, they'll speculate." Her tone was frost laden as she added, "And I *will* not have any scandal attached to the family name. If you and your sister are to secure suitable matches, you must not put a foot wrong. You do understand that, don't you?"

"Yes, I do." And she honestly did. *But...but...* She ground her back teeth together. Society's hypocrisy rankled her no end. Men like the Duke of Dartmoor and Lord Gascoyne could do whatever they liked, whenever they liked with impunity, but women were never free of etiquette's tight yoke.

Unless and until the rules of society changed, women would always be constrained by restrictions men were not subject to. Their choices in life would always be limited. Why couldn't she have an obligation-free romantic liaison—or even take a lover—if she wanted to? She wanted the freedom men had, God damn it.

Most of all, she wanted to make a difference, even if it was only in a small way. And she would do that when she started her college. Somehow, some way, she would make it happen. If only she didn't have a dragon of a chaperone like Aunt Roberta breathing down her neck all the time, watching her every move. She'd truly had enough.

And then a mad, mad idea drifted through Artemis's mind. A way to free herself from her aunt's tight sphere of control, once and for all.

As soon as Artemis could meet with Lucy and Jane to discuss her plan, she would.

Chapter Ten

"YOU WANT TO DO WHAT?" ASKED LUCY, HER EYES WIDE with incredulity.

"I must say, Artemis, it sounds a trifle risky," added Jane.

Artemis regarded her friends across the afternoon-tea-laden table in Mr. Delaney's parlor. "I know, but if I can make this work, with your help"—she caught each of her friends' gazes in turn—"I will be truly free to pursue my goal of finding a patroness for my academic college at long last. And because Aunt Roberta will have washed her hands of me, she'll focus all her attention on finding a husband for Phoebe instead."

"Your reasoning is sound and no one could doubt your motives, Artemis, but…" Jane, always the sensible one, looked unconvinced. "It could all go horribly wrong."

"There won't be any issue at all with you staying with me as a companion once your aunt disowns you, Artemis," added Lucy. "So I don't want you to worry on that score. But have you thought about how you will persuade the Duke of Dartmoor to go along with your plan? Do you think that he will?"

Artemis had already disclosed her attraction to the duke and their prior encounters, including their tryst at the Castledowns' ball the night before. "Well, as I mentioned, he did ask to see me again."

"Yes, but for a romantic liaison, Artemis," said Lucy. "What you are suggesting is something else entirely."

"In the interest of full disclosure, I think you must tell him about your scheme and ask for his consent to participate," added Jane. "He has a right to know what he might be getting himself into."

"Because he's a man—and a nobleman at that—the risk to his reputation is minimal," said Artemis. "But you're right. I should ask him if he's willing to be involved." She tried to imagine what the duke might say to her proposition but couldn't. Would he say yes or dismiss her outright? He might even laugh at her. Oh, how lowering that would be.

"I'm glad you agree," said Jane. "Now, the next important step in your plan is to work out strategies to minimize the risk to you. As you said, this needs to be a strategic ruination."

"Yes. I can't actually be ruined in a public sense," agreed Artemis. "If my reputation is destroyed in truth, there is no way on earth that I will be able to open my college. Who would send their daughter to an establishment with a hussy for a headmistress? Aside from that, I don't wish to spoil Phoebe's chances at finding a match. That wouldn't be fair."

"Have you thought of telling your aunt that you are already deflowered? I mean *we* know you're not," said Jane. "But if she believes your white lie, she might disown you outright anyway."

Artemis's cheeks grew hot. Oh, if only her friends knew that she'd lost her virginity long ago! But to make such a confession would mean recounting her affair with Guy de Burgh, and she couldn't do it. The humiliation would be too much. "I *could* fabricate a story for Aunt Roberta," she said at length, "but I don't think it would make a difference. Because no one else knows that I'm not as pure as the driven snow, it wouldn't really matter to her. Unless I fell pregnant. But of course I'm not with child so…" She shrugged.

"Hmmm. I see your point," said Lucy. "It's the *threat* of a public ruination that is important here, not the actual deed. Still, it will certainly be a delicate operation."

Jane tapped her chin. "What if we lead Lady Wagstaff to where Artemis and her duke are having their tryst, and she discovers them in flagrante?" she said. "Then, all you and I have to do, Lucy, is make lots of noise along the lines of 'Oh no, look someone's coming this way. What if they see something? What if someone tattles to one of the gossip rags?' You know, make a bit of a kerfuffle that impresses upon Lady Wagstaff that word about the tryst *will* get out and that imminent social disaster is nigh, even if it isn't."

Lucy clapped her hands. "Excellent idea. This might just work. Now, all we have to do is decide which ball this staged ruination will take place at, arrange invitations for all of us, and you, my dear Artemis…"

Artemis sighed. "I need to speak with the Duke of Dartmoor. And pray that he agrees."

Jane settled her green gaze on her. "I have to ask the question though… Have you thought of approaching the duke and asking him to be your school's patron? You could avoid risking your reputation altogether if you could obtain the funding you need. Then you can do what you like."

"I have. Briefly but…" Heat flooded Artemis's cheeks. "After our encounter last night, it feels odd to be asking the duke for money. I worry that I'll come across as mercenary and perhaps even a little grubby doing so. Of course, we've only exchanged kisses but…" She shrugged. "A woman who so readily agrees to romantic trysts at the drop of a hat with a man she barely knows is hardly a paragon of virtue. And I can't help but think he might not want to support a controversial cause given his own notoriety. And vice versa. No doubt the public endorsement of a forward-thinking noblewoman of influence might serve me better than that of a man known as 'the Dastardly Duke.'"

"Hmmm, true, but surely it couldn't hurt to mention your project to him," said Jane. "He could be a silent partner if nothing else."

"I suppose I could do that, and if he makes an offer to help of his own volition, I'd seriously consider it. But if he doesn't"—Artemis gave a wry smile—"I must forge ahead with my ruination scheme no matter what."

"And there's no chance at all your aunt would consider becoming a patroness of your college?" asked Lucy.

Artemis shook her head. "Never. She firmly believes that all women should marry and that a finishing school education is all that is necessary. That it's against the laws of nature to do otherwise." She released another sigh. "Even if the Duke of Dartmoor or indeed someone else offers to invest in my school, I suspect that my aunt will continue her crusade to see me wed. I'm equally certain my sister will never get her Season until I capitulate. Yes"—Artemis gave an emphatic nod—"Aunt Roberta must disown me completely. This needs to be a clean break. And the only way to achieve that end is for her to catch me red-handed. It's the shock of seeing me in the arms of a man, along with the *threat* of a monumental scandal that will do the trick. She'll be so horrified by my lack of remorse and refusal to wed that it will be the last straw."

———————

Dominic always enjoyed having dinner at Northam House, even though the occasions were few and far between. His sister employed a damn good cook and her husband, Edward, kept an impressive cellar.

He also enjoyed seeing his two youngest nephews, Teddy and Jasper, high-spirited twins aged seven years old. The two older boys—Rupert and Henry—were now at Eton, but Dominic always made time to visit the nursery to chat with the twins, even though it was a bittersweet exercise. As he listened to the boys prattle away about their favorite toys and games and books and what mischief they'd been up to, he tried not to think about all the might-have-beens with Juliet. It was only natural that the tight reins on his control would loosen, and he would find his thoughts wandering to the son they would never have.

The babe they'd lost... If things had been different, he would have been almost old enough to attend Eton too.

Dominic was always grateful that Horatia and Edward's company was most diverting at dinner. Edward's claret during the meal, followed by a nip or two of French cognac, always helped to dilute his grief, at least for a little while.

Just like a certain flame-haired siren who had the ability to make him forget about his all-too-painful past whenever he was with her. As he accepted a third glass of cognac from Edward, he wondered if she would actually agree to meet with him again. Would she be insulted that he'd propositioned her? He would understand entirely if she was.

But her kisses had been sublime. The taste and feel of her. The way she'd moaned and responded to every flagrant thing he'd done. But it wasn't just that. He was stimulated by her conversation. Her boldness and pithy observations. Even the occasional slip of her tongue.

Good God, her deliciously tart tongue.

One thing was patently clear: Dominic needed to spend

more time with her. It had been so long since he'd felt such a passion for anyone or anything other than his business affairs and managing his vast estate. And it was becoming more than evident that Miss Artemis Jones might be more addictive than his brother-in-law's very good spirits. It was as though she was the opiate his soul desperately needed to assuage his pain.

And his ever-present guilt.

Horatia's return to the dining room interrupted his brooding.

"Are the boys all settled?" asked Edward as he waved a footman over to pour her a sherry.

"Yes, at last," she said before turning her attention to Dominic. "And you'll be pleased to know, dear brother, that Celeste is still quite happily installed in the library with Miss Sharp and a fresh pot of tea. We had a brief chat about what it means to be a duke's daughter and the importance of maintaining one's reputation, and she was most receptive to everything I said." Horatia grimaced. "At least I think so. Adolescent girls are so hard to decipher."

"I know what you mean." Dominic sighed. "But I'm glad Celeste listened to you. Perhaps we've seen the worst of this strange moody stage she's been going through."

Indeed, earlier this evening, he'd been nothing but pleased when Celeste had readily agreed to accompany him to her aunt and uncle's house without making a huge fuss. By fuss, he meant a bout of histrionic crying and accusations that he was being grossly cruel and unfair to make her sit through a boring family dinner when all they ever talked about was politics and business and horses and estate management. And how could she possibly go out when none of her gowns would do, yet he'd refused to provide her with a new wardrobe for the Season?

No, she'd smiled sweetly and had murmured, "Yes, Papa," when he'd told her what he expected. It had been almost *too* easy.

Dominic hoped that she wasn't up to something. However, he'd talk to Miss Sharp tomorrow to reassure himself that everything was indeed all right.

Horatia sipped her sherry, then settled a measured look upon him. "So, I hear you made quite a splash at the Castledowns' ball last night."

Dominic cocked a brow. "I have no idea what you're talking about."

"Of course you do. My friends were simply abuzz with gossip about the Duke of Dartmoor during all my morning calls. About the huge stir you created with your dramatic entrance last night—how the entire room stopped and stared. And then how you singled out a mysterious redheaded woman in a bright-red gown and asked her to waltz. You're the talk of the town. It's in all the papers."

"Sorry, old chap, but I'm afraid I also heard a few fellows talking about you at my club this afternoon," added Edward.

Dominic grimaced. "It would be naive of me to hope that my name, or some bastardized version of it, hadn't appeared in the newspapers this morning." He'd avoided looking at any of the social pages because he knew he'd be irritated by whatever manufactured version of "the truth" appeared. As far as he was concerned, it would all be unmitigated rubbish.

"Everything I came across tended to focus on the fact you've come out of hiding to hunt for a new duchess," said Horatia. "Which is true. None of the pieces I saw mentioned the word 'dastardly' or were disparaging in any way, if that's what you're worried about. Although..." She cast him a knowing smile. "I'd like to know the identity of this ravishing redhead. No one of my acquaintance seems to know."

Dominic sipped his cognac. "She's no one of consequence," he said after a moment. "Just someone who caught my eye." Even though he trusted Horatia not to spread gossip, he suddenly felt rather protective of Miss Jones.

How decidedly odd.

But his sister wasn't going to let him off that easily. She gave a small snort. "I thought you wanted my opinion on anyone who sparked your interest. How am I to help if I'm kept in the dark?" Her expression turned sly. "I could always ask your hostess, Lady Castledown. I'm sure *she* would know this mysterious woman's name."

Dominic sighed in resignation. Horatia wouldn't leave him alone if he didn't share a few bread crumbs. "She's a bluestocking. The daughter of a vicar, but her aunt is a dowager baroness. Lady Wag-something."

Horatia's eyes glinted with interest. "So she's not entirely bereft of connections. And you seemed to have gleaned quite a bit about her during your waltz."

"You're making far too much out of this, Horatia. Yes, I shared one dance with the woman. That's all."

"But by all accounts, you didn't dance with anyone else," she countered.

"I was tired," he returned. "I've had a lot on my mind of late. And I wasn't in the mood to be rejected by umpteen blushing chits or their gaping mamas or outraged fathers."

"From what I've heard, this woman wasn't a mere chit. *And* she didn't reject you." Horatia sent him a speaking look. "I wonder why."

"Because she has better taste than most? She's not the shy,

retiring type? Because she doesn't listen to idle gossip or believe everything she reads in the newspapers? I don't know."

"I'm sure you do but you won't say," said Horatia. "And I think your unwillingness to talk about this woman speaks volumes. I think she *is* someone of consequence. To you at least."

Curse Horatia and her nosy questions and deuced perceptiveness. To stop himself from snapping at his sister—she didn't deserve that—Dominic drained his cognac and pushed his glass toward Edward. "If you wouldn't mind indulging me, old chap…"

"Of course." Edward's expression was a study in neutrality as he unstopped the crystal decanter and dispensed a double nip.

Horatia smirked at him but didn't say anything else.

Exasperation simmered inside Dominic's veins. "I like red," he conceded at last. "And she stood out in the crowd. That's all there is to it."

His sister inclined her head. "If you say so. But just know I'm always here if you do need my opinion about this redheaded bluestocking or anyone at all."

Conversation turned to a race meet that Horatia was keen on attending, and after Dominic finished his cognac, he repaired to the library to collect Celeste.

It appeared Miss Sharp had nodded off in a window seat. Celeste who sat by the fire, dark head bent, was apparently engrossed in *Pride and Prejudice*.

Dominic smiled as he approached. He was pleased Miss Jones's recommendation was proving to be popular. "Celeste…"

She jumped and squeaked and dropped her book. And a piece of paper slid out from between the pages as it hit the floor. "Oh, you startled me," she said, and then her cheeks immediately turned bright pink when her gaze fell to the rug. "Oh…"

Celeste's guilty expression made Dominic swoop down to retrieve the book and the paper before she could.

Suspicion prickling beneath his skin, he examined the sheet in his hands. It was a handwritten note. And then anger thundered in his veins as he took in the words.

My darling, beautiful Celeste, it began. *I count the hours, nay the minutes and seconds until I can see you again...* He could barely bring himself to read the remainder of the note that was full of vulgar suggestions and highly impassioned praise for his daughter's "attributes," but he did. The ridiculously florid passages seemed to float in a red haze.

It was signed with the single initial, *T.*

Somehow tamping down his roiling emotions and the urge to rip the paper to shreds and cast the pieces into the fire, Dominic said softly and very carefully, "What is this? Who is this 'T'?"

Celeste's countenance was now as pale as the snow-white lace at her throat and the love letter he held up for her to see. She swallowed. Licked her lips. "I... It's..."

Miss Sharp, who'd been startled awake by all of the commotion, drifted closer. Her eyes were huge in her ashen face as she took in her charge's reaction. "You must answer your father, my lady."

"Do you know who 'T' is, Miss Sharp?" Dominic demanded, his voice harsh with barely restrained ire. "Because he's penning highly inappropriate, illicit love notes to my fifteen-year-old daughter!"

The governess's throat worked in a nervous swallow. "I...I'm sorry. I have no idea, Your Grace," she whispered. "But I will endeavor—"

Dominic held up a hand. "Enough. We're leaving," he

snapped. Fury and frustration made him uncharacteristically impatient. "Celeste. You and I are going to have a talk when we get home. Between now and then, I expect you to recall 'T's name. Do I make myself clear?"

"Yes, Papa." Tears shimmered like moonlight in her silver-gray eyes as she rose shakily to her feet, but Dominic would *not* feel guilty about making his daughter cry. He was protecting her, God damn it.

If this 'T' had laid one filthy finger on her, taken any sort of liberty with the Duke of Dartmoor's daughter, the dog would be mincemeat.

A fraught hour and a river of tears later, Dominic was no closer to learning the identity of 'T,' and he was so damned furious, he could smash something.

When she wasn't sobbing incoherently, Celeste had remained steadfastly tight lipped about the identity of her paramour or where she'd met him or how long their "affair" had been going on. Or how far things had progressed. Miss Sharp had been tearful yet stoic; but in the end, she hadn't added anything useful to the discussion. No doubt the governess feared she'd lose her position because she hadn't been watching Celeste as closely as she ought to. Celeste's maid, Yvette, hadn't been able to provide any useful intelligence either. Neither had Morton or the housekeeper. There was one footman on staff at Dartmoor House by the name of Tod, but by all accounts, the young man could barely sign his own name, let alone pen a letter.

Even though he'd already had far too much to drink, Dominic retreated to his beloved library and poured himself a sizable dram of whisky. He needed something damnably strong to quell the fire blazing through his bloodstream. He was a bundle of thwarted energy. A barely contained firestorm about to rage. A volcano about to erupt. A grenade about to explode.

Yes, he needed an outlet, a way to vent steam, and right at this moment, it seemed that alcohol was the only thing that would do.

He was on his second dram when something on the edge of his desk's leather blotter caught his eye. An unopened envelope that bore his name in a flowing script that he didn't recognize. Putting down his whisky, Dominic reached for it and then sliced the flap open with his silver-bladed letter opener.

And then he smiled.

Your Grace,

If you had time to meet with me at Delaney's Antiquarian Bookshop tomorrow at four o'clock sharp, I would be most grateful. I have a proposition for you.

I'll be waiting by the Gothic novels.

A.J.

First thing in the morning, Dominic would ask Morton to clear his late-afternoon schedule. This was one appointment he did not want to miss.

Chapter Eleven

ARTEMIS HOVERED BY THE TOWERING SHELVES OF GOTHIC novels in Delaney's and tried to peruse Selina Davenport's *Italian Vengeance and English Forbearance*. According to her pocket watch, it was five minutes to four, and her heart was galloping faster than a runaway horse. Or perhaps, more aptly, a hapless heroine fleeing the clutches of a wickedly handsome but evil libertine.

After she'd spoken with Jane and Lucy yesterday, she'd quite boldly sent a message to Dartmoor House, inviting the duke to meet with her, but he hadn't responded. Of course, he might not have seen the need to. It might also be the case that the duke's servants hadn't passed on her missive. She'd bribed Phoebe's maid with a half crown to deliver it. Single young women of marriageable age shouldn't call on dukes, even to impart messages—not unless they wanted to start a scandal.

But perhaps the duke had simply changed his mind about wanting to see her again.

In any event, that meant she could be lingering here in Delaney's, a tightly knotted bundle of agonized uncertainty, for nothing. Her plan to free herself from Aunt Roberta's clutches could very well come to naught, a possibility that didn't bear thinking about.

With a deep sigh, Artemis slid Selina Davenport's book back into place, then randomly chose another. Whenever the shop's doorbell tinkled, she jumped and then looked over the railing to see if it was the duke. But so far, the only customers who'd entered had been a somberly suited gentleman who'd asked for an appraisal of a seventeenth-century atlas and a middle-aged woman who'd been picking up a restored family Bible. Jane and Lucy were upstairs in Mr. Delaney's parlor. As much as they wanted to catch sight of the Duke of Dartmoor, they'd promised they would wait patiently until Artemis joined them.

To wait patiently. Now that was something Artemis had never been able to do. For what seemed like the thousandth time, she glanced at her watch—it was two minutes to four—and then the doorbell rang once more and she heard the duke's distinctive baritone.

At the sound of the duke's heavy footfalls on the stairs, Artemis inhaled a calming breath and ran her damp palms down the skirts of her new bronze silk gown. When he appeared, she almost ceased breathing altogether.

Mephistopheles's member, the Duke of Dartmoor was sinfully, heart-stoppingly gorgeous. His superbly tailored coat and trousers showed off his lean, muscular form to perfection. And the wolfish grin he flashed made her bones as soft as sunwarmed butter. Especially when his gaze wandered over her with frank appreciation. Perhaps she *would* melt into a puddle at his feet this time.

"Miss Jones," he murmured as he approached. "You look lovely today."

Artemis swallowed. "So do you, Your Grace. I mean, you look well. More than well…" She bit her lip to stop herself from blathering. "You look very handsome," she concluded with a soft smile. There was no point in acting like a coy maiden. It was time to employ her so-called Jezebel wiles. And stroking the duke's not inconsiderable male pride couldn't hurt.

"Hmmm." Drawing near, he removed his top hat and placed it on the shelf above her head. He was so close, Artemis could see bright flecks of silver and pewter in the deep-gray depths of his eyes. Smell his delicious cologne and the starch of his collar. "You think I'm handsome?"

She arched a brow. "You arrogant peacock. You know you are."

"Arrogant peacock?" Even though his gaze had narrowed and he was regarding her through slitted, heavy lids—rather like a predator about to devour its prey—his voice was laced with sardonic amusement. "Am I supposed to be flattered by that remark?"

"You're not?" she asked with a coquettish flutter of her eyelashes. "I thought the defining characteristic of a duke was arrogance. And aren't peacocks the epitome of avian virility?"

His mouth twitched. "You think me virile?"

"Well, now, we've only shared a single kiss. You can't expect me to be *entirely* certain based upon that measure alone."

Something hot and intense like lightning flashed in the duke's eyes. He placed one hand on the shelf by her head. Leaned in until his mouth hovered just above hers. "I'd be happy to remove any doubt from your mind, Miss Jones. By whatever means you so desire. Just say the word."

Artemis's breath quickened, and beneath her corset, her nipples tightened into hard, aching points. She was playing with fire. It was exhilarating. Beyond intoxicating. But she wasn't ready to set the spark to the tinder *just* yet.

"I'm sure you could," she murmured huskily, then ducked beneath the duke's arm. As she deliberately sauntered down the narrow aisle between a set of bookcases, heading away from the stairs, she called over her shoulder, "But as you know, Your Grace, I have a proposition I'd like to discuss with you first."

She was certain she heard him mutter, "Minx," before he followed.

At the end of the sheltered aisle, Artemis spun around and leaned against the bookcase at her back. A soft shaft of late-afternoon sunlight filtered through a high window, highlighting the spiral of dancing dust motes in the air between them. The pleasant scents of beeswax polish and old books enveloped her and the duke as he drew close for a second time.

"I'm listening." His voice was a low, soft purr. "I will confess, I am more than a little curious."

She smiled. "I'm pleased to hear it." And then she willed herself to forge ahead with what needed to be said. "I have a request. A favor to ask that is on the unusual side, to say the least."

His eyebrows rose, but only for the briefest of moments. A corner of his wide mouth kicked into a smile. "Now I'm thoroughly intrigued."

"Of course, you are under no obligation to say yes to what I'm about to suggest." She clasped her hands together, bracing herself to continue. "I want to stage my own ruination so that my aunt, Lady Wagstaff, will stop hounding me to wed. I'm so very tired of being under her thumb and—"

The duke's brows plunged into a frown. "What the deuce? You want me to ruin you? Surely you don't mean that."

Artemis raised her chin. "Actually, I do. But not in a public manner. In a calculated, strategically planned manner so that the damage to my reputation is minimal. Simply being alone in a room with you is all it would take, but to leave my aunt in no doubt at all that I've been compromised, she needs to catch us while we're sharing a passionate kiss or two. Of course, you are under no obligation to offer for my hand. Actually, I'm counting on the fact that you won't. I just have to convince my aunt that I'm ruined so that she cuts ties with me. No one else need know."

Dartmoor crossed his arms and rocked back on his heels. "And how do you propose to manage all this exactly? Specifically, the 'no one else need know' part?"

"I have it all worked out," she said and then proceeded to describe the plan she'd hatched with Lucy and Jane. "Scandal is what my aunt fears most, so even though she'll disown me, she will never divulge the real reason for our estrangement. Of course, I still need to sort out when and where this staged event will happen. Everyone who is involved—Lucy, Jane, my aunt and sister, myself, and you, if you agree to participate—will need to secure invitations to the same function. A ball perhaps. Unless you don't wish to participate, Your Grace. I–I would understand if you were opposed to taking part in such an underhanded, potentially risky venture."

Dartmoor snorted. "Considering my reputation is already tarnished, there is hardly any risk to me, Miss Jones. No one would bat an eyelid if the Dastardly Duke was discovered debauching a woman at a ball and then refused to do the right thing. Most of high society expects dishonorable behavior from me. You, on the other hand"—his penetrating gaze searched hers—"you are risking everything if your plan goes awry. Are you really prepared for that?"

"I am. You see, it's not just marriage that I'm trying to avoid." Ignoring the tripping of her heart, Artemis inhaled a deep breath, then ventured, "I have other, quite significant plans for my future." As she shared her idea of establishing an academic women's college, the duke listened, his expression thoughtful.

"Being constantly scrutinized by my aunt is hampering my ability to find a much-needed sponsor," Artemis continued. "She will never support my endeavors. In fact, she might even undermine them. So it's best for everyone if we cut all ties sooner rather than later. You might think I'm foolish and reckless, but I must have my freedom. Indeed, for the chance to make my dream a reality, I would risk almost anything."

Artemis studied the duke's face, waiting in breathless anticipation for him to respond. If he had any inclination to lend his support to her cause—financial or otherwise—now would surely be the time for him to say so.

"I can see how passionate you are," he said after a short, tension-filled pause. "And while some might consider your idea controversial, I, for one, admire your vision. I have no doubt whatsoever that you have the drive, intelligence, and tenacity to succeed."

"Thank you," she said, hoping she didn't sound disappointed. Which was silly because she hadn't actually asked him to be a sponsor. At least he hadn't laughed at her plan.

"However," the duke continued, "while I'm inclined to become involved in your ruination scheme, I'm afraid my participation is conditional. I'll accept your proposition with one proviso."

Her interest piqued, Artemis arched a brow. "Oh, yes…"

"As you know, I have a fifteen-year-old daughter. Her name is Celeste. And even though she has a governess—Miss Sharp—who possesses excellent qualifications and references, I'm concerned she's not quite up to the task of keeping Celeste sufficiently stimulated—in an academic sense. My daughter is bright with an inquiring mind, and quite frankly, I'm concerned that she's bored. And because of that she's been"—the duke paused as if searching for the right word—"difficult of late. A little rebellious and inclined to get up to mischief not befitting a young lady of her station."

"Ah, I see," said Artemis. "Like reading salacious Gothic novels perhaps?"

"Exactly." The duke smiled his approval. "So I'm rather hoping you will agree to talk with Miss Sharp. You appear to have some expertise when it comes to the education of young women, and I have every confidence that you will be able to provide recommendations to improve the governess's tutelage. So that Celeste is more engaged."

"Hmmm." Artemis considered the duke's request and couldn't think of any reason to refuse. But she also had a suggestion. "Perhaps it would also help if I actually spoke with your daughter about her academic interests, Your Grace. I'm sure she will be able to clearly articulate what she likes or doesn't like about her studies. It would help me to pinpoint any issues or concerns that Miss Sharp hasn't identified."

The duke rubbed his chin as he considered her proposal. "I think that could be arranged."

"And I'd suggest that when I visit Dartmoor House, I do so discreetly. A single woman like me shouldn't show up on the doorstep of a very eligible duke in the middle of the day or, even worse, at night. If I'm recognized, it could spell disaster. And I can't have that."

He grinned. "I'm flattered that you think I'm eligible. And of course, I'll make sure that your visit is unobserved and that your identity is protected. I'll have Morton, my secretary, set it up."

"So, does that mean we have struck a bargain, Your Grace?"

His mouth slowly curved into a wide grin. "We do, Miss Jones." And Artemis suddenly felt like she'd made a deal with the devil himself. Especially when the duke leaned close and his heated gaze locked with hers. "What say we seal our pact with a kiss?"

———

Miss Jones inhaled a long, slow breath, and Dominic's blood thrummed with anticipation. *Intrigued* didn't seem like quite the right word to describe how he felt at this moment. And it wasn't just this woman's innate sensuality that had him so hooked. It was her keen intelligence. Her openness and brazen willingness to take risks for something she wholeheartedly believed in.

Perhaps *captivated* was a better word. Or *mesmerized*.

Wanting definitely fit the bill.

God, how he wanted…

His gaze drifted to Miss Jones's delectable mouth, her crushed-berry lips so ripe and plump and inviting. A wash of sunlight from a nearby window drew his attention to a tiny dark mole, a natural beauty patch, right beside the corner of her mouth. He had no idea why he'd never noticed it before, and now that he had, it was damnably distracting. Like an erotic exclamation mark inviting him to stop and take note.

To pause. To linger…

"You haven't answered my question." His gaze flicked up to her eyes, where shards of deep gold and caramel glinted in their dark-brown depths. "Shall we kiss, or—"

He got no further as Miss Jones gripped his lapels with such force, he had to put out a hand to steady himself against the bookcase. And then her mouth crashed into his.

Christ. Her kiss was hard and intense, almost bruising. There was nothing gentle about the fierce press and desperate slide of her lips, or the way her tart, slick tongue curled around his.

Yes, it was an all consuming, turbulent kiss filled with heat and passion, and it fired his ravening need to blazing proportions. Her scent, a bewitching combination of sweet things like roses and vanilla with a musky feminine undertone, wrapped around him, ensnaring him in its tendrils. Fanning the flames of his lust.

He slid a hand behind her nape and tipped her head back to allow him better access to the hot, honeyed cavern of her mouth. He delved and tasted and feasted with the urgency of a man starved of sustenance. And perhaps he had been. For years. Miss Jones's tempestuous kiss was like sweetest manna from heaven, and right here, right now, he intended to have his fill.

When she flagrantly crushed herself against his chest and twisted her fingers into his hair, she pulled a deep groan from his throat. Beneath his trousers, his already half-hard cock leapt and twitched. If they were any other place than a bookstore, he'd devour her neck and rip open the buttons of her damnably confining bodice and corset. Free her full breasts…

Perhaps sensing the precarious position she was in and how aroused he was, Miss Jones suddenly broke the kiss.

When she spoke, her voice was soft and breathy. "I trust that was satisfactory, Your Grace." Her lips were as dark as the dew-slick petals of a bloodred rose and her pupils were so dilated, Dominic swore he could drown in them.

"Satisfactory? I'd say that kiss was incendiary, Miss Jones." He gently tucked a loosened curl behind the delicate shell of her ear. "And perhaps, given the circumstances, I may be so bold as to call you Artemis?"

Her cheeks, which were already flushed, turned a deeper shade of pink, and Dominic was strangely charmed. "Of course, Your Grace."

"And you may call me Dominic. If you would like to."

"I would." Her smile lit her eyes. "Dominic."

Dominic couldn't help but smile back. It seemed like forever since a woman had spoken his Christian name, especially in such a soft, throaty voice. The intimacy of it made his chest ache with something akin to longing.

Dear God. He should be terrified. He wasn't looking for tenderness or love or happy endings, just a sensible woman of his own class who'd be quite content to enter into a marriage of convenience. The unconventional, entirely unsuitable Artemis Jones was *not* going to be his next duchess.

Was she?

He swallowed to alleviate a totally unexpected tightness in his throat. "So my wild, sweet Artemis, I should probably bid you adieu before I do actually ruin you in a spectacularly public fashion." Releasing her from his hold, he took several steps back.

Artemis blew out a shaky breath and ran her hands down her slightly rumpled skirts. "Yes." When the shop's front doorbell tinkled, she slid deeper into the shadows of a nearby bookcase. "If you go on ahead, I'll follow in a few minutes."

Grateful that his arousal had subsided, Dominic tilted his head. "Very wise."

"Don't forget your hat," she called softly after him. "I think it's near the 'horrid' novels by Dalton, D'Aubigne, and Davenport."

Chapter Twelve

"IS HIS GRACE IN?" ARTEMIS ASKED MR. MORTON AS HE ushered her into Dartmoor House via the servants' entrance. Even though it was something of a cloak-and-dagger arrival— the duke's personal secretary had arranged for an unmarked carriage to pick her up from Cadogan Square—a footman appeared to collect her hooded cloak, bonnet, and gloves as though she'd walked through the front door.

Morton shook his head. "I'm afraid not, Miss Jones. Business meetings will keep him away from the house for most of the day. But he did ask that I pass on his regards. His Grace also wishes you to know that if you require anything at all during your visit with his daughter and Miss Sharp, you only need ask and you shall have it."

"Thank you." It had been almost a whole week since Artemis had met with Dominic at Delaney's, and she couldn't suppress a ripple of disappointment. Not only would she have to wait longer to hear about the next phase of her ruination plan—whether Dominic had been able to arrange invitations for a suitable event and when that event would be—but in all honesty, she was also crestfallen that she wouldn't see him this afternoon after all.

She was *not* besotted, she told herself firmly as another footman led her into an enormous entry hall and then up an imposing marble staircase with exquisitely carved balustrades. No, she was simply brimming with unfulfilled lust.

The way Dominic had kissed her between the bookcases, indeed, the whole wicked encounter had fueled her erotic fantasies every single night. When he'd asked if he could use her first name and had invited her to call him Dominic, she knew at that precise moment that they would become lovers.

Because she'd decided long ago that she wouldn't deny her sensual self if a man she truly desired came along, she wasn't daunted by the prospect of becoming a powerful duke's paramour—far from it. She didn't believe in marriage or happily-ever-afters, so there was no risk to her heart. As long as she and the duke were both discreet, the opportunity to become his lover was one she would fully embrace.

Indeed, it was only society that believed an unmarried woman couldn't eat her cake and have it too. Well, just as she always had, Artemis would thumb her nose at what society thought.

She would have as much darn cake as she wanted.

At the end of an upstairs gallery, the footman showed Artemis into a pretty, feminine parlor decorated in tasteful pastel shades.

A chambermaid appeared and bobbed a curtsy. "Miss Sharp has been expecting you, Miss Jones. If you would like to take a seat, she'll be with you as soon as she can. Would you like some tea while you wait?"

"Ah, yes, thank you. That would be lovely."

How odd that I should be kept waiting by the governess, thought Artemis as she drifted to the hearthside to study a landscape painting depicting a bleak moorland featuring craggy, mist-wreathed tors. She wondered if Miss Sharp had taken offense at the duke's decision for an outsider to scrutinize her charge's lessons. If she, Artemis, were in the same position, she would probably be chagrined too.

In any event, she would do as Dominic had asked. How could she not? She still couldn't quite believe that he *had* actually agreed to her outrageous proposition. Of course, this was a quid pro quo—his participation in her faux ruination *was* dependent upon her agreement to speak with Miss Sharp and his daughter. But she didn't mind. Indeed, if Artemis were perfectly honest with herself, she would admit that she was curious to meet Lady Celeste. It had been her experience that when parents described their daughters as "bright" but "a little rebellious," it generally meant their children had turned into evil, demanding witches. And any "mischief" they created was usually a coded word for "havoc."

The tea arrived, and after Artemis had poured herself a steaming cup, she settled into a comfortable armchair by the fireside and studied the leaping flames. If she knew Miss Sharp was going to take *this* long, she would have brought her notebook and continued working on *Lady Mirabella and the Midnight Monk*. Artemis had last left her heroine on the brink of ecstasy, and the poor woman needed a release sooner rather than later. She just needed to decide upon the wicked technique the Midnight Monk would employ to help Lady Mirabella slip over the edge and what euphemisms she would use. She was always careful to only give a suggestion of what was happening beneath the sheets. Her love scenes weren't really all *that* lurid, despite popular opinion.

The parlor door snicked open, and Artemis immediately closed the mental door on her characters' amorous shenanigans.

"Miss Jones?" A petite, attractive woman about Artemis's age approached. She wore her smoothly parted, light-brown hair in tightly coiled braids beside her ears, and her Prussian blue gown with black military style frogging was appropriately sedate for someone of her station. "I'm Miss Rosalind Sharp, Lady Celeste's governess. My apologies for keeping you waiting."

"That's quite all right, Miss Sharp." Artemis put down her cup and rose to her feet. "It has been quite pleasant sitting here by the fire, taking tea. May I pour you a cup? The pot is still quite hot."

"Why, thank you. Yes," replied the governess. Her manner was cordial if not altogether warm. Her smile, superficially pleasant. "I take it without sugar or milk."

"Wonderful," said Artemis. They sat opposite each other like combatants in a game of chess or cards. At least Artemis formed that impression. It also felt decidedly odd playing hostess when she was the visitor, but nevertheless, she dispensed Miss Sharp's tea.

The governess took it with murmured thanks, sipped delicately, then placed the cup and saucer down upon the mahogany table between them. "Now," she said, folding her hands together in her lap in a prim fashion, "I understand His Grace has asked you to speak with me about Lady Celeste and her studies with a view to improving their quality. For that reason, I thought it best that we speak first before you meet my lady."

"I cannot fault your reasoning," returned Artemis.

That insincere smile again. "That being said," continued the governess, "I will admit that I am a trifle confused about His Grace's request. I was not aware that there was an issue with Lady Celeste's tutelage. And I hope you'll forgive me for saying this, Miss Jones, but I'm also uncertain what makes *you* so uniquely qualified to make such an assessment and any subsequent recommendations."

Artemis frowned. She'd been expecting Miss Sharp to query

her professional credentials, but perhaps in not quite so blunt a fashion. At any rate, it was out on the table.

"I have been a governess and finishing school teacher for a number of years," she said carefully. "Nine actually. And my last appointment was at the very well-regarded Avon Academy for Young Ladies of Quality in Bath." Well regarded by members of the upper middle-class at least. Highly ranked peers wouldn't deign to send their daughters to such an establishment.

Miss Sharp's lips pursed; she clearly wasn't impressed either. "In my two previous posts, I served as governess for the daughters of a viscount and then an earl."

Artemis had to stop herself from rolling her eyes. She didn't have time for this sort of petty rivalry. Still, she needed to assert she had something of value to offer. She didn't want to fail Dominic. "Most admirable." Artemis gave a gracious inclination of her head. "But might I ask, what ages were your previous charges?"

The light in Miss Sharp's hazel eyes hardened. "I don't think that's at all relevant, Miss Jones."

"Perhaps it is. Otherwise, why would His Grace have sought my advice? It's been my experience that young ladies in their adolescent years can be quite a different breed with their own particular set of behaviors, likes, and dislikes, when compared to younger children. Managing them can be a delicate operation, regardless of how well connected or elevated their families are."

Miss Sharp picked up her tea and took several sips. Her eyes glittered with resentment.

"Perhaps you could simply tell me what subjects Lady Celeste is studying," ventured Artemis after a lengthy, prickly-as-a-hedgehog-caught-in-a-briar-bush pause. "What accomplishments has she attained? I'm sure she has many."

The governess put aside her cup and then ran her palms over her skirts. "Lady Celeste studies everything that is necessary for a young lady of her station," she said stiffly. "Literature, French, a little German, mathematics, history, geography, painting and drawing, embroidery, music—she plays the pianoforte beautifully—and dancing. And of course, etiquette lessons. She is adept at anything she puts her hand or mind to."

"Of course. But to clarify, you do not teach any scientific subjects? The physical sciences? Botany or zoology perhaps?" Artemis dared not ask if they ever discussed politics or progressive topics such as a woman's right to higher education, property holding, or suffrage.

Miss Sharp sniffed. "We occasionally discuss flora when practicing flower arrangement, or if we are out and about on an excursion, say to Kew Gardens. But as a general rule, no."

Artemis nodded. "I see. You mentioned literature. I assume that you discuss deeper meaning such as themes, symbolism, and literary devices That there is some analysis of plot, characterization, and the author's purpose or message."

"Of course."

Artemis knew she was playing with fire before she even asked her next question, but she couldn't help herself. "And does Lady Celeste enjoy reading a wide range of books, including novels? His Grace informed me that she particularly likes anything by Jane Austen. And Gothic novels."

"Yes, she does. Although, she does not read anything in the latter category," said Miss Sharp with a moue of displeasure. "Not if I can help it. Indeed, I would say that the vast majority of Gothic novels are utter rubbish. Especially anything by that shocking author, Lydia Lovelace, who seems to be all the rage. Heaven knows why." The governess gave a theatrical shudder before her narrowed gaze settled on Artemis. "Miss Jones, I hope you'll for-give me for changing the subject, but I must confess, I'm more than a little curious about you. How is that you and His Grace became acquainted? If you don't mind me asking, of course."

"No, I don't mind. We met through mutual connections, quite recently," Artemis replied smoothly even though she was reinventing history ever so slightly. "The Countess of Castledown and my aunt, the Dowager Baroness Wagstaff."

There, you're not the only one who can lay claim to knowing members of high society, Miss Rosalind Sharp.

As Artemis nonchalantly sipped her tea, she didn't fail to notice the tightening of the governess's mouth. This meeting was not going the way Artemis had anticipated. For one thing, she really should stop baiting the woman. They weren't in competition, and as far as Artemis knew, Miss Sharp's job was secure. Indeed, Miss Sharp clearly cared for the well-being of her charge and the subjects she taught her were the usual fare for a peer's daughter.

Although Artemis had no overt reason to doubt the govern-ess's instructional skills, she also sensed that the woman was a bit of a stickler. She understood that not everyone enjoyed reading her Gothic romance books, but to dismiss them *and* the entire genre as utter rubbish... Now *that* rankled.

Yes, perhaps the duke's assessment was accurate: Lady Celeste *was* bored. And maybe it was because Miss Sharp was just a little too staid and stuffy. She struck Artemis as some-one who was unwilling to discuss anything that was the least bit unconventional and would never question the status quo. Which might mean her conversational exchanges with Lady Celeste were uninspiring on an intellectual level. Especially if Lady Celeste had the inquiring mind the duke claimed.

While Dominic had asked her to speak with Miss Sharp, Artemis felt that it was only his daughter who could actually shed any helpful light on the situation.

———————

When Miss Sharp ushered in Lady Celeste Winters a short time later, Artemis was immediately struck by how much the young woman reminded her of her father.

Not just in terms of her physical features—like the duke, she was tall with black hair and arresting gray eyes fringed with enviable dark lashes—but the way she carried herself. There was a quiet confidence about her that was appealing. When Miss Sharp effected the introductions, Lady Celeste spoke with grace and her smile seemed genuine. She was neither shy nor too loud or overbearing. Indeed, she was scrupulously polite, and Artemis couldn't detect any signs of rebelliousness or waspishness or an unwillingness to take part in this interview.

As they all prepared to take seats at the fireside, Artemis addressed the governess. "Miss Sharp, I know this may seem irregular, but might I speak with Lady Celeste on her own?" She smiled at the duke's daughter. "If that's all right with you too, my lady."

Miss Sharp's brows knit into a ferocious frown. "I hardly think that is appropri—"

"Of course, that would be perfectly fine with me, Miss Jones," said Lady Celeste. She turned her attention to Miss Sharp. "Leave us, please."

"But—"

"Miss Sharp"—now it was Lady Celeste who was frowning—"Papa informed me that Miss Jones may like to converse with me in private. But I believe you already knew that, so I see no reason for you to raise an objection. I will ring for you when I am ready."

"Yes, my lady." The governess dipped into a respectful curtsy, then retreated. Even though the door closed behind her, Artemis wondered if the woman might actually disregard the dictates of decorum and try to eavesdrop through the keyhole.

If she heard anything she didn't like, then it would serve her right.

Lady Celeste sank with studied poise onto the opposite settee. She smoothed her rose-pink taffeta skirts with pale, elegant fingers, then fixed Artemis with an expectant look. It was only then that Artemis noticed the slight shadows, like lilac bruises, beneath the girl's eyes. Perhaps there was even a hint of puffiness to her eyelids and the tip of her nose was slightly pink. Had she been crying?

When Artemis offered to pour her a cup of tea, Lady Celeste's brows dipped into a slight frown. "Oh, let us order a fresh pot. And some petit fours and sandwiches or pastries. I don't know why Miss Sharp didn't organize something a little more lavish for you in the first place." She leaned forward and added in a low voice, "I shouldn't say this, but I often think my governess can be a bit parsimonious. Particularly when it comes to cake."

Artemis tried very hard to maintain a neutral expression, but feared she'd failed abysmally when the duke's daughter offered her a conspiratorial smile in return.

Lady Celeste rang for the maid, who appeared almost immediately, then after ordering a proper afternoon tea, her full attention returned to Artemis.

They engaged in general chitchat for a short while—about the weather, the latest fashions featured in the *New Monthly Belle*

Assemblée (of which Artemis knew little about), who were London's best modistes (Artemis had only heard of Madame Blanchard), their favorite tea shops (Lady Celeste loved Gunter's)—until Artemis broached the subject of why she was here.

"Yes, my father mentioned you were a finishing school teacher with considerable expertise," said Lady Celeste, "and that you have quite progressive views about the education of women. To be perfectly honest, I am most intrigued by that."

"Yes, I do have progressive views. But I'm not here to talk about my educational beliefs precisely." Even though Artemis was impressed that Dominic had been so frank with his daughter, she was fairly certain he wouldn't want her to discuss the controversial stances of women such as Mary Wollstonecraft, Olympe de Gouges, and Bessie Raynor Parkes. "Your father wondered if it might be worthwhile if I chatted to you about *your* education. If there's anything you feel that you are missing out on in terms of your own lessons.

"I've had a quick conversation with Miss Sharp, but perhaps it would help if you could share with me what you enjoy—or, to be more precise, what particular topics you would like to know more about. Is there something you have a passion for that you haven't had an opportunity to study?" Artemis moved to the edge of her seat. "I know you do not know me, but whatever you say to me, you can be assured of my utmost discretion. I'm here to offer advice and support. That is all. I believe your father only wants what is best for you."

Lady Celeste's expression grew pensive as she regarded Artemis. Or was there a shadow of reluctance or wariness in her eyes? Perhaps even a flicker of resentment. "What's best for me," she repeated. She opened her mouth as if to add more, but then the afternoon tea arrived. Once the new tea service had been set out just so, Lady Celeste assumed the role of accomplished hostess, dispensing tea and serving cakes and sandwiches with aplomb. Miss Sharp's etiquette lessons had clearly been taken on board.

Deciding she might need to take a different tack to help Lady Celeste open up, Artemis drew her into a conversation about novels, particularly those by Jane Austen. She steered clear of talking about Gothic novels, considering they were a bone of contention with both Dominic and Miss Sharp. Artemis didn't wish to create any discord. By degrees, the duke's daughter began to smile and chat freely, right up until the point Artemis mentioned she and her two very good friends were members of a book club, and that their favorite pastime was to discuss the novels they loved over tea and cake—just like she and Celeste were doing now. Then a look of sadness and intense longing clouded Lady Celeste's soft gray eyes.

"Friends…" The duke's daughter dropped her gaze to the crumbs left upon her cake plate. "Now that is one thing I would like more of," she murmured. "Actually, having at least one friend would do."

"Oh…oh, I had no idea, my lady," stammered Artemis. Her brow knit with confusion and heartfelt remorse. "I'm sorry if I've said the wrong thing. It was not my intention to upset you."

"No. It's all right. You weren't to know." Her mouth twisted into a small wry smile. "Being the daughter of the Dastardly Duke of Dartmoor is not conducive to making friends. My aunt, Lady Northam—that's Papa's sister—has tried to help on occasion, but she can only do so much. Once a reputation is tainted so badly…" Lady Celeste shrugged a shoulder.

"Yes, I imagine that has made things extremely difficult for you. You have my sympathy, Lady Celeste."

"I'm sure you've heard all of the horrible gossip and rumors about my parents," continued Celeste. "Everyone has. Even though I was only six when my dear mama passed away, I do know that my parents loved each other. Very much." She picked up her teacup but instead of taking a sip, toyed with the handle. Her gaze drifted to the fire and her mouth curved with a soft, sad smile. "I have a memory of them at Ashburn Abbey. It's like a poignant painting, etched into my mind. Or perhaps I should say photograph. They were sitting before the enormous fire in the drawing room, and Papa was holding Mama in his arms like she was the most precious thing in the world. He was stroking her hair…"

She sighed and her gaze returned to Artemis. "I don't know why I'm saying all of this to you, Miss Jones. I suppose I see something in you that I like. You seem to be a direct, no-nonsense sort of person, and I don't think you would be here if you believed all the cruel things said about my father. And I want to assure you that none of it is true. Of course, Papa will pretend that he doesn't suffer, that he's immune to it all, but that's not the case. Like me, I think he's lonely."

Lonely… Artemis frowned into her tea. She'd never thought of the Duke of Dartmoor as that. He was so vital, almost larger than life. When he walked into a room, the very air around him seemed to vibrate with electrical energy. By all accounts, he was a ruthless business magnate who possessed the wealth of Croesus along with a vast estate. But perhaps on a personal level, he *was* isolated, socially shunned by many of his peers. Especially their wives and daughters of marriageable age. And by association, so was Celeste.

Something tugged inside Artemis's heart in the most peculiar way. To some degree, she knew how it felt to be an outsider.

She'd never quite fit in at the Avon Academy. But she'd never felt alone. Not when she had a sister who loved her—despite their differences—and dear friends she could count on, no matter what.

If Lady Celeste was both bored and lonely, it might explain why she'd been testing the boundaries of late. She was looking for something—anything—to divert her.

A short time later, after Artemis had bid farewell to Lady Celeste and Miss Sharp, she began to rack her brain about ways to help the girl find friends of her own age, but she could think of nothing useful. She didn't move in the same social circles, and if Dominic's sister had been unable to assist in that regard, it would be virtually impossible for Artemis to make a difference.

As she followed a maid toward the main stairs leading to the entry hall, she heard her name called. "Miss Jones?"

Dominic.

Her heart leaping, she spun around. And there he was, standing by an open set of oak-paneled doors. He was informally attired in a fine cambric shirt, navy silk waistcoat, and gray trousers. His black neckcloth was loosened and his sleeves were rolled up, exposing his forearms. Good Lord, even Dominic's forearms with their corded muscles and light dusting of dark hair were mesmerizing.

"Miss Jones," he repeated, his commanding voice sending a shiver of delicious anticipation through her, "if you could spare a moment, I'd like a word before you leave." To the chambermaid he said, "Mary, you may go."

Chapter Thirteen

THE BLUSHING MAID BOBBED A CURTSY AND SCURRIED away—heaven knew what she thought of the highly irregular situation—and then Artemis dropped into a sedate curtsy herself. "Of course, Your Grace." She couldn't naysay Dominic, not when she'd been secretly hoping she might see him.

He stepped back from the doorway, and Artemis could see that the room beyond was an elegant, very masculine library. The light of the brightly leaping fire in the gray marble fireplace glanced off the glass fronts of several oak bookcases, the brass fixtures of an enormous, elaborately carved desk, and a gilt-framed mirror above a mahogany sideboard. When Artemis traversed the fine Persian rug, she caught the rich scents of leather, woodsmoke, and coffee; a fine bone-china cup sat beside a silver coffeepot and a pile of papers on the desk's dark-red blotter.

The door closed behind her with a soft click, and Artemis's pulse capered when she realized they were completely alone.

She turned, and almost at once, Dominic caught her about the waist with his large, warm hands. His dark-gray eyes burned with an intensity that made her breath hitch.

"Artemis. God, how I've missed you." And then his mouth was on hers, demanding and fierce. He tasted of coffee and desire, and within seconds, he'd backed her into one of the glass-fronted bookcases. His large, hard body pressed heavily against hers, crushing her skirts, trapping her. But she didn't want to be anywhere else.

Her fingers curled around his biceps, and she couldn't suppress a moan when the hard, bulging muscles flexed beneath her palms. How well they fit together. How glorious the feel of his wicked mouth possessing hers. One of his hands clasped the back of her neck while the other skimmed over her ribs and then covered her breast, kneading with gentle urgency. His tongue was hot and slick as it stroked every inch of her mouth with ruthless, studied purpose, enflaming her own desire.

How could it be that this man's kisses and wicked caresses instantly turned her into a wanton, mindless creature? She'd been kissed before, but never like this. Had never experienced such heady, decadent sensations. Like she was intoxicated, and her head was spinning. Like she was melting and aching and wanting and burning up with need.

When Dominic at last drew back to drag in some much needed air, Artemis was also panting. Her knees were so weak that she clung to his shoulders, and perhaps Dominic felt a little overcome too; he rested his forehead against hers as if he didn't wish to move.

"I hope you can forgive me," he murmured, his voice low and hoarse. "When I saw you in the hallway just now, I knew I had to see you. To kiss you. I–I can't stop thinking about you. Truth to tell, I've been having fantasies about kissing you all day."

"The fantasies are mutual," she whispered. She reached up and stroked his jaw. Light stubble rasped against her fingertips. "You need a shave."

He chuckled softly. "I'm a beast."

"Well, it's a good thing that I happen to like beasts. Fairy-tale princes are rather boring."

He lifted his head. "Yes. You like monsters and scowling misanthropes. I suppose I'm lucky that I fit into the latter category."

"You're not scowling at the moment." Indeed, Dominic was smiling down at her and a soft glowing warmth lit his gray eyes. A frisson of fear curled around Artemis's spine.

No, the Duke of Dartmoor couldn't be developing tender feelings for her, could he? She suddenly felt like they were both on a treacherous slope, sliding headlong into perilous, uncharted territory. But Dominic wasn't a prince with noble intentions, she sternly reminded herself. And she wasn't a sweet, virginal maiden looking for a hero to save her or take her to wife.

She almost laughed aloud. No, she wanted this "hero" to ruin her.

The cold, hard truth was, they were both simply lust riddled. Artemis's kiss had temporarily appeased the duke's strong carnal urges. Yes, that was the only reason the mighty Duke of Dartmoor had suddenly been rendered as soft and malleable as unfired clay. He was just pleased that she was so receptive to his amorous advances. That she would readily climb into his bed if he asked her to.

And she would. The man was impossible to resist.

But they weren't in his bedchamber. They were in his library at four o'clock in the afternoon. His daughter and her governess were not far away, and the whole house was filled with an army of servants.

She needed to go home before Aunt Roberta missed her and kicked up an almighty fuss and asked too many questions about where she'd been.

But first, she had something to tell Dominic. "I suppose you're wondering how my meeting with Miss Sharp and your daughter went."

"Yes. I am." Dominic at last stepped back and gestured at a pair of leather wingback chairs beside the fire. "Won't you take a seat?"

Once they were settled, Artemis filled him in on the details—scant though they were. "Celeste wasn't particularly forthcoming about her studies. She didn't mention anything was amiss, so that's reassuring. Although I did note Miss Sharp isn't keen on teaching scientific subjects. There only seems to be a smattering of botany." Even that was being generous.

Dominic frowned. "Hmmm, that's interesting. I happen to know Celeste is particularly interested in astronomy. One of her favorite pastimes at Ashburn Abbey is to stargaze, weather permitting. I'll have a word with Miss Sharp. Celeste is to have a first-rate, comprehensive education, and that includes all of the sciences, not just a 'smattering' as you put it. I expect her to be able to converse intelligently on any topic."

"I agree…" Artemis hesitated, unsure if she should bring up the other detail she'd learned about the duke's daughter. But really, what was the point of staying tight lipped? She wasn't lily livered and the duke *had* sought her help, no matter how unpleasant the truth she discovered might be. Stiffening her spine, she continued, "You might already be aware of this, but Lady Celeste also hinted that she is lonely. That she lacks friends her own age because of…" She grimaced. "I hope you can forgive me for being blunt, but it's because of your own notoriety. Undeserved, of course. But yes, I do wonder if that might be the reason your daughter has been difficult of late."

Dominic scraped a hand through his hair, ruffling the thick black locks into spikes. "Yes, I've also recently begun to suspect that might be the root of the problem. And you have just confirmed it." He blew out a sigh, and exasperation roughened his voice. "The frustrating thing is, there's not a great deal I can do about the situation. And it seems it's not just female companionship Celeste has been seeking." His troubled gaze met hers. "A little over a week ago, I discovered that Celeste has a secret admirer. Someone who calls himself 'T.' He's been sending her suggestive, highly inappropriate love letters. I have no idea who it is and as far as I know, nothing else untoward has occurred. Thank God.

"Celeste's maid, Miss Sharp, and indeed all of the servants have been watching her movements like a hawk. There are not many men she comes into contact with beyond the footmen, one or two grooms from my stables, and her middle-aged dancing master, and for various reasons, I don't suspect any of them. But still…" He thumped his clenched fist on the arm of his chair.

"I also blame those bloody books by Lydia Lovelace that she got her hands on—the ones with the all-too-graphic love scenes. Too graphic for my daughter, at least. Celeste must have got it into her head that a little bit of romance and excitement will cure her low spirits. But it won't. It will only make things worse if she gets herself into trouble. She's only fifteen, for Christ's sake." Dominic bared his teeth. "When I find out the identity of the dog who's been attempting to seduce my daughter…"

Artemis dropped her gaze to her lap where her hands were clasped as tightly as Miss Sharp's. She understood Dominic's anger. A man who attempted to seduce a fifteen-year-old girl was a blackguard through and through. But it didn't seem fair to blame her alter ego, Lydia Lovelace. There were so many different arguments she could mount to defend her books, but then she might say too much and reveal who she was. And she couldn't do that. Not when Dominic had promised to help her free herself from her aunt's controlling rule.

"I agree that Lydia Lovelace's books are probably not appropriate for someone your daughter's age," Artemis conceded. "And I understand your frustration and concern. I do sincerely hope that you can find out who's been secretly corresponding with Lady Celeste and attempting to take advantage of her. It's not right. He must be the worst kind of scoundrel."

"Yes." Dominic's wide shoulders rose and fell with a heavy sigh. "Now, enough about my familial woes. You have delivered on your part of the bargain, my dear Artemis, and I must now endeavor to fulfill mine." He leaned forward, his bare forearms resting on his muscular thighs. "You'll be pleased to hear that my sister, Horatia, has agreed to throw a masked ball in a week's time at Northam House. Given the short notice, and my much maligned reputation, the guest list won't be a mile long, but"—he caught her gaze—"you, along with your aunt, your sister, and your two coconspirators, Miss Bertram and Miss Delaney, and their respective chaperones, are definitely on that list. Indeed, the invitations are being sent out as we speak. Your ruination is imminent."

"Oh…" Artemis smiled. "That's wonderful. Thank you to you and your sister. I'm most grateful."

"No, I should be thanking you, Artemis." Dominic's mouth curved with a devilish grin. "It's not every day a man is invited to take part in a debauching."

"I'm glad that you trust me. That you're not concerned that something might go wrong."

"Hmmm." Dominic frowned. "Actually, I would be lying if I didn't own that I have some niggling reservations. Not about my involvement—that's assured—but what the ramifications might be for you if the worst should happen and word *does* get out that you've been compromised, and there's no proposal in the offing. I have firsthand experience of how cruel and unforgiving society can be. That being said"—his smile returned—"I respect your decision to do what you think you need to. I'm certain that you and your friends' planning has been meticulous."

Artemis gave an emphatic nod. "It has."

"Good. And of course"—Dominic's smile grew wider—"once you part ways with your aunt, you'll be free to start your college. In fact, you'll be able do whatever you like, whenever you like."

With me. The words were unspoken, but no doubt that's exactly what the Duke of Dartmoor was thinking. Because it was precisely what Artemis was thinking as well. At least until she secured the funding to start her college.

She could hardly wait for Lady Northam's masked ball.

Chapter Fourteen

"ARE YOU REALLY GOING TO GO THROUGH WITH THIS, Artemis?" asked Jane in a low voice. Behind her elaborately decorated mask, worry clouded her green eyes.

"Yes," added Lucy. Her gaze was also shadowed with apprehension. "As much as I would adore having you as my companion, I would understand if you wanted to change your mind, even now. Severing all ties with your aunt in such a dramatic fashion is not something to be sneezed at. There will be no turning back once you and the duke are discovered together."

"I know," said Artemis. "And I'm nothing but grateful for your concern. Truly. But I'm afraid there *is* no other way." She inhaled a steadying breath. Her stomach might be aswarm with butterflies, but she had never been so determined. And if she were honest with herself, she would also acknowledge her blood was humming with excitement at the mere thought of Dominic's kisses. They'd already shared a waltz this evening, and she couldn't wait to be in his arms again. "This must be done," she continued. "Tonight. Everything and everyone is ready to play their parts. Our preparations couldn't be more perfect. The Duke of Dartmoor is just waiting for my signal."

They were presently gathered on a secluded balcony that overlooked the main ballroom. Despite Dominic's notoriety, at least two hundred guests, if not more, had accepted Lord and Lady Northam's invitation to attend. Beneath crystal chandeliers, waltzing couples spun about the dance floor creating a brilliant kaleidoscope of color, while tight knots of other masked guests watched or conversed with great animation. Champagne and laughter flowed, and the swelling strains of the orchestra provided a constant lively undercurrent to it all.

Indeed, the entire room was brimming with a gay, almost licentious air that reminded Artemis of a masquerade ball at Mardi Gras. Perhaps it was her imagination, but the very air around her seemed to vibrate with expectation...

Artemis turned to Jane, who looked truly lovely this evening—not that she didn't always look lovely, but like Artemis, she'd often had to make do with less than fashionable attire. Tonight, she'd borrowed one of Artemis's brand-new ball gowns—a confection of emerald-green silk taffeta and lace—and the sweeping feathers and ribbons that adorned her mask helped to conceal the worst of the scarring on her cheek. Clusters of artfully arranged ringlets courtesy of Lucy's clever lady's maid completed the look. Of course, Jane was resigned to the stares of strangers, but tonight, she'd stated that she wanted to blend in as much as possible; she didn't want to create a stir.

No, that was Artemis's job. And the time to do exactly that had arrived. She touched Jane's arm. "I think it's almost ten o'clock. Will you let His Grace know that I'll be in the library in a few minutes?"

Jane offered a smile. "Of course, my dear friend. And good luck."

Lucy watched Jane quit the balcony. "Goodness, I'm rather glad you asked Jane to speak with the Duke of Dartmoor. I'm sure I'd faint before I even reached his side. The man is too handsome for words. All that brooding intensity..." She flicked open her silk fan and fluttered it madly for effect.

"I agree," said Artemis. She was hard pressed not to stare like a starry-eyed fool whenever she caught sight of him. Attired in a black-as-midnight evening suit with a matching black velvet mask and a red satin–lined domino, he reminded her of the wickedly handsome and charismatic antihero she'd created for her book *Lady Violetta and the Vengeful Vampyre*. "I still can't quite believe that he agreed to take part in my scheme when he easily could have said no. But I'm so glad that he did."

Lucy gave her a nudge. "He obviously likes you. Perhaps more than you think."

Artemis snorted. "I doubt it. In any case, I can't afford to dillydally about here any longer." She winked at Lucy and then picked up her mazarine-blue skirts so she could safely negotiate the winding staircase to the floor below where the Northams' library was located. "The show is about to begin."

———————

When Artemis entered the library, she discovered it was deserted, just as they'd planned. Dominic had discreetly stationed one of his own footmen at the door to discourage other guests from entering. If anyone else was intending to have a romantic rendezvous this evening, they'd have to go somewhere else.

She surveyed the well-appointed room with its floor-to-ceiling bookcases and decided that the best place for Dominic to "seduce" her would be a brocade-upholstered settee that graced the Turkish hearthrug before the fire. It also faced the door. Anyone who walked in couldn't fail to miss a romantically entangled couple sprawled across its plump, claret-colored cushions.

As Artemis approached the fireside, she removed her

velvet-and-lace mask and placed it on a side table. Although the mask was pretty, it would get in the way when Dominic and she were kissing. Besides, she wanted Aunt Roberta to see that it *was* her wayward niece, no one else, being debauched upon the settee. Her aunt mustn't have any doubts.

The Boulle clock on the mantel chimed ten o'clock, and Artemis's pulse began to race and reel faster than a polka. She trusted Dominic wouldn't be too much longer. Every minute counted. Once Jane had delivered her message to the duke, she and Lucy were tasked with rounding up Aunt Roberta, and Phoebe too, if she hadn't been asked to dance. Artemis had last spied them near the entrance to the supper room chatting with Dominic's sister. Jane was to quietly inform Aunt Roberta that she'd seen Artemis enter the library with a gentleman in hot pursuit. That was sure to get Aunt Roberta's attention.

Although her aunt and dear Phoebe would both be upset, Artemis believed it was better to rip off the bandage as quickly as possible. To make a clean break. Then, when the dust settled and the resultant damage was found to be minimal, all of them could get on with life in ways that made each of them happy. Phoebe would marry. Artemis would find a sponsor for her school. And Aunt Roberta could continue to freely meddle in *other* people's lives. Just not her nieces'.

Artemis subsided onto the settee and then fidgeted with the curls brushing her bare shoulders and the cameo attached to a dark-blue velvet ribbon at her throat. Even though she'd usually berate herself for fussing with her appearance, tonight, a wholly feminine part of her did indeed want to look attractive for Dominic.

She needn't have worried because the moment he stepped into the library, his gaze wandered over her with frank apprecia-tion and his mouth slid into a lopsided, rakish smile.

"Miss Artemis Jones." His voice was a low growl as he kicked the door shut, then prowled toward her. "Fancy meeting you here." He tugged off his gloves and threw off his cloak with a theatrical flourish and then joined her on the settee.

Artemis couldn't help but laugh. "Have you been practicing your entrance, Your Grace? It's very dramatic. I approve."

Behind his black mask, Dominic's eyes glinted, not just with mischief but something keener and hotter. Smoldering expectation perhaps. "One has to make an impression, Miss Jones. A ruination, staged or not, must be done right. And with great zeal."

"I won't disagree with you. Shall I remove your mask, or would you like to keep it on?"

"What do you think?" he purred. He leaned in close and brushed a bare fingertip along the edge of the ribbon, just above Artemis's collarbone, raising gooseflesh. "I'm at your complete disposal. I'll do whatever you want."

Dominic was clearly taking delight in playing the role of wicked seducer; despite the fact he was overacting, his performance was working. Flutters of desire began to gather in Artemis's lower belly. "Although I cannot see all of your handsome face, I rather like how you look with it on," she murmured. "It lends you an air of mystery and adds an element of excitement to our illicit encounter."

"Ah, then I shall keep it on," he said, his voice as soft as dark velvet. One of his hands slid around her bare shoulder. "The question is, how illicit do you want this encounter to be? You suggested a passionate kiss or two would suffice, but I'm amenable to almost anything if you are... Tell me what you truly desire."

"Oh..." Artemis's pulse raced hard and fast as her imagination began to run wild. She slid her fingers up Dominic's silk-lined lapels until they came to rest upon his broad shoulders. "Well, passionate kissing is definitely permitted," she murmured huskily. "And perhaps a little caressing and fondling. Some nibbling and licking. But all of our clothes should remain on. I don't want my aunt to have an attack of apoplexy."

"Understood. However…" Dominic swept aside her curls and placed a whisper-soft kiss on her jaw. "Is a degree of mussing and rumpling allowed?" Another kiss, this one in the secret, sensitive hollow just below her ear. "It will be difficult to make a ruination look convincing otherwise."

Artemis arched into Dominic as he continued to drop teasing kisses down the line of her neck and across her shoulder, making her shiver. "I'll allow it."

"Good," he said. And then he gently cupped her jaw and pressed his mouth to hers.

His kiss wasn't hard and wild, but gentle and teasing. A seductive slide of firm yet satin-smooth lips with only an enticing flicker of his tongue. Artemis moaned her frustration, and he drew back a little and chuckled softly. "What's wrong, my dear Artemis?"

"You're teasing me," she returned with a playful pout.

"I might be." He caressed her cheek with the back of his fingers. "I find that a little teasing makes the pleasure sweeter." He placed a featherlight kiss at the corner of her mouth, right near her mole. "Don't you?"

"That's all well and good, but I was led to believe there'd be some mussing and rumpling of my person. And right now, I don't think a single hair on my head is out of place."

"Impatient minx." Dominic smiled against her lips.

"Well, we don't have all night."

"No, we don't." His dark-gray gaze locked with hers. "But I wish we did."

Oh. My. Goodness. Liquid longing pooled between Artemis's thighs. "So do I," she whispered. And then at long last, Dominic claimed her mouth in exactly the way that she wanted.

He kissed her with a fierce urgency, his mouth hot and demanding, his tongue a slick, delicious lash as it plunged and stroked and twined with hers. As he pushed her down onto the cushions of the settee, his fingers speared into her hair, scattering pins. One hand roughly dragged at her sleeve, exposing more of her shoulder, and then he was feasting upon her neck with decadent licks and hot, ferocious, open-mouthed kisses.

Dear God. This wasn't just a ruination. It really *was* a debauching.

And it was magnificent.

Dominic moved, taking his weight on one leg. And then Artemis felt his hand slide beneath the multiple layers of her skirts and stiff petticoats and along her fine lawn drawers until he found the juncture of her thighs. There he paused, long fingers stroking her hip in small maddening circles. "Are you wet and wanting, Artemis?" he whispered, his voice low and raw with lust. "Can I stroke you here?" One of his wicked fingertips danced over the gaping slit in her drawers, ruffling her curls.

Artemis bit her lip. She should say no. Her aunt might walk in at any moment.

But hell's bloody bells, she wanted Dominic's touch right there so very badly. She wanted it so much, she was trembling. Quivering like a barely set blancmange. She couldn't deny him or herself. She wasn't strong enough. Not when she felt like this, so wanton and abandoned and wonderful. "Yes," she managed, her voice no more than a thread of sound between jagged, panted breaths. "To everything."

A low growl of approval rumbled in Dominic's throat. And then his mouth was on hers, absorbing her moan as he slid his finger between her slick folds and then began to mercilessly tease her clitoris. He expertly rubbed and flicked and pinched that little nub of throbbing flesh, working her into a mindless frenzy. And all the while he murmured coarse yet deliciously erotic words of praise and wonderfully filthy suggestions in her ear—about what he was doing to her; about what he would like to do with her if they were somewhere else and completely alone…

Oh, sweet heaven. Never, in all her life had Artemis been so aroused or so skillfully pleasured that within mere moments, she'd plunged headlong into a cataclysmic release. Dizzying, thought-robbing bliss rushed through her body in a hot spectacular wave. If she cried out, she wasn't aware of it.

As her body's quaking eased and her breathing slowed, Dominic continued to gently nuzzle the hollow of her neck. Even though his hair was a little ruffled and his black silk cravat askew, somehow, his mask was still in place.

Artemis, on the other hand, was disheveled beyond repair. She was a thoroughly rumpled, highly satisfied mess. And she couldn't stop smiling…right up until the moment the library door flew open, and she heard Aunt Roberta snap in a voice as harsh as a whip, "Artemis Jones! What in God's name are you doing with *that* man?"

Chapter Fifteen

THAT MAN?

As Dominic sat up, he found it a challenge to maintain a straight face. And he really shouldn't be laughing given the gravity of the situation. Not only was Artemis about to be verbally flayed by her aunt, but *he* was sporting a rather inconvenient cockstand. Indeed, he was so hard, he could probably drive a nail through a plank of wood and into next week. Although when he turned and took in the outraged expression on Lady Wagstaff's face and then the equally shocked looks on the three other young women hovering in the library doorway, he quickly discovered that being gaped at was the mental equivalent of a dousing with ice-cold water.

"Aunt Roberta," Artemis began as she struggled to simultaneously push her bunched skirts down and push herself up from the depths of the settee. "I can explain—"

"No. You cannot," declared the middle-aged dowager baroness. She was bristling with so much anger, the peacock feathers adorning her mask were shivering like autumn leaves in a gale. "I'm speechless. Flabbergasted. Dumbfounded. So shocked and mortified, I can barely speak."

If only that were true, thought Dominic with a sigh. "Lady Wagstaff." He rose and then helped Artemis to her feet. "Your niece is not to bl—"

"Oh, yes I am. I am to blame," Artemis rejoined. "I take full responsibility for my own scandalous behavior leading to my complete and utter ruination. I was the one who lured the Duke of Dartmoor here—"

All of sudden, one of Artemis's friends, Miss Delaney perhaps, gasped in a most melodramatic fashion, "Oh, no! Viscountess Seagrove and a few of her friends are headed this way! And everyone knows what frightful gossips they are."

"*Lady Seagrove?*" Lady Wagstaff cried. "Oh dear Lord." She pressed a gloved hand to her forehead as though she were about to faint. "Quickly, Phoebe. Shut the door before the viscountess or anyone else sees what's going on in here. Your sister's name cannot be linked with that of the Dastardly Duke. No offense, Your Grace." She gave a slight nod in his direction.

"None taken," he said with mock solemnity and an equally slight tilt of his head.

"Oh dear, Lady Wagstaff. I'm afraid the footman stationed at the door has seen rather a lot," ventured Artemis's other friend, the one with the blond curls and a tendency to blush. "In fact, he's still looking," she added in a stage whisper. "Let's hope he's not the sort of man who'd sell gossip to a scandal rag like the *London Tatler* for the right price."

"Oh God. You're right, Miss Bertram," wailed Lady Wagstaff. "Oh, what a disaster." Then she scowled at Dominic's footman. "You, young man. Be off with you." Then to her niece. "What are you doing, Phoebe? Do you want everyone to witness your sister's shameful conduct? Close the blasted door. At once!"

"Everyone's crinoline skirts are in the way," the young woman in question cried and then she began to make frantic shooing movements with her hands. "Move. Inside. Quick sticks. Hurry up."

Dominic had to bite the inside of his cheek to stop himself

from laughing again. He felt like he was taking part in a comedy of errors. Although the ending for Artemis might not be a happy one. Even though she had good reason to sever ties with her aunt, he couldn't help but worry that in years to come, she might regret their estrangement. Of course, it wasn't his place to judge.

He cast a glance her way. Her lovely face was flushed, her lips were kiss-bruised, and her curls in hopeless disarray. Her silk gown—a distinctive shade of indigo that was the perfect foil for her dark auburn hair and pale-as-cream skin—was horribly crushed and courtesy of his depredations, one of her sleeves had slipped so far off her shoulder, the snowy edges of her corset and chemise were showing.

There was no denying what had happened in this room tonight. Even if no one else ever found out, the incontrovertible truth was he *had* ruined Miss Artemis Jones.

The question was: Was he going to set aside what she wanted in favor of pushing his own agenda instead?

———

Artemis's plan had been executed perfectly…so far. Aunt Roberta was absolutely horrified—this *had* to be the last straw, and at any moment, she would declare that Artemis was nothing but a wicked hussy and she would disown her.

Of course, Artemis felt guilty that Phoebe had to be put through this ordeal. Once her sister wrestled the library door shut and turned to face Artemis, her expression could only be described as stricken. A mixture of panic, bewilderment, fury, and deep disappointment. But as time went on and it became clear that perhaps there *wouldn't* be a monumental scandal attached to the family name, her sister would rally and be able to resume her husband hunting in earnest.

Both Lucy and Jane had played their parts beautifully. Though, perhaps they hadn't expected Artemis to throw herself into the role of "ruined heroine" with quite so much gusto, given that Jane was looking steadfastly at the Turkish rug beneath her feet and Lucy was blushing furiously.

As for Dominic…his idea to station one of his trusted footmen outside the library—someone who'd be viewed as a potential snitch and a threat by Aunt Roberta—was nothing but inspired.

And then of course, he'd been true to his word and had well and truly compromised Artemis. There could be no doubt in anyone's mind. Indeed, Artemis's body still hummed with the afterglow of Dominic's thoroughly attentive ministrations. She'd never been so well pleasured in all of her life. Even now, she couldn't quite believe that she'd let herself get so carried away by the moment.

Now, all he had to do was declare he *wouldn't* do the right thing and go on his merry way. And then she would go off on hers.

Simple.

Artemis sensed that Dominic was looking at her, so she leaned closer and gave him a little nudge. "Now it's time for you to tell my aunt that this has all been a big misunderstanding," she murmured, "and that while you never intended to besmirch my honor, you have no intention of proposing marriage."

"Yes. About that…" began Dominic but then Aunt Roberta spoke.

"Here. What are you two both whispering about?" she demanded in a querulous tone.

Artemis lifted her chin. "Aunt Roberta, as I mentioned before when you first burst in, I am entirely to blame for this mess. I was the one who brazenly and quite recklessly invited His Grace to the library for a romantic tryst, knowing full well it was entirely improper and that I was risking my reputation and, indeed, that of the whole family. That's how terrible and willful I am. And because of that—"

"Yes, because I *did* agree to meet with you, Miss Jones," said Dominic in such a grave manner that Artemis's heart began to thud most uncomfortably in her chest, "I find that it is incumbent upon me, as a gentleman and peer of the realm, to ensure that your reputation is *not* sullied. It is *I* who compromised you and therefore"—he removed his mask, then turned to face her—"I must make amends. You will not be ruined. I will not let you suffer such a cruel fate."

And then the Duke of Dartmoor did the unthinkable. He took both of her hands in his and dropped to a bended knee. "Miss Artemis Jones," he intoned with great solemnity, "will you do me the untold honor—"

"What are you doing?" Artemis hissed, yanking her hands away. Confusion and anger and horror surged and roiled inside her. "This is *not* what you're supposed to do. You're supposed to agree that I led you astray and that you have no obligation whatsoever to offer for my hand. And then you're supposed to leave! Remember?"

"Artemis! What is wrong with you?" cried Aunt Roberta. "The Duke of Dartmoor is proposing to you, you stupid gel! Let him finish."

"No. No, I will not," she snapped back. "And since when did you become such an ardent admirer of the duke, dear Aunt?" Artemis was suddenly so furious, she could break one of the Northams' fine porcelain vases that sat atop the mantelpiece over Dominic's far-too-handsome head. Or better yet, she should run him through with the poker sitting in the fire-iron stand by the hearth. "The Duke of Dartmoor is a dastardly, duplicitous scoundrel," she continued in a voice that shook with the force of her outrage, "and I do not want to hear one more word from his wicked, lying mouth."

And then she picked up her skirts, pushed past her aunt, her sister, and her friends, and fled the library before the scalding tears flooding her vision began to fall.

She didn't get very far. Not when she was encumbered by so many ridiculous skirts threatening to trip her up with every step and a determined, long-legged duke on her heels.

Artemis hadn't even reached the end of the hallway when Dominic caught up to her.

A pox on this bloody gown and the Duke of Dartmoor, she mentally cursed as he grasped her by the upper arm and all but dragged her through a nearby door into a room that contained a pianoforte and harp. A music room.

Her blood boiling, she wrenched herself free and rounded on the man who'd just betrayed her. "Damn you to Hades, Dominic Winters," she cried, poking him in the chest and forcing him to back up against the closed door. "How dare you go against your word? You…you promised to ruin me, not wed me! What in heaven's name are you thinking? Ugh!"

She spun away and began to pace back and forth across the polished wooden floor, the heels of her silk pumps clicking angrily. "What am I supposed to do now? Aunt Roberta won't leave me alone until I say 'yes.' She'll plague me until the end of my days. Beelzebub's ballocks." Artemis deposited herself onto the velvet-lined pianoforte stool. "I should never have trusted you. You're almost as bad as Lord Gas—" She clamped her mouth shut at that. Not even Dominic deserved that sort of insult.

"Lord Gascoyne?" He cocked a brow. "I'm not a saint by any means, but I don't think I'm quite that level of awful."

"No, you're not," she conceded through gritted teeth. "But that doesn't mean that what you just did isn't despicable."

"Since when is a marriage proposal considered despicable?"

"When it's not sincere!"

"But it is."

"Oh, you expect me to believe that?" Artemis sprang to her feet again. "Dukes do not sincerely propose marriage to women like me."

He crossed his arms over his chest. "What do you mean 'women like you'?"

"Rebellious bluestockings. Jaded spinsters. Almost thirty-year-old women who are not virginal or pure or blue blooded but have sharp tongues and radical ideas who never want to marry. That's who I mean."

"You're making a lot of assumptions about what I do and don't want in a wife." Dominic's mouth tilted into a sardonic smile. "For one thing, I happen to like your tongue."

She snorted. "I'm sure. Oh, and I forgot to add, I'm not even certain that I want children. Don't you want lots of rosy-cheeked, happy babies to fill the ducal nursery? At the age of twenty-nine, I'm far too old to be anyone's brood mare."

Something flickered in his gaze. A flash of hurt, perhaps even anger, but then it was gone. "My sister, Horatia, was about your age when she gave birth to twin boys," he said.

Artemis planted her hands on her hips. "That's all well and good, but I still don't understand why you are proposing to begin with. Rumor has it that you're hunting for a new duchess, but I am not, nor will I ever be suitable. Aside from that, and it's probably the most important point: I. Don't. Want. To. Wed… Ever!"

Dominic rubbed his chin, his expression contemplative. "I think you need to think this through, Artemis, before dismissing me out of hand. Consider all of the possibilities. You know, there might be some benefit to you. And just because we become engaged, it doesn't necessarily mean that marriage will follow."

Artemis threw her hands up in the air. "Oh, so now you're proposing an engagement of convenience? It seems to me that you are as inconstant and changeable as the wind, Your Grace."

"I'll admit this proposal has seemingly come out of nowhere, but as I mentioned, it might actually be worth your while to say yes. I propose we make another deal."

"At this point in time, I'd rather make a deal with the devil," muttered Artemis. "It seems to me that the Prince of Darkness himself would be more trustworthy."

"I can understand why you'd think that way, but all I ask is that you hear me out."

"Very well." Artemis crossed her arms and fixed him with a hard stare. "I'm listening."

Dominic crossed to the fireplace, then took up a wide stance on the hearthrug as though he owned the room and everything in it, including her. "If we become engaged, a few things will happen. First of all, your aunt will stop haranguing you. Second, your aunt's unreasonable caveat preventing your sister, Phoebe, from marrying will be removed. Third, your reputation won't be at risk of being ruined at all. I know your planning has been meticulous, but there might be a few here tonight who do actually suspect something highly irregular has passed between us.

Not only did we dance together tonight, but you've just made a rather large to-do in the hall outside the library. Several other guests witnessed your dramatic exit and my pursuit. They know we're in here right now. And that we're alone. Part of me can't believe you thought this scheme would actually work."

"Humph." Artemis was still too cross with him to concede that he was right. It had been beyond foolish to lose her head like that and to dash madly from the room, but she'd been so overwhelmed with emotion, she'd let herself succumb to the urge to run away and hide. "Tell me, Your Grace," she said after a slight, taut-as-a-piano-wire pause, "what other benefits are there on the table? What are the precise terms of this deal?" She narrowed her eyes. "What do you want from me?"

"I was nothing but impressed with the way you handled Miss Sharp and Celeste. Celeste has always found it particularly difficult to share her thoughts and feelings with others, but you managed to gain her confidence in a very short time. If you spend even more time with her, I'm confident that you'll be able to find out who this confounded 'T' is. Miss Sharp certainly hasn't been able to. Indeed, I'm starting to lose faith in her abilities, and that's not helpful when time is of the essence. I'm worried Celeste will do something even more dangerous than simply trade love letters with a would-be seducer, and then there will be no going back."

"You want me to spy on your daughter?"

"That's rather a blunt way of putting it, but yes, essentially I am asking you to gain her confidence—to befriend her—to see if you can glean any useful intelligence. And perhaps you can also guide her. Help her to see reason. That this 'T' does not have her best interests at heart. That he's a scoundrel seeking to take advantage of her."

Artemis gave him a flat look. "You want me—the woman who just did something completely outrageous—to help Lady Celeste see reason?"

"You claim you have radical views, Artemis, but I believe you have a superior intellect, and for some reason I can't quite explain, I trust you. Perhaps it's your forthrightness I find so appealing. You might also be surprised to learn that I don't disagree with you on most of the things you believe in. I *do* think women are as intelligent as men. I do think they should be able to study whatever they want to at university. I do think women should be able to seek a divorce. I do think married women should be able to own property in their own right."

"You do?"

"Undoubtedly. If you don't believe me, I'll show you a copy of the Matrimonial Causes Act that received my vote in Parliament last year. It ended church interference in the process of divorce and instead made it a secular matter for law courts. It hasn't removed all of the unfair barriers women face, but at least it's a start."

Artemis paced over to the pianoforte, then back again. Then back and forth once more. Her mind was whirling, tumbling with a million thoughts, and she couldn't seem to pin any of them down. If she accepted Dominic's proposal, what would her life be like?

If…

"You know, if you just found a suitable wife from someone who hails from your own class, Your Grace, I'm sure she would be able to befriend and guide your daughter too," she said at last.

"The thing is, Artemis, I haven't found anyone else. It's you who's caught my interest. You're not as unsuitable as you seem to think."

Oh... Artemis's brow knit into a deep frown. He couldn't mean that. But then, he didn't know that she was really Lydia Lovelace who'd written all of those salacious Gothic romance novels he seemed to despise so much. Books that he believed had corrupted his adolescent daughter's mind. He wouldn't think she was a suitable role model then, would he?

If she told him the truth, would he withdraw his ridiculous offer of marriage? In fact, if she did, she was certain he'd want nothing to do with her, ever again.

But... She held her tongue and started to pace again. Could she trust him with such an incendiary secret? She'd trusted him with her ruination plan. And look how that had turned out.

However, if he learned that she was in fact, Lydia Lovelace, he might be so furious, he'd tell others. And once her anonymity had been destroyed, so would her dream of starting her own academic college.

No, she couldn't do it. She couldn't take the risk.

"What are you thinking, Artemis?"

She stopped and faced him. "You still haven't told me what I can expect in return for accepting your marriage proposal. And what will happen if I decide to end our engagement of convenience."

"I will guarantee financial support for your college regardless of whether you become my wife or not," he said. "And I will ask Horatia, who has many influential connections—despite my notoriety—to become a patroness. If you would like her to."

Artemis's pulse began to leap about like someone had let off a Catherine wheel inside her. "You, and your sister, you would really do that for me?"

Dominic inclined his head. "You have my word. I also suspect that if you decide to jilt me, no one will blame you for it. I am the Dastardly Duke after all. For you, there will be no negative consequences. What do you have to lose?"

Artemis studied his face. His dark-gray eyes. His gaze was steady, his expression watchful while he patiently waited for her to respond.

Her heart was beating so wildly, she thought it might burst. Indeed, she felt like she was balancing on a very narrow precipice. She could have everything she'd ever wanted if she was willing to step over the edge. She just needed to take a leap of faith and trust Dominic again.

Inhaling a shaky breath, she asked, "How long do we need to be engaged?"

"It's up to you, but I would hope you would remain my fiancée long enough to help me with Celeste. And if you two should become close, I wouldn't expect you to end your association with my daughter if you and I parted ways. That wouldn't be fair to either of you."

Artemis released a sigh. "You've given me a lot to think about."

He moved closer. "I understand what a shock this has been. I–I did turn the tables on you quite unexpectedly. But to be perfectly honest, I had been thinking of doing so from the outset. It was clear to me that your scheme would never work—that it was full of potential pitfalls. That you could ruin your reputation irrevocably despite all of your careful planning. And when all is said and done, I could never ignore my duty as a gentleman." He shrugged a shoulder. "And just think"—his mouth curved into a wicked smile—"if we're betrothed, you and I will undoubtedly be seeing a lot more of each other." His voice dropped to a low, seductive purr. "You can't deny that what happened in the library wasn't spectacular."

Artemis's cheeks burned hotter than the flames dancing in the grate. "No, I can't deny it," she admitted. Indeed, the sensual part of her was thrilled by the idea that she would be able to openly spend more time with Dominic. To be alone with him, in his arms again... Oh, she could readily agree to that.

She stared into the fire, thinking about everything that had occurred tonight and what Dominic had promised. Despite the fact he'd changed the rules of their arrangement without warning, she couldn't stay angry with him for long. He was too damn irresistible. And generous and...ugh...reasonable and open-minded and *informed*.

"So, my dear Artemis, what's it to be? Will you become my fiancée, even if it's just for a little while?" Dominic's voice was a gentle nudge, but surprisingly, it also contained an appealing, hesitant note, as though he was suddenly nervous about what her answer would be.

As though she mattered.

Artemis raised her gaze to his. "Very well, Dominic. I will agree to an engagement of convenience. I will help you with your daughter, and at the end of our arrangement—"

"You shall have your college." Dominic was smiling at her, and Artemis felt her mouth lift into a smile as well.

"Yes," she said softly.

"And we might even have a little fun along the way?"

"Oh, I hope so," she replied with a laugh. "But not right now. I've caught a glimpse of myself in that mirror over the mantel, and it's going to take me a few minutes to repair my hair before I venture out of this room."

"You look lovely." Dominic drew behind her as she began to smooth her curls and repin various sections. His hands settled at her waist.

"I look like a ravished hussy who just tumbled out of bed."

"Mmm. As I said, lovely." He bent his head and kissed her neck, making her shiver.

"That is not helpful, Dominic," she chided gently.

Looking up, he caught her gaze in the mirror and flashed her a devilish grin. "Isn't a man allowed to kiss his fiancée?"

"Not when she's trying to make herself look respectable so she can go and face her aunt and everyone else outside. I can't even begin to think what Aunt Roberta is going to say to me."

Another teasing kiss, this one in the hollow behind her ear. "Your aunt didn't seem all that bothered when I was proposing to you. In fact, I think she was rather in favor of it."

"Yes." Artemis grimaced as she slid the last pin back into place. Her hair still looked a little ruffled in places, but it would have to do. "I suppose it shouldn't surprise me though. She's always been a mercenary creature."

"And so am I. I say, sod your aunt. She and everyone else can wait for our return. This man wants to kiss his fiancée properly."

He turned her about so she faced him. And then he crooked a finger under her chin and kissed her. It was a soft, sweet, sensual kiss, nothing like the many they'd shared before. It was beguiling and gentle and made Artemis's heart ache in the most peculiar way. She'd never been kissed like this before. With such tender reverence. As though she was precious.

She imagined it was the sort of kiss you bestowed on someone you loved.

But no, this was not, nor would it ever be a love match, Artemis sternly told herself as they quit the music room to, ironically, face the music. It was a relationship based on obligation-free lust and fun, and a degree of mutual respect and liking. And now there was a transactional nature to it as well. Everything about it was "convenient." That was all.

She'd best remember that in the coming days.

Falling in love with the Duke of Dartmoor was not an option.

Chapter Sixteen

"HOW COULD YOU DO THIS TO ME, ARTEMIS? HOW COULD you?"

Artemis kicked off her pumps and propped her aching feet on the plump ottoman in her bedroom. She'd already loosened the tapes securing her crinoline cage about her waist and had dumped it and the rest of her ball gown's petticoats on the floor by her bed. "I don't see why you're so upset, Phoebe. Aunt Roberta is over-the-moon happy that Dom… I mean, that His Grace and I are betrothed. Now there are no impediments stopping you from finding a suitable match and getting married this Season."

"But that's just it, Artemis. How am I to do that when your fiancé is the Dastardly Duke?" Phoebe threw her a baleful glare that was so sharp, it could have sliced flesh from bone. "All Aunt Roberta can see is a way for you to escape ruin and the money you'll bring into the family. And I don't want someone to pursue me and then propose just because my aunt and newly ennobled sister are both richer than Solomon. I want him to propose to me because he *loves* me."

"If he loves you, he won't care about the gossip surrounding the Duke of Dartmoor. And that's just it, Phoebe. It's nasty, entirely unfounded gossip. Dom…" She took a breath. There was no point pretending that she and the duke didn't have a more intimate relationship. "Dominic is not dastardly at all. He's really rather noble."

Phoebe snorted. "You're just bedazzled by his dukedom and his enormous wealth and handsome face."

"Bedazzled? Hardly."

"Then why did you say yes to his proposal? You told me that you never wanted to wed. That you wanted to start your own school for women."

"Because I'd been well and truly compromised, Phoebe. And I'm doing everything I can to minimize the damage to the family's reputation." This last point wasn't entirely true. She'd been more than willing to endanger the family name and her own reputation to some extent in order to gain her freedom. But Artemis wasn't about to admit that the only reason she'd accepted Dominic's proposal was so that she *could* get her school.

"By marrying someone with the worst reputation in England," cried Phoebe. "Artemis, he murdered his wife! If you're going to get caught in a compromising situation with someone, at least choose a man who isn't dangerous."

"The coroner ruled otherwise, and that's good enough for me. It should be good enough for everyone else too," returned Artemis with a flash of annoyance.

Phoebe scowled. "Aren't you the least bit suspicious or concerned that he did actually kill her?"

"Not at all. Underneath all of his arrogance, I do think he's a good man. He's just misunderstood."

Phoebe's eyes narrowed. "I always thought of you as supremely intelligent. But now I think you might be the biggest fool in all of Christendom." She marched to the bedroom door. "And don't expect Hetty to come and help you out of your corset or pick up your things." She gestured at the pile on the floor with an angry stab of her finger. "She'll be assisting me and that's all. Good night."

The door slammed, and Artemis let her head drop onto the cushioned back of the chair. Poor Phoebe. Tonight had been such a tumultuous ride for all of them, including her sister. She'd calm down in time. Especially when articles crowing about the Duke of Dartmoor's engagement began appearing in papers like the *London Tatler*. And that the duke's fiancée happened to have a very eligible younger sister. Of course, there might very well be fortune hunters and other unscrupulous sorts who would attempt to court Phoebe. But Aunt Roberta would make short shrift of them if they had nefarious rather than genuine intentions.

At least Artemis hoped so. Although Aunt Roberta didn't seem to mind that Artemis was now betrothed to a duke with "the worst reputation in England."

Artemis sighed. It shouldn't surprise her that her aunt would do just about anything to be rid of her. It seemed the urge to part ways was both strong and mutual.

———

The following day, Dominic sent Artemis a massive bunch of deep-red roses with a note stating how much he was looking forward to seeing his "gorgeous fiancée." He also mentioned that he would call on her at four o'clock sharp to take her on a jaunt about Hyde Park in his new tilbury.

Indeed, he was acting like a lovestruck fool in the full throes of courting a woman, but he couldn't seem to help it.

He kept telling himself the real reason for his visit to Cadogan Square was that he merely wanted to ask Artemis to speak with Celeste as soon as possible. And that wasn't *entirely* untrue; he really did need some clarity around this troubling business with 'T.' But before Artemis saw Celeste, he'd have to break the news to his daughter that he was engaged. According to Morton, there would be several formal announcements appearing in the newspapers on the morrow, so time was of the essence.

He had no idea how Celeste would react—whether there'd be slammed doors and tears or smiles and heartfelt congratulations—so he'd been procrastinating and effectively putting it off all day.

Instead, he was now playing the part of besotted fiancé, lingering in Lady Wagstaff's drawing room waiting for Artemis to arrive. His pulse was elevated, his body on edge as he drummed his fingers on the edge of a windowsill. He'd given up trying to lounge with calculated carelessness against the mantelpiece or in a doorway like a young buck trying to impress a woman with his Corinthian's physique and abundant nonchalance. Although, in a way, he *was* trying to impress Artemis. God only knew why. He'd donned a new charcoal-gray coat that fit like a glove, and his waistcoat was an appealing shade of cobalt blue. And in his pocket was a betrothal ring—a massive square-cut ruby surrounded by smaller diamonds that he'd purchased from Asprey's earlier that morning.

Anyone would think he was in love. Which was ridiculous. He'd been in love once—with Juliet—and he *never* wanted to be in that agonizing state of being again.

No, I'm simply in lust with Artemis, he told his reflection in the windowpane, even as he was adjusting his necktie. *And I want something from her—her expertise. There's nothing else to this arrangement.*

Indeed, his blood began to thrum with expectation when she entered the room a moment later and then uttered his name in that delightfully sultry voice of hers, a voice that reminded

him of honeyed whisky and illicit encounters like the one
they'd shared the night before.

Pushing down the urge to immediately sweep Artemis into
his arms and kiss her until she was breathless with want, he
turned and greeted her with a smile. "What, no chaperone?" he
asked, glancing past her shoulder.

She laughed. "No, not this afternoon. Aunt Roberta has
a megrim. I think she drank too much champagne after our
betrothal was announced at Northam House. And Phoebe has
taken off with her maid somewhere to run errands."

Dominic briefly contemplated seducing Artemis here in
her aunt's drawing room—there was a wonderfully overstuffed settee by the hearth that would do nicely—but then
thought better of it. She was attired in a stylish carriage gown
of claret velvet with a matching little hat perched on top of
her elaborately arranged auburn curls. He didn't think she'd
appreciate him mussing up her appearance like he was some
randy dog who couldn't control his lustful urges. Instead, he
said, "Well, I'm pleased I shall have you all to myself. And to
that end…" He removed a small, velvet-covered box from the
breast pocket of his coat and opened it with a small flourish. "I suppose now would be an opportune time to give you
this…"

Artemis's eyes widened. "Oh heavens, Dominic. That ring is
truly magnificent. But you really shouldn't have. You don't need
to spoil me by sending roses—although they *are* lovely—or
giving me jewelry. We're not courting. You don't need to sweep
me off my feet."

"I should and I have. And you will accept my betrothal
ring—a token of my esteem for you—with good grace." He
took the ring from the box and slid it onto Artemis's slender

ring finger. "There. It fits perfectly. And now everyone will know you are the Duke of Dartmoor's fiancée."

"Thank you." Artemis's cheeks were as red as her gown and the ring she now sported. As she turned it this way and that to admire the gemstones, they caught the late-afternoon sun pouring in through a nearby window and threw off brilliant glints of light. "I've never owned a piece of jewelry that's quite so beautiful. Or expensive. I'm quite honored." Her gaze, as warm as sunlit treacle, met his. "And touched."

"Think nothing of it. Now"—he tucked her hand into the crook of his arm and escorted her out of the drawing room—"let us away before I decide to have my wicked way with you on your aunt's settee."

She laughed. "I wouldn't mind if you did."

"Wench." He stopped and turned to face her. "You are…"

She smiled. "Enchanting? Enticing? Enthralling?"

"Yes. All of those things." And then he kissed her, right in the middle of her aunt's vestibule because he simply couldn't resist. It was a soft, sensual, calculated kiss that spoke of his burning desire. The things he wanted to do with her in the heat of the night filled his head, and he had to pull away before he did drag her back into the drawing room or throw her over his shoulder and cart her back to his bed at Dartmoor House.

Egads, this woman was temptation personified. Perhaps she should have been named Aphrodite rather than Artemis. Or even Hecate because he was starting to suspect he'd been bewitched.

As he leapt into the seat beside Artemis in his tilbury carriage and then urged his bay gelding into a smart trot, he briefly let himself contemplate what it would actually be like to be married to a woman like her. The more he thought about it, the more he liked the idea even though she wasn't precisely the sort of woman he'd initially had in mind for his duchess. She was outspoken; there was no denying it. She possessed radical views about womanhood—but he didn't disagree with her on any of the points she'd raised in his presence. In a word, she was passionate.

And he liked that very much. Maybe *too* much.

If she decided to end their engagement, he realized he'd be deeply disappointed.

Now that was a sobering thought.

But maybe if he wooed Artemis, convinced her that marriage to him wouldn't be such a bad thing, that she could have everything she wanted and more... She was such a fearless young woman, he had no doubts that becoming a duchess wouldn't daunt her. He could well imagine her giving Queen Victoria herself a good run for her money.

No, he was getting ahead of himself. He didn't just need a duchess; he wanted a wife who would also be a mother to Celeste and who'd willingly bear him an heir. And Artemis wasn't sure that she wanted children. She was a free spirit who valued her independence above all else.

He'd best stamp out this budding warmth inside his chest before it flared into something uncontrollable. He needed to be more circumspect. Guarded.

Developing any sort of tender feelings for Miss Artemis Jones was not an option.

Artemis didn't think she'd ever enjoyed herself quite so much. Seated beside the darkly handsome Duke of Dartmoor as they barreled through Hyde Park in his fast and light carriage, with the wind in her hair and the afternoon sun in her face, she almost felt as if she were in a dream.

Or to be more precise, someone else's fairy-tale dream—a young schoolgirl's romantic fantasy where true love existed and wishes came true.

At least one of her wishes would happen. Her college. When this wild, fantastical ride with Dominic was over, she would have that to sustain her in the years ahead.

Dominic reined in his horse beside a stand of beech trees not far from the Serpentine.

"What now, Your Grace?" Artemis asked.

"Other than creating a stir amongst the aristocratic hoi polloi when they see me promenading with the most beautiful woman in London, I have no plans." Then a shadow crossed his countenance. "That's not entirely true. I did want to talk to you about Celeste and when you would be willing to speak with her again. Sooner rather than later, if possible."

"You're worried about her."

"Yes…" His brooding gaze wandered to the lake. "Celeste has been quite maudlin of late, mooning around the town house, barely speaking two words to me. I expected her to be upset after I confiscated her would-be suitor's letter. But it's worse than I ever anticipated. Miss Sharp came to me this morning and shared some intelligence that I found most disturbing. Apparently, Celeste has lost her appetite—she only picks at her food—and she's not sleeping well. It's like she's suddenly become some sort of lovelorn wraith and"—he ran a hand down his face, his expression haggard—"it's simply heartbreaking to witness.

"I keep telling myself it's for the best. If the mysterious "T" was indeed a fortune-hunting ne'er-do-well, he's probably moved on. I suspect Celeste somehow warned him that I'd uncovered their illicit liaison. Of course, if he now views her as a lost cause, he'll no doubt be searching for new prey in fresh hunting grounds. But I can't be sure, so that's where you come in. Only..."

His chest rose and fell with a heavy sigh. "I've never seen Celeste in such low spirits before. Over the years, I've avoided speaking to her about my duty to remarry one day. Which has been a mistake on my part. She was only six years old when her mother passed, and of course, she loved her a great deal." He shook his head. "I'm afraid I've been a coward for not broaching the subject of my obligation to wed again until now. Because of my own pain, I suppose."

After another fraught pause, he caught Artemis's gaze. "Even though Celeste seemed to warm to you after your first meeting, I'm concerned about how she will react when she learns that we are engaged and that you will be her stepmother. Well, *might* be her stepmother," he amended with a wry smile. "I'm worried I'm going to inadvertently make things worse for her instead of better."

A sliver of guilt penetrated Artemis's heart at the thought she would be misleading Celeste. To gain her trust but then break it when she ended things with Dominic seemed unnecessarily cruel. Of course, that was not Artemis's intention. And Dominic *had* said she could maintain her relationship with Celeste if one developed.

When all was said and done, she was trying to help an impressionable adolescent girl. She didn't want Celeste to make the same mistake *she* had all of those years ago with Guy de Burgh. How ironic that particular cad was the girl's uncle. "As to whether Celeste accepts me or not, I suppose we will just have to see what happens," said Artemis gently. "Regardless, I will do my best to find out who this man is and if his apparent abandonment has led to this troubling bout of melancholy."

"Thank you," Dominic said gravely. "Your understanding means a lot."

He reached out a gloved hand and squeezed one of Artemis's, and her heart skipped about in her chest. There was that strange sensation again. That she somehow mattered to Dominic. But she must ignore the feeling. It was only an illusion. Her overactive imagination was attributing far too much significance to Dominic's words and actions.

He was using her and she was using him. Such was the way of the world, and she should know better than to be gulled into believing a man like Dominic could truly care for a woman like her, despite his words of support the night before. She was opinionated and difficult and unconventional, and she wouldn't change.

She was not what he needed.

To break the strange sense of intimacy surrounding them, Artemis withdrew her hand and turned the conversation to safer, practical matters. "When would you like me to call on Celeste?"

"Tomorrow, if your schedule permits."

"It does."

"Excellent." He smiled. "I'm afraid I'm quite busy with meetings et cetera and won't be in, but I'll send one of Horatia's carriages around to collect you at around one o'clock if that suits. That way everyone, including your aunt, will think my sister is chaperoning."

"You are very good at subterfuge."

"It comes with playing politics in business for so long. One does what one must."

"It seems we are both of a pragmatic nature."

"Yes, I think we are. And with that in mind"—he smiled—"I suggest that I take you home before your aunt Roberta has conniptions."

Artemis laughed. "I agree. She's been known to have them before, and it's not a pretty sight."

Dominic released the brake on the tilbury, flicked the reins, and then they were off again, bowling merrily down one of the carriage drives toward Hyde Park Corner.

They were just rounding a bend that led to the Wellington Arch when Artemis caught a glimpse of a young woman in a cabriolet that was racing past in the opposite direction, and she emitted a gasp.

"What is it?" asked Dominic, slowing his horse. "Is everything all right?"

"I..." Artemis leaned out of the tilbury and glanced backward from whence they'd come, but it was too late. The other carriage had disappeared around the corner. "I could have sworn that I just saw Phoebe...with...with a man."

Concern laced Dominic's voice as he said, "Do you want me to turn around and follow?"

Artemis settled back into her seat. "I... No. No, it's all right. I must have imagined it was her. It's not the sort of thing she would do—go off with a gentleman without telling anyone."

Unless Phoebe is more like you than you think, Artemis. And you already know her maid can be bribed...

"Did you see who the man was?"

"No. They flew by so quickly, I didn't see his face. It was all rather a blur." Artemis touched Dominic's arm. "Honestly, there's no point in making a fuss. Besides, Phoebe is twenty-four and more than capable of looking after herself. And as I said, I'm not even certain it was her. I'm sure I'll find her back at Cadogan Square."

But Phoebe wasn't at home, and when she stepped through the door an hour later, Artemis thought she looked rather windblown and far too flushed. And were her lips a little kiss bruised?

When Artemis tried to question her in her bedroom, her sister sent her a cold, hard glare. "I'm still not speaking to you, Artemis," she said stiffly. "But I'll make you a deal. I'll keep my nose out of your business if you keep your nose out of mine. Now, I'll ask you to leave. I'm rather tired, and I'd like to rest before dinner." Turning her back on Artemis, she then deposited herself on the seat at her dressing table and proceeded to unpin her hair. "Hetty, after you've seen my sister out, I'd like you to organize my bath."

The lady's maid gave Artemis an apologetic smile as she gestured toward the door.

Artemis sighed. "Phoebe, I don't understand why you're so angry with me. Yes, I'm engaged to a man you don't approve of, but in time you'll see that it isn't such a terrible thing. In the meantime, just know that I'm always here for you if you need me. Please believe me when I say that I want you to be happy." And then she quit the room.

There was no point in arguing with her sister when she was in a pout. But now, more than ever, Artemis was convinced that Phoebe had a secret paramour.

She just prayed it was someone suitable.

"How could you do this? Try to replace *my* mother? With, with…well, with anyone. I don't care about the sodding dukedom. You and Miss Jones can go hang for all I care!" The sound of Dartmoor House's library door slamming shut was immediately followed by the sound of receding footfalls and racking sobs.

Bloody blistering ballocks. That could have gone better. Dominic downed the whisky he had at the ready and then tipped his head back to stare at the ceiling. The cavorting cupids above him were still impervious to the drama that had just played out in this room.

It was his own fault of course, that he hadn't discussed his intentions with Celeste until now. It didn't sound as though she had any particular objections to Artemis per se. She simply didn't want him to marry at all.

With a sigh, he poured another whisky from the bottle at his elbow. Despite Celeste's volatile outburst, he would still encourage her to accept a visit from Artemis tomorrow. He'd broach the subject after she'd calmed down. He was certain she'd see reason. Surely she'd give Artemis a chance.

He also trusted that his clever fiancée was experienced enough to weather the swiftly changing, oft-times turbulent moods of an adolescent girl. Perhaps Artemis would easily smooth things over and help Celeste to see that her stepmother-to-be wasn't wicked or evil. In fact she was genuine, understanding, and could be amusing company.

Dominic ran a hand down his face. There was the rub. There was no guarantee that Artemis *would* become Celeste's stepmother. And that would be disappointing. He *did* genuinely like and admire her. There was no denying his desire for her. But could it be more than that?

He sipped his whisky. He'd never thought that he'd find love a second time. Or more to the point, that he'd ever have the guts to give his heart completely to someone again. And he still didn't. No matter that Artemis beckoned and beguiled like a flickering will-o'-the-wisp or pixie light in the far distance, he wouldn't follow. He wasn't ready to let down his guard again and he might not ever be.

He'd endured enough heartbreak to last a lifetime.

In any event, he'd warn Artemis that Celeste might be less than amenable to any of her overtures. She had a right to know that she was potentially walking straight into the line of fire on a battlefield on the morrow. And if she decided not to come straightaway, he would understand that too.

Chapter Seventeen

"I BELIEVE CONGRATULATIONS ARE IN ORDER, MISS JONES."
Miss Sharp's smile was as sincere as that of a Cheapside coster-
monger trying to off-load a cart of bruised apples or yesterday's
fish.

Nevertheless, Artemis graciously inclined her head. "Thank
you, Miss Sharp." She'd just arrived at Dartmoor House in Lady
Northam's carriage, sans chaperone, as Dominic had planned.
He'd sent word to Cadogan Square early this morning confirming the details of her visit and that his daughter had been far
from happy to learn that he'd be marrying again. "I trust Lady
Celeste is well?" The governess's answer would determine
whether Artemis needed to don full battle armor or not.

In the distance, she could hear the light tinkling notes of
a pianoforte. She assumed it was Celeste playing the jaunty
tune—some sort of polka or mazurka. Perhaps armor wouldn't
be required after all.

"Oh, as well as can be expected under the circumstances,"
the governess replied cryptically.

Under the circumstances. Did the woman mean, as well as can
be expected given Lady Celeste's secret paramour had apparently deserted her? Or that her father had just announced his
betrothal to a veritable nobody who used to be a lowly finishing
school teacher? Artemis had no idea, but it was clearly a petty
swipe. And unhelpful.

"I see," said Artemis carefully. "I take it that she is still willing to receive me? Dominic—I mean, His Grace—informed me that it was all arranged." As she spoke, she raised her bare left hand to her throat to quite unnecessarily fiddle with the lace of her collar. Drawing Miss Sharp's attention to her ruby and diamond engagement ring was equally as petty, but Artemis couldn't seem to help herself. The governess was infuriatingly supercilious.

Miss Sharp made a show of looking at the watch pinned to her bodice. "I'm afraid she's currently having a dancing lesson with Signor Giovanni Moretti. It was a last-minute change of plans. He's one of London's finest dancing masters, and because his time is precious, one doesn't quibble. If you'd like to wait…" She gestured toward a tiny parlor near the front door.

Artemis almost laughed at the woman's audacity. She was certain who was responsible for the last-minute change of plans. "No, I'm happy to observe the lesson if Lady Celeste doesn't mind. After all, she *is* expecting me, so I wouldn't want to disappoint her. Or Dominic. I mean, His Grace."

Miss Sharp pursed her lips. "Yes. Certainly. This way." She swept from the entry hall and led Artemis down a wide gallery toward a grand set of doors flanked by two liveried footmen. The music grew louder, and Artemis heard a light feminine laugh.

She frowned. For someone who was reported to be vacillating between "lovelorn" and "seething with anger and resentment," Lady Celeste clearly enjoyed her dancing lessons.

As soon as Lady Celeste saw Artemis, she stumbled and stepped on the toes of her middle-aged dance master—Signor Giovanni Moretti, Artemis presumed—and the music stopped. But Signor Moretti wasn't the only man in the room. Seated at a pianoforte in a far corner by an arched window was an attractive young male with tousled black hair, olive skin, and dark soulful eyes. And Artemis's senses were immediately on high alert.

"Who is that?" she murmured to Miss Sharp, but the woman ignored her question.

"Lady Celeste"—the governess bobbed a curtsy—"Signor Moretti, Master Antonio"—this last remark she directed toward the man at the piano—"my apologies for the interruption. Miss Jones here insisted on observing. She didn't think you'd mind, my lady."

Artemis inwardly rolled her eyes. To the duke's daughter, she curtsied then said, "Lady Celeste, it was not my intention to disrupt your lesson by any means. Please do carry on. Our engagement…" She inwardly winced. Why on earth did she use *that* word? "Our appointment," she amended, "can wait until later."

Lady Celeste inclined her head. However, her gaze was decidedly cool as she said, "Of course, Miss Jones. My father mentioned you were paying another visit. And that I am to receive you." Then she turned back to Signor Moretti. "Shall we continue with the mazurka, Signor, or should we try that new style of Viennese waltz that's all the rage?"

Her message to Artemis was loud and clear: *You might be my father's fiancée, but that is of little consequence to me. Of so little consequence, I'd rather have a dancing lesson than speak with you. And when I do so, it will be under sufferance.*

And Artemis had thought it was Miss Sharp's idea to reschedule Lady Celeste's dancing lesson.

She followed the governess across the marble floor and took a seat by one of the windows to observe. Although Miss Sharp didn't seem all that interested in the proceedings because she picked up a book and began to read.

Interesting. Artemis turned her attention back to Lady Celeste. The girl was graceful and a quick study. In no time at all she'd mastered a new set of intricate steps and was whirling about the ballroom with Signor Moretti.

The pianist was excellent too. He hadn't missed a note of the fast-moving waltz. And that was despite the fact that his eyes never left Lady Celeste. Artemis leaned toward Miss Sharp. "Master Antonio, is he Signor Moretti's regular pianist?"

The governess lowered her book. "Yes. He's Signor Moretti's nephew. He comes to every lesson."

"And how old is he?"

"I'd say nineteen or twenty."

Hmmm. Artemis studied his expression. His dark gaze was rapt as he watched the duke's daughter spin around the room, her elegant movements swathed in undulating swirls of lilac silk. "And do you always observe Lady Celeste's dance lessons?"

The governess gave a haughty sniff. "Most of the time. If I'm not here, Lady Celeste's maid, Yvette, is. And there are always footmen at the door. My lady is never on her own." The woman's gaze narrowed and she whispered, "You're not suggesting that Master Antonio is my lady's mysterious paramour, are you?"

Artemis sent the governess a speaking look. "Since I've been here, he hasn't stopped watching her. And she keeps casting lingering glances his way too."

"What rot. If that were the case, I would have…" Miss Sharp's voice trailed off as she caught sight of her charge sending Master Antonio a secretive smile over Signor Moretti's shoulder as they whirled by the piano. "Oh…" The governess swallowed and put down her book altogether. "But his name begins with 'A,'" she murmured. "He can't be 'T.'"

"Why not? Tonio, Toni, and Tonino are common enough diminutives of Antonio. Using a shortened, more intimate version of one's name would be entirely fitting for a love note."

"I… Well…" Miss Sharp's face had turned scarlet. "I never considered it, but perhaps…"

"I have an idea," said Artemis. "Do you play the pianoforte?"

"Yes. But—"

"Could you manage something like a Scottish reel? Nothing *too* quick though."

"I suppose so. If I had some sheet music to follow. Why—"

"Follow my lead."

Artemis stood as the waltz ended. "Signor Moretti, I understand you are one of London's, if not England's, finest dancing instructors," she said with a bright smile meant to charm.

The gentleman bowed. "Miss Jones. I have heard that said, and more than once, yes."

"Well, I wondered if you would mind teaching me the steps of the latest Highland schottische. I came across it the other night at Lord and Lady Northam's masquerade ball, and I must confess, it rather confounded me. Of course, Lady Celeste should learn it too."

"I…" The dancing master's heavy brows slid into a frown. "I am not sure if that would be permitted, Miss Jones. The duke—"

"I'm certain His Grace wouldn't mind. I am his fiancée after all."

"His fiancée?" A ruddy flush spread across the man's cheeks before he folded into a deep bow. "Forgive me, Miss Jones. I was not aware of your betrothal to His Grace. Congratulations to you."

Artemis waved away his apology. "That's quite all right.

How were you to know? It was only announced publicly in the papers this morning." She glanced at Lady Celeste who was fuming so much, steam was practically shooting out of her ears. At the risk of raising the girl's ire further, she added, "But rather than steal *you* away from Lady Celeste, perhaps I could dance with your nephew, Master Antonio. I take it he dances too…"

"*Si.* Yes. *Molto bene.* Very well. But—"

Artemis clapped her hands and beamed. "And Miss Sharp will accompany us on the pianoforte. Won't you, Miss Sharp?"

The governess tilted her head. "I will do my best."

Master Antonio vacated the piano stool with obvious reluctance and approached Artemis. "Miss Jones," he said as he executed an elaborate bow. "It would be an honor to dance with you."

As the young man took her in his arms in the required position for the dance, Artemis caught a glimpse of Celeste's face. If looks could kill, Artemis would have expired then and there. The young woman was livid. Her mouth was compressed into a flat, angry line and her gray eyes were bright with glittering anger.

Sadness gripped Artemis's heart. She derived no joy from discovering who Celeste's secret paramour was. She didn't want to upset her. Young love was intense and to rip it away was going to wound the girl deeply. But it had to be done. She was far too young to have an affair. Or worse still, elope. It could only end in disaster.

As for Master Antonio, Artemis couldn't quite work out whether the young man's affections were genuine or if he was a fortune hunter seeking to take advantage of a well-connected but lonely adolescent girl.

He was light on his feet and nothing but charming as he

partnered her in the Scots-style polka. He'd stopped staring at Celeste, which only seemed to make the duke's daughter more incensed. By the time the scottische ended, Lady Celeste's cheeks were flaming.

"Thank you, Master Tonio. I mean *An*tonio. That was most enjoyable," Artemis said as they drew apart.

"I… It was my pleasure, Miss Jones," he muttered, his gaze darting to Celeste, then away again to some distant place on the far side of the ballroom. Bright color stained his high cheekbones. If Antonio Moretti were a dog, his tail would be between his legs right now.

The lesson came to an end and after the Morettis took their leave, Lady Celeste excused herself. "I have a terrible megrim," she declared. "So I'm sorry, Miss Jones, I won't be able to speak with you today after all."

"That's quite all right, my lady. I understand," returned Artemis gently. "Perhaps we might speak another day." Dominic had asked her to befriend Celeste, to guide her, but it seemed she had just done the opposite and made an enemy.

As soon as Celeste disappeared, the governess grasped Artemis's arm. "You were right. I found this"—she thrust a piece of folded paper into Artemis's hand—"hidden amongst the sheet music in Master Antonio's folio when I was searching for a Scottish reel to play."

Artemis opened the sheet.

My darling Tonio,

I know you asked me to wait, that I must be patient until we can be together when I am at least sixteen, but I simply cannot. Being without you is intolerable. I cannot eat, I cannot sleep, and now that I have found out—just last night—that my father is to remarry and I am to have a stepmother, I do not think I can bear it. Even though Papa's fiancée is not altogether objectionable, I cannot even begin to contemplate living with someone who is supposed to replace my own beloved mama, let alone endure it. It isn't fair of him to expect me to do so. I thought he loved my mama with all his heart. And now he is breaking mine by betraying her memory.

But if we were to elope to Guernsey, you and I could wed at once and be blissfully happy together, just like my parents once were. I have some pin money saved—enough to purchase our train tickets to Southampton and then our passage to the island. I can also pawn several pieces of jewelry. I'm certain it would be enough for us to live off, at least for a little while until you're able to secure work. Or until Papa forgives me...

Oh, goodness. What on earth was Celeste thinking? It didn't sound like Antonio Moretti was the villain here. To be sure, this love affair was doomed to fail, and he should know that. Impoverished nephews of dancing masters did *not* wed duke's daughters. Indeed, it was Celeste who was urging the young man to abscond with her, not the other way around. It was also abundantly clear that she had no idea how hard it would be to give up her sheltered, privileged life and instead live a hand-to-mouth existence. Because that's the situation she and Antonio were bound to end up in. Celeste was ensnared in a schoolgirl's fantasy, and that fantasy was about to come crashing down.

"What should we do?" murmured Miss Sharp. Her face was ashen. No doubt she was worried that she would lose her position because of what Celeste had been up to on her watch.

"We have to send word to His Grace," said Artemis. "At once. He must be informed. About everything."

The governess nodded. "I will make sure Lady Celeste is watched every single minute until His Grace arrives home."

"Good. And thank you for helping. I'll be sure to let His Grace know that you were the one who found Lady Celeste's letter and brought it to my attention."

Miss Sharp's cheeks pinkened. "Thank you, Miss Jones. I would appreciate it."

"It will be no trouble at all."

Chapter Eighteen

Dominic sloshed cognac into a crystal tumbler with a hand that was none too steady. "Would you like a brandy too?" he called over his shoulder to Artemis. Like a cat, she'd quite unrepentantly claimed the best spot before the library fire—his favorite leather wingback chair—and he knew he wasn't going to get it back. Strangely, he didn't mind. "Or there's sherry," he added. "I know it's only four o'clock in the afternoon, but given the circumstances, I do think a drink is in order."

"Sherry, thank you. And I agree, drinking something alcoholic is very appropriate. Tea certainly won't do the trick."

Dominic repaired to the fireside with their drinks and then slumped into the matching chair beside hers. "You did the right thing, sending word to me straightaway," he said after he'd taken two sizable slugs of his cognac.

Artemis winced. "Morton said you were in some sort of board of directors meeting."

"Yes, but nothing is more important than my daughter and her safety. If you and Miss Sharp hadn't discovered what Celeste was planning…" Dominic dragged a hand across his mouth and shook his head. "Christ, I can't even begin to imagine what would have happened if she'd run off with that boy."

Guilt sliced deep, straight to the bone as he drained his glass and then discarded it. "It's all my fault," he said, his voice ragged and raw. "She's lonely because of me. Because of what happened to her mother. Because I couldn't stop..." His hands clenched into fists on his thighs. Artemis didn't need to witness his verbal self-flagellation. Besides, he didn't wish to revisit his far-too-painful past right now. "If my reputation wasn't so stained with mud, Celeste would have friends. She wouldn't be seeking affection from an entirely unsuitable, virtually penniless boy."

Artemis reached out and touched his arm. "I can see you have both suffered, and continue to suffer, immensely. And I will continue to do what I can to help. How was Celeste when you left her?"

After Dominic had confronted Celeste about her plans to elope with the dance master's nephew, she'd erupted into a violent storm of tears and had fled to her rooms. "Inconsolable," he said grimly. "Especially after I declared that she would have to return to Ashburn Abbey because she couldn't be trusted not to ruin herself. I did learn that Yvette, her maid, is the one who's been passing notes between Celeste and Moretti, so she's in tears too. Miss Sharp made Celeste a sleeping draught to try and calm her down, but she tossed it across the bedroom."

"Ah, that was the crash I heard," said Artemis.

Dominic grimaced. "I suppose she'll eventually cry herself to sleep."

"I would offer to go and see her, but I imagine a visit from her stepmother-to-be wouldn't be well received. Besides, I'm not very good at dodging flying objects. Unless you have a shield or a medieval helmet I could borrow. Perchance, there is a suit of armor lingering in a shadowed corner of Dartmoor House?"

"I wish I did because *I* might very well need it." Dominic sighed heavily. "But, honestly, you've done more than enough already in such a short time. I'm nothing but impressed and grateful, even if my daughter isn't."

"I'm happy I could help."

The library's longcase clock marked the quarter hour and Dominic contemplated replenishing his cognac. But he had much to do before he quit London—there was no way in Hades that he was going to send Celeste back to Ashburn on her own—and he needed a clear head. It didn't help that an insistent pounding had begun in the vicinity of his left temple and alcohol would surely make it worse.

He rubbed his forehead and Artemis frowned at him. "Are you all right?"

"It's only a headache," he said. "I'll live."

Artemis rose and moved behind his chair. "Nonsense," she murmured. "Let me help." Her cool fingertips touched his temples, massaging gently, applying just the right amount of pressure, and almost immediately the tension in his muscles started to ebb away.

He closed his eyes and groaned. "Good God. Where did you learn to do that? You have precisely one hour to stop."

She laughed softly and transferred her attentions to his scalp, her talented fingers kneading and stroking. "I suspect you'll be asleep within ten minutes. Perhaps five."

Dominic didn't doubt it. The woman's touch was magical. He let his head drop against the back of the chair and allowed himself to revel in the luxurious feeling of being taken care of. It seemed like forever since he'd been indulged like this. Most of the mistresses he'd engaged in the past—professional courtesans—were all business and he'd never been one to linger long in their company. Those relationships had been purely transactional and carnal. He'd never been interested in cultivating any sort of intimacy. His battered heart, his scarred soul, wouldn't allow him to.

But this…with Artemis. It was different.

Oh God, he was in a bad, bad way. The fortified walls he'd built around his heart after Juliet had died were in danger of being breached, of even crumbling completely, yet he could do nothing but *wallow*.

If he didn't stop Artemis's ministrations very soon, he *would* fall asleep.

Or worse…fall in love.

He caught one of her hands. "Come here," he said gruffly and pulled her across his lap. She came willingly, settling into his chest as though she belonged there.

He rested his forehead against her temple, inhaling her delicious fragrance—roses and vanilla, and something else that was entirely Artemis. "You smell good," he murmured against her ear.

She chuckled softly. "So do you."

He raised his head and captured her jaw. "Come with me. To Dartmoor. Let me show you Ashburn Abbey. It will only be for a week. I'm sure your family and friends can spare you."

Her mouth curved in a smile and mischief danced in her dark eyes. "You're more determined than me to create a scandal."

"I'll get my sister to come. To chaperone. So it all appears aboveboard."

"She would do that?"

"She loves the country. Horses and dogs and wide-open moors are her particular idea of heaven. And it will allow you to spend more time with Celeste. To establish a bond with her and to provide the support and guidance and, indeed, the female companionship she's been missing so desperately." Dominic was aware he was unfairly spinning things out, snaring Artemis in a web of obligation when she'd already done what he'd asked her to do—by all accounts, she'd discovered who "T" was in less than an hour. If she wanted to, she could end their engagement right now and ask him to provide the funds for her college.

Though he rather wished that she wouldn't.

She dropped her gaze to his neckcloth and her fingers flirted with the black silk folds. "At this stage, I'm not sure if I will help or hinder."

"You've said that before, yet you've already done so much. I have no doubt at all that you'll continue to help Celeste. She may not recognize that now, but she will."

"I'm glad you think so. She probably thinks I'm as monstrous as Cinderella's stepmother."

"I'm sure she doesn't. Give her time." Dominic's gaze dropped to Artemis's delectable ripe-as-a-summer-plum mouth. The desire to kiss her was an insistent tattoo in his blood. He slid his hand about her slender torso and flexed his fingers, wishing he could explore what lay beneath the confines of her bodice and corset. "I'd ask you to stay and dine with me, but I have mountains of work to get through before I depart tomorrow." He wanted to spend the entire evening with her, so very much. The urge to spirit her up to his bedroom, to get lost in her for a few blissful hours, was strong. An irresistible force.

A bone-deep ache.

But he couldn't. As always, duty called.

"I understand you're busy." She stroked the hair off his forehead. "No rest for the wicked?"

His mouth twitched with a wry smile. "Something like that." He stroked his fingers up the long, elegant line of her back, then curled them around her nape. A thick, silken curl that had escaped the confines of pins and combs brushed his skin. Even her goddamn hair was tormenting him. "You still haven't answered me, Artemis. Will you come? To Ashburn?"

His eyes searched hers, hoping to find a need as strong as his. If she said no...

She smiled. "I would love to, Dominic."

He couldn't suppress a grin of triumph. "Excellent. I'll have Horatia pick you up in her carriage to ferry you to Paddington Station. I have a private railway car that will take us to Newton via Exeter. Ashburn Abbey is only an hour's carriage ride away from there. I hope eight o'clock isn't too early?"

"No, that will be quite—"

The door to the library burst open, and Morton charged in as though the British cavalry were on his heels. "Your Grace, you said to let you know when these documents from the Home Office arrived. Oh..." Dominic's private secretary halted in the middle of the Persian rug. Behind his spectacles, his face had turned as red as the decanter of claret on the sideboard. "I humbly beg your pardon, Your Grace. Miss Jones. I–I had no idea Miss Jones was still here."

Artemis slid off Dominic's lap and smoothed her slightly rumpled skirts. "That's quite all right, Mr. Morton," she said, her manner cooler than a cucumber. "I was just leaving anyway."

No, it wasn't all bloody right, but at least Artemis had handled the situation with her usual aplomb. Dominic rose too. "Morton, will you send for an unmarked carriage to take Miss Jones home?" Horatia's coach had already gone back to Northam House.

Artemis waved a hand. "There's no need. I'll walk."

"Walk?"

She laughed. "You know, to amble, to stroll, to saunter. That thing we do when we put one foot in front of the other and we're carried forward. Cadogan Square isn't far. A mere half mile. I'm certain I can manage it."

Cheeky wench. "I'm sure you can, but are you sure? It's no trouble at all."

"I'm positive."

"I'll send a footman with you."

"Honestly, Dominic," she chided gently. "I'll be fine. I've managed to walk about London and elsewhere on my own for more than a decade. And if anyone notices me leaving here unaccompanied, it won't bother me. We *are* engaged so I'm sure a degree of latitude is permitted."

He sighed. "Very well."

She leaned in to kiss his cheek. "I'll see myself out. And I'll see you tomorrow."

Minx. Dominic could hardly wait.

———

The Bertrams' rented town house in Wilton Crescent wasn't far from Dartmoor House in Belgravia Square; it meant Artemis would only need to make a slight detour on her way back to Aunt Roberta's town house. If she was going to quit London, she really had to let Lucy know that she wouldn't be able to accompany her to functions over the next week.

As soon as she stepped through the Bertrams' front door, Lucy appeared and then straightaway ushered Artemis into the drawing room at the front of the house. "I'm so glad you got here so quickly," her friend said without preamble. "I only sent a note to Cadogan Square fifteen minutes ago."

It was then that Artemis noticed how pale Lucy's complexion was and the dark shadows beneath her eyes.

Prickles of alarm spiked inside her. "My darling friend, what's wrong?" She touched Lucy's arm. "Why, you're shaking. What's happened?"

Lucy swallowed. "I…I'm not exactly sure, but something terrible has happened. Between Papa and Monty. They had a horrible argument late last night." Tears welled in her eyes, and she pulled a lace-edged handkerchief from her sleeve. "I'm sorry. It's all been so stressful and awful."

"Here, come and sit down." Artemis led her over to a plump sofa by the bow window. "I'm here to listen to anything you want to tell me." If Lucy needed her, she wouldn't be going to Devonshire tomorrow.

Lucy emitted a watery laugh that was more of a hiccup. "I wish there *was* more to tell. All I know is that after Papa and I returned from the theater, I retired to my rooms to get ready for bed. Not long after that, there was a burst of dreadful shouting. When I opened my door, I could hear it was Monty and Papa, but when I approached Monty's room, Papa came out and ordered me back to my own bedchamber. I-I've never seen him so angry. And this morning…" Lucy dabbed her eyes. "Monty was gone. And he hasn't returned home. And I'm worried that he won't."

"Oh, no. I'm so sorry, Lucy. Perhaps Monty has gone to stay with a friend until things calm down?"

"Perhaps. There are things missing from his wardrobe and dressing table. Some clothes and a valise. His pocketbook. His shaving set. According to his valet, at least. The worst thing is, Papa refuses to talk to me. I have no idea what the argument was about. But it *is* something terrible because…" Lucy reached for Artemis's hand. "I feel just awful telling you this, Artemis, but Papa wants us to quit London at once and return to Heathwick

Green. He's declared my Season is over, and Cousin Mabel is to go home to Shropshire. In fact, I've been packing all afternoon and we're leaving first thing in the morning."

Goodness... "I can't deny that I'm surprised, and I'm nothing but saddened to hear your brother and father are estranged. But in a way, I'm also greatly relieved for you, Lucy. You never wanted a Season to begin with, let alone a husband."

"That's true, but, Artemis, you quit your post at the Avon Academy because of me. You've only been in London a few weeks, and now I'm effectively deserting *you*. I feel so guilty. I'm a terrible, selfish friend."

"Oh, no, you're not, my darling Lucy. And don't you dare feel guilty. I don't regret resigning from that academy at all. It was time for me to move on, and now, because of my engagement to Dominic, I will have my college." Both Lucy and Jane knew about her quid pro quo arrangement with the duke, and they were nothing but supportive of her decision to consent to an engagement of convenience.

Lucy's mouth trembled with a smile. "Are you certain?"

"I most definitely am. Truth to tell, the reason I came by was to let you know that I will be quitting London tomorrow too. But only for a week." Artemis filled her friend in on what had transpired at Dartmoor House during the afternoon and that Dominic had asked her to accompany him to Ashburn Abbey to help with Celeste. "As soon as I return, I will come to visit you at Heathwick Green. It's not far."

"Oh, but that's wonderful." Lucy squeezed Artemis's hand. "Not about the duke's difficulties with his daughter. But it does sound as though your fiancé can't bear to be without you." Her expression turned sly. "Are you *sure* you don't want to marry him?"

Artemis laughed. "Entirely sure. He might be handsome and generous and wonderful company, but we want different things. It will never work."

Lucy didn't look convinced, but nevertheless, she didn't say anything else. They bid each other a fond farewell along with more promises to meet again soon, and then Artemis set out for home.

As she entered Cadogan Square, she caught sight of a young woman being handed down from a smart-looking cabriolet that had drawn up in front of Aunt Roberta's town house. *Phoebe.*

And then Artemis froze, rooted to the spot when she glimpsed the gentleman who escorted her sister to the door.

Old Nick's nob. It couldn't be…

Artemis's stomach pitched and then all but plummeted to the ground.

It was none other than Lord Gascoyne.

He bid Phoebe a far-too-familiar farewell that involved a kiss upon her cheek while a sly hand curled about her waist, and then he sauntered back to his carriage, whistling a jaunty tune. As he leaped back into the seat, Artemis started forward. Ice-cold fury frosted her voice as she called, "Lord Gascoyne, a word." How she'd managed to use his real name and not some variation on "disgusting-vile-swine-who-should-be-castrated-with-a-blunt-fish-knife," she didn't know.

He turned and his mouth lifted into an infuriatingly smug smile. "Why, Miss Jones. Isn't this a pleasant surprise?"

"Yes, about as pleasant as discovering an enormous spider in one's shoe," she returned. "What in the devil's name are you doing courting my sister?"

"And why shouldn't I? She's rather fetching, amiable company, and of age." He leaned forward and dropped his voice.

"I'm not sure if she's quite as amorous as you just yet, but we'll see."

Artemis clenched her fists to stop herself pummeling him with her reticule. "You're contemptible..." she hissed. "Stay away from her. Or I'll—"

"You'll what? Go running to your *contemptible* fiancé? A man who just happened to murder my sister? I don't think he has any moral high ground to stand on. Or you for that matter, Miss I'll-drop-my-drawers-for-the-chance-of-a-title-or-fortune."

Artemis ignored the crude insult. "Why are you doing this?" she demanded in a furious whisper. "And why choose Phoebe? There are hundreds of other eligible young women in London you could chase after. Or should I say defile and betray?"

He smirked as he took his horse's reins from the liveried tiger who stood at attention at the back of the cabriolet. "Ah, but where would be the fun in that? Au revoir, my dear Artemis." And then he tipped his hat in a mocking salute, flicked the reins, and moved on without a backward glance.

Just like he always did.

———

Artemis found Phoebe in her room, seated at her dressing table with Hetty at her feet, helping her to remove a stylish pair of blue leather half-boots.

As soon as Phoebe saw Artemis's face, she ordered her maid to leave. "What is it?" she asked, her tone flat with bored weariness.

"Don't pretend you don't know. I don't have the patience." Artemis shut the door to stop the lady's maid eavesdropping. "You must not see that man," she said in her best schoolteacher's voice. "He's not what he seems."

Phoebe gave a derisive snort. "Just like your duke?"

"Phoebe." Artemis narrowed her gaze. "I mean it. He's dangerous."

Her sister shot her a skeptical look as she removed the hat pin from the flimsy confection of lace and feathers that was perched upon her elegantly arranged curls. "And how would you know? Unless you're relying on secondhand intelligence from your highly questionable fiancé. I have it on good authority that anything he says should be taken with a grain of salt."

Artemis studied the flowers in the Axminster carpet at her feet. She couldn't tell Phoebe everything, not about all of the things she'd done with Gascoyne in the name of love. A love that proved false. It was far too humiliating "Please," she entreated. "Just trust me. I *know*."

Phoebe sniffed and turned away, loosening the lace cuffs on her gown. "I'm afraid that's not good enough, dear sister."

Artemis swallowed, her mouth dry. "We… Ten years ago, during my debut, we…he and I…we shared… We were intimate…"

In the mirror, Artemis saw Phoebe roll her eyes. "Guy told me that you would say some sort of rubbish just like this. He said that even back then you were jealous of his budding relationship with Evangeline Gibbs. That at every you turn, you sought to sabotage—"

Artemis thumped the door so hard it rattled. "He's lying," she cried. "That's not the case at all. I wasn't jealous of Evangeline then, and I'm not jealous of you now. He promised me the world, then broke my heart, Phoebe."

Her sister studied her, her look long and assessing. "Well, even if he did," she said after a fraught pause, "that doesn't mean he will break mine. He's charming and amusing and—"

"And a cad and a bounder and an untrustworthy, manipulative snake. Please, you must end this courtship or affair or whatever you want to call it. At once."

Phoebe lifted her chin. "I cannot. I will not. I have no reason at all to distrust him. You, on the other hand, have a fiancé who's been dripping poison in your ear about Lord Gascoyne. Your Dastardly Duke is the one you should be wary of."

Artemis ground her back teeth together. How could her sister be so blind? Or was she like poor Celeste, starved for affection and jumping at the first man who came her way, even if he was wicked to the core? "I'll go to Aunt Roberta."

Phoebe released a bored sigh. "She already knows about Lord Gascoyne. And she approves."

What? A cold, sick feeling settled in the pit of Artemis's stomach. "You must be joking," she whispered.

"I'm not." Phoebe began to pull the pins from her hair, tossing them onto the dressing table, willy-nilly. "Go and ask her if you don't believe me."

Artemis did and it proved to be true. Aunt Roberta *did* know that Lord Gascoyne was courting Phoebe, and she'd given her consent.

Artemis stood in the middle of the drawing room rug, her heart pounding erratically. Her stomach churned with nausea. "Aunt Roberta, you must listen to me. Lord Gascoyne... His intentions cannot be honorable. He's not to be trusted."

Aunt Roberta fed a sweetmeat to her terrier Bertie. "Phoebe warned me that you would take this tack. And so did Lord Gascoyne himself. Your duke has turned you against the man."

Somehow Artemis tamped down the urge to take Aunt Roberta's prized collection of Ming vases off the mantelpiece and hurl them, one by one, onto the porcelain tiles of the hearth. Lord Gascoyne had clearly been busy "dripping poison" in everyone else's ears. "That's not true. He was the one... When I had my debut..." Artemis paused to gather the scattered, tumbling pieces of her thoughts. "All those times that I stole away with someone during my debut—the times you recently said you *knew* about—it was with him. Lord Gascoyne. He promised me love and hinted he was going to propose whenever we—" She bit her lip as a scalding blush flooded her cheeks. "Suffice it to say, he lied. About everything. And I'm worried he's going to take advantage of Phoebe and ruin her just because he can."

Aunt Roberta sniffed. "I have not one iota of sympathy for you, my gel. Why should he have bought the cow if said cow was intent on giving him all the milk he wanted for nothing? At least your sister isn't so naive or foolish."

"You have no way of knowing that. Lord Gascoyne is very convincing. And a master of seduction. Phoebe must be on her guard or else he'll take away her innocence without a second thought."

"Enough." Aunt Roberta held up one ring-encrusted hand. "I don't wish to hear any more. Phoebe and I met Lord Gascoyne at the Castledowns' ball, and you cannot convince me that his intentions are nefarious. He has not put a foot wrong. You, on the other hand, continue to stumble though life, making poor choices and blundering from one disaster to another, most of them of your own making. So you'll understand why your opinion matters not one jot to me."

"And vice versa," returned Artemis. "You'll be pleased to know that I will be gone from this house for the next week. I'll be spending time at Ashburn Abbey, the Duke of Dartmoor's house in Devonshire. And your chaperonage will not be required."

There, make of that what you will.

Artemis turned on her heel and stalked away. She had packing to do, and she wasn't going to waste another breath on trying to convince her aunt or her foolish sister that Lord Gascoyne was the worst kind of blackhearted blackguard.

It seemed they were going to have to learn that themselves, the hard way.

Chapter Nineteen

BENEATH A LOWERING, LEADEN SKY, THE TRAIN FROM London to Newton raced through verdant fields and scattered stands of trees. It was certain to rain.

Indeed, the atmosphere of gloom seemed to penetrate the Duke of Dartmoor's private rail carriage where everything was veiled in a dull, gray light. The car had been divided into two distinct sections; the large front compartment was furnished with several luxurious settees and an elegant mahogany dining setting. The aftward compartment had been fashioned into a private study, complete with an ornate desk, a set of cabinets, and a cozy arrangement of leather armchairs and a sofa.

Even before they'd departed Paddington Station, Dominic had sequestered himself in his study to work on a particular pressing business matter while Lady Northam, Lady Celeste, Miss Sharp, and Artemis had occupied the front compartment. Well, Lady Celeste had taken over one entire corner of the carriage; she was lounging upon one of the settees, staring out of the window, watching the passing countryside in sullen silence. Beside her on a low table sat an untouched plate of sandwiches and petit fours and an unopened book—part one of Dickens's *Nicholas Nickleby*.

Artemis had never been an admirer of Charles Dickens's work. The way he sentimentalized many of his central female characters, making them as pure as the driven snow, annoyed her no end. She'd rather read about a plain yet intelligent and resilient governess or flawed and passionate Cathy Earnshaw any day than perfectly sweet and noble Kate Nickleby or impossibly selfless Amy Dorrit.

Aware that several hours had ticked by and Lady Celeste had refused to have anything to do with her—well, other than utter a stiff greeting that had been prompted by Dominic when Artemis boarded the train—Artemis decided she had to do *something* to bridge the yawning gap dividing her and the duke's daughter. She'd been chatting pleasantly with the affable Lady Northam for most of the journey—who'd insisted Artemis call her Horatia within the first five minutes of Artemis entering her carriage—but the countess had since nodded off to sleep on the opposite settee. And Miss Sharp appeared to be entirely engrossed in her own novel—another tale by Dickens, *Bleak House*.

Artemis carefully pulled her careworn carpetbag from the overhead luggage rack, then removed two of her favorite novels—*Jane Eyre* and *Wuthering Heights*. And then she placed them on the table beside Lady Celeste. The girl turned her head and glanced at the covers. "I have a book," she said, her manner dismissive.

"I know. But I thought you might find these titles a little more diverting." Artemis offered her a gentle smile. "I don't know about you, but I always find Dickens to be far too dogged in his sermonizing. I don't disagree with some of his social commentary on the Church, evangelism, and charitable concerns, but I'd much rather read a sweeping love story any day."

And then Artemis moved on to Dominic's study. She'd had enough of being ignored by her fiancé. Appearances be damned. She wanted his company and a kiss.

She found him not at his desk but sprawled upon the dark-brown leather sofa. Even though it wasn't even midday, his long fingers were wrapped tightly about a crystal tumbler that contained a deep amber-hued liquor. His head was tipped back, his eyes closed, but when the door shut behind her, he looked up.

And Artemis had to suppress a gasp. His expression was nothing but haggard. Indeed, she'd never seen him look so exhausted and rumpled. Deep lines bracketed his mouth and eyes, and there were bruise-like shadows of fatigue beneath the dark sweep of his lower lashes. Even though he regarded her through half-mast lids, his mouth quickly kicked into a smile.

"Artemis," he murmured. "I was just thinking about you."

"I hope I haven't disturbed you," she said, still hovering uncertainly by the door. He'd discarded his jacket, waistcoat, and necktie—they lay in a crumpled pile on another chair—and was only dressed in his shirtsleeves, braces, trousers, and bespoke leather shoes. His sleeves were rolled up to reveal his strong forearms, and the way his shirt gaped open at the neck, revealing a tantalizing glimpse of flesh and a scattering of dark hair in the gap between the undone buttons... Artemis's pulse leapt but then she berated herself for blatantly ogling him.

"Not at all. I needed a break." He scrubbed a hand through his already disheveled hair, then patted the spot beside him in invitation. "Come here. You're too far away."

She immediately joined him. "Did you get any sleep last night?" she asked softly, smoothing a stray lock of his silky black hair away from his forehead.

"Mmm, maybe an hour or two."

"You work too hard, Your Grace," she gently admonished.

"I won't disagree." He caught her hand and brought it to his lips. "Can I get you anything?" He raised his glass. "A drink? I know it's probably too early for brandy, but I seem to have lost all track of time."

"I wouldn't mind a kiss," she said with a smile. "If you can spare one."

"I think I can spare more than one," he returned, his voice soft and low. From between slitted lids, his dark-gray eyes gleamed with a carnal light.

He placed his drink on a nearby table, then turned his body to face her. Leaning in close, he cupped her jaw and his thumb brushed across her lower lip. "Dear God, you're gorgeous," he murmured, his breath fanning across her mouth, teasing her with the promise of what was to come. "Do you know how much I want you?"

"Why don't you show me?" she whispered.

"With pleasure." His kiss was gentle yet possessive, and Artemis immediately yielded to him, opening beneath his lips on a soft sigh, reveling in the strokes of his hot, slick tongue. He tasted of the sweet but fiery brandy he'd been drinking, and very soon Artemis's head was spinning as though she were intoxicated. Drunk with desire.

Her hands rested against the hard, unyielding wall of his chest, and her fingers flexed against the linen; she wanted to explore the smooth, hot flesh beneath, to trace the crisp whorls of hair. If she could rip this shirt from his body, she would. But now was not the time and place for anything else. Not when there were others—Dominic's daughter and sister and a governess—just beyond an unlocked door.

Perhaps Dominic had the same thought because all too soon, he broke the kiss and drew back. "That was just what I needed," he said with a languid smile. "Thank you. And I'm so glad you decided to come. Not just for Celeste's sake, but for mine. Ashburn Abbey…" He sighed and his fingers absently toyed with a lock of her hair that had come loose. "It holds such bittersweet memories for me. While part of me dreads return-ing, another part longs to be home."

"I can't even begin to fathom what you and your daughter have been through," Artemis said. "It can't be easy returning to the place where you lost your wife. The first time I met Celeste, she told me that you and Juliet loved each other very much."

His smile was small, almost broken. "We did. That being said, it wasn't the easiest of marriages. Juliet…" His voice trailed off. "Juliet was unwell at times, and despite the best of care…" He grimaced and reached for his drink. "I'm sorry; I'm sure you have questions about my first wife. I don't mean to be evasive. It's just that it's difficult to talk about."

Artemis's heart clenched. Of course she *was* curious about Juliet and what had happened to her, but she didn't want to pry. Aloud she said, "If it helps you to talk about it, I will listen. And gladly. But if it causes you too much pain, I understand that too."

He nodded. "Thank you. If I seem a little withdrawn and morose at times when I'm at Ashburn, you'll know why. I've never been one to share how I feel about things, and in recent years I haven't found anyone to—" His voice cracked, and perhaps to hide his emotion, he tossed back the remainder of his brandy in one large swallow. He dragged his hand across his mouth as he stared at the empty glass before carefully and deliberately putting it aside. "I will admit that I sometimes tend to reach for the demon drink to drown my sorrows. But more often than not, I throw myself into work to avoid dealing with anything that's difficult or painful." His mouth twisted, and Artemis wasn't certain if his expression was a grimace or a smile. "There you have it. I'm not a particularly easy man."

"I see a man who is not only hardworking and dedicated to his Queen and country, but a wonderful, caring father. But I do understand what you are saying. I'm not a particularly easy woman. I'm headstrong and far too brazen, and because of that, I have a tendency to rub others the wrong way."

Dominic's smile slid into something dark and wicked. "I like brazen." His voice was a low purr as he wrapped her escaped curl around one of his fingers. "As for rubbing…"

She laughed. "If I were brazen right now and locked that door to the other cabin, would you be shocked?"

"Not at all. I'd be nothing but intrigued."

Her pulse racing faster than the hurtling train, Artemis latched the door, then turned back to face her handsome-assin fiancé. Dominic's arms were stretched out along the back of the sofa, his long, muscular legs spread wide as though he was the master of all he surveyed. His gaze was dark and burning as it traced over her, lingering on her mouth, her breasts, her waist, then drifting lower to her skirts, as though he could see what was beneath all of the layers. How she pressed her thighs together in a futile attempt to ease the ache there.

Lucifer's love truncheon. Dominic's confidence was breathtaking. And Artemis loved how he made her feel so desired. As though he had eyes for her and her alone. That she could do anything—be completely wanton and wild in his arms—and he wouldn't think less of her. That maybe he'd want her even more.

Rain lashed the windows, and it suddenly felt like they were completely alone in their own private world. Artemis could hear nothing but the downpour, the gallop of her own heart, and the rhythmic *clickity-clack* of the train upon the tracks. The carriage rocked gently as she contemplated what she would do next. What her plan of attack would be.

The Duke of Dartmoor was exhausted and tense, and she wanted to take that all away, at least for a short while. He deserved to feel desired too.

With calculated slowness, she lifted her silk skirts. Dominic's gaze smoldered as she untied the tapes securing her petticoats and crinoline cage. The cumbersome garments slid down her hips and over her drawers, puddling around her booted feet. Picking up her skirts, she then neatly stepped out of the voluminous pile and sashayed back to Dominic.

Her fiancé looked up at her, watching and waiting. He might appear to be patient, but she could see the heat and hunger in his eyes, the coiled tension in his muscles, feel the lust radiating from his body. Her gaze fell to his lap, and she couldn't fail to notice the outline of his erection; from the way it tented his trousers, she knew he was thick and large and ready for her.

She licked her lips and then dropped to her knees on the carpeted floor before him. The Duke of Dartmoor had proclaimed he didn't mind that she was brazen.

Well, she was about to see if that were true.

She looked up at him through her lashes, deliberately playing the seductress. Leaning forward, she slid Dominic's burgundy-red braces off his broad shoulders and down his arms, relishing the feel of his bulging biceps beneath her palms. The tickle of the hair on his forearms. Oh, what she could do with a man like this.

When she tugged his shirt from the waistband of his trousers and her questing fingers found the hot, taut flesh of his abdomen beneath, his muscles twitched at the contact and he groaned. She smiled.

"Tease," he rasped.

"Of course." And then she bent forward and placed her

mouth on his left pectoral muscle, alternately sucking and then laving the thin fabric with her tongue, tormenting the nipple beneath until it was a tight nub.

"Witch." He grasped the back of her neck, as though he wasn't sure whether he wanted to keep her there or pull her away.

She laughed and transferred her attentions to his other nipple. At the same time her fingers found the buttons securing the fall of his trousers and she began to slide them free. She so very badly wanted to hold and stroke the hot, hard, heavy length of him in her hands. To take him in her mouth, to taste him, and to hear him gasp and hiss and groan until he lost all control. She licked her lips as the last button came undone—

"Artemis." He caught her chin with gentle fingers. "You don't have to do that."

"But I want to," she said with a coquettish pout.

"Believe me, I would love you to, but if you do, I'll probably spill within five seconds. It's been far too long since anyone…" He brought her hand to his lips. "I want you far too much," he said. "And I don't want to come too quickly. Here." He urged her to rise. "Hop on my lap. Straddle me."

Gathering her skirts with one hand, Artemis did as he asked. She was more than willing to go along with whatever Dominic wanted. Right at this moment, her sole purpose was to give him pleasure. But with her legs parted and her sex hovering over his rigid length, it took all of her willpower not to grind against his cockstand to find her own pleasure.

One of Dominic's hands settled on her waist, holding her steady while his other hand dragged her down for a searing kiss. "I have to see you," he murmured hoarsely against her lips as the hand spanning her torso slid to her bust. His thumb circled her straining nipple. "I want to know what you look like. The shape of your breasts. The color of your nipples. What your sweet flesh tastes like. When I'm alone at night, pleasuring myself, I want a precise picture of you in my head."

Oh my. How could she say no to such a wonderfully wicked request? Excitement curling in her belly, Artemis slid open the jet buttons of her dark-green bodice until the top half of her gown sagged open, revealing her cream silk corset and the lace-edged chemise that barely covered her breasts.

"Corsets are the devil's work," muttered Dominic as he battled with the first few hooks and eyes, but within moments the tightly fitting, boned garment loosened and then he hauled down her chemise, exposing her breasts to his heated gaze.

"Sweet Jesus," he whispered hoarsely, cupping her flesh gently. "I hope you can forgive my crudeness, but your breasts are spectacular, my wild, sweet Artemis. My imagination hasn't done them justice. At all."

A hot thrill coursed through Artemis at the thought that he liked what he saw. And that he'd been imagining what she looked like naked. "I happen to like your crude compliments and suggestions," she returned, her own voice ragged with unbridled need. When he pinched one of her already tightly furled nipples, then gently rolled it and tugged, Artemis had to bite her lip to suppress a whimper of delight. But then the hot cavern of his mouth engulfed her other nipple, and there was no way on heaven or earth she could contain her moan. As his knowing tongue flicked and circled the taut, aching peak, as his teeth scraped and his lips suckled, Artemis had to clutch at his shoulders to keep her balance. He made her dizzy and so mad with desire she knew she would do anything that he asked. Anything at all.

One of his hands slid beneath her bunched-up skirts and

found her drawer-clad inner thigh. Her legs were trembling. Could he feel how wet she was through the thin fabric?

Her throat was tight with lust as she whispered, "Please touch me, Dominic. Don't make me wait." And then she gasped as his fingers hooked into the slit of her drawers and he gave a determined yank, tearing the lawn asunder.

A hot tremor of pleasure shot through her as one wicked fingertip stroked along the damp furrow of her sex before settling unerringly on her swollen, throbbing core. And then he rubbed her right where she needed him, his fingers dancing over her exquisitely sensitive flesh in tiny tormenting circles. She began to rock her hips, grinding shamelessly against Dominic's hand and his straining, still partially trapped erection. And then she felt him fumbling with his trousers right before he dragged his hot, rigid shaft along the length of her slick folds.

"I promise that I won't spend inside you," he whispered raggedly against her ear. "I won't get you with child."

Too breathless with want, all Artemis could do was nod. She buried her face in his neck and gave herself over to the shockingly rude thrill of sliding and rubbing against Dominic's sleek, hard, bare cock. Her orgasm began to build, the tension inside her coiling tighter and tighter. Her whole body was trembling, and she was panting and gasping and...

Oh God. Dominic found her clitoris again, and with one exquisite pinch, she was overwhelmed by a wave of ecstasy. As ripples of mind-numbing, pulsating pleasure radiated through her, she sank her teeth into Dominic's shoulder to stop herself from crying out.

Beneath her, Dominic's hips lifted and then he shuddered and jerked and groaned, his hot seed bathing the inside of her quivering thighs.

As his breathing slowed, his arms came up around her, cradling her, and he pressed his mouth to her temple. "We're a good fit, you and I," he murmured. "In fact, I think we rub along rather well together, if you'll pardon my pun. I'm sure if you changed your mind and agreed to be my duchess, we'd both be very satisfied."

Artemis froze. Her throat tightened. The bliss still thrumming through her veins dissipated, shocked dismay taking its place. Drawing back, she searched her lover's drowsy, sated gaze. "Dominic, I'm not sure if I want children," she reminded him, her tone gentle. "And you need an heir."

A troubled frown creased his brow and her heart cramped. The urge to kiss away those lines was alarmingly strong, but she ruthlessly pushed it away.

"Yes, there's that." Dominic's mouth tipped into a rueful smile. "I wouldn't worry, love. The sweet aftermath of our lovemaking has simply addled my brain."

Yet…Artemis *was* worried. He'd called her "love," and she wasn't certain if it was an endearment he routinely used with his paramours or a more telling slip of the tongue.

Even more alarming was the fact her brain was addled too. Because for the first time ever, she had begun to seriously wonder what it would be like to be Dominic's wife. To share his life and to bear his children. To cultivate a true relationship with Celeste with a view to becoming her stepmother.

It's just sated lust talking, she told herself as she tidied herself up. *You're not really his "love."* No doubt the golden glow both she and Dominic were drifting in would fade and before long they would begin to feel like their usual selves again.

Yes, she couldn't think straight because she'd simply shared a highly erotic, sexually fulfilling interlude with a man who was a superb lover. A *considerate* lover—the fact he'd taken care not to spend inside her meant everything. It meant that she could end this engagement and walk away from him whenever she wanted to.

The question was: Could she do that?

She had to. *You're not the woman he needs, Artemis Jones*, she sternly reminded herself as she entered the main rail carriage and took a seat by the window, opposite Celeste. The girl had her nose buried in *Jane Eyre*, while Horatia continued to nap in another corner.

Artemis ignored a disapproving look from Miss Sharp. Instead, she turned her gaze to the landscape rushing by in a dull, green-gray blur. Watched the incessant rain sliding down the slightly fogged windowpane. She wasn't an impressionable, lovestruck governess, and Dominic wasn't Mr. Rochester. So she needed to stop trying to live in her own Gothic romance novel. That way lay madness and certain heartbreak.

Chapter Twenty

THE LIGHT WAS RAPIDLY FADING AS DOMINIC'S COACH turned into the gravel-lined drive leading to Ashburn Abbey. During the one-hour journey from Newton to the village of Ashburton, which lay close to the ducal estate, Artemis and Dominic traveled alone while Horatia, Lady Celeste, and Miss Sharp followed in another carriage. Yet another coach conveyed all their luggage and several other servants.

Artemis leaned forward and peered through the gathering gloom to get a better glimpse of the enormous sprawling manor house. The rain had petered out to a light drizzle, but a mist had begun to roll in from the surrounding moors. It wreathed the towering oaks lining the drive and the abbey itself, but Artemis could still make out the house's looming bulk. In many ways, it reminded her of a grander version of the Thornfield Hall in *Jane Eyre* that had lived in her imagination for so long.

While it had a touch of Gothic to it—the stone rainspouts appeared to be fiercely faced gargoyles—it was essentially Elizabethan in style with three separate wings branching off the main body of the house. Ivy clambered with abandon over the gray stone walls and about the numerous high-arched windows. There were even several crenellated towers, and above the gatehouse hung a huge bell.

"What do you think?" asked Dominic. He lounged

negligently in the opposite seat, but his gaze was filled with keen interest as he studied her face.

"It's…it's lovely," she said.

"Liar," he returned with grim amusement. "It's a monstrosity, but it's my home. The place where Horatia and I were born and grew up. Where Celeste was born and where…" His voice trailed off. "Juliet wasn't particularly enamored of it. She always thought it was haunted. I take it you don't believe in ghosts or other supernatural beasties, despite your penchant for Gothic novels?"

"While I've never seen a ghost myself, I do generally subscribe to Hamlet's view: 'There are more things in heaven and earth, Horatio, than are dreamt of in your philosophy.'" Artemis shrugged. "One might say that I'm quite open-minded. And you? Do you believe in ghosts?"

He smirked. "Not really. Not now. But that didn't stop my childhood nurse from trying to fill my head with local tales of ghosts and witches and pixie lights on the marshes and spectral black hounds on the moors. The bridge we crossed at Ashburton supposedly has an evil sprite named Cutty Dyer who lives beneath it. He slits the throats of unsuspecting drunks and then after drinking their blood, hurls them into the river below."

Artemis shivered theatrically. "How wonderfully grisly. I must make note of that for my—"

Oh God. Artemis slammed her mouth shut. She'd almost said, "for my next novel."

Dominic raised a quizzical brow but then the carriage drew to a halt outside the abbey's grand front entrance and thankfully they were caught up in the hubbub of arrival.

Dominic escorted Artemis into the imposing main hall where the soaring vaulted ceiling was clearly an original part of the abbey. Artemis had barely any time to take in the saints depicted in the stained-glass windowpanes or the gruesome medieval weaponry mounted on the hall's far wall before Dominic was introducing her to the entourage of smartly uniformed servants as though she were already his bride and the new mistress of Ashburn.

It was a situation she hadn't anticipated when she'd first agreed to this visit, and the weight of her decision sat uncomfortably on her shoulders. It made her think that perhaps she was becoming too enmeshed far too quickly in Dominic's life. The last thing she wanted to do was play Dominic and everyone else in his life false. But here she was, and for the moment, all she could do was smile and nod and act the part of the dutiful duchess-to-be.

A no-nonsense-looking housekeeper showed Artemis to her bedchamber in the east wing on the third floor. Apparently, it wasn't all that far from the master's suite of rooms, according to the young chambermaid who prattled away as she stirred the logs in the massive stone fireplace, plumped the fat cushions and pillows on the equally massive tester bed, and made sure the heavy damask curtains were adequately drawn against the chill, damp evening. The rain had set in again, heavier than before, and Artemis was grateful for the fire.

Once the maid departed, Artemis retrieved her notebook that contained her current manuscript. She'd managed to write a few words on the train this afternoon, but she was nowhere near the end of her novel. No doubt her publisher, Chapman and Hall, would have something to say if she didn't finish it on time; her editor was expecting a completed manuscript by the end of May. Of course, she no longer needed the income from her books now that she'd made her deal with Dominic, but she felt that she owed it to her devoted readers to finish *Lady Mirabella and the Midnight Monk.*

She glanced at the clock on the mantel, and because it was only half past five, she decided she might be able to squeeze in a little writing time before dinner. One thing was certain: she dare not leave this notebook lying about for anyone to stumble across. Indeed, her silly slip of the tongue in the carriage could have landed her in all sorts of strife with Dominic. For all of his kindness and consideration, she knew he would be horrified if he discovered her secret career.

Ashburn Abbey's dining room was very much like every other room Artemis had seen so far—spacious and magnificently appointed with an abundance of rich furnishings and gleaming wood paneling. A beautifully rendered tapestry of a hunting scene graced the wall opposite a black marble fireplace that was so enormous, it could have accommodated a whole roasted boar. Artemis was certain she was going to get a permanent crick in her neck from staring at all the highly ornamented ceilings—gilt moldings, crimson Tudor roses, and the Duke of Dartmoor's heraldic badge were everywhere—and there wasn't a gaslight in sight. It was like she'd stepped back in time to Elizabethan England. If a ghost of a departed monk or one of Dominic's ancestors floated by, Artemis wouldn't have been the least surprised.

While the rainstorm continued to rage outside the abbey, all was cozy and warm inside. The blazing fire and numerous beeswax candles provided a soft flickering light. It glanced off the silverware and crystal wineglasses and picked out glints of gold in the gilded picture frames of past ancestors who glowered down at whoever was seated at the vast mahogany dining table. Indeed, the table could have comfortably seated at least two dozen guests, not the current party of four—Dominic, Lady Celeste, Horatia, and Artemis—who were sequestered at the end nearest the fireplace.

Alas, it might have been quite a merry gathering but for the duke's daughter. Celeste responded politely enough to any questions directed her way, but her doleful silence in between those moments created a strained, awkward atmosphere. Despite everyone else's best efforts, conversation was stilted. Horatia chatted sporadically about her dogs and horses and the current mounts in Ashburn's stables. Dominic, who also seemed more subdued than usual, spoke a little about the estate and the tenants and the village and what he hoped to accomplish over the next week.

Eventually, when there was a decidedly uncomfortable lull in the conversation filled only by the wail of the wind and rain outside, Artemis drew a fortifying breath and began to talk about her plans for establishing her college. How as a duchess, she'd love to sponsor a venture that was so dear to her heart. While she was aware that she wouldn't be able to teach anymore once she'd wed—she was careful not to let slip that she may not actually marry Dominic—she could certainly provide expert advice on the curriculum. And she could petition various universities to allow women to sit for their entrance exams.

She was heartened that Horatia seemed quite impressed with her vision, despite the controversial nature of it. The countess even mentioned she'd consider becoming a patroness if Artemis would like.

While Dominic didn't say much, she felt him watching her with keen interest. Artemis even sensed that Celeste was listening. At one point she asked Artemis if scientific subjects like astronomy would be part of the curriculum, and Artemis was happy to reply that yes, they would be as well as botany, chemistry, zoology, and physics. "Anything that young men study, our female students will too," she said. "I firmly believe that women should have professional careers if that is what they want."

Celeste nodded and returned to her meal, her expression thoughtful as she sliced into her roast beef. At least her appetite appeared to have returned. She'd taken a portion from every platter presented at each course and ate everything on her plate. Artemis knew the girl's heart was still broken—how could it not be?—but she hoped that with the passage of time, Celeste would come to realize that eloping with Antonio Moretti would have been a terrible mistake.

In the coming days, she would do what she could to ease the girl's melancholy. Even now, she liked to the think that the books she'd shared with Celeste were helping a bit.

After the dessert course was cleared, both Horatia and Celeste bid Dominic and Artemis good night, claiming they were exhausted from the journey.

Dominic looked exhausted too, but once his sister and daughter had quit the room, he reached for Artemis's hand and raised it to his lips. "Join me for a postprandial port in the drawing room," he said, urging her to rise. It wasn't a question, but Artemis didn't mind. Spending quiet hours alone with Dominic was addictive, and she wanted to relish every moment while this affair lasted.

Because that's all it was. A wonderful, thrilling, once-in-a-lifetime affair, and Artemis was certain she would cherish these memories long into her dotage when all she had were her books and maybe a few cats for company.

Once they were settled in matching leather wingback chairs before the fire, glasses of port in hand, Dominic leaned his head against the padded headrest and closed his eyes. "Celeste seems to be coming out of her shell. She likes you, you know."

Artemis laughed. "How can you tell?"

His eyes opened. Mirth sparked briefly in the deep-gray depths. "For one thing, she didn't hurl the butter boat or her knife at you."

"Very true. And I'm glad." Artemis hesitated but then admitted, "I like her as well. She's a lot like you, you know. Intelligent, gracious, sharp witted. I sense she feels things keenly."

"Yes…" Dominic sipped his port, then studied the ruby-brown depths as he held the glass up to the firelight. "Although, perhaps she gets that from her mother too."

Artemis didn't know what to say to that. Of course, now that she was at Ashburn Abbey, she was more curious than ever about Dominic's first wife and all of the mystery surrounding her untimely passing. But she didn't want to bring up painful memories. She'd already noticed a change in Dominic's demeanor since they'd arrived.

The dancing light of the fire highlighted the stark lines of fatigue etched around his eyes and mouth. But there was something else about Dominic—the way he carried himself, the shadows in his gaze—that suggested it wasn't just exhaustion weighing him down.

It was grief.

Dominic claimed Ashburn Abbey wasn't haunted, but Artemis was certain these walls, this entire place, must be haunted with sorrow. This man had lost the woman he loved, the mother of his child, in the most tragic of circumstances. By all accounts, she'd disappeared from Ashburn Abbey—vanished without a trace—and he'd had to wait for seven years before she could be declared dead. Artemis hadn't yet spied a portrait of the last Duchess of Dartmoor at Dartmoor House or here. And she wondered what that might mean.

Perhaps Dominic had sensed the direction of her thoughts, because at length he said, "I suppose you'd like to know more about Juliet."

"I'd be lying if I didn't admit that I have thought about her and what happened. What your marriage was like. But as I said earlier today, I understand how hard it must be for you. I'm happy to wait until you're ready to share such intimate details."

"No, it's all right. You have a right to know everything. I don't want you to think I'm keeping secrets from you." Dominic's gaze drifted to the fire and grew distant as he said, "Juliet and I were both young when we wed. I was twenty-two and she was only nineteen. She hadn't even had her debut at court or a Season. Her family—the de Burghs—hailed from Exeter, and when she and I met through mutual friends at a local ball, we were both instantly smitten."

His mouth quirked with a small smile. "It was as though Cupid had struck us with an arrow simultaneously. So we courted, and then we wed—with the mutual consent of our families—and we were blissfully happy until..." He emitted a deep sigh, and his next words were weighted with immeasurable sadness as he continued, "Until Juliet had Celeste...and then everything changed."

"You mentioned that she'd been unwell."

"Yes..." His fingers clenched and unclenched on the arm of his chair as though he were bracing himself to continue. "After Celeste's birth, Juliet became ill almost overnight, but not in a physical sense. It was as though a dark fog rolled in off

Dartmoor itself and surrounded her, and she could never seem to escape from it. The physicians said it was some sort of terrible melancholia, and it lasted for months. Years…"

"Oh no, Dominic. My heart weeps for all of you. For Juliet, for Celeste, and for you."

Dominic nodded, then swallowed. His voice was hoarse as he continued. "But it wasn't only sadness that consumed Juliet. She also suffered terrible attacks of strange, sometimes irrational behavior that the doctors described as mania. I tried to keep her safe. Consulted the very best medical minds that I could find, and money was no object. She did have periods when she seemed well again, but then something would trigger another episode. Her friends would announce they were pregnant or talk about their recent additions to the nursery, and the fog would descend once more.

"She went through years of endless treatment, and in the end, it was to no avail. All because of me." Dominic dragged a hand down his face, his expression haggard with remorse. "I wasn't strong enough for both of us. I should have said no, but I told myself she was well at long last and that giving her another child would make her happy again. So I gave in and when she lost the babe—a son who came far too early—she became ill. Even worse than before."

"Oh, Dominic. I had no idea. I'm so, so sorry for your loss." Artemis didn't know what else to say. "I can't even begin to imagine what you've been through."

His eyes gleamed with tears as he met her gaze. "Thank you," he said softly. "We named him Alexander, and if he'd lived, he would have been nine by now. After we'd laid our son to rest, Juliet began to see and hear things that weren't real all of the time—it was as though she'd gone mad—and for her own safety, I had to have her confined to her own suite of rooms. Even though she was watched around the clock by nurses, one night she somehow managed to escape."

"She strayed onto Dartmoor?"

"Yes…yes she did. She'd tried to abscond on other occasions, each time claiming there was an evil witch on the moors who'd stolen our son, and the pixie lights in the marshes and bogs would lead her to him. Although I have no proof, I believe that's exactly what Juliet did. She went searching for our boy. I was away, had been called to London on urgent business and was only supposed to be gone for a night, but I was held up and stayed away for two. During my absence, she apparently wandered out onto the moors and got lost and strayed into a mire…"

Dominic's voice cracked. He pinched the bridge of his nose and shook his head. "I can't bear to think of her suffering out there. The way she died, all alone, frantic and fearful. I sometimes have nightmares. That she's calling to me, and I can't reach her. Especially when I'm here at Ashburn. And perhaps I deserve to be tormented so because what happened is all my fault. I shouldn't have gone away. Not when she needed me."

"Dominic. I'm so sorry." Tears filled Artemis's eyes and her own heart clenched with pain. "That's so, so tragic and terrible, and I don't know how you bear it. But I'm sure that you did everything that you could."

He shook his head. His expression was bereft, his voice leaden with grief and self-recrimination as he said, "Not enough. Nowhere near enough. Perhaps I am as dastardly as everyone says."

"I don't believe it for a minute." Artemis abandoned her seat and knelt on the floor before him. Took his hands in hers and squeezed them. "You are a good man, Dominic Winters. I sense it and I have done so from the very first moment I met you. And I won't have you thinking anything else. No one is perfect. You couldn't have been at your wife's side every waking minute of every day. From what you've just told me, you did do everything that you possibly could to protect Juliet. The laws of this land have exonerated you from any wrongdoing, even if your ignorant peers haven't. You need to do the same and forgive yourself."

He gave a crooked, heartbreaking smile. "I wish that I could."

"Oh, Dominic…" She cupped his square jaw. Her fingertips could feel the tension vibrating through him, the muscles pulsing in his lean cheek. "I wish I could take your pain away. I wish…" *I wish that I could be the woman you need and deserve.*

His expression changed. The darkness in his eyes cleared as though bright sunlight had just burst through the clouds. "You do. When I'm with you, you make me forget. You make me believe that I might find some sort of happiness again."

Artemis's breath caught. *Oh God. Please don't fall in love with me,* she prayed. *I don't want to break your heart when I leave you.*

To escape the tenderness in Dominic's gaze, to break the tendrils of this intimate spell that seemed to be binding them together, Artemis slid her hands up Dominic's muscular thighs and then higher until they came to rest upon his rock-hard pectoral muscles. Through his silk waistcoat and fine linen shirt, she could feel the steady thud of his heart. The rise and fall of his chest.

His heat.

"I can think of the perfect way to keep you occupied and your mind diverted," she murmured. "Come to my room. If you're not too tired…"

Lust flashed in his gaze and then he caught her face between his hands and kissed her. "For you, my beautiful Artemis, I'd stay up all night."

Artemis arched a brow, her expression entirely skeptical as she teased, "Really, my arrogant peacock of a duke? With a pronouncement like that, you're going to have to prove it."

He grinned. "Oh, don't worry. I will."

Chapter Twenty-One

WHEN DOMINIC ENTERED ARTEMIS'S BEDCHAMBER HALF an hour later, he found her alone, waiting for him in an armchair by the fire. And his heart began to beat double time as she greeted him with a knowing, feline smile and said his name in that rich voice of hers that never failed to stir him.

He adored her self-assurance. How unashamed she was.

She'd never looked so beautiful.

Her glorious auburn hair was unbound for once. It cascaded about her shoulders in wild disarray like a curtain of autumnal fire. She'd changed out of her evening finery into a robe of sky-blue satin, and as far as he could see, she wore nothing else. At all.

Thank God. If he'd had to deal with corsets and crinolines and bloody drawers again, he'd have gone mad.

His cock, which had already been at half-mast just at the idea of spending the night with Artemis, practically sprang to full attention beneath his loose silk trousers and banyan as he crossed the floor to the fireside. Their sexual encounter on the train had been nothing short of thrilling, but now that he'd a taste of Artemis in his arms, he wanted more. At long last, *tonight*, she would be completely naked and completely his, and he wouldn't be satisfied until she was crying his name to the heavens.

She reached out a hand and he brought it to his lips. "You've been writing," he observed and when she gave him a quizzical look, he added, "You have ink on your fingers. It wasn't there at dinner."

"Oh, yes…" To his surprise, she blushed. "I finished off a letter to one of my friends. You know, just filling in the time until you arrived."

He lowered his voice. "I can think of more interesting ways to fill your time."

"Only my time?" She arched a brow. "I hope you can fill more than that."

"It will be my absolute pleasure to give you a complete demonstration." He caught her other hand and drew her out of the chair. "But first things first…" He gently tugged at the tie securing her robe and it slowly slid undone. "We need to dispense with this."

He raised his gaze to Artemis's. "May I?" he asked as he reached for the blue satin lapels.

Her breathing had quickened and her brown eyes were dark with longing. "You may."

Lust hurtling through his veins, Dominic pushed the robe off Artemis's shoulders, and it slid with a whispered rush to the Turkish rug beneath her elegant bare feet.

"By God." His voice was laced with awe as he fully absorbed Artemis's naked beauty for the very first time. Every exquisite part of her was gilded by firelight. Her full breasts tipped with rosy nipples as delectable as raspberries, her slender waist flaring into generous hips. The smooth plane of her belly and the thatch of fiery curls at the apex of her thighs. Her long, shapely legs. "I'm speechless."

"I'm pleased you like what you see," she purred. Her hands lifted to his silk-clad shoulders. "Now your turn, Your Grace."

She slid off his banyan and then smiled when she caught sight of the tented front of his trousers. The frank admiration in her gaze, combined with the light caress of her fingernails through his chest hair and then down the taut ridges of his abdomen, somehow made him even harder. "Actually, it seems to me that you like what *you* see. A lot."

"Damn right I do." Dominic caught her about the waist and pulled her flush against him. She was soft and warm with skin smoother than the satin robe he'd just removed. And the way her bare sex rubbed against his throbbing cock when he seized her delectable derriere and pressed her closer... Through the silk of his trousers, he could feel she was already wet, and he couldn't wait to claim her in all the ways he'd been dreaming of for so long.

He captured her chin. "But I don't just want to look at you. Let me show you how much I burn for you. How much I need you." And then he kissed her.

It was a hot, hard, crushing kiss, and as his mouth ruthlessly plundered hers, he pushed a hand into her unbound hair, gripping the back of her head. He wanted her breathless and moaning and weak at the knees. He wanted her to feel just as lust-ridden and desperate as he was.

And perhaps she was already. Artemis clutched his bare shoulders and kissed him back with an urgency that matched his own. Her sweetly tart tongue tangled with his, and she ground herself against him, writhing her hips as though she couldn't wait for him to be inside her.

He coaxed her to the floor, encouraging her to lie on the rug, and then his body covered hers. He wanted to taste her everywhere. Touch her everywhere.

His mouth slid to her jaw, and he laved the sweet hollow

behind her ear. Traced the shell-like curves with his tongue. He scraped his teeth along her neck, then rained hot, feverish kisses across her shoulder and lower until he reached her breasts. And then he feasted and gorged upon those plump, sweet mounds and their ripe, rude peaks, tugging and sucking and licking and relentlessly tormenting her flesh until Artemis was moaning and arching and twisting beneath him with mindless abandon.

But it wasn't enough. He wanted Artemis rendered boneless. He wanted her pleasure-soaked cries and frantic gasps. Despite his own fierce need—his ballocks were aching and his cock was already leaking seed—he pressed on. This passionate onslaught was far from over.

He dragged his mouth down her torso and across the soft, silken plane of her stomach. His tongue dipped into the hollow of her belly button and traced the outline of each hip bone.

And then he moved lower and feathered kisses across the tangle of red curls hiding her sex. Glancing up the length of her body, he caught her heat-filled gaze. "Open for me, Artemis. Let me taste your sweet honey."

She complied without hesitation, spreading her thighs, and Dominic immediately wedged his shoulders between them. Her glistening sex was on full display, and the musky scent of her arousal surrounded him in a sensual cloud, making his mouth water and his blood pound.

She gently rolled her hips in blatant invitation. "Don't be cruel, Dominic. Don't make me wait," she whispered huskily.

"Shhh," he murmured, sliding his finger through her nectar, spreading it along each plump fold and then up to the pearl of her clitoris. "I'm enjoying the view."

"Might I suggest less sightseeing and more, oh…"

Dominic blew across her swollen nub of pleasure, then

dragged his tongue along her drenched cleft. And then he suck-led delicately, right where she needed him, pulling a moan from her throat.

Yes.

Dominic raised himself, sitting back on his haunches, and after grasping Artemis's luscious derriere with both hands, he lifted her hips and devoured her thoroughly delectable pussy, licking and nuzzling and savoring her slick dew. How sweet she tasted, like succulent summer peaches. How glorious the sound of her ragged pants and moans. The feel of her fingers twisting tightly in his hair, her unabashed surrender to his wicked minis-trations were everything he'd dreamed of and more. And when her whole body spasmed with ecstasy and she came on a great shuddering sigh, he was filled with the sweetest, most wonder-ful sense of triumph.

He lowered her gently, then crawled up her body. Nuzzled her neck and stroked her hair away from her face until she came back to him. Her lids fluttered open and her eyes were like deep, dark pools as she stared into his. "Even though you've completely devastated me with pleasure, I want you inside me, Dominic," she whispered. "Right now. This instant."

He smiled. "How could I possibly say no?" He was so aroused, his voice was thick with lust. And his cock was so primed and ready to plunder her lush heat that he was shaking.

With rough, jerky movements, he all but tore off his trou-sers, then slid over Artemis. She wrapped her arms about him and pulled him down for a blistering kiss. "Take me," she whis-pered when he came up for air. "Fill me."

"I will." Nudging her thighs apart, he took his weight on one forearm and then dragged the head of his cock through the welling moisture at her entrance. But before he pushed inside, he captured her gaze. "I promise I won't come inside you," he said solemnly.

"I trust you," she whispered, and her hands slid to his buttocks. "And I'm ready."

"Good." With one long, smooth thrust, he entered her and she sighed as though in welcome.

Lowering his head, he claimed her mouth once more while he set up a slow, steady rhythm, gliding in and out of her slick, satiny sex. It sucked greedily at his rock-hard length, grasping and squeezing, and it felt so damned good to be inside her. Too damned good. Dominic knew it wouldn't be long before he lost all control. He increased the pace of his thrusts, plunging hard and fast, urging Artemis to come with him. She wrapped her legs about him, matching his pace on this fast and furious ride to bliss.

He knew she was getting close to heaven too when she curled her fingers into his back, her nails scoring his flesh, marking him. Her breath was coming in frantic gasps. Her rhythmic moans were music to his ears. But best of all was the sound of his name on her sweet lips as she clenched around him. Her climax was so strong, so powerful that he couldn't help but follow. With a harsh cry, he pulled out and his seed spilled all over her belly in a series of hot, hard spurts.

He collapsed on the rug beside her, panting and gasping, and smiling. Pleasure pulsed through his veins, suffusing every fiber of his body, right down to his very bones. With one arm, he gathered Artemis in to his side and kissed her cheek. "Good God," he rasped. "Or should I say, Lucifer's love truncheon?"

She gave a soft laugh and her nails raked over his chest. "At the risk of inflating your already considerable self-esteem, I think I might begin to exclaim 'The Duke of Dartmoor's titanic truncheon' from now on. Your manhood is certainly worthy of note. Not only for its size and girth, which are most impressive, but what you can do with it when you wield it."

He was grinning like a youth who'd just had his first bout of bed sport. "'Dartmoor's titanic truncheon.' I like the sound of that. And I'm glad you think I wield it well."

"Most definitely." She walked her fingertips down his torso toward his groin, and to Dominic's surprise, his spent member twitched. "I also hope you'll make good on your earlier promise and stay 'up' all night with me," she murmured huskily.

"I'm not going anywhere except your bed, love."

Was it his imagination or did Artemis tense in his arms? He couldn't see her face because her head was resting on his shoulder. "Is everything all right?" he asked softly, brushing a tendril of her wild hair away from her cheek.

Outside the storm continued to rage, and he wondered if she hadn't heard him.

After a moment though, she raised her head and bestowed a tender kiss upon his lips. "Never better," she said, and Dominic silently prayed she'd spoken the truth. There was nowhere he'd rather be right now than in this bed, making love to Artemis. Not just tonight, but for countless nights to come… And then all at once, a tremor of unease slid through Dominic's chest as a disconcerting realization hit him. Indeed, it shook him to his core.

Despite his deep reservations about falling in love again, it seemed there was nothing he could do to stop himself. He was tumbling headlong into something deep. Something inevitable. Something he had no hope of escaping even if he wanted to. Perhaps the most terrifying part of it all was that he had no idea if Artemis felt, or would ever feel, the same way.

Chapter Twenty-Two

WHEN ARTEMIS WOKE THE FOLLOWING MORNING, IT WAS to discover that she was alone in her bed. Dominic must have left during the wee small hours to return to his own room. Even though they were engaged, it wouldn't do for the staff to discover them in bed together. The last thing she needed was for Dominic's servants to begin spreading gossip about her once their engagement ended and she started her college.

Artemis smiled to herself as she stared up at the bed's canopy of scarlet damask. She was exhausted, a little sore in places, but utterly satisfied. She'd lost count of how many times she and Dominic had made love. In fact, it had been the most wonderful night of her life. Her fiancé was a brilliant lover—attentive, considerate, adventurous, and with the stamina of a warhorse. A bubble of laughter formed in her throat whenever she recalled her pet name for Dominic's remarkable cock. *Dartmoor's titanic truncheon*. It was a pity she couldn't use it in one of her books.

Her book…

With a yawn, Artemis pushed herself up against the pillows. As much as she'd like to lounge around all day, reminiscing about all of the things she'd done with Dominic last night, she had words to write. Lady Mirabella wasn't going to find her happily-ever-after with her Midnight Monk unless Artemis put pen to paper.

And of course, she must endeavor to spend more time with Celeste.

She dug out a nightgown—if any of the chambermaids found Miss Jones naked in bed, that, on its own, was bound to raise an eyebrow or two—and then slipped it on before ringing the bellpull to request fresh water for bathing.

And then she pulled open the curtains and sat in the window seat with her notebook and pen and let her imagination run free.

———

After breakfast—a quiet affair in the morning room with Horatia—Artemis accepted the countess's kind offer to show her about Ashburn Abbey. Dominic had headed out early for a ride, as was his usual custom at Ashburn, and Horatia believed he would be sequestered with his steward in his private study going over the estate's ledgers and accounts for the rest of the day. "To be perfectly honest, my dear brother works far too hard," Horatia said as they quit the morning room and headed for the main staircase. "But he never listens to his nagging little sister. Perhaps you'll have more luck at getting him to change his ways when you're married, my dear."

Artemis offered the Countess of Northam a weak smile. "Perhaps." Guilt pinched and she began to wonder if this tour was such a good idea after all if at every turn Horatia made mention of her engagement and a marriage that wasn't going to happen.

Even though the rain had abated, the morning was still cold and drear as Horatia escorted Artemis through Ashburn's main apartments. "Ashburn was originally founded by an order of Cistercian monks in the thirteenth century," she explained as she showed Artemis through the great hall. "Queen Elizabeth gifted the land and the abbey—which had been seized during the dissolution of the monasteries—to one of our ancestors for his service to the Crown."

"Goodness, belonging to a family that can trace its lineage back so far is mind-boggling," said Artemis.

Horatia laughed. "Believe me, it quite boggles my mind too."

They moved on to the family's main living quarters and then a picture gallery containing portraits of distinguished family members, including the first Duke and Duchess of Dartmoor. At the very end of the gallery, Horatia paused before a painting of a lovely young woman with luminous green eyes that were huge in her heart-shaped face. She wore a fine gown of light-green silk, and a crown of orange blossoms and jasmine adorned her dark-brown hair.

Artemis immediately knew who it was. "It's Juliet Winters," she murmured.

"I thought you might like to see her likeness." Horatia's voice was nothing but kind. "That you'd be curious."

"I am. Thank you." She offered Dominic's sister a grateful smile. "I feel honored that Dominic recently shared a little about Juliet's illness with me. How she died. To think that he lost both a baby boy and then his wife…" She shook her head. "My heart breaks for him."

"There are not many who have afforded my brother with such understanding." Horatia's gaze was direct, her manner warm as she added, "Dominic *is* a good man—the very best of men—and I'm so pleased that you see that. For what it's worth, I think you will make a wonderful duchess, Artemis. Indeed, I think Dominic is very lucky to have found you. You make him happy. I can see that whenever he looks at you. And I believe, in time, that Celeste will warm to you as well."

A blush heated Artemis's cheeks. "Thank you for your kind words. I'll do my best to make him happy too."

Oh, but that was a terrible bald-faced lie, and guilt twisted Artemis's stomach as she followed Horatia outside to take a tour of the conservatory, the orangery, and the stables.

After Horatia established that Artemis was not much of a horsewoman—in Heathwick Green, she'd never ridden anything larger than a pony on the odd occasion—they began to wander back to the house. An icy wind had picked up, and it threatened to flatten the tulips and daffodils as the two women wended their way through the neat beds of a knot garden. They'd just passed through a gap in the boxwood hedge to follow the gravel path that would lead them back to the abbey when Artemis spied a rotunda-like outbuilding with a domed roof off in the distance. It sat on a slight rise and Artemis suspected that it would afford a sweeping view of the moors.

"What's that?" she asked. "Is it a folly of some kind?"

"No, it's actually an observatory. Juliet used to like to stargaze. Dominic had it built for her when they were newlyweds. There's a wonderful telescope inside and Celeste still sometimes goes there to use it. I think she fancies herself as a bit of an astronomer."

"I recall she asked if astronomy would be one of the subjects on offer at my college."

"Yes. It's a shame that such an option isn't feasible for someone like Celeste. Duke's daughters don't attend schools or colleges of any kind, I'm afraid."

"Yes, it is a shame. Celeste strikes me as a very intelligent young woman. I've been meaning to talk to Miss Sharp about expanding her studies to include more of the natural sciences."

A freezing blast of wind straight off the moors caught at

their cloaks and bonnets and crinoline skirts, threatening to bowl them over like they were skittles.

"If you don't mind, Artemis, I'd rather like to go back inside for a spot of tea," said Horatia. "There's rain in the air too. Oh, look, speak of the devil, here comes my niece." And then she frowned. "Where are you off to, young lady?" she called down the path. "And where is your governess?"

Celeste drew closer and Artemis could see her countenance was pale and pinched with cold. But her gray eyes were clear and held no trace of melancholy or anger as she said, "She told me she was feeling poorly with the beginnings of a head cold, but I wanted to go for a walk." She lifted her chin mulishly. "I take it that is permitted if it's only about the grounds."

"I'll accompany you if you'd like," offered Artemis, and Horatia beamed.

"That sounds like a capital idea," said the countess. "I shall see you both anon. You'll most probably find me in the drawing room if you need me, toasting my half-frozen toes and fingers before the fire."

Artemis and Celeste farewelled the countess and then continued along a branch of the path that led to the observatory.

Artemis was beginning to worry that this walk would be as frosty as the wind that continued to buffet them, but then Celeste broke the stiff silence. "It's your fault I'm here," she said, her voice as hard as flint.

"Yes…" Artemis kept her eyes ahead. "I will readily admit that I was the one who uncovered the identity of your secret beau. And that's why your father sent you here."

"It was none of your business," she shot back. "You shouldn't have interfered."

"Your father asked me to—"

Celeste stopped in the middle of the path and rounded on her. "What does he care?" she challenged. Her mouth was twisted with bitterness. "He's always so busy. With his work and now with you." She started walking again. "You'd think he'd be glad to be rid of me. I'd be one less issue for him to worry about. One less item on his endless list of things to do."

"He loves you very much, Lady Celeste. I'm convinced he only wants what is best for you. And even though you may not believe it, I do too."

"He wants what's best for me," Celeste repeated, her tone flat with resentment. "You've said that before, but it's absolute rubbish. How can that be true when he takes away everyone and everything that I love? When he banishes me to the middle of nowhere indefinitely? I feel so alone, I may as well be on the moon."

"I'm so, so sorry you feel that way," said Artemis gently. "Being lonely is indeed a terrible thing. But surely you realize, now that you've had some time to reflect upon everything that has happened, that fifteen is far too young to wed, and Anthony Moretti could not have truly cared for your well-being if he had agreed to your plan to elope. He has not the means to look after you. Not in the way you are accustomed to, and it wouldn't be long before you both regretted your decision. Even though it sounds cruel of me to say it, at your age, you know hardly anything about the world and the way it works." She halted and when Celeste did too, she cast the girl a searching look. "I hope you'll forgive me for being so blunt, but what if you were to get with child? You're not even out of the schoolroom yourself."

The duke's daughter blushed bright red, but her eyes flashed with indignant anger as she snapped, "How dare you speak to me about such things. Besides"—her chin lifted a notch—"I know enough about how babies are made to keep me safe from such an eventuality. At least until I'm ready to have children."

"Oh, really?" Artemis arched a brow. "And where did you learn about such things? By observing the livestock and dogs on the estate or in books by Lydia Lovelace? Your father told me he'd confiscated all of her titles," she added gently.

"Both," Celeste said stiffly. "And yes, he did take all of her books away after Miss Sharp found them in my room. She's too much of a fussy busybody sometimes."

Artemis ignored this last remark because she suspected Celeste was right. "Well, I know all about Lydia Lovelace's books too. In fact, she is one of my favorite authors. And while her characters might make love on occasion, she uses only the vaguest of descriptions and highly euphemistic terms. Her books are definitely not supposed to be a lady's guide to understanding how sexual congress works. She certainly doesn't talk about how to prevent conception."

Celeste blushed again. "I know enough," she said mulishly.

"But I'm not sure that you do," said Artemis. "Reading about the sexual act is one thing. Engaging in sexual intercourse and then having to deal with the consequences are quite another. For instance, have you even heard of a French letter—also known as a condom—or a sponge? Do you know about withdrawal? And that there are serious diseases such as syphilis and gonorrhea that one can contract if one happens to have intercourse with an infected person?"

Celeste turned on her heel and began walking back toward the house. "And how would you know about such things? You're not even married, *Miss* Jones."

"No, that's very true," she said. "But I'm nine-and-twenty and well educated. And when I was nineteen and made my debut…" She stopped and faced Celeste. "When I was nineteen, I met the wrong sort of man and learned about some of these things the hard way. In fact, I was very lucky that I didn't end up with child. Even so, I wish I'd known more so that I wasn't taken advantage of.

"Sadly, I lost my own mother when I was about your age, and as my father was a vicar—and quite a sanctimonious one at that—I had no one to teach me about men and the ways of the world. About its dangers and pitfalls. But after my one and only Season, I came across a most helpful title, *Every Woman's Book; Or, What is Love?* by Richard Carlile, at my friend's bookstore. While the book is not perfect, it does explain the nature of sexual congress and different ways to prevent conception. Perhaps one day when you're old enough, I can lend you my copy and we can talk about it."

Even though Lady Celeste's face was still aflame, she inclined her head. "I–I would like that, thank you."

By this time, they'd gained the short expanse of pristine lawn that led to the abbey's back terrace.

"Miss Jones, do you mind if I ask, why have you never married before now? I know you met the wrong man when you were nineteen, but did you not want to wed in all of those intervening years? You are very beautiful, so I can't imagine you haven't had other offers."

"Thank you for the compliment, my lady. And no, I don't mind if you ask…" Artemis paused, trying to order her thoughts. Now that she'd begun to exchange confidences with the duke's daughter, she was loath to let slip that she didn't really intend to marry Dominic. "I suppose you could say I never found the right man after my first and only Season. And I wasn't convinced that I ever would. And so, I decided to remain unwed and instead devote my time and energy to educating young women so they could have all the opportunities in life that men have. I firmly believe that knowledge is power."

Celeste nodded. "I like your philosophy. But now that you've met my father, that's all changed. The getting-married part, that is."

"Yes…" Artemis glanced downward and focused on lifting her skirts so she could safely negotiate the terrace steps. "I'm very grateful that he supports my idea for starting a ladies' college. Not many noblemen in his position would." It wasn't a complete lie.

"I think I would like to attend a college like that," said Celeste wistfully. "I'm enjoying *Jane Eyre*, by the way. In fact, I'm finding it hard to put down."

"I'm pleased to hear it," said Artemis as they stepped into a wide, stone-flagged hallway. "When you've read *Wuthering Heights*, you must tell me which book you prefer. My bookish friends and I have very firm opinions on the matter."

Celeste tugged on her bonnet strings and pulled her hat off. "I will," she said, then pressed a hand to her forehead. "Oh dear, I think I might be coming down with Miss Sharp's cold. My head's begun to ache frightfully and I feel quite hot, even though I'm cold."

"Oh, no." Artemis frowned. "Perhaps we shouldn't have gone on that walk."

"It's not your fault," said Celeste with a weak smile. "Once I get an idea into my head, I can be particularly stubborn about changing my mind." They followed the corridor back toward the great hall. "However, if I'm going to be confined to my bed for several days, I wondered if you might have something else I could read?"

Artemis smiled. "I do. And I will bring my books to your room later this afternoon if you'd like. Would you also like me to arrange some tea or soup for you?"

"Tea and soup would be love—" The duke's daughter pressed a gloved hand to her nose, then sneezed. "Oh, I beg your pardon. It's definitely a cold. I hope you don't catch it."

"I'm sure I'll be fine. After working as a governess and a teacher for so long, I have the constitution of an ox. Now off you go to bed, my lady. Standing about in drafty halls isn't conducive to getting better. I'll order that tray."

As Artemis watched Lady Celeste scale the stairs to the upper floors, she released a sigh, pleased that she'd made some progress with befriending the girl. She trusted the duke's daughter would be all right. And for some reason she couldn't quite put her finger on, she believed she could trust Celeste not to divulge her past history with the "wrong man." Not that she would particularly mind if Celeste said something to her father about the fact his fiancée *wasn't* a virgin. Dominic had probably worked that out for himself within no time at all, and he'd never passed judgment on her for not being the epitome of chaste womanhood.

She smiled. Last night had certainly confirmed it. Although, she wasn't certain if she was ready to disclose how she'd lost her virginity. Or more to the point, with whom… Perhaps in time when the moment felt right.

Hopefully, Miss Sharp would keep her nose out of her charge's books because Artemis was of a mind to pass on some of Lydia Lovelace's titles. Celeste was not only nursing a cold, but also a broken heart, and she deserved some cheer in her life. Besides, it wasn't as though she hadn't already read most of them.

And one day, she would lend Richard Carlile's book to Celeste. Continuing to keep a young woman in the dark about anything pertaining to sexual congress wouldn't do her any favors. Celeste's naivety could have landed her in all sorts of trouble if she *had* run off with Antonio Moretti.

Artemis was also sure Dominic would never have a frank conversation about where babies really came from. That sort of discussion was always left up to a girl's mother or her more worldly married friends, and at present, Artemis was probably the closest to either of those things that Celeste had.

And if Dominic found out and protested about his daughter's reading choices…well, Artemis would tell him the same too. Books were never the problem. Ignorance and prejudice and blatant narrow-mindedness were, and the world would be a much better place without them.

Chapter Twenty-Three

AFTER ARTEMIS SHARED A LIGHT LUNCHEON WITH Horatia before the drawing room fire, she decided to see how Lady Celeste was faring. Dominic sent word that he was touring the estate and visiting several tenants—despite the fact it was now pouring again—and wouldn't be back at the abbey until dusk. Artemis hoped *he* wouldn't catch cold.

Once she'd delivered her books to the duke's daughter in the west wing—the housekeeper had provided Artemis with directions—she'd retire to her own room to continue with Lady Mirabella's tale. She was sure she'd have a few quiet hours to herself until she needed to prepare for dinner. She had no doubts that Dominic would want to visit her again tonight. As long as he was well, of course. The man really did like to burn the candle at both ends. As his wife, *she* certainly wouldn't put up with—

Artemis stopped dead still in the middle of the west wing's hallway, clutching her books to her chest. What on *earth* was she thinking? She wasn't going to marry Dominic. She was a jaded spinster. She didn't believe in love matches. She wanted to establish a college. She didn't have time for a husband or babies or stepdaughters or the countless duties of a duchess.

Did she?

But Artemis, as Dominic's wife you'd have everything you'd ever need. You'd have the funds and the staff to do whatever you wanted.

But most importantly of all, you'd have a husband who supports you. A man with power at your side who could influence those members of society who are actively stopping women from gaining entrance to the hallowed halls of higher learning. Places that are presently the sole province of men.

All you have to do is say yes…

A small noise—a creak perhaps—barely discernible above the sound of the rain lashing the abbey, caught Artemis's attention. Turning her head, she saw that a door to one of the rooms was slightly ajar. A bedroom perhaps? And then she frowned. She was certain all of the doors had been shut when she'd entered the hallway. And wouldn't she have noticed the light spilling out of the room onto the Turkish floor runner if the door *had* been open?

The hair at her nape prickled and a shiver slid down her spine. She suddenly felt as though someone was watching her, and the air around her had turned frigid. Dominic had said Ashburn Abbey wasn't haunted. But what if it was?

And then she admonished herself for being so ridiculously fanciful. There was one simple way to reassure herself that she was not, in fact, being spied upon by an actual someone or something that perhaps wasn't corporeal.

Drawing a bracing breath, Artemis crossed to the open door and entered the room. And then blinked as wonder followed by a wave of great sadness washed over her.

It wasn't a bedchamber or sitting room or parlor. It was a nursery.

Despite the grayness of the day, the room was light and airy. Chintz curtains of pale blue framed the windows, and most of the furniture was fashioned from lustrous satinwood. The plush Aubusson rug that Artemis padded across was in soft pastel shades, and the diaphanous lace hangings cascading over the empty cradle were so fine and delicate that they were almost transparent.

As Artemis approached the cradle, her vision grew misty. Dominic and Juliet's baby boy, Alexander, would have lain here if he hadn't arrived too early. And no doubt Dominic and Horatia and Celeste had all slept in this cradle too.

She definitely felt Juliet's presence here, because above her head was the most exquisite trompe l'oeil of the heavens she'd ever seen. The moon and sun had been painted in the center of a powder-blue sky, and tiny constellations of twinkling stars were scattered around the edges of the ceiling where the blue melded into shades of dusky pink and lavender. But sweetest of all was the border of white, pillowy clouds, where rosy-cheeked cherubs lay sleeping.

A soft sound, like someone humming a lullaby, drifted past Artemis's ear. The sweet scent of orange blossoms and jasmine filled the air. And then the lace netting about the cradle shifted, as though a breeze had just wafted through the room.

Her heart pounding, Artemis stepped back from the cradle. There was no one here, no one at all but her. There must be a draft somewhere. That would explain the soft whisper of sound and the movement of the lace.

Turning on her heel, Artemis quit the room, and then shut the door quietly behind her.

She had books to deliver and a book to write. She didn't have time for fanciful imaginings about ghosts.

When Artemis entered Lady Celeste's bedchamber a short time later, she found the duke's daughter already tucked up in bed with *Jane Eyre* in her hand and a cup of tea and plate of buttered toast at her elbow.

Even though Miss Sharp was unwell, she was apparently ensconced in the adjacent sitting room, curled up in an armchair with her own book—probably something grim and depressing by Dickens. The communicating door was ajar, and Artemis called a brief greeting to the governess before she crossed to the bed. "How are you feeling, my lady?"

"Horrid." Indeed, Celeste looked and sounded quite under the weather; although her face was pale, her eyes were unusually bright, and her voice had a raspy quality. "I didn't have much of an appetite for the soup, but the tea with lemon has been quite soothing for my scratchy throat."

"I'm sorry you're feeling so awful. But here…" Artemis placed her small pile of books on the bed beside Celeste. "I brought these along for you." She dropped her voice. "Besides *North and South* by Elizabeth Gaskell, I've also sneaked in a few of Lydia Lovelace's titles. I don't know which ones you've read but choose whatever you'd like."

"Oooh, thank you so much," whispered back Celeste. Her eyes danced with delight as she picked up the topmost volume. "*Lady Fanny and the Fantastical Phantasm.* Now I have read that one as well as *Lady Violetta and the Vengeful Vampyre.* Of course, I'd happily read them again, but I haven't come across *Lady Guinevere and the Ghastly Ghost,* nor this one…" She flipped open the small, leatherbound volume that had been on the bottom of the pile, and Artemis almost died.

It was her notebook that contained her unfinished manuscript.

"Oh, no! Not that one." Artemis tried to take back the book, but Celeste quickly turned away from her and extended her arm toward the center of the tester bed so that the book was beyond Artemis's reach.

"*Lady Mirabella and the Midnight Monk*?" said Celeste. "This looks interesting."

Old Nick's nob. This couldn't be happening. How could she have been so foolish as to accidentally add her manuscript to the selections? It must have ended up on the bottom of the pile when she was sorting through her books. Artemis's pulse was racing so frantically, her throat was so tight with horror, that she almost couldn't speak. "I'm so sorry," she managed. "That book wasn't supposed to be included. Please don't read it. It's not—"

"It's handwritten." Celeste leafed through the pages until she reached Artemis's last entry. "'Lady Mirabella laid her hand on Count Bellugio's chest,'" she read under her breath. "'Beneath her trembling fingertips, his heart thudded—'" Her brow knit. "But...is that it?" She turned to the next page and the next, which were blank. "It's not finished. It's just a manuscript." Her gaze shot back to Artemis. "Are *you* writing this? Is this yours?"

Artemis blushed. "I... Yes, it's a manuscript. But—"

"But it says on the front page that *Lady Mirabella and the Midnight Monk* is by Lydia Lovelace. Wait a minute..." Celeste's eyes widened in shock, and then she whispered, "Miss Jones, are *you* Lydia Lovelace?"

Artemis gaped. "I... No. No, I'm not," she lied, but it seemed she wasn't convincing enough. The entirely skeptical look on the duke's daughter's face clearly indicated that she didn't believe her.

Celeste's next words confirmed it. "You are. I know you are." Her gaze narrowed. "I saw you writing in this book when we were on the train on the way here. When you thought I wasn't looking. Does my father know about this? Who you are?"

Artemis swallowed. Her face was burning. "No, no he doesn't."

Celeste nodded once. "Good. I promise I won't tell him because if he does learn you're Miss Lovelace, he might stop you writing your wonderful books. And I can't have that, Miss Jones. You are one of my favorite authors, so you needn't worry." She dropped her voice to a dramatic whisper. "Your secret is safe with me. I will take it to the grave if necessary."

Artemis released a shaky breath as she tried to rein in her runaway panic. It was no use. Now that the cat was well and truly out of the bag, she was going to have to concede defeat and put her faith in Lady Celeste to keep her word. "I... Thank you, my lady. For keeping my secret and for the lovely compliment about my writing. It means a lot to me." Her gaze darted to the sitting room doorway, but no one was there. She trusted Miss Sharp hadn't been eavesdropping. Surely, she would have noticed the governess lingering about the threshold.

"Do you have somewhere you can hide all these?" she added, keeping her voice low. "I'm worried Miss Sharp will confiscate them again."

"I do." Celeste nodded toward the other side of the room. "See that window seat? There's a secret compartment underneath and a locked chest inside. Bring the chest here and I'll hide the books straightaway. I'll only read them at night after Miss Sharp has retired to her own rooms."

Artemis fetched the chest and Celeste, who'd already retrieved the key from her bedside table drawer, unlocked it and then began to put the books away.

"I'll need to take this one back with me, my lady," said Artemis, picking up her manuscript.

"Understood." Celeste's gaze firmed. "You *must* finish it

because I want to read it. And please, do stop calling me 'my lady.' If we are to be family, you must call me Celeste."

"And you may call me Artemis. Miss Jones makes me sound like some stuffy old schoolteacher or your ancient maiden aunt."

Celeste smiled warmly. "Artemis then." She locked the box and Artemis returned it to its hidey-hole beneath the window seat.

"I promise to gift you a signed copy of Lady Mirabella's tale as soon as it's published. Hopefully before Christmastide," she said when she returned to Celeste's bedside.

Christmastide... That seemed like such a long way away. Where would she be living by then? What would she be doing? Would she be "Miss Jones, Proprietress and Head Teacher" at her new ladies' college somewhere in London? Alone, penning Gothic romances by the fire in her small but adequate bedroom with a single glass of sherry and a crumbling piece of plum pudding at hand to provide her with a semblance of seasonal cheer?

An image of her spending Christmas with Dominic, Celeste, and Horatia and her family leapt into her mind. They'd all be clustered around the enormous fire in Ashburn Abbey's drawing room, and there'd be a towering Christmas tree in the corner. There'd be a wassail bowl and an extravagant roast dinner and singing and laughter and lively conversation—

A fierce, searing longing shot through Artemis's chest, taking her breath away. What was wrong with her? Ashburn Abbey, Dominic, and indeed his entire family were starting to weave some strange enchantment over her. Before she knew it, she'd be doing something ridiculous like saying yes to Dominic at the altar.

But was it that ridiculous?

As she farewelled Celeste, then hurried back to her room—the door to the nursery still firmly shut, thank goodness—she vowed to herself that from now on, she would keep an open mind about what was to come. While she didn't believe in love, perhaps Dominic had a good point. They *did* rub along well together. Perhaps a marriage of convenience with him wouldn't be such terrible a thing…if she could find it in her heart to give him the heir he needed.

And if she could also find the courage to tell him about her writing career. She didn't want a marriage based on secrets and lies. She was sure Dominic wouldn't want that either. But under the circumstances, what choice did she have?

If she *did* confess that she was Lydia Lovelace—or if Celeste broke her promise and gave her secret away—Artemis's musings about any sort of future with Dominic, along with her dream of establishing a college, would be all for naught. Of this, Artemis was absolutely certain. She couldn't imagine Dominic would happily give her the funds and the moral support he'd promised, let alone marry her, when he learned the truth. When he learned she'd been duplicitous all along.

She could continue to lie to a good man and have everything she wanted. Or she could be open and honest with him and lose it all. But if she did want to marry him, there was no doubt in her mind that disclosing her secret was the one risk she *would* have to take.

Chapter Twenty-Four

"I'm sorry I didn't spend more time with you today," murmured Dominic drowsily. He was lying naked in bed, sated and curled beneath the tousled covers with an equally naked Artemis in his arms. The incessant rain had stopped, and the only sounds in Artemis's bedroom were the faint tick of the mantel clock, the crackle of the fire, and the soft sound of Artemis's breathing. Indeed, at this late hour—almost midnight—the whole of Ashburn Abbey seemed hushed and asleep.

For a moment, he wondered if Artemis had fallen asleep too, but then she murmured, "That's all right. I know how busy you are."

Dominic sighed, and his voice was as bleak as the moorland beyond Ashburn's grounds as he said, "No. It's not all right." It was dark when he'd returned to the abbey, and because he'd attended to a few telegrams and letters about pressing business matters, he hadn't seen Artemis until dinnertime.

And then, of course, Horatia had been present. Ordinarily, he'd welcome his sister's congenial company, but throughout the dinner service, all he could think about was spending time alone with Artemis and what he would do with her. How he'd dismiss all of the servants and then make wild love to her on the very table. Or on the rug before the fire. Or on one of the settees in the adjoining drawing room. His desk in the library.

There would be time to make love in all of those places, and more, if they married. And he could talk with her for hours, whenever he wanted to, wherever he wanted to, without having to worry about bloody chaperones and "appearances." Stealing in and out of her bedroom in the dead of night like he was some sort of sneak thief in his own home was becoming old very quickly. He wanted Artemis in his bed—or better yet, a bed that they could call theirs—every single night.

Dominic suppressed a sigh because there was no guarantee they would wed, was there? Artemis was as skittish as a cat on a hot bakestone whenever he mentioned their future.

Although right at this moment, she was more like a coquettish kitten. "You've more than made up for your absence," she purred as she playfully scraped her nails over his chest.

Dominic caught her hand and brought it to his lips. "You make light of the situation, but the plain, cold truth is, I do neglect those who I care about most in this world."

Artemis raised her head and scowled. "Dominic Winters, you are *not* neglectful."

"It's very gracious of you to defend the indefensible, but you're wrong. Take Celeste, for instance. I've ignored her isolation and failed to fix her situation for so long, it almost ended in disaster. And in my quest to hide from the past, I've forgotten to take care of myself. I've buried myself in work at the expense of everything and everyone else. I certainly haven't done enough to clear my name. Simply ignoring my brother-in-law's concerted smear campaign—hoping it will all just eventually go away—hasn't done me any favors.

"But that's about to change and it's all because of you, Artemis." Dominic raised himself onto one elbow and cupped her face. "You've changed me. You've made me see things so very differently. And I'm nothing but grateful." He leaned in and kissed her with lingering tenderness, knowing that if he called her *love* or said anything more about how much he'd come to care for her, she'd retreat from him. He didn't want to frighten her away with the strength of his feelings. And they *were* strong. He'd given up trying to deny that she meant so very much to him. He wasn't sure if the emotion budding inside his chest was love *just* yet, but it was damn close.

Regardless of his burgeoning feelings, he needed to convince Artemis that she could be happy if she chose to marry him. That perhaps this could be *more* than a marriage of convenience. Now, more than ever, he sensed that a softly-softly approach was required to win her. And he had the rest of this week to change her mind. To give her a glimpse of the future that *could* be.

"I wouldn't be such a bad husband, you know," he said, his tone as light and teasing as he could make it. "Especially now that I've come to realize that I need to change my ways and make my family my priority, not estate management, business, and politics."

To Dominic's relief, Artemis didn't drop her gaze from his. Indeed, her eyes were as soft as brown velvet as she murmured, "I'm pleased to hear it, Dominic. But most of all, I'm pleased for Celeste."

He caught one of her curls and wound it around his finger. "The change you've wrought in her in such a short time is nothing short of miraculous, and I'm truly astounded. I'm glad I trusted my instincts about you. The fact that Celeste will now let you use her first name shows how much she likes and respects you. When I visited her room tonight before dinner, I could tell that she's in much better spirits even though she's unwell. Again it's all your doing, Artemis. You're remarkable."

A soft pink blush suffused Artemis's cheeks. "Well, I don't know about that."

"Trust me, you are." And then Dominic kissed her again because he couldn't help himself. He was beginning to think that even if they shared a lifetime together, he'd never have his fill of her. She was that damn addictive.

———————

I wouldn't be such a bad husband you know... As Dominic kissed her with such sweet and thorough gentleness, Artemis couldn't help but wonder if he might be right.

But this wasn't just about forming a union; it was about creating a family and continuing a legacy. And all of those things would affect Artemis's choices in the future. She might have her college, but she wouldn't be able to continue to teach, and she may not be able to continue to write if she became the Duchess of Dartmoor. Could she sacrifice those things she held dear for this man? A man who was only now realizing that he often buried himself in work to hold everyone at arm's length and might do so again and again?

A man who *appeared* to be falling in love with her, but there was no doubt in her mind that he'd also constructed defensive walls around his wounded heart to protect it. She should know because she'd been fiercely guarding her own heart for so long too.

He desired her. He *liked* her a great deal. Would that be enough for her in the years ahead if he couldn't offer her love? Could she let herself love him back?

She was nothing but torn. Dominic had been so forthright with her that she felt as though she owed him some sort of explanation as to why she was so circumspect and reluctant to commit to a life by his side.

"You're probably wondering why I eschew marriage and everything that comes with it," she said when their kiss ended and she was lying once again in the comforting warmth of Dominic's arms. "Last night you shared your own past with me. So, because of that, it's only fair that I tell you about mine. I hope it will help you to understand why I am the way that I am. Why I value my independence and find it hard to believe in love and happy endings."

"You don't have to"—he kissed her temple—"if it's too difficult or painful. I do have an inkling that my scoundrel of a brother-in-law might be involved."

"No, I want to tell you," she said firmly. "You deserve to know. And it's not just Gascoyne who is responsible for my cynical views. In many respects, my parents are to blame too. They were as unhappily married as a couple can be."

"I'm sorry," he said. "My parents were not unhappy at least. They were *comfortable* with each other. They knew what their duties were and amicably adhered to them, as is often the case with society marriages." He gave a slight huff as though he were disgruntled. "But now I've rudely interrupted you. Please, go on."

"No, it's all right," she said. "I appreciate how candid you are." Artemis wasn't sure if Dominic was hinting that he expected their marriage to be like his parents', but it was something she should take into account—that peers of the realm often wed for convenience alone, and after the heir and the spare were produced, husbands and wives led very separate lives. Dominic had never promised her anything more than that.

Gathering her thoughts again, she continued. "My mother, Clara, and her older sister, Roberta, came from a moderately wealthy family with solid connections. But for some reason

I've never been able to fathom, my mother chose to marry a genteelly impoverished vicar rather than to pursue a gentleman of rank and wealth. But she was miserable being a vicar's wife. She was so very intelligent—as smart as ten professors—and she read all the time. And widely. I clearly received my love of books from her.

"My father's passion was the Bible and doing good works for the community in and around Heathwick Green. Of course, my mother did participate in charity work—visiting villagers, helping out at the parish school, and the like. But for the most part, I think she was bored being Mrs. Obadiah Jones. At best, my parents were politely distant. At worst..." She shivered. "My father was a hard, pernickety man, and disdain was his bedfellow far more often than my mother was."

"Forgive me for being so blunt, but do you think that your mother *had* to get married?"

Artemis shrugged. "I can't imagine my father ever did anything that wasn't proper. I'm sure he never seduced her and got her in the family way before they wed. Yes, why they married is a complete mystery to me. I'm sure my aunt knows, but she would never tell.

"In any event"—she released a sigh—"observing how unhappy they were, I never formed a very positive opinion about marriage, even before I was forced to have a Season."

Dominic brushed a curl away from her cheek. "You didn't want a London Season? You never dreamed of finding your own Mr. Darcy or Mr. Rochester or Mr. Thornton?"

She smiled at that. She liked it that Dominic paid particular attention to everything she said. "Once upon a time when I was Celeste's age, I suppose I did. But I soon came to realize that Byronic heroes only exist in books and I wasn't likely to find someone who fit the bill in a London ballroom. But after my mother passed away when I was fifteen, Aunt Roberta assumed the role of female guardian, and she was determined that I would marry, and well. Then I met Guy de Burgh."

Artemis couldn't suppress a shudder. "He was so very handsome and charm personified. For the space of a month and two days, I really did believe I might have found my very own Mr. Darcy. I had no clue that everything he told me—that he wanted to make me his, that he adored me—was a lie. He seduced me, and once he'd had enough of me—when someone far richer by the name of Evangeline Gibbs came along—he cast me off like I meant no more to him than a harlot he'd thrown a few coins to after he was done." A bitter laugh escaped her. "In a way, his ill treatment of me was worse than that because I didn't even get paid. I was such a naive fool, but I was so caught up in the thrill of having a clandestine romance—and thwarting my aunt—that I was willing to risk everything. Thank God I didn't fall pregnant because I had no idea about how to prevent conception. Guy certainly didn't care enough to take precautions."

"I could kill him for treating you so badly." Dominic's voice was such a harsh growl, like oncoming thunder, that Artemis lifted her head.

"I'm sure you don't mean that. Besides, it was a decade ago now." Although Artemis had thought about doing Gascoyne bodily harm when she'd seen him with Phoebe, she wouldn't really hurt him. But Dominic sounded so fierce. The quicksilver flash in his gaze, the set of his jaw, the way a muscle flexed in his cheek spoke of an anger that was formidable.

"If he were here right now," continued Dominic in a voice so low and soft with menace that a shiver of foreboding slid through Artemis, "I'd happily pummel him into dust. Or better yet, gut him with a blunt butter knife and then feed him to the worms."

While Artemis had always contemplated telling Dominic about her sister's ill-advised affair at some stage, she definitely wouldn't tell him now. Not after this disclosure and the manner in which he'd delivered it. Indeed, at this moment, she was deathly afraid of what he might do if Gascoyne actually *did* ruin Phoebe and he found out. "Noblemen" called each other out at the drop of a hatpin, and she didn't want her sister's foolishness to be the tipping point that resulted in any sort of bloodshed between Dominic and his vile brother-in-law.

Phoebe was *her* responsibility, and she'd warned both her sister and Aunt Roberta about what a snake Gascoyne was. Phoebe had made her bed and now she'd have to lie in it. If anything untoward happened, it was on her head and no one else's.

"You've gone all quiet, Artemis," murmured Dominic. "I'm sorry if I've upset you with my display of temper."

"You haven't upset me," she replied. Although she couldn't deny she was unsettled. "I certainly understand how easy it is to be infuriated by Lord Gascoyne. Let's not talk about him anymore."

"Agreed." Dominic's fierce frown lifted and his eyes gleamed. "What shall we do instead?"

"I can think of something." While part of Artemis simply wanted to distract Dominic to avoid further discussion about a perilous topic, she also couldn't deny her own insatiable need for this man. It was so strong, she wasn't sure she'd ever be able to give him up. But she didn't want to think about having to face another upsetting prospect right now.

While she was in his arms, she'd live in the moment.

With a smile, she extricated herself from the tangled sheets, then straddled Dominic. She undulated her own hips, and the damp cleft of her sex glided over his already half-aroused cock. "Will this do?"

One of Dominic's hands slid possessively to the back of her head, and he pulled her down for a kiss, not gentle this time but full of heat and rough, raw lust. His mouth commanded hers—his tongue stroked deeply, a tantalizing prelude to what they were about to do. His teeth nipped and pulled at her lower lip, and then he gave a low growl. "Most definitely."

"Good." After raising her body slightly, Artemis grasped Dominic's now fully erect cock and then sheathed him, her greedy sex enveloping all of his long, steel-hard length in one slow, smooth glide. And she moaned.

Oh dear Lord, his possession felt good. He filled her so well and so completely that she could already feel tremors of pleasure rippling through her. The way his burning gaze trapped hers as he plunged in and out of her was sublime. It was no wonder at all that she never wanted this feeling of being Dominic's and Dominic's alone to end.

But all too soon, pleasure claimed both of them. When Dominic reached between their sweat-slickened bodies and thumbed her core, Artemis's whole body bowed as pure ecstasy shot through her. And then Dominic pulled out with a mighty roar, spilling his seed onto the sheets instead of inside her.

Just like he always did. Just like they'd agreed upon.

Dominic wrapped her in his arms, kissed her tenderly, and Artemis reveled in the warmth of his embrace and the deep satisfaction humming through her veins. But as their breathing slowed and Dominic slipped into sleep, a niggling feeling—a pang of sorts—penetrated her contented, dreamy languor.

For the first time ever, she almost regretted the fact that Dominic had withdrawn from her when he'd spent. Since

Gascoyne had used her so terribly, and after she'd somehow escaped the terrible fate of becoming an "unwed mother," she'd never once let herself indulge in the fantasy of having children. For so long, she hadn't believed in love or marriage, so babies were not for her.

While she hadn't had sexual intercourse in the intervening years, she'd educated herself and knew how to guard against conception if she ever did take another lover. She had physical needs after all and never intended to live the life of a nun.

But now…what if she *had* found the right man? Not the dark and brooding unattainable hero of her girlish daydreams, but a real man, a *good* man who would care for her? Who believed in her and supported her goals? Maybe she *could* have a baby given the right set of circumstances.

Her thoughts drifted to the lovely nursery here at Ashburn, and her mind conjured up a beguiling image of herself and Dominic laying their own baby in that cradle. That pang—a strange, sweet ache—squeezed her heart again, and instead of ruthlessly rooting it out and crushing it like she'd always done in the past, she let it linger. Let it come to life and then take shape and blossom. The promise within that vision was so strong and so poignant, tears sprang to Artemis's eyes.

And then a sigh of regret slid out of her. What was the use of dreaming about babies and nurseries and a life with Dominic if he learned the truth about her and decided she was not the sort of woman he could marry after all? He didn't know everything about her. Not yet…

The problem was that she didn't trust him enough—not with her powder keg of a secret.

Finding the courage to share that she was Lydia Lovelace might be the hardest thing she'd ever have to do.

Chapter Twenty-Five

THE NEXT FOUR DAYS AT ASHBURN WERE SO ENJOYABLE, they passed all too quickly for Artemis. The weather improved, and both Celeste and Miss Sharp recovered from their colds. Indeed, Artemis was heartened that Celeste actively sought out her company to chat about *Jane Eyre* and *Wuthering Heights*—like Artemis, Celeste preferred *Jane Eyre*—and one evening, she even showed Artemis how to use the telescope in Ashburn's observatory. The duke's daughter had pointed out all of her favorite constellations and stars and had confided that one day, she longed to be awarded a gold medal by the Royal Astronomical Society of London, just like Caroline Herschel. Artemis secretly vowed to herself that if she could make Celeste's dream come true, she would.

Best of all, Dominic was true to his word and spent less time making rounds of the estate and reading endless documents and more time with her, Celeste, and Horatia.

He took Artemis on a tour of the estate's grounds and the picturesque village of Ashburton. Everyone they encountered greeted Dominic with due deference, and they were nothing but warm and welcoming upon meeting his fiancée. At least in this part of the world, there was no obvious distrust of the Duke of Dartmoor. In fact, Artemis gained the impression that he was not only well respected but liked. It seemed Lord Gascoyne's pernicious influence only extended so far.

When Dominic did have to work, or if the weather was inclement, Artemis continued to work on *Lady Mirabella and the Midnight Monk*. Hopefully she'd finish writing the first draft of her manuscript within the next week.

Of course, Artemis would have enjoyed herself more if she hadn't felt quite so guilty all the time. The fact that she was keeping part of herself hidden from Dominic weighed heavily on her mind, and she regularly castigated herself for not being brave enough to tell him about her writing career. Part of her believed it would almost be a relief if Miss Sharp *had* eavesdropped on her conversation with Celeste and then tattled on her to Dominic. But the governess had been nothing but pleasantly courteous in the ensuing days. If she did know that Artemis was Lydia Lovelace, surely she would have said something to her employer.

And then on her sixth morning at Ashburn Abbey, Artemis received a telegram. Ashburn's butler brought it into the morning room where she was sharing breakfast with Horatia and Celeste.

As soon as Artemis picked up the piece of paper and glanced at the name of the sender, her blood ran colder than the icy winds whipping across Dartmoor itself.

Artemis, you were right about Lord G. Please come home. Don't delay. P.

Horatia put down her marmalade-slathered toast. "Is everything all right?"

"You've gone awfully pale." Celeste's brow was creased with worry.

"I… My sister needs me," Artemis whispered. Guilt skewered her heart more effectively than the wickedly sharp pewter letter opener beside Horatia's small pile of correspondence.

"I'm sorry." She pushed to her feet so abruptly, the table shook and the freshly poured tea brimming in her teacup spilled all over the saucer. "Please excuse me. I must find Dominic."

———————

As it was, it wasn't hard to find Dominic. Even though he'd just come back from his early morning ride, he was ensconced in the library, at his desk, still wearing his riding attire of a hunter-green coat, buckskin breeches, and boots.

As soon as he laid eyes upon Artemis, he rose from his chair. "What is it? What's wrong?"

Artemis rushed to the desk and proffered the telegram with a shaking hand. "Something's happened between Lord Gascoyne and my sister. I'm afraid I need to return to London at once and...and I wondered if you could spare a carriage to take me to Newton train station."

Concern etched lines around Dominic's eyes as he lifted his gaze from the telegram. "Of course you can. You can have anything you need. It won't take me long to get ready. We should be able to make the train that departs at midday if we leave within the hour."

"You're...you're coming as well?"

Dominic's brows arrowed into a deep frown. "You don't want me to? I'd always intended to leave Celeste here with Miss Sharp and return to London tomorrow with you and Horatia. I can only speculate about what has happened between Gascoyne and your sister, but whatever the case may be, perhaps I can help."

"I don't want to disrupt your plans. And I would understand if you didn't want to have anything to do with Gascoyne. It's why I didn't mention—" Artemis broke off. She'd all but admitted that she'd already known something had been going on but hadn't thought to confide in Dominic.

Her fiancé's gaze narrowed dangerously. "Didn't mention what exactly?"

Artemis swallowed. Her mouth was drier than the sand in the silver pounce pot on Dominic's desk. "That Gascoyne was courting my sister." She raised her chin a notch. "I only found out about it the night before we quit London."

"God damn it, Artemis." Frustration flickered in Dominic's eyes. "Why didn't you tell me about all of this beforehand?"

Indignation stiffened Artemis's spine. "I'd thought about doing so, but you had enough to worry about with Celeste," she returned heatedly. "And when I did tell you about my own painful past with Gascoyne, you reacted with such anger, I was afraid you might do something rash. Something that would harm your reputation even more. Besides, Phoebe is *my* sister. She's my responsibility. I did warn her about Gascoyne, but she was so caught up in the thrill of their courtship that she wouldn't listen. Neither would my aunt Roberta. What's even worse, they'd taken that scoundrel's side over yours. They believed his lies about you. At the time, the night before I left, I really didn't think there was anything you could have done that would have made a difference. I still don't."

"You don't know that." Dominic's expression was thunderous. "And the only reason you didn't come to me for help is that you don't see this"—he gestured between them—"what we have, as a real betrothal."

Artemis gave an impatient snort. "But it's *not* real."

"Isn't it, Artemis?" In two strides, Dominic was only inches away from where she stood frozen in the middle of the Turkish rug. His gray eyes blazed as they locked with hers. "Because after this week, it feels damn real to me, despite the bargain we made."

Artemis searched Dominic's face. She'd never seen him like this before—so tense and so angry. With *her*. "That's not fair," she whispered. "You make it sound as though I'm reneging on a promise. One that I should remind you, I never made."

He emitted a frustrated huff, then stalked across the room to one of the library's windows and gave his back to her. Beneath his finely cut coat, his shoulders were a rigid line. "You know, you've already fulfilled your part of the deal, Artemis," he said in a voice so clipped and cold, a shiver chased down her spine. "You can leave whenever you want to. I'll write a damn cheque to fund your college right now if you like. All you have to do is name your price."

Artemis's throat was so tight she could barely swallow. Why was he so furious with her? And why did he suddenly seem intent on driving her away when he'd just said this engagement didn't feel like one based on convenience alone anymore?

But she knew the answer. He was upset and lashing out because she hadn't trusted him enough to come to him for help. She was acting as though she didn't need him. As though she didn't care.

She'd *hurt* him.

The stark implication of that took her breath away. And it begged the question: When had this seemingly straightforward arrangement turned into a relationship with actual emotions tied up in it?

When had they both begun to fall in love?

"I…I'm not ready to make a decision yet," she managed at last. Even to her own ears, her voice sounded high and thin and brittle. "I need a little more time to make up my mind…about whether to end things or not. I–I don't know what I want."

Dominic turned back to face her. A muscle worked in his jaw as his turbulent gaze held her in its grip. And then the fight went out of him. He dragged a hand down his face and then he sighed. "You're right, Artemis. I'm sorry for losing my temper. And for pressuring you to make a decision when you're not ready. Particularly now. It's incredibly arrogant and selfish of me to expect you to." Another sigh. "It's just…I wish you'd trusted me enough to confide in me about Gascoyne's involvement with your sister."

"I know. And I'm sorry too. Truly I am. I didn't mean to upset you. I decided to keep it to myself because I thought it was for the best. As I said, I thought you had enough to deal with, with Celeste."

He nodded. Once. And then his mouth twisted with a wry smile. "It seems we both have family members who are hell-bent on turning us old before our time."

She offered him a small smile in return. "Yes."

"I shall see you in an hour in the great hall."

And then he turned back to his desk and Artemis quit the room.

Chapter Twenty-Six

IT WAS JUST AFTER NINE O'CLOCK IN THE EVENING WHEN Artemis arrived back at Cadogan Square. Even though she and Dominic seemed to have called a truce after their tense exchange in Ashburn's library, there were long periods of strained silence on the journey back to London. Horatia, who'd decided to return too, had done her best to make conversation, but at best, it was stilted. When Artemis alighted from Dominic's carriage, she'd simply farewelled him and Horatia rather than invite them into her aunt's house. But she had promised to speak with Dominic on the morrow.

"She's in her bedroom," said Aunt Roberta without preamble as soon as Artemis set foot in the drawing room.

"How is she?" asked Artemis, pulling off her gloves and bonnet and dumping them on a chair. Trepidation tripped through her when she took in her aunt's slightly disheveled appearance—lace cap askew, iron-gray hair sliding from its pins, no jewelry at her throat or upon her fingers. Such a look was completely out of character even for this relatively late hour. "What's Gascoyne done?"

Aunt Roberta absently patted Bertie who sat beside her on the sofa. "She won't say precisely, though I fear that the blackguard has stolen her virtue," she said in a voice that was weak and frail rather than brimming with self-assurance. "But it's even worse than that, I'm afraid."

The barely restrained fear inside Artemis bolted clean away.

She had to inhale a lungful of air before she could make her voice work. "Please speak plainly, Aunt Roberta."

Her aunt gestured at a pile of newspapers beside her crystal bowl of sweetmeats. "Take a look for yourself. It's on page seven in the gossip...I mean the 'social' column of the *London Tatler*. The whole family's reputation is ruined."

Oh no.

Artemis picked up the infamous scandal rag and flipped to the page her aunt had indicated. And then her heart stuttered and all but stopped.

Miss P.J. of C. Square forsaken by the Dastardly Duke's nemesis!
But who will have the last laugh?

She couldn't bear to read any more than that. "How did this happen?" she asked, her voice shaking with anger.

Aunt Roberta shrugged. Her wrapper slipped down her arm, but she didn't seem to notice. "I have no idea. Whenever I try to talk to Phoebe, she bursts into tears. But I'm sure she'll speak with you. She sent for you after all."

Artemis started toward the door but as she reached for the handle, her aunt spoke again. "I don't blame you, you know. In case you were wondering. You did try to warn us."

"How very gracious of you," returned Artemis over her shoulder. "It's just a pity that neither of you believed me until it was too late."

———

Artemis found her sister slumped in an armchair by the fire. And she was in an even worse state than Aunt Roberta.

Her cheeks were pale, but her eyes and nose were red. Her brown hair hung in limp tangles about her sagging shoulders, and in one hand she clutched a linen kerchief.

"Thank you for coming so quickly," Phoebe murmured, then sniffed. "I wasn't sure if you would, under the circumstances."

"Oh, Phoebe." Artemis rushed to her sister's side and gathered her into a hug. "I'm so sorry I wasn't here for you. And of course I was going to come home as soon as you messaged me."

When she drew back, she sank onto the ottoman at Phoebe's feet and took one of her sister's pale hands in hers. "Aunt Roberta has shared a little about what's happened. If you want to tell me more, I'm here to listen."

Phoebe nodded and a sigh shivered out of her. And then a tear slid down her cheek. "It's not fair, Artemis. All I ever wanted to do was marry and have children, and I've been waiting for so, so long. But now that will never happen. Who will have me now?" The expression in her eyes was nothing but haunted. "What if I'm with child?" she whispered, her bottom lip trembling. "Every time I think about it, I feel sick."

"Are you sure that he—"

"Yes, he did, Artemis. I'm not stupid," Phoebe snapped, making Artemis jump. And then she immediately looked contrite for her outburst. "I'm sorry. It's not your fault. None of it is."

Apprehension squeezed her chest as Artemis asked gently, "This question may be difficult for you to answer, Phoebe, but Lord Gascoyne didn't hurt you, did he? Force himself on you?"

Phoebe sniffed again and then dabbed at her red eyes. "No, no he didn't. Well, it hurt a little when he first… When he began to, you know… I'd expected it to though. But that's not the worst part." She lifted her chin. "It's the betrayal and the humiliation and the fact I was such a gullible little fool that stings the most. Because I wanted to *do* it with him after he told me that he adored me, and of course, he knew a lie like that would work. We were at a rout at Lord and Lady Everton's, and when he asked me to meet him in the gardens, I did. I was so swept up in the moment. I was in love, and it was all so wild and wonderful and exciting and romantic, and I thought that he *loved* me—" She broke off and drew a shallow breath. "Have you seen the *London Tatler*?"

"Yes. Aunt Roberta showed me the article."

Phoebe shook her head. "I don't know what possessed me. To follow him to his club and to make such a public to-do that it all ended up in that horrid paper. When he didn't respond to my messages the day after the Evertons' rout, or the next, I was just so desperate to see him again. His silence confused me. I was so certain that he would be here on the doorstep, first thing in the morning after we…" A crimson blush stained her cheeks. "I thought he would ask to speak to Aunt Roberta and then seek a private audience with me to ask for my hand. But when he didn't, I sent him a message. And then another. And then I thought that perhaps some horrible, pernickety servant at Gascoyne House simply hadn't passed my messages on. Hetty swore she delivered *all* of them. But it turned out that wasn't the problem at all.

"Late yesterday afternoon, one of the footmen told Hetty that his master was avoiding me and that if I went to his club, Brooks's in St. James's, in the early evening, I might catch him. So I did." Her eyes glinted and her mouth flattened. "When I confronted Gascoyne in the street before he went inside, he laughed at me and claimed that the mere idea of someone like him, a viscount, marrying someone like me, was delusional. That he'd never cared for me. That it was all in my head. We'd had our fun, but now it was time for both of us to move on."

Fury gripped and twisted Artemis's gut. The sick bloody

bastard had said almost the exact same things to her a whole decade ago. Somehow, she managed to keep her tone even and relatively gentle as she said, "Someone in the street must have overheard your exchange and sold the story to the *London Tatler*."

"Yes. I said I wasn't stupid, but I am, Artemis. Gascoyne is a snake and a blackguard and a swine and a cad…" Phoebe's voice cracked on a sob. "I hate him, Artemis. I hate him. But most of all, I hate myself. For being so weak and so naive and so needy." And then her whole face crumpled, and she collapsed onto the arm of the chair in a storm of tears.

The sound of Phoebe's weeping was heartrending, and Artemis's own vision blurred. She hated Gascoyne too, but other than giving him a verbal flogging, she had no idea what to do to make him pay for treating Phoebe so badly. So she simply stroked her sister's back and murmured soothing words until Phoebe's paroxysm of crying eventually abated.

Then she summoned Hetty and asked her to fetch a pot of chamomile tea and some toast, and once Phoebe was tucked up in bed and had fallen asleep, Artemis farewelled Aunt Roberta and then walked the short distance to Dartmoor House.

―――――

Dominic was replacing the crystal stopper on the whisky decanter when there was a knock on the library door. *Bloody hell.* He glanced at the longcase clock. It was nearing ten.

"What is it?" he called. It had been a long, draining day, and he wanted nothing more than to sit before the fire, dram in hand, until the alcohol did its job and blunted all his sharp edges. Until he stopped thinking about Gascoyne and what he'd like to do to the sodding prick for all of the damage he'd done and the pain he'd caused over the years.

Until he stopped yearning for Artemis. Christ, if she would have him, he'd be the happiest man alive.

And then, as though the Lord above had answered his prayers, the butler opened the door and announced, "Miss Jones to see you, Your Grace."

Dominic immediately put down his tumbler and crossed the floor, his legs devouring the distance between them in a handful of strides. "Artemis."

Her face was pale, and there were shadows beneath her dark-brown eyes. And he just knew in his gut that Gascoyne had ruined her sister. Forcing himself to smother his simmering anger and to maintain a calm exterior, he added, "I thought I wouldn't see you until tomorrow."

"I know," she said grimly. "But I needed to talk to someone about Phoebe and Gascoyne, and I didn't think you'd mind if I dropped by at this late hour."

"Of course not. Here. Take a seat." He gestured toward the fireside. "I just poured myself a whisky. I take it you'd like a sherry?"

"Yes, please." She cast him a grateful smile, and when she claimed his favorite chair again, he didn't complain. In fact, he rather liked it.

No, it was more than that. He loved it. Artemis belonged in his favorite chair in his library. In his bed and by his side. As soon as this business with Phoebe and Gascoyne was effectively dealt with, he'd somehow make her see that she *could* trust him. That she could be happy with him. That choosing to be his wife and duchess and, if she wanted it too, the mother of his children, wouldn't be a mistake.

Once Dominic was installed in the opposite wingback chair, and they were both nursing their drinks, he said, "Tell me what's happened. All of it." And Artemis did.

By the time she'd finished, he was filled with so much glacial fury that he felt as though his blood had all but frozen in his veins. His hands had formed into fists on his thighs, and his resolve was harder than freshly forged steel that had just been plunged into a bucket of ice-cold water.

His mind was crystal clear.

"Dominic?" Artemis's voice was laced with hesitancy. "What are you thinking? I have this horrible feeling I've just made a terrible mistake by confiding in you. Please promise me that you won't do something rash and ridiculous to punish Gascoyne. Like calling him out."

Dominic made himself smile but suspected the expression on his face was more of a grimace. "If I *did* decide to call Gascoyne out, it wouldn't just be to avenge your sister's honor. It would be for the callous, reprehensible way he treated you too, Artemis, when you were a debutante. And for all of the loneliness Celeste has had to endure because of his relentless campaign to socially destroy me. I can't forgive him for any of that. I've had enough."

She nodded. "I have too. But he's not worth losing your life over. I certainly didn't come here to ask you to take revenge against Gascoyne for ruining my sister. Both she and my aunt bear some responsibility in all of this too. I simply wanted to share what had happened." Her voice softened. "Most of all, I didn't want to shut you out."

"I understand," he said. "And it means a lot—more than I can say, in fact—that your first thought was to come to me."

"It was." She smiled, then put down her barely touched sherry as the longcase clock struck the hour. "Now that I'm reassured that you're not going to turn into a slavering beast of retribution, I suppose I should go."

"Yes..." She was right of course, about leaving. For the sake of appearances, she should return to Cadogan Square.

She rose and he followed her to the library door. "I can see myself out," she began, but then Dominic caught her hand as she reached for the handle.

"Wait."

She raised a quizzical brow. "What is it?"

"I..." He sucked in a breath. Beneath the ice-cold anger crystallizing his veins, he felt something else. Something hot and potent, surging through his blood. Hardening his cock.

Lust and longing and something else he dared not put a name to.

"I want you," he said, his voice low and rough. And then he pushed her up against the door, crowding her in with his body, crushing her ridiculously full skirts with his hips and his legs. His mouth grazed hers. "Let me love you."

Because he *was* going to call Gascoyne out, despite everything he'd just said to Artemis, and if this was his last night on earth and his very last opportunity to make love to this extraordinary woman, by God, he was going to make the most of it.

———

Let me love you...

Artemis's breath quickened and her heart contracted painfully in her chest. Oh, what did Dominic mean by that? He meant "make love," didn't he? Not actually the "I love you" sort of love.

She had no more time to reflect on such an earth-shattering notion because Dominic was kissing her with such searing passion that all of her thoughts scattered like embers in the wind. His hands were cradling her face, and his tongue was in her mouth, stroking deeply. His hips pushed so hard against hers, she could easily feel his arousal, even through all of the layers of her skirts and petticoats.

She was aroused too and needed to lose herself. To feel something other than anger and anguish and dread. To experience something that was real and true and uplifting, which in her heart of hearts she knew she could find only with Dominic.

She burned for him so much that she was already hot and wet and slippery between her thighs. Her nipples were as tight and hard as pearls even before he cupped her breasts. When he skated his thumbs over those aching nubs and then pinched them through her bodice and corset, she moaned, rendered helpless with the strength of her own desire. "Take me," she whispered hoarsely.

He lit her up so quickly, so effortlessly, that she couldn't help but succumb to the fire blazing between them.

He growled his approval, then yanked the woolen skirts of her traveling gown up to her waist. "Help me take off these damn petticoats and drawers."

And she did. At once.

As soon as the garments were pooling around her ankles, Dominic was on his knees, nudging her thighs apart, pressing his wicked mouth to her sex. His hands held her hips captive as his tongue delved between her folds, licking and swirling and tasting her wetness, tormenting her clitoris, driving her to the edge of reason. In no time at all, her knees were trembling, and she was gasping and gripping his head, holding on for dear life as he sent her hurtling into bliss.

But there was to be no respite from Dominic's sublime assault on her senses. Before the aftershocks of her pleasure had subsided, he was climbing to his feet and unfastening his trousers. He ruthlessly raised one of her legs, notched the head of his rigid cock at her dew-slick entrance and, with one powerful thrust, seated himself inside her, all the way to the hilt.

Artemis's core quivered around his hot, steel-hard length and she closed her eyes and clutched at Dominic's shoulders. How could it be that she was ready to come again so soon?

"Look at me," he commanded. His stormy gaze burned into hers as he began to drive into her slick heat, again and again. Harder and faster, making the door rattle with each exquisite incursion. One of his hands grasped her about the nape, holding her steady. And then his mouth was at her ear, whispering coarse, delicious, wicked words about how much he wanted her and her alone. How much he adored being inside her. How much he loved hearing her pants and sweet moans... And when he pressed a scorching kiss to her throat, Artemis shattered and broke on an ardor-drenched cry, pleasure engulfing her, carrying her heavenward in a great, pulsating wave.

Clinging to his neck, she buried her face in Dominic's shoulder. Except for the harsh gust of his breath and the rise and fall of his chest, he'd gone completely still. And then he slid himself free with one hand, jerked his hips once, then twice and with a low, guttural animal groan, he found satisfaction too. As he pushed against her, shuddering and quaking and gasping, his seed coated her inner thigh.

"Artemis," His whisper was harsh and raw, almost desperate as he drew back to look at her, and Artemis frowned.

Something about him—the stark expression in his gaze as it wandered over her face as though memorizing her features, the way his fingers brushed over her lips, then down her cheek, set off of a frisson of alarm. "Is something wrong?" she asked softly.

And when his mouth curved into a lopsided smile, and he

murmured, "Nothing, nothing at all, love," she didn't quite believe him.

"Are you sure? Because—"

"I'm sure. I'm just tired and you must be too. You must go home and get some sleep."

He pulled out a handkerchief from his jacket pocket, and after wiping her thigh clean and tidying himself up, he helped her to put her attire back to rights.

"Good night, my sweet Artemis," he said in a voice so soft and low and filled with tenderness it made her breath catch. "We'll talk more tomorrow." Then they exchanged one final light and lingering kiss before she quit the library and made her way down the stairs to Dartmoor House's entry hall.

As Artemis donned her bonnet and pulled on her gloves, she had the distinct impression she was being watched, but when she turned around and looked back up the stairs to the first floor, there was no one there. At least she didn't think so. It was difficult to see into all of the shadowy corners beyond the wooden balustrades. The night footman stationed by the front door certainly didn't seem to notice anything.

Her fatigue and all of this horrid business with Gascoyne had clearly unsettled her. Her mind was playing tricks on her just like it had in the nursery at Ashburn Abbey.

Dominic was right.

She needed a good night's sleep.

Chapter Twenty-Seven

THE LATE-NIGHT AIR WAS DANK AND CHILL, AND THE streets were enveloped by a roiling fog as Dominic strode through St. James's. According to the intelligence he'd gathered from several colleagues who frequented Brooks's gentlemen's club, Lord Gascoyne had moved on to the nearby Firebrand Club, a gaming hell with a notorious reputation for high-stakes play that was situated in nearby Duke Street.

There was but one stuttering gas lamp illuminating the corner of Duke Street and the narrow cobblestoned laneway near the Firebrand Club's entrance, so it was easy for Dominic to take up residence in the dense, fog-laden shadows. He was neither a coward nor a fool—venturing inside when he wasn't a member and creating a scene would likely result in him getting kicked out by one of the club's burly doormen. So, he'd wait for Gascoyne to emerge.

Hopefully, he wouldn't take all bloody night; according to Dominic's pocket watch, it was well after midnight already. Even wrapped up in his greatcoat, Dominic was cold—he'd lost most of the feeling in his booted toes—and the pewter flask of whisky he'd brought to warm him up from the inside out wasn't helping much either.

But needs must when the devil drives. Ever since Juliet had died, Gascoyne had been a cankerous thorn in Dominic's side, and it was about time he did something about it.

Minutes crawled by, and a feeling of inevitability settled over Dominic while he watched the club's distinctive red door and the comings and goings of various gentlemen—none of them Gascoyne unfortunately. In many respects, challenging the bastard to a duel was reckless as hell. Especially considering Dominic had so many responsibilities—to his dukedom, his country, his businesses, and all of the tenants connected to the Dartmoor estate. To his daughter, of course, and his beautiful Artemis…if she would have him.

Failing to do anything about Gascoyne wasn't an option either.

Not only would he continue to plague Dominic—forever blaming him and maligning him for a crime he didn't commit—but he was certain to harm those Dominic cared about. Indeed, Dominic feared that one day, Gascoyne might do the unthinkable and hurt Celeste in some tangible way, just for the sheer perverse pleasure of it. If Artemis did agree to become his wife, Gascoyne could very well make her a target to avenge Juliet's death. No doubt he'd see it as taking an eye for an eye.

Dominic firmly believed that Phoebe Jones had entered Gascoyne's sights simply because she was connected to him via Artemis. The headline in the *London Tatler* all but proclaimed it.

In any event, he would confront Gascoyne about his ill treatment of Phoebe and see what the blackguard had to say for himself before he threw down the gauntlet. Dominic was a damn good shot, and given his determination and sangfroid, he was unlikely to miss his mark in a duel. And then of course, Gascoyne was a coward at heart and might simply turn tail and run when Dominic confronted him, even if the terms of the duel were to only fight until first blood.

One thing was clear: some sort of comeuppance for Gascoyne was long overdue, and Dominic wasn't afraid to dish out some well-deserved just deserts. Artemis may not have wanted him to go down this path, but he had to. To not act, to not take a stand, was, in his mind, unconscionable.

It was his duty.

The nearby clock tower of St. James's Church had just proclaimed the hour, one o'clock, when the Firebrand's crimson door swung open again. This time, it was Gascoyne who stepped into the weak pool of light spilling from the club's interior. And he was alone.

Perfect.

As his former brother-in-law paused on the pavement, adjusting the collar of his greatcoat, Dominic called out to him. "Gascoyne. A moment if you would."

The viscount turned and shot a scowl Dominic's way. "What the fuck are you doing here?" he growled, striding toward him like a mongrel on the attack. "And what makes you think I'd want to talk to you? You're lucky I don't darken your daylights instead."

Dominic took a few steps back into the alleyway, luring Gascoyne farther into the murky shadows. While dueling was still a largely accepted practice amongst gentlemen to settle matters of honor, by law it was illegal and the fewer people who might overhear this conversation, the better. "I'm here because I'm utterly sick of you and the harm you inflict on other innocent parties in my sphere."

The uncertain light cast by the gas lamp at the head of the alley revealed Gascoyne's mouth twisting into a snarl. "Oh, my heart weeps for you, Dartmoor. Don't tell me that you're here to avenge the honor of your slut of a fiancée's equally promiscuous sister?"

That was the last straw. Something inside Dominic snapped, and within the space of a heartbeat, he'd thrown Gascoyne up against the rough brick wall of the alley, his arm at his throat. "You're a vile, contemptible excuse for a man, and I should take you apart piece by piece for what you just said."

Gascoyne clawed at his sleeve. "Get…off me," he choked out, and Dominic dropped his arm and stepped back a pace. It wouldn't do to the kill the bastard before he met him on the so-called field of honor.

"Fuck you," Gascoyne spat out, pulling at his collar and rubbing at his neck. "And you have the audacity to call me vile and contemptible when you're the one who murdered my sister!"

Dominic ignored his accusation. There was no point. Gascoyne had made up his mind a long time ago. But there was one thing he wanted to know before he issued his challenge. "You set up that whole supposedly accidental encounter outside of Brooks's, didn't you? You knew Phoebe Jones would take the bait and make a public scene. You probably even fed the *London Tatler* that ridiculously dramatic headline."

Gascoyne's whole demeanor changed, a smirk replacing his scowl. Thrusting his gloved hands into his greatcoat's pockets, he rocked back on his heels. "I'd say it's rather inspired and also quite accurate because who's laughing now?"

"You certainly won't be when I extract a pound of flesh or two from you, you malicious bastard," Dominic growled. "Meet me at dawn. Pistols at Hampstead Heath. We'll fight to first blood."

Gascoyne's eyes narrowed to slits. The man's whole body seemed to vibrate with hatred. "God, I'm so bloody sick of you and your whole 'I'm the honorable Duke of Dartmoor' act," he gritted out from between clenched teeth. "Because I know what you did, despite what the coroner decreed. You killed Juliet and then dumped her body in a bog, didn't you?"

"That's *not* what happened. I would never have harmed a single hair on Juliet's head. I loved your sister. I did everything I could—" Dominic broke off. What was the point of continuing this argument? Gascoyne would never believe he was guiltless. Not after all this time. "Are you going to accept my challenge or not?" he demanded, his voice harsh in the freezing dark. "Or are you too much of a sniveling coward? A depraved weakling who'd rather prey upon an innocent young woman than—"

All of a sudden, Gascoyne stepped forward until he was almost nose to nose with Dominic. "No, I'm not, because only gentlemen fight duels. You're the one who's depraved and a murderous cur. A pathetic dog. So I'm going to put you down like one."

Too late, Dominic felt the press of a cold steel muzzle in the vicinity of his heart. Horror gripped him as he grabbed Gascoyne's arm. Tried to twist away. And then a shot rang out and Dominic stumbled backward, reeling. Searing pain bloomed in his chest.

His head hit the brick wall, and as he slumped to the filthy ground, a flash of sharp regret about what might have been with Artemis penetrated his mind. And then the dark fog of oblivion claimed him.

Chapter Twenty-Eight

"MISS JONES, MISS JONES!"

Artemis opened her eyes and blinked with confusion into the gray, early morning gloom of her bedroom. *What on earth?*

Apprehension knotting her stomach, she pushed herself up against the pillows as the woman's voice—Hetty's by the sound of it—came again along with a barrage of urgent tapping on the door. "Miss Jones!"

"Come in," Artemis croaked in a voice rusty with sleep as she slid from the cocoon of warm covers and reached for her robe. Was something wrong with Phoebe?

Her sister's maid stuck her head around the door. "Miss Jones, you must come quickly. There's a gentleman asking for you. He's downstairs in the entry hall. He says it's urgent."

Artemis cinched her robe tightly over her nightgown. "Is it my fiancé, the Duke of Dartmoor?"

Because who else could it be?

But Hetty was shaking her head. "No, Miss Jones. He says he's the Earl of Northam."

Artemis frowned as she thrust her feet into slippers. *Lord Northam? Horatia's husband? Here about an urgent matter?*

Oh dear God.

As Artemis sped through the house—even before she reached the entry hall and saw Lord Northam's face—she just knew in her heart that something had happened to Dominic.

"My lord, what's wrong? What's Dominic gone and done?" she asked in a voice breathless with panic and rushing as soon as she reached the earl's side.

Lord Northam, a tall, slender gentleman, sketched a slight bow before he spoke. "Miss Jones, I apologize for calling at such an unseemly hour, but Horatia insisted that I come at once to tell you that Dominic has been hurt. Quite badly, I'm afraid."

"Hurt. Quite badly," Artemis repeated dumbly through stiff lips. It suddenly felt as though her chest was in a vise and all of the air had been squeezed out of her lungs. "In what way?"

The earl winced and glanced down at his top hat in his gloved hands before he met her gaze again. "Shot. And…he also has a serious concussion after sustaining a blow to the head. Probably from a fall."

"Oh…"

Artemis must have looked as though she were about to faint because the earl reached out and gripped her elbow. "Miss Jones, do you need to sit down?"

She shook her head, then pushed a tangled strand of hair behind her ear with trembling fingers. "No. No, I'm all right. I mean, I'm not all right because Dominic is…" She swallowed, hard. "How did it happen? Was he dueling? With Lord Gascoyne?"

But Lord Northam was shaking his head. "No. It wasn't a duel. He was found in St. James's. Wounded in a side street, not far from his clubs. Scotland Yard is investigating—I've spoken with them already, but I suspect they'll want to question you also considering you have pertinent information." His brow wrinkled. "Why would you think he was dueling?"

"Last night, he found out that Lord Gascoyne deliberately ruined my sister. He was so very angry."

"Ahh." Lord Northam nodded as though he understood perfectly. "I see." To his credit, his gaze didn't stray once to Artemis's disheveled hair and crumpled night attire as he said, "I will wait here for you while you get ready. I have a carriage waiting outside to ferry you to Dartmoor House."

"Thank you, my lord," she said. And then, because she couldn't help herself, and she had to know the worst, she added in a whisper, "Will he live?"

Lord Northam's frown descended into frightfully solemn territory. "The physician who's been in attendance is not certain, I'm afraid. He removed a bullet from Dominic's left shoulder, and apparently he was lucky that it didn't nick anything vital. However, there's always the risk of purulence setting in. And then it's worrying that Dominic hasn't regained consciousness yet. The doctor thinks that the thick fog last night—a miasma—may have contained noxious humors that have worsened his condition. And then, no one is entirely certain when he was wounded and how long he lay there before he was discovered."

Artemis's hand fluttered to her throat. "Oh God." To think of Dominic, bleeding and abandoned, lying insensible in a cold, dark alleyway for hours and hours made her stomach twist with horror. She had to see him. At once. "My lord, give me five minutes."

Lord Northam bowed his head. "I'll be here. We'll leave whenever you're ready."

———

Artemis felt like she was drifting in some strange sort of nightmare and at any moment she would wake up as she hurriedly followed Lord Northam up the stairs to the floor where

Dominic's bedchamber lay. A tense hush pervaded Dartmoor House, lingering in each corridor and every shadowed corner, reminding her of the dismal chill fog that continued to shroud London's streets and squares outside.

When they reached Dominic's suite, the earl knocked gently on the door, then admitted her to the softly lit room. The blue velvet curtains were still drawn against the gray morning but a fire crackling merrily in the grate and several lamps provided sufficient light. A warm golden glow illuminated the four-poster bed that dominated the center of the chamber.

The scene would have been quite cheery under different circumstances. But not now. Not when a pair of chamber-maids was collecting soiled clothing and linens and towels from the floor beside the bed and a male servant—Dominic's valet perhaps—was removing a basin of bloodied water. A gray-haired, bespectacled gentleman—who had the look of a physician about him—was in the process of rolling down his shirtsleeves and fastening his cuffs.

And then there was Dominic, lying so still beneath the bed-covers. Just knowing that he was fighting for his life, not simply sleeping, filled Artemis with stone-cold dread.

Horatia, who was sitting by her brother's side holding his limp hand, rose as Artemis approached.

"Thank you for sending for me," Artemis murmured.

Horatia gave a weak smile. "Of course, my dear. I hope you can forgive me for not sending for you sooner, but while the physician, Dr. Hamilton, was working on Dominic's shoulder, I thought both Edward"—she nodded toward Lord Northam—"and I should be present."

"Of course," said Artemis. "I understand."

Her gaze strayed to Dominic. The covers hadn't been pulled

all the way up to his chin, so she could see that he was bare-chested save for the white linen bandage wrapped around his left shoulder. There was another bandage wrapped about his forehead. In stark contrast to the dark stubble on his jaw, his complexion was an unnatural chalky white, and his lips were as bloodless as a marble statue's.

Artemis drew a shaky breath, willing herself not to cry. "How…how is he?"

Dr. Hamilton, who'd just shrugged on his coat, stepped forward. "While the bullet has been removed and the wound cleaned with a weak solution of chlorinated lime—it's a relatively experimental treatment I've been employing to help stave off infection—I'm afraid His Grace did lose quite a lot of blood before I stitched him up, Miss…"

"Jones," supplied Horatia. "Miss Artemis Jones is my brother's fiancée."

"Ah…Miss Jones." The doctor nodded. "I will add, if it hadn't been so cold last night, things might have been far worse. His Grace probably would have lost even more blood. But my main concern at this stage is that His Grace hasn't regained consciousness. I've bandaged the gash on his forehead, but I suspect the blow he sustained to his head was quite significant.

"I'm afraid there's little else we can do at this stage but wait for him to rouse. In the meantime, watch over him for any changes in his condition—send word immediately if he deteriorates or becomes feverish—and periodically check his wound and keep it and the dressing clean. I've left a bottle of chloride of lime on the washstand for you to use. You'll know His Grace is beginning to improve if he reacts to the cleaning solution when you apply it." The doctor grimaced. "It smarts like the very devil."

After Dr. Hamilton had collected his leather physician's bag and taken his leave, Horatia gestured toward the armchair at Dominic's bedside. "You take it, Artemis," she said. "As much as I'm loath to do it, I need to send word to Celeste and tell her what's happened. Edward will catch the nine o'clock train to Newton to fetch her." A worried frown knit her brow as her gaze drifted to her brother. "I think it's best."

Artemis agreed. She couldn't even begin to imagine how Celeste would react to the news. "Please, let me know if I can help in any way."

Horatia gave her a wan smile. "I will. But for now, stay with Dominic. He needs you."

The Northams and the rest of the servants quit the room, and within moments, Artemis was left all alone with her fiancé.

Her vision misted with tears as she approached the bed on unsteady legs and then sank into the armchair. Dominic didn't stir at all when she took his large hand and threaded her fingers through his.

Entwined them.

"Oh, Dominic, my love," she murmured, caressing his bandaged brow, gently brushing a lock of his thick black hair away from his eyes. "Who did this to you?"

But Artemis knew. Knew to her very bones that it was Gascoyne. After she'd quit Dartmoor House last night, Dominic must have gone searching for him to confront him about what he'd done to poor Phoebe. It was the sort of thing an honorable, good-hearted man like him would do.

Retaliating—lashing out in the worst possible way—seemed exactly like something Gascoyne would do too.

Of course, she could be wrong. Perhaps Dominic had simply gone to one of his clubs in St. James's and had been set upon by an opportunistic footpad on the way home. But as far as Artemis knew, St. James's really wasn't the sort of area where footpads roamed, looking to attack gentlemen who were high in the instep.

And footpads didn't usually shoot their marks, did they? She suspected they'd be more likely to pick a toff's pocket or use a snatch-and-grab tactic rather than employ excessive violence in the pursuit of a handful of guineas or a watch. Why draw attention to oneself by discharging a pistol shot?

It *must* have been Gascoyne. As far as Artemis knew, no one else held such an intense grudge against Dominic. She trusted that Scotland Yard would do a thorough job investigating who was behind this despicable attack. It wasn't every day that someone attempted to murder a nobleman of such high rank.

"Whoever hurt you, I will make sure they are brought to justice," whispered Artemis. She pressed her cheek to Dominic's hand where it lay motionless upon the counterpane. "Please don't die. I couldn't bear it if—" She bit her lip to stem a tide of weeping that threatened to breach the brittle wall of stoicism she'd erected around her heart. She wouldn't give into despair.

Dominic was strong and vital, both in body and spirit. He would pull though this.

He had to because she loved him.

I love him...

The long overdue acknowledgment of how she really felt about this wonderful man should bring her joy. But it didn't. Not in this moment. The bittersweetness of her realization threatened to cleave her heart in two.

She loved Dominic, but he might die.

She loved him, but if he survived and she did decide to marry him—right now in this moment she longed to do so—she'd have to be honest with him about her writing career. But then she might lose him if he couldn't accept her for who she truly was.

A tear slipped down her cheek. And then another.

All of a sudden, the bedcovers shifted slightly and then she felt Dominic's hand move. It came to rest lightly upon her head. Even though her pulse leapt, she froze, not even daring to take a breath as his fingers stroked over her hair in a ghost of a caress. "Artemis…" Her whispered name, a mere thread of broken sound on his lips, was the sweetest, most beautiful thing she'd ever heard.

And then his hand slid back onto the bed. Ever so slowly, Artemis raised her head. Dominic's eyes were closed, and his breathing was shallow. Sweat sheened his upper lip. "Dominic?" she murmured and squeezed his all but lifeless hand. "Can you hear me?"

But he didn't respond, and when Artemis touched his cheek, she noticed he was warm. Perhaps too warm. He was covered with several blankets as well as the heavy counterpane and the fire was burning brightly.

Surely Dominic didn't have a fever. Not yet. However his hand, which had been cool only moments ago, now felt hot and clammy too…

Panic seared through Artemis's chest, stealing her breath. Despite Dr. Hamilton's best efforts, what if infection *had* set in?

She rose from the chair and, with the utmost care, loosened the bandage covering Dominic's left shoulder. The wound, although small, looked angry and red beneath the neat stitches. The doctor had only finished attending to it a short time ago, but he'd also suggested applying more chloride of lime if there were any concerns.

And if the solution stung, maybe Dominic would stir again.

With trembling fingers, Artemis soaked a fresh pad of gauze in the astringent-smelling liquid. Returning to the bedside, she carefully removed the old gauze from underneath the loosened bandage and slid the new one into place. Dominic immediately flinched and then his eyelids fluttered open a split-second before he grasped her wrist, his grip surprisingly strong. "Bloody, blistering ballocks, Artemis," he muttered from between clenched teeth. "What the devil are you doing to me?"

Relief whooshed through her in such a great wave that Artemis felt giddy. "Being cruel to be kind," she said, pressing the pad firmly but gently against the wound. This earned her a hiss and a deep groan. "Now lie still and be a good patient."

"What…what happened?" Dominic was peering at her from beneath heavily hooded lids. But his gaze was lucid. "Sweet Jesus, my head hurts." He raised his right hand to the bandage covering his gashed forehead. "And my shoulder. It feels like someone's taken a mace and a flaming broadsword to me."

"You don't remember?" she asked, trying to keep her tone light even as a frisson of worry slid through her.

A deep furrow formed between his brows. "No…I–I remember you. Here. You told me about your sister and then we said good night…" His mouth twitched with a smile. "You didn't run me through with a poker, then hit me over the head with it because I said something inappropriate, did you?"

She couldn't help but smile in return as she tightened the bandage and secured the ends. "Well, it wouldn't be the first time you've done that. But no, it wasn't me who hurt you." Her eyes met his. "Someone shot you, Dominic. You were found in the vicinity of Duke Street."

Confusion clouded Dominic's gaze. "Shot? In Duke Street?"

"Yes. You don't recall what happened?"

"No. No, I don't," he said faintly. "Not a thing. Other than I was furious with Gascoyne for what he'd done to your sister. I might have gone to look for him...but I'm not sure. I don't remember anything after you left. My mind is drawing a complete blank." He turned his head slightly and winced. "Is there something to drink? I'm parched."

"Of course. How thoughtless of me not to offer you something straightaway." Artemis filled a tumbler with water from the pitcher on the washstand.

She'd just eased Dominic back down onto the pillows after he'd had a few sips when there was a light knock at the door and Horatia and Edward entered.

"Dominic! You're awake!" Horatia cried, rushing over to the bed. "Oh, thank God."

"Nice to see you back with us, old chap," remarked the earl. "I'm off to Ashburn in a tick to bring Celeste back. If that's all right with you. Horatia and I thought it might be a good idea under the circumstances."

"Yes. Of c-course." Dominic had sunk back against the pillows. The grooves bracketing his mouth were deep and his teeth had begun to chatter. It was clear the infection was taking hold.

After making sure Dominic was as comfortable as possible, Artemis drew Horatia and her husband aside. "Even though Dr. Hamilton has just left, perhaps we should summon him again," she said and shared her concerns. "Dominic might need some laudanum to help him with the pain too. I also learned he doesn't recall anything about the attack. Nor why he was in Duke Street."

"Hmmm," said Lord Northam. "The blow to his head must have caused a degree of memory loss. I think you're right about sending for Hamilton. We should hire a nurse too. The more hands on deck, the better."

"I agree," said Horatia. "I will arrange everything. You'd best set off for the station, Edward. Otherwise you'll miss your train."

"I c-c-c-can hear you all whispering about m-m-me." Dominic's eyes were closed, but his ears were obviously still working. "It's rude t-t-t-to whisper, y-y-you know."

"And you should be resting, not fretting," Artemis chided gently and returned to his side. She nodded a farewell to the Northams, then felt Dominic's hot cheek. "Do you need anything? A cold compress perhaps?"

"Only y-y-your hand," he murmured, slipping his out from beneath the covers. "Stay with me," he whispered as she slid her fingers through his.

"I'm not going anywhere," she returned softly. "I'm here for you."

She'd never been more sincere about anything in her life.

Chapter Twenty-Nine

ARTEMIS FOUND THAT THE NEXT FEW DAYS PASSED BY IN A horrid, nightmarish blur as she watched Dominic battle the infection rampaging through his body. It was heart-wrenching to see such a powerful man reduced to such a state of helplessness by incessant pain and a raging fever. The idea that he might not survive was anathema to her. She would do whatever she could to get him through.

However, according to Dr. Hamilton, little could be done for Dominic other than providing him with assiduous nursing care that included regularly applying chlorinated lime in the hope that it would lessen the severity of the localized infection at the wound site. He suspected the purulence had spread to Dominic's bloodstream, but as Dominic had already lost a good deal of blood, the doctor was loath to drain away any more to purge the ill humors from his body.

Artemis was grateful Dr. Hamilton didn't want to try such a treatment.

The doctor also suggested, much to Artemis's dismay, that it wouldn't hurt to pray.

Not caring what anyone thought—either at Dartmoor House or at Cadogan Square—she stayed by Dominic's side for endless hours, taking turns with Dominic's devoted valet and Horatia to help the no-nonsense nurse, Miss Quincey, look after him. Artemis lay endless cold compresses on Dominic's fevered brow and sponged his neck, arms, and torso with cool water. Covered him with extra blankets when his body quaked with chills. Even though it pained her to see Dominic hiss and flinch when she applied chlorinated lime to his inflamed bullet wound and the gash on his forehead, she gritted her teeth and did so because she had to. She offered him sips of water and weak broth if he could manage it. Whenever the pain and blazing fever became too much and he groaned and writhed in agony and could barely speak, she gave him carefully measured doses of laudanum. And when he eventually slid into a drug-induced slumber, she held his hand. Whispered to him in quiet moments when they were all alone that he mustn't die. That she simply wouldn't let him.

Because she loved him.

Guilt twisted her heart whenever she made such a declaration. The plain, far-too-ugly truth was that she was too scared to say "I love you" when he was lucid. Because then he might think that she would marry him, but how could she when he didn't know everything about her? And now certainly wasn't the time to confess anything of import. As much as she feared telling him about her writing career, she would when the time was right.

An officer from Scotland Yard, a Detective Lawrence, would interview Dominic when he was alert enough. The detective had already spoken with Horatia, Edward, and Artemis, and on the basis of their statements, he'd also questioned Lord Gascoyne as to his whereabouts at the time of the shooting. Apparently Gascoyne had been seen at the Firebrand Club, a notorious gaming hell in Duke Street on the night in question, but several gentlemen attested that the viscount had been gaming with them the whole night, so he couldn't have been the shooter. The Firebrand's doorman couldn't specifically recall the comings and goings of Gascoyne, and he hadn't heard the pistol shot.

Lawrence reported that he would have interviewed Phoebe as well, but she and Aunt Roberta had repaired to the dowager baroness's country house, Highfield Hall, in Berkshire, and in the end, he'd told Artemis and the Northams that her testimony wouldn't add much to the case. Lord Gascoyne's ongoing slur campaign directed at Dominic wasn't in and of itself sufficient evidence to bring a charge of attempted murder against the viscount. Dominic's inability to recall what had befallen him, along with a lack of witnesses at the time of the incident, meant Scotland Yard's hands were effectively tied for now.

If Dominic could only remember...

Unfortunately, Dr. Hamilton believed that the blow to Dominic's head might have driven all memories of the event from his mind. And they might never return. It rankled Artemis no end that Gascoyne might get off scot-free. She was certain he'd tried to take Dominic's life. Nothing else made sense.

But just like Scotland Yard, her hands were tied. Even if she stormed round to Gascoyne's town house and demanded he confess, he'd either lie to her or laugh in her face. Probably both. And no doubt some dreadful headline would appear in the gossip columns the very next day, smearing the character of the Dastardly Duke's fiancée. All Artemis could do was pray that Dominic made a full recovery and that his memories of that night were restored.

At least Artemis could thank the Lord above for the gift of her friends. On the afternoon of the third day since her world and Dominic's had been turned upside down, Lucy and Jane arrived at Dartmoor House bearing a basket of fruit, an enormous bunch of hothouse flowers, and a small bundle of novels wrapped in scarlet ribbon.

"I know presents won't do much to help, but we wanted you to know that we are both thinking of you and your duke," said Lucy after she'd released Artemis from an enormous hug. Her brow creased when she took in Artemis's disheveled appearance. "Just look at you, my dear friend. Anyone can see that you're exhausted. I hope you're eating well even if you're not getting enough sleep."

"Yes, it wouldn't do for you to get sick too," added Jane.

Artemis summoned a smile to reassure them she was all right, even if she was weighed down with worry. "Why don't I ring for a spot of afternoon tea?" she said. In actual fact, she couldn't recall the last time she'd eaten anything substantial, so a cup of tea and a sandwich or two would be most welcome.

While they waited in the drawing room for the tea things to arrive, Artemis filled her friends in on what had happened to Dominic and the severity of his condition. Lucy and Jane had only picked up the scantest of details from the newspapers.

"I've got my fingers crossed that Scotland Yard will soon have enough evidence to arrest Lord Gascoyne," said Jane gravely.

"And I hope His Grace's memory returns soon," added Lucy. "It must be so disconcerting and horrible for you all."

"I won't lie. The last few days have indeed been testing. For all of us," agreed Artemis. "But you haven't had an easy time of late either, have you, Lucy? I've been thinking of our last meeting and how upset and worried you were. Have you heard from your brother?"

A shadow flitted across Lucy's face. "I'm afraid not. Since his argument with Father, I've not seen hide nor hair of Monty.

He seems to have disappeared off the face of the earth. I keep hoping that he'll write to me, but so far he hasn't. And every time I try to broach the subject with my father, he cuts me off. It's all so terribly frustrating."

"I'm so sorry." Artemis reached for Lucy's hand and gave it a gentle squeeze. "I trust Monty will reach out to you soon."

"I hope so," said Lucy with a sigh. "Father's still grumbling about the need for me to marry and that he might have some-one particular in mind. But you all know how I feel about mar-riage. I'd much rather be left to my own devices than bartered off like I'm a barnyard animal."

Lucy shuddered, and even though Jane and Artemis tried to reassure her that surely that wouldn't happen, Artemis wasn't so certain. Sir Oswald needed money, and the fastest and easiest way to gain it would be to marry his lovely daughter off to a wealthy man.

Afternoon tea arrived, and the next hour passed far too quickly. By the time Artemis bid her friends farewell, a cold, dismal evening had begun to descend. As she gained the gloomy hall outside the ducal suite, Celeste emerged from her father's rooms.

The duke's daughter had returned to Dartmoor House in the company of Miss Sharp three days ago. When she first came upon her beloved papa in a delirious, almost insensible state, she'd been beside herself. Between heartfelt sobs, she begged him to live and promised that she would never, ever cause him grief again. That she would never run away. That she would always do her duty.

As the days wore on, Celeste fell into a pattern of reading aloud to him when he was resting a little more comfortably— usually after the laudanum had taken effect and he'd slipped into sleep. More often than not, she'd choose passages from her new favorite book, *Jane Eyre*.

Sure enough, Celeste was holding Charlotte Brontë's book in her arms. "I think Papa could hear me today," she said when Artemis approached. "I'm sure he even smiled a little at one point."

Artemis imbued her voice with a quiet confidence she sadly didn't feel. "That's wonderful. I'm sure your father can hear you too," she lied. But she had to, to spare Celeste's feelings. Indeed, Artemis was almost entirely certain that Dominic was completely oblivious to his surroundings most of the time. After he'd taken a dose of the strong opiate, his sedative-laced sleep always appeared unnaturally deep to her.

Celeste nodded and hugged *Jane Eyre* to her chest like a talisman that might ward off further misfortune or evil. Even though a pair of footmen were in the process of lighting the wall-mounted gas lamps, their soft golden radiance didn't quite dispel the deep shadows that were gathering like ghosts. Raindrops slid like tears down a nearby windowpane.

Beneath Celeste's veneer of quiet courage, Artemis detected an undercurrent of apprehension, and she wanted to offer comfort. She reached out and touched the girl's arm. "I'm afraid I must return to Cadogan Square. Just to pick up a few things that I need. But when I return, shall I join you for dinner? We could have trays sent up and dine in your sitting room if you'd like." Horatia and Edward had already repaired to their town house for the evening to see their boys and for some much-needed rest.

Celeste's mouth lifted into a thankful smile. "I would like that. Very much." After glancing about to perhaps ascertain that they were completely alone—the footmen had since disappeared through a nearby jib door leading to the servants' stairs—she leaned closer to Artemis. "I've finished rereading *Lady Violetta and the Vengeful Vampyre* and *Lady Guinevere and the Ghastly Ghost.* But if you happened to have a spare copy of *Lady Sophia and the Seductive Sorcerer,* I'd be most grateful if you could lend it to me," she said in a low voice. "It's the only book by Lydia Lovelace that I haven't read. Well, aside from *Lady Mirabella and the Midnight Monk.*"

"Of course, I'll bring back a copy," said Artemis. "Miss Lovelace will even sign it for you."

At last, Celeste's smile lit her eyes. "I would love that." But then her brow creased. "I hope it doesn't sound dreadful to say this, but your stories provide a much welcome respite from everything that's going on with Papa. I know he doesn't approve of your books, but I need them."

Artemis offered a reassuring smile. "It's not dreadful at all, and I know exactly what you mean. We all need a little diversion sometimes, and I, too, rely on a good book to help me escape from reality time and time again. I might even venture to say that the reason I took up writing in the first place was that it gave me a fantasy world of my own creation to run away to whenever life seemed too hard."

"I'm so glad you understand. Honestly, I don't know what I'd do without you."

To Artemis's amazement, Celeste leaned forward and placed a swift kiss upon her cheek. "Hurry back, won't you?" she said. "It's getting dark and it's horrid outside and we can't have you catching a cold. Papa needs you. And so do I."

With that utterly astonishing pronouncement, the duke's daughter stepped away and then hurried down the hall toward her own suite of rooms.

"Well, I never," murmured Artemis. Despite all the fear and uncertainty that seemed to be her constant companions, she felt her mouth curving in smile. And her heart glowed.

Celeste clearly loved her books, but maybe the girl—no, young woman—might possess a little bit of affection for her too.

A pleasant warmth still humming through her veins, Artemis turned, intending to head toward the main staircase, but then a soft creak behind her made her pause. Glancing over her shoulder, she saw that the jib door had swung open, and Miss Sharp was emerging from the deeply shadowed recess, her wide-as-a-church-bell skirts swaying with each smart, purposeful step she took. "May I have a word with you, Miss Jones?" she called.

Frowning, Artemis turned back. The governess's tone was frosty, her expression as hard as arctic ice, and a shiver of apprehension slid over Artemis. Nevertheless, she stayed her ground and said with relatively smooth politeness, "Of course, Miss Sharp. What can I do for you?"

"I know who you are," the governess fired at her without preamble. "And I know you gave Lady Celeste copies of your foul, poorly written books."

Oh, Beelzebub's ballocks. Artemis attempted to swallow past a boulder-sized lump of fear jamming her throat. "I–I don't know what you mean—" she began, but Miss Sharp cut her off with a slice of her hand.

"Don't even bother trying to lie to me. You can deny it all you like, but I overheard your conversation with Lady Celeste in her room at Ashburn Abbey. When she was ill and you gave her a pile of your wicked books to make her feel better. You might purport to be a forward-thinking, open-minded blue-stocking, but I *know* that you've been hiding the fact you're that vulgar author, Lydia Lovelace. Indeed, you confirmed it again mere moments ago."

Artemis's own temper flared. "And you were eavesdropping on a private conversation. Again. You seem to have made a habit of listening at keyholes, yet you have the nerve to accuse *me* of being vulgar."

Indignation flashed in Miss Sharp's eyes. "And it was a good thing that I did eavesdrop. Someone has to protect Lady Celeste from someone like you. A sinful woman who's invaded His Grace's home and infected his innocent daughter's mind with her vile books and even viler presence. To think that you were once a governess and a teacher at a young ladies' academy." Her mouth flattened with contempt. "You make me sick."

"If you've known all this for so long, why didn't you say anything sooner? To me, or to His Grace for that matter? Before we even quit Ashburn Abbey? You had days to expose my secret."

The governess glared at her through slitted lids. "I kept telling myself it wasn't my place to interfere. That I'd already created enough friction between Lady Celeste and her father when I first brought your hideous books to his attention weeks ago. But after hearing your exchange with Lady Celeste just now, I realize how deep your hooks have become embedded in her. How insidious your wicked influence. How much you've corrupted her mind. I'm certain it was your ridiculous books that put ideas in her head about love and romance and running away in search of an adventure in the first place. She never even looked at Antonio Moretti before then. But all of this, your sway over her, has to stop."

"What do you mean 'stop'?"

Miss Sharp advanced and poked a finger at Artemis's chest. "I want you gone from here. Out of her life and the duke's."

"You ask the impossible. I can't just abandon Lady Celeste and His Grace. Not now when he's fighting so hard for his life. It wouldn't be fair to either of them."

"And you expect far too much. For someone of your inferior station—with such a shocking profession and clearly no morals to speak of—to think that you could rise above all of that and become the next Duchess of Dartmoor, let alone the patroness of a young ladies' college, you must be stark-raving mad. You're not fit to empty the duke's chamber pot. In fact, you're no better than a street whore. Indeed, the way you've been carrying on with the duke behind closed doors…" Her mouth twisted with derision. "Don't think the rest of the staff haven't noticed. They might have remained tight-lipped about your wanton behavior, but I certainly wouldn't be doing *my* duty if I didn't try to protect Lady Celeste from your pernicious influence." She set her fisted hands on her hips and lifted her chin. "Call off your engagement and leave. At once. Or else."

"For goodness' sake. Speak plainly," Artemis snapped. "Or else what?"

"I'll go to Lord and Lady Northam and tell them everything. And His Grace when he is well enough. And your aunt, Lady Wagstaff. I'm sure she doesn't know. I might even go to the newspapers myself. Imagine the humiliating headlines. *Salacious Gothic Romantic Novelist's Identity Revealed.* Your reputation will be ruined forevermore. You will *never* be able to open your college."

"And in the process, you would also damage the reputation of the duke—your employer," Artemis fired back. "Do you really think that's such an astute move to make?"

"The scandal would be short lived, for him at least, and worth it to cut you out of his life and Lady Celeste's."

Artemis's hands curled into fists within the folds of her skirts. Outrage warred with her hard-to-restrain mulish streak along with a sizable dose of fear. She didn't want to capitulate, but it seemed that for the moment, she had little choice but to yield a fraction. The consequences would be dire if she didn't. She'd never survive a public scandal of such magnitude. All of her dreams would be shattered beyond repair. Ground to dust beneath the booted heel of a far-too-smug, sanctimonious governess.

"All right, Miss Sharp," she managed from between stiff lips. "I will remove myself from the environs of Dartmoor House. For now. But when I hear that His Grace is on the road to recovery, I will return and tell him myself that I am Lydia Lovelace, at which point, our engagement will undoubtedly end. What I *won't* do is leave a note and skulk away like some spineless thief in the night. His Grace deserves an explanation. To his face."

Miss Sharp studied her for one long moment. Her gaze was assessing, her eyes as hard as flint. "Very well," she said at last.

"And I will say goodbye to His Grace before I leave tonight."

The governess arched a haughty brow. "I don't think so."

"This is not negotiable. I care for him. Very much. If he succumbs to the infection—" Artemis's breath hitched. She swallowed, fighting to control her voice. To eliminate the telltale quaver. She would *not* cry in front of Miss Sharp. She would not give such a petty, vindictive, narrow-minded snitch the satisfaction. "You will afford me this opportunity to bid His Grace farewell. It might be my last chance."

Without waiting for the governess to reply, she pushed past her and returned to Dominic's room. Nurse Quincey, who was in the process of adjusting the bedclothes, looked up as soon as she entered. "Miss Jones. I hadn't expected you to return so quickly." Her incisive gaze narrowed. "Is everything all right?"

"I…" Artemis forced herself to smile as she approached the bed. "Yes. I simply wanted to see His Grace again before I left. I…" She drew a steadying breath and spouted the only lie she could think of that might be believed by the nurse, Lady Celeste, and the Northams. "I've just received word from my aunt in Berkshire that my sister is asking for me—she's not feeling particularly well after all of the recent hullabaloo about her in the newspapers—and so I need to quit Town for a few days. In light of that, would you mind if I spent a few moments alone with His Grace?"

The nurse offered her a kind smile. "Oh, I'm so sorry to hear that. And of course, I'll make myself scarce. Actually, I left my spectacles in my room, and I really can't function without them. This seems like the perfect opportunity to retrieve them."

As soon as the bedroom door shut behind the nurse, Artemis sank onto the mattress beside Dominic.

Her aching heart stumbled and faltered as her gaze traced over his beloved features. Despite the ravages of the fever and everything else he'd been through, his austere masculine beauty was in no way diminished. Not to her. Apart from the mottled bruising about the healing gash on his forehead and the purple shadows beneath the sweep of his lashes, his countenance was as pale as marble. Indeed, he lay so still underneath the bedclothes that he seemed almost lifeless, like the statue of a Greek god or the stone effigy upon a knight's tomb. Infinitely noble and handsome yet disconnected and somehow otherworldly.

She had to remind herself that it was just the strong opiate he'd taken an hour ago that made him appear so. That if she slid her hand beneath the covers, he would still feel warm to the touch and his heart would beat steadily against her palm. His chest would rise and fall with each breath he took.

With a shaky sigh, she gently took one of his limp hands, cradling it between hers. She didn't even bother to dash away her tears as her fingertips traced the patterns of Dominic's knuckles and the veins on his palm. She couldn't bear to leave him, but she must. Her whole future hung in the balance. The fact that Miss Sharp had forced Artemis to make such an agonizing choice at this juncture—stay and face public ruination, or go and risk never seeing the love of her life ever again—was both heartless and cruel in the extreme. And it wasn't just her reputation that would be destroyed. Her aunt's and Phoebe's would be too. And Phoebe had already suffered enough.

But Artemis had no power to bargain here. Not one whit. The self-righteous governess held all of the cards. As much as she was loath to do so, Artemis must say goodbye to Dominic, for now, or she would lose everything.

"I'm afraid I have to bid you adieu, my darling," she murmured thickly. "But I pray that it's only for a little while. Just until you're out of the woods, so to speak."

Another sigh escaped her; the laudanum was both a blessing and a curse. It took away Dominic's pain and reduced his fever, but right at this moment, Artemis wished he could hear her next words. "You were right, you know," she continued. "This engagement *is* real. But I've been such a coward, lying to myself and to you. Not only have I denied how I feel about you for far too long, but I've also been hiding who I really am. When you are awake and aware and out of danger, I promise you that I will profess all."

She lifted his hand to her lips and kissed it. Her throat was so clogged with emotion, her voice emerged as a fractured croak as she whispered, "And I *know* that you will get better, my darling Dominic. You must. Because I want you to hear me say that I love you. And I want you to know that I will marry you, and that I yearn to give you a son and heir...if you'll still have me after you learn the truth."

She kissed Dominic's hand once more, then laid it carefully on the counterpane. She placed a kiss on her fingertips and then touched them to his lips. "Good night, my love," she whispered. "I will not say farewell because this is not goodbye."

It can't be. It mustn't *be.*

Gathering the last remnants of her disintegrating will around her, Artemis forced herself to rise and quit the room. She was leaving Dominic in good hands, she told herself as she swallowed her tears and repaired to the library to dash off a quick note to Horatia. He would survive this. Berkshire was not so far away—it was but an hour and a quarter's journey on the train. She was certain Horatia would send word if Dominic took a turn for the worse.

She just had to keep Miss Rosalind Sharp happy for a few days. And then one way or another, everything would be resolved.

Chapter Thirty

DOMINIC PRIED HIS HEAVY LIDS OPEN WITH WHAT FELT LIKE a Herculean effort and attempted to focus on his dimly lit bed-chamber. His eyes felt gritty, his vision was blurry, but for once, his head wasn't throbbing, and his body didn't feel like it was ablaze and stretched to breaking point on a torturer's rack.

He swallowed, his mouth dryer than the ashes gathered at the bottom of the grate. "Artemis…" he rasped, turning his head this way, then that. He could have sworn she'd been here not that long ago, holding his hand, stroking his brow. Whispering soothing words in his ear. His heart kicked at the memory of her professing that she loved him.

Or had that all been a fever dream? Wishful thinking on his part?

He exhaled shakily, then pinched the bridge of his nose. He had no idea how long he'd lain in this bed, insensible to his surroundings. Between the delirium, the pain, and what seemed like an eternity of drug-induced sleep that was fathoms deep, he'd lost all sense of time. Whether it was day or night or indeed, how long it had been since he'd been shot. It could have been a few days, a week, or a millennium.

Another memory stirred and flickered like a tiny lick of flame. He remembered the alleyway off Duke Street. How cold it had been. His breath frosting in the air. The thick rolling fog. The sharp bite of whisky on his tongue and the resounding chime of a church tower clock. The red doorway of the Firebrand Club. But then the image in his mind fizzled away to nothing, floating away like a tendril of smoke from a snuffed-out candle.

Perhaps that wisp of a memory had all been a dream too.

Or a nightmare.

He groaned with frustration and then struggled to push himself up into a sitting position against the pillows. The movement sent a bolt of pain through his wounded shoulder and a hiss escaped him. And then all of a sudden he felt a gentle hand at his back. A cool palm pressed against his forehead.

"Dominic. You're awake. And your fever's broken. Thank God."

Dominic squinted up into the face hovering above him. "Horatia," he croaked. "I think you might be right."

She beamed. "I'm so, so relieved. You have no idea how worried—" Her voice cracked and then she shook her head. "Here, let me help you to sit up. You must be parched."

"I am." After he gratefully accepted a few sips of water from a tumbler, his unsteady gaze shifted about the room again. There was a fire and several low-burning lamps, but the curtains were drawn. He couldn't make out the face of the mantel clock. "What time is it?" he asked. "Is Artemis about? I seem to recall she was here…"

Horatia's lips pulled tight. "It's nearly half-past one in the morning," she said. "And Artemis was here, but I'm afraid… She had to leave. Two days ago. She's…she's at her aunt's house in Berkshire. Apparently, her sister needed her. I assumed the matter was urgent because she only left me a hastily scrawled note. But Nurse Quincey, who saw her briefly before she departed, mentioned that she seemed quite upset and was clearly reluctant to leave you."

She'd been reluctant to leave him... Even so, a sliver of acute disappointment pierced Dominic's chest at the knowledge that Artemis wasn't actually here. "Oh..." He drew a breath. "Did she say when she'd return?"

"No." Horatia sat on the bed next to him. "But in the days before she left, she was devoted to you. She barely left your side. She worked even harder than Nurse Quincey. Although I have wondered if something happened—something we don't know about—and if the need to visit her sister was merely a convenient excuse."

Dominic's gaze met Horatia's. Concern began to simmer in his blood. "Do you have any idea what?"

His sister shook her head. "None at all." She sighed. "In any case, I think it might be a good idea to send word to her in the morning to let her know you're on the mend. I'm sure she's been worried sick, and no doubt she'll want to return as soon as she is able."

"Yes..." Dominic reached for the tumbler of water again. It wouldn't do to work himself into a lather, stewing needlessly about Artemis when she *was* probably safe and sound in Berkshire with her family. There was no reason to think otherwise. Given his own recent ordeal, he supposed it was only natural that he'd jump to wild conclusions and start at shadows.

Even so, something was niggling him. Pricking and scratching like a burr in his mind. Something to do with Phoebe Jones and the night he was shot. He'd seen Artemis—made desperate love to her like it was his last night on earth. And then he'd gone looking for Gascoyne to call him to account.

To call him out.

Gascoyne. Bloody Gascoyne.

White-hot anger blazed through Dominic's veins and his

fingers tightened around the tumbler. Indeed, his hand shook so much, he splashed water onto the counterpane.

Gascoyne had called him a pathetic dog and had pulled a pistol on him. Had pressed the muzzle against his chest. They'd struggled and then...

He looked at Horatia. "Gascoyne. It was Gascoyne who tried to kill me," he said. "I remember everything. Every last detail."

"Oh my God." Horatia's face blanched. "I'll send word to Scotland Yard immediately. I'm certain Detective Lawrence will want to speak with you as soon as possible." Her brow dipped into a frown. "If you're up to it, that is."

"I am," Dominic said grimly. Of course, he would have liked nothing more than to go and pay a visit to Gascoyne himself, right now, this minute, but he was far too weak. His limbs felt like they were weighted with lead. He could barely sit up or lift a glass to his mouth. And who knew what Gascoyne would do if confronted again. Cornered dogs did tend to go on the attack.

The man was clearly unhinged, with an unquenchable thirst for vengeance. It wasn't beyond the realms of possibility that he could try to finish the job he'd started in a dark, filthy alley.

No, it would be beyond foolish to tackle Gascoyne again on his own. For now, Dominic would just have to trust in Scotland Yard and the legal system to deal with the cur effectively.

———

"We'll catch him, Your Grace. Mark my words." Thus proclaimed Detective John Lawrence before he departed Dominic's bedchamber with a grim expression and a determined stride.

As the door shut, Dominic sighed heavily and sank back against the pillows. He was exhausted but satisfied that the Scotland Yard detective would bring Gascoyne to justice.

Lawrence's plan was to arrest Gascoyne straightaway. He was going to send men to the viscount's town house, his usual clubs, and even his current mistress's lodgings, as it was Gascoyne's habit to carouse well into the early hours. All going well, the viscount would be in custody before the sun rose.

Even though Dominic felt as though he'd been hit by a train, his mind was so abuzz, he was unable to sleep and so he dragged himself from bed at dawn. With his valet's assistance, he washed, shaved, and donned a banyan, and then ate his first proper meal in days at a table in his sitting room—a coddled egg and toast washed down with a cup of tea. Nurse Quincey wouldn't let him have more than that, claiming his stomach might reject anything more substantial.

He'd just finished dictating a telegram to Morton— Dominic wanted to let Artemis know he was out of danger and that Gascoyne would be apprehended—when Dr. Hamilton arrived at seven o'clock to check on him.

"While you certainly seem to be on the road to making a full recovery, Your Grace, you mustn't overtax yourself," the doctor warned as he tucked his stethoscope into his medical bag. "I prescribe plenty of bedrest and frequent but light meals for the moment. And it might pay to wear your arm in a sling to support your injured shoulder—at least for a week or two. I'll also have Nurse Quincey continue to apply chlorinated lime to keep the healing wound free of purulence. All going well, I'll remove the stitches in a few days."

"Excellent. I can't thank you enough, Doctor," said Dominic with heartfelt sincerity. "You've saved my life."

However, as soon as he bid the good doctor farewell, Dominic rang for his valet a second time. Bedrest be damned. He was still extraordinarily restless and no doubt he had a thousand things piled up on his desk that required his attention. Besides, perhaps a bit of light paperwork would keep his mind off Gascoyne and, of course, how much he missed Artemis.

Although it felt like an enormous effort, he added a shirt, shoes, trousers, and a sling to his "ensemble" and then descended to Dartmoor House's library on legs that felt as unsteady as a newborn foal's. By the time he collapsed into the chair behind his desk, he was sweating and slightly nauseous, but he was certain he was no longer feverish. He'd simply over-exerted himself. He'd just rung for a pot of tea and had settled in to tackle a pile of correspondence when Miss Sharp stepped into the library, a bundle of books in her arms.

Upon seeing Dominic, she halted abruptly and promptly blushed. "Your Grace, I'm so happy to see you up and about. We've all been so worried."

"Thank you," he began but got no further because Morton poked his head around the door.

"Ah, Your Grace, my apologies for the interruption, but I wanted to inform you that one of Detective Lawrence's consta-bles delivered a message. Apparently the Detective Inspector will return at 10:00 a.m., or thereabouts, to let you know how things are progressing."

Dominic frowned as a frisson of unease traveled down his spine. He'd hoped for news about Gascoyne's arrest sooner than that. He prayed that nothing had gone wrong. Tamping down his undoubtedly needless apprehension, he said, "Before you go, Morton, I trust that you managed to get that telegram off to Miss Jones?"

"Yes, I did, Your Grace."

"The moment she replies, let me know."

"At once, Your Grace. Is there anything else?"

"No, that will be all."

The door closed behind Morton and then Miss Sharp ventured closer to the desk. The flush still hadn't left her cheeks. "It's such a shame Miss Jones had to go," she said quietly. "I'm not one to listen to rumors, but I heard it had something to do with her sister and that awful article that appeared in *the London Tatler*..." Her words trailed off and then her mouth slid into a coy smile. "Goodness. What on earth am I saying, Your Grace? In any event, I hope it's nothing too serious."

Something about the young woman's expression—a sly look in her eye—and a slight note of insincerity in her voice made Dominic frown. Was the governess really fishing for gossip about Artemis and Phoebe Jones? Would she truly be that impudent and, quite frankly, foolish? And then another peculiar thought entered his mind. Had Miss Sharp taken a disliking to his fiancée? And if she had, why?

"Yes," he said carefully, watching the woman's face for further signs of disingenuity. "I hope it's nothing serious either." Wanting to change the subject—Artemis's situation was none of the governess's business—he added, "I know it's early, but do you know if Celeste has risen yet? I should like to see her. And I'm sure she'd like to see me."

"Oh, I'm not certain. But as soon as I return to her rooms, I'll check." She adjusted her hold on the books in her arms, and Dominic had further cause to frown when he glimpsed several of the titles. *Lady Violetta and the Vengeful Vampyre* was uppermost. "You've taken to reading Lydia Lovelace's books, Miss Sharp," he observed.

The blush staining the young woman's cheeks was now the same deep-red hue as the leather blotter on his desk. "Oh no. No, I haven't. Not me, Your Grace. I would never read anything so dreadful. I'm disposing of them. Well, not disposing of them exactly because they're not mine… I thought to hide them in the shelves somewhere. Behind something obscure like Homer's *The Iliad*. For Lady Celeste's sake."

"I see… But where did they come from? I thought you'd confiscated all of Celeste's copies weeks ago."

A strange look crossed the governess's face. It could have passed for regret but for a pernicious twinkle in her hazel eyes. "I'm afraid to say that they belong to Miss Jones, Your Grace. And I'm so, so sorry that you had to find out about her reading preferences this way. It must come as quite a shock. If I'd had any inkling you were in here, I wouldn't have barged in like this—"

He cut her off. Miss Sharp's manner was really rankling him now. "What makes you think that I don't already know about my fiancée's 'reading preferences'?" he asked coldly. "Unlike Celeste, she is a grown woman and quite free to read whatever she pleases, even if I don't share her taste in literature."

"Oh…" The governess's blush faded and her grip tightened around the books.

"Leave them here." He nodded curtly at the desk.

"Of course." She placed the pile on one bare corner, then stepped back, clasping her hands primly at her waist as though she were bracing for her knuckles to be rapped.

"And Miss Sharp," he continued, "I would remind you that someone in your position shouldn't take it upon yourself to dispose of *anything* that belongs to my fiancée. And you certainly shouldn't spread gossip about her."

"Yes, yes of course," she murmured, her eyes cast downward. "You're right. My sincerest apologies. It's just… Even though it's not my place and I shouldn't interfere…and…I really don't want to say anything that might cause further trouble..." She lifted her gaze briefly before it dropped to the floor again. "I'm loath to make an unwarranted accusation, but—"

Dominic's irritation flared into full-blown exasperation. "An accusation? About Miss Jones? What the devil are you talking about?"

"I'm...I'm so sorry, Your Grace," stammered the governess. "It's really none of my business. I've said far too much already. I'll fetch Lady Celeste, shall I?" Then without waiting for his reply, she scurried away, leaving Dominic floundering in a sea of frustrated bafflement.

Chapter Thirty-One

Highfield Hall, Berkshire

"YESTERDAY EVENING'S NEWSPAPERS HAVE ARRIVED AT long last," said Aunt Roberta as Artemis entered the fussily furnished morning room of Highfield Hall. Her aunt, enthroned upon a Queen Anne dining chair with her beloved Bertie on her lap, put down her teacup and waved a beringed hand toward a stack of broadsheets at the end of the table. "I thought you would want to know," she added in a surprisingly gentle tone.

"Thank you." It had been two whole days and nights since Artemis had left London, and not a moment passed without her thinking about Dominic and wondering how he was faring. Had his fever abated? Had he asked for her? Did Celeste and the Northams believe the reason she'd given for her sudden departure?

Of course, she was sure Horatia or her husband would have sent word if Dominic's condition had deteriorated. Unless they were angry with her because Miss Sharp had already gone to them and disclosed her authorial identity, and now they refused to have anything to do with her...

There was no way to tell, so in the absence of any messages from London, Artemis had taken to scanning all of the broadsheets both morning and night for any news about Dominic, just in case the worst had happened and no one had wanted to inform her.

She picked up the papers and claimed a cushioned window seat. It promised to be a fair spring day—there was only a hint of clouds on the horizon—but the delightfully bucolic view of Highfield's pristine grounds set against a backdrop of wooded rolling countryside held little interest for Artemis as she carefully perused all of the newspapers from front to back.

There was nothing about the Duke of Dartmoor or his fiancée, or her alter ego Lydia Lovelace, for that matter. Which in many ways was a relief, but also entirely frustrating. Being kept in the dark about Dominic's condition was almost too much for her heart to bear.

Part of her—the all-too-reckless part—wanted nothing more than to throw caution to the wind and catch the next train back to London. How dare Rosalind Sharp hold her to ransom? It was unfair and malicious, and she had no right. But there was no doubt in Artemis's mind that the woman would carry out her threat to expose her if she did return to spend endless hours beside Dominic's sickbed. She couldn't risk it, no matter how much she yearned to return to Dartmoor House.

Could she?

Her gaze wandered to her aunt's rose garden, but the bright blooms became as hazy as a watercolor as her eyes filled with tears. She suddenly longed for a different view—one of the desolate, windswept moors and gnarled woods that surrounded Ashburn Abbey. Most of all, she longed for Dominic. For his strong arms about her, the scent of his cologne. The warmth of his breath against her ear as he whispered low, soft words that made her pulse race and her toes curl. The sound of his laughter, rich and deep, when she said something that amused him.

She wiped away a tear that had slipped onto her cheek, and

when she looked up, it was to find that her aunt was studying her.

"You love him, don't you?" observed her aunt in the softest, kindest voice that Artemis had ever heard; she thought she might lose all control and dissolve into a weeping mess right then and there.

Somehow, she swallowed past the ache in her throat and murmured, "Yes. I do."

"Then why are you here?"

"I…" Artemis briefly contemplated then discarded the idea of confessing all to her aunt. She might be displaying uncharacteristic sympathy, but if she learned about the sort of books Artemis wrote, that sympathy might dry up faster than a drop of water beneath the Sahara sun in midsummer. So she settled on saying. "I'm afraid it's rather complicated."

Her aunt nodded knowingly. "It always is, especially for someone as complicated as you, my gel. I'd venture to say that in many respects, you're a lot like your mother. Too smart for your own good and far too bold and passionate. And stubborn."

Artemis abandoned the window seat and settled herself upon a chair near her aunt. Aunt Roberta had never once spoken about her younger sister, Clara, and Artemis was intrigued. "I'm definitely all of those things," she agreed. "Actually…I've never really understood why my mother married someone like my father. She was so lively, at least when I was young, and he was always so serious and self-righteous. It was obvious to me, even when I was a child, that they didn't suit."

"No," said Aunt Roberta, feeding Bertie a discarded corner of toast dripping with butter and egg yolk. "They didn't." She paused, but only for a moment. "Your mother *had* to marry, if you take my meaning. And because beggars can't be choosers and Obadiah Jones made an offer…"

"My mother was pregnant with me before she wed?"

"Yes. She was." Her aunt's gaze was unflinching as she added, "And not from Obadiah Jones but another man."

Oh… Artemis inhaled a fortifying breath as so many puzzle pieces of her disordered upbringing fell into place in her mind. She was ostensibly a bastard. Another man's by-blow. "Well," she said at last, "that explains why my father never seemed to warm to me. It must have been difficult for him to raise another man's child. Did…did he know my mother was pregnant when he proposed?"

Aunt Roberta wiped her fingers on a linen napkin. "Yes, I believe he did. He was the vicar in our village and had been smitten with Clara for some time, even before she had her London Season. Like you, she was quite gorgeous with her flaming-red hair and siren's smile. But Obadiah couldn't seem to see past her looks and that she would never be suited to the life of a village vicar's wife. When Clara discovered she was in the family way, so to speak, and she hadn't a fiancé, he was more than ready to jump in and play her knight in shining armor."

Artemis nodded. "Do you know who my actual father is, then?"

Aunt Roberta sniffed. "Yes. Your mother confided the truth to me, just after your birth. Your father was a rakehell. And quite the Corinthian to boot. They fell in love during her one and only Season—indeed, everyone expected him to issue a proposal, including me—but then the idiot, who was fond of a wager by all accounts, went and got himself killed in a curricle race. Lord Roger Blakeney was his name. The second son of the Marquess of Sudley."

Artemis blinked in astonishment. Her grandfather was the Marquess of Sudley? Her real father had been the son of a nobleman?

Not that it matters now, she told herself. Indeed, if Obadiah Jones hadn't done the honorable thing, she'd have been labeled baseborn her entire life. Or perhaps her mother would have "gone abroad" and then Artemis would have been adopted out to some distant relative or, worse, placed in an orphanage. Clara and Roberta's parents had hailed from the ranks of the landed gentry, and Artemis had always been led to believe they'd been comfortably well-off. But after Clara's marriage to Obadiah, it appeared that her parents had cut ties with their daughter. Even though she'd wed, she was clearly a disappointment to them and no doubt Artemis was a source of shame. She might bear the surname Jones, but she was obviously still tainted by the stain of illegitimacy.

It suddenly occurred to Artemis that despite Roberta's meddling when it came to her and Phoebe, she'd always supported Clara and she'd never abandoned her nieces. Artemis looked at her aunt with new eyes.

"It's a lot to take in," Artemis said at length. "I suppose it explains so many things about my parents and why I am the way that I am."

Aunt Roberta's smile was wry. "And now I'm sure you understand why I've been so insistent that both you and Phoebe wed. Especially you, given your rebellious streak. I didn't want you to suffer the same fate your mother had—marrying a man she didn't love because she had to. Or worse, becoming an unwed mother."

"Then why didn't you listen to me when Lord Gascoyne began to court Phoebe?" asked Artemis. "I warned you that he was a despicable cad and that his intentions were not honorable."

A look of remorse crossed Aunt Roberta's face. "Yes, it was a mistake on my part," she said. "A terrible lapse of judgment. I suppose it was a combination of factors. First of all, I thought your fiancé's poor opinion of Lord Gascoyne had influenced yours. And yes, I know, Gascoyne had seduced you all those years ago, but it takes two to dance the polka, and part of me believed that you were also to blame. In my eyes, you'd gone looking for trouble, just like you'd always done in your youth.

"Phoebe, on the other hand, has always been cautious, and Lord Gascoyne appeared to be openly courting her, like a gentleman should, not running off into the shadows with her. Well, not at first." Her aunt's expression changed, became wistful. "I'd never seen her so happy, and I didn't want to spoil her chance to find a love match, not when I'd been forcing her to wait for her Season for so long."

Aunt Roberta sighed heavily. Her eyes were filled with sadness, perhaps even regret as she continued, "I know you think ill of me, Artemis, but I'm really not that much of a tyrant. I've been a monumental fool, and I'm ashamed of my role in Phoebe's ruination. And I'm ashamed about how I've treated you. Not only did I dismiss your warnings about Gascoyne because my pride and arrogance made me think I knew better, but I underestimated how manipulative he could be. I hope you'll accept my heartfelt apology for doubting you."

"I..." Artemis swallowed to clear her throat. "I will admit that I'm more than a little flabbergasted by all of your disclosures and your apology. But yes, I will accept it, Aunt Roberta. And gladly. There has been discord between us for far too long. I would like it to end."

Her aunt inclined her head, and for a fleeting moment, her eyes seemed suspiciously bright. "Thank you, my dear gel. You might deny it, but I think you are a romantic soul. And even though I don't know what happened in London to make you leave, I hope that you will be able to return to your fiancé's side sooner rather than later. I'm sure that he needs you. More than your sister does at present. Whatever happens, I will take care of her."

Artemis smiled. "I know you will. Speaking of my sister, I should go and check on her. If the weather stays fine, perhaps I can coax her to take a turn about the gardens."

"That sounds like a capital idea," said Aunt Roberta. "I'm sure a bit of sunshine would do her the world of good."

Since Artemis had arrived at Highfield, Phoebe had rarely emerged from her bedroom. She'd taken to solitary pursuits, reading or sewing or pressing flowers, and any food that was sent up came back barely touched. Artemis was terribly worried about her.

Upon entering Phoebe's room, Artemis found her sister still curled up in bed in her nightgown. But she was smiling broadly.

"Good news, Artemis. My courses have arrived," she announced in a loud whisper as though one must never ever speak of normal things like menstruation, even in one's bed-chamber in front of one's sister or lady's maid.

Nevertheless, Artemis rushed to Phoebe and embraced her. "Oh, I'm so glad and relieved for you," she said. And she meant it.

"Me too," said Phoebe. The light had returned to her soft brown eyes. "My reputation might still be tarnished, but at least I've escaped from this business with Gascoyne relatively unscathed. And who knows, perhaps in time I might find a decent man. Someone like your darling duke who won't give a fig about my past."

"Perhaps you will. In fact, I'm sure of it." Artemis sat upon the bed and stroked a tangled strand of hair away from her sister's cheek. "I'm glad your opinion of Dominic has changed."

"It has. If you think he's a good man, he must be. You've always been an exceptional judge of character, Artemis. I shouldn't have doubted you." A line appeared between Phoebe's brows. "I've been so caught up in my own woes that I haven't thought to ask how the duke is. And why you're here and not in London. Aunt Roberta told me he'd been attacked and wounded in the street. You must be so worried about him."

"Yes…I am. But I'm sure he's improving by now," Artemis said with false brightness. "I'm certain his sister would have sent word if he was in any imminent danger."

"You should find out for yourself," said Phoebe. Her frown deepened. "Unless there's something you're not telling me." She clasped Artemis's arm. "What's wrong? What's happened? After all we've been through, you can share anything with me. You know that, don't you?"

Artemis fiddled with the tassels on one of her sister's bed cushions. "It's complicated," she said after a brief pause. Even to her own ears, her reason had begun to sound more like a feeble excuse.

"You love him," said Phoebe gently. "And if he loves you too, which I suspect he does, it's rather simple really. Love is what matters, nothing else. You should be with him."

"You're right," said Artemis. But then Rosalind Sharp's ugly words passed through her mind.

Imagine the humiliating headlines. Salacious Gothic Romantic Novelist's Identity Revealed. *Your reputation will be ruined forevermore. You will never be able to open your women's academic college.*

Even if Dominic didn't care that she was Lydia Lovelace, there was no telling what Miss Sharp would do.

There was only one way to found out.

Artemis gave Phoebe another hug. "It looks like I have some packing to do," she said. According to the mantel clock, it was only eight o'clock, so she'd easily make it to Pangbourne Station to catch the first train to London which departed at ten. There wasn't a reason in the world stopping her.

She simply had to be brave.

Chapter Thirty-Two

EVEN THOUGH DOMINIC'S CONVERSATION WITH MISS Sharp had been nothing but peculiar, the governess had at least done as he'd asked and had passed on his message to Celeste.

"Papa," she cried, dashing across the library to where he'd installed himself upon a settee. "I'm so, so relieved you're going to be all right."

Her exuberant hug made Dominic gasp and flinch, but he didn't mind. "I am," he said, drawing back to smile at her ecstatic face. "And I have no doubt at all that your frequent visits to my room to read to me helped."

"You remember that?"

"Bits and pieces. To be honest, my memories are rather hazy, but you read from Charlotte Brontë's *Jane Eyre*, did you not?"

"Yes. I did." Her smile was brighter than a midsummer sunrise as she settled herself into the chair beside his. "Artemis wasn't sure if you could hear me after you'd taken a dose of laudanum, but I was certain you could. Well, I *hoped* that you could." A shadow crossed Celeste's countenance as she added, "You've probably heard that she isn't here."

Dominic grimaced. "Horatia mentioned she had to see her sister. That it was an urgent matter."

"Yes…" A furrow etched itself between Celeste's fine black brows. "I'll admit I was surprised by the way she left so suddenly, without really saying goodbye. And while it's only been a few days since she quit Town, I've come to realize that I miss her." She offered him a smile that was touched by melancholy. "I'm sure you miss her even more. It must have been a shock to find out she wasn't here when you woke up."

Dominic studied her for a moment. The sense that something was amiss still nagged at him but he couldn't quite put his finger on it. "I can't deny that I'm disappointed. But you'll be pleased to hear that I've already sent a telegram letting Artemis know my fever has broken. With any luck"—he summoned a smile—"she'll return soon. Hopefully today."

Celeste's smile brightened. "I'm sure she will. How could she not?"

Dominic's answering smile was less certain. That worrisome niggle returned. It was like a pebble in his shoe or a dog nipping at his heels. Why *had* Artemis left so unexpectedly? Of course, her aunt or sister *could* have simply sent a message entreating her to come to Berkshire, at once. Artemis loved Phoebe and would do anything for her.

But then, what if there *was* another plausible explanation for Artemis's sudden departure? One closer to home...

His mind returned to his odd conversation with Miss Sharp a short time ago. Of all the innuendos and evasion. And the not-so-subtle insinuation suggesting Artemis had done something wrong beyond having a taste for questionable literature. How had Miss Sharp framed it? *I'm loath to make an unwarranted accusation...*

He caught his daughter's gaze. "When and where did you last see Artemis?"

Celeste's brow creased in thought. "Two nights ago. In the hall outside your rooms. We'd been talking about how we'd have dinner together after she returned from her aunt's town house. She was going to pick up a few things—fresh clothes I expect—and she also promised to bring back one of her books. A signed copy of *Lady Sophia and the Seduc—*"

Dominic frowned as a deep blush spread across Celeste's cheeks. "*Lady Sophia and the Seductive Sorcerer*? By Lydia Lovelace?"

Celeste's throat bobbed in a nervous swallow. "I… Yes, that's the one."

"I see… Perhaps you should check the books on my desk to see if it's there," he said, though he knew that particular novel wasn't. He watched Celeste's face closely as her gaze landed on the small pile. How her eyes widened in horror.

"Where…where did they come from?" she whispered.

Dominic raised a brow. "Miss Sharp brought them in earlier. She told me they belong to Artemis."

Celeste's nod was barely perceptible. "They do."

Dominic narrowed his gaze as another thought occurred to him. "Is there anything you wish to tell me, Celeste? About the books *you've* been reading lately? While I don't have a problem with my fiancée reading anything penned by Lydia Lovelace, you know exactly how I feel about *you* reading them."

"I'm sorry, Papa, but…" Celeste inhaled a shaky breath. "Yes, I have been reading them…but only because I've been so unhappy and anxious and Artemis's books—I mean, Lydia Lovelace's books—bring me such solace. They're gripping and romantic and wonderful and take me to another time and place. They make me forget all of my worries." She lifted her chin. "I don't wish to create discord between us, especially after everything that you've been through, but I happen to adore Miss Lovelace's books and nothing you can say or do will stop me from feeling that way. Ever."

Discord. There'd been enough of that between him and Celeste. And far too much sorrow and heartbreak. Enough to last a lifetime. Dominic blew out a sigh. "I don't want us to be continuously at loggerheads either," he said gently. "And I do understand how difficult things have been for you of late. How lonely you've been."

"I've been far less lonely since Artemis entered our lives. And I really do hope that you can forgive her for lending me some of Lydia Lovelace's books. Because when all is said and done, they're just books, Papa. Books that are really not as salacious as you and Miss Sharp seem to think they are. In fact"—Celeste shifted forward on her seat, her face alight with eagerness—"you should read one. Properly. Not just skim through it, looking for all of the so-called naughty bits, but from cover to cover."

"Perhaps I should," Dominic said wearily, adjusting his position on the settee to take the strain off his wounded shoulder. Even though Artemis was intelligent and discerning when it came to other matters, he was suddenly ashamed that he'd continuously dismissed her favorite books as a load of tripe after only the most cursory of inspections. He'd believed Miss Sharp's assessment over his fiancée's. Yes, perhaps it was time to put his own preconceived notions aside about what constituted a good book and trust Artemis's taste in literature too. And his daughter's.

"Honestly, I'm certain you'd enjoy them," said Celeste, her eyes glowing with enthusiasm. "They're all exceptionally well written. Artemis is a very talented auth—" As she broke off for a second time, her whole face turned a blazing shade of crimson.

"A very talented what, Celeste?" Dominic pinned his daughter with a hard look. Suspicion prickling along every nerve, he leaned forward. "An author? Are you telling me that Artemis Jones—*my* Artemis—is really Lydia Lovelace?"

Tears shimmered in Celeste's eyes. "Yes," she said after a tense-as-a-bowstring pause. "I–I found out by accident. When we were all at Ashburn Abbey. Her latest manuscript, *Lady Mirabella and the Midnight Monk*, was caught up in the pile of books she gave to me to cheer me up and, well, it wasn't hard to put two and two together. But I promised Artemis that I wouldn't reveal her secret—hardly anyone else knows at all— and now I've been an unthinking idiot, blathering on about how much I love her books, and in the process, I've betrayed her." She reached out and grasped his forearm. "Please, Papa. Please don't be angry with Artemis. If you're going to be angry with anyone, it should be with me for reading forbidden books behind your back."

Dominic dragged a hand down his face. He suddenly felt exhausted beyond measure. Saddened and chastened. He covered his daughter's hand with his and gave it a reassuring squeeze. "I'm not angry with you, Celeste. Not after everything that's happened." He offered her a small smile. "After the near-miss that I've just had, it rather puts things into perspective. About what's important in life and what isn't. I hate to think that you see me as some sort of terrible ogre or tyrant. A man to fear. And I'm beginning to wonder if my fiancée sees me in the same way."

"Oh, Papa, you're not an ogre, or any kind of monster for that matter, and I'm sure Artemis doesn't think that either. I swear she loves you very much. She rarely left your side. Aunt Horatia told me that she was so worried about you, she barely ate or slept for days."

Dominic's gaze wandered to the window. The curtains had

been pulled back and a wash of pale morning light spilled over his desk, over Artemis's books, illuminating the embossed gold lettering of the titles. If he closed his eyes, he knew he would be able to hear Artemis whispering how much she loved him. That he had to live. That he couldn't die. That she wouldn't let him...

But she'd kept a secret from him. *A significant secret.*

One that could be used against her.

He caught Celeste's eye. "You said that hardly anyone knows about Artemis's clandestine writing career. But could someone else have found out? Someone like Miss Sharp?"

"Perhaps..." Celeste worried at her lower lip. "If she overheard our conversations... The first time, Artemis and I were in my bedroom at Ashburn and Miss Sharp was next door in the sitting room, so she might have listened in. Our second conversation, as I mentioned before, took place in the hall outside your rooms. But I didn't think there was anyone else around. Well, I did notice a pair of footmen lighting the lamps, but then they left."

"Via the jib door to the servants' stairs near my suite?"

"Yes." Celeste's eyes widened. "You don't really think that Miss Sharp eavesdropped on us, do you? And then threatened Artemis in some way?"

"I'm not sure, but I'd certainly like to find out," said Dominic. "Your governess would know that a secret like that could do irreparable damage to Artemis's reputation if it got out."

"And we both know she disapproves of Lydia Lovelace's books," added Celeste. She made a moue of displeasure. "I've always had the feeling she doesn't particularly like Artemis either. That she sees her as some sort of rival. Perhaps it's because they're both teachers. Miss Sharp seemed quite put out when you first asked Artemis to talk to me about my academic interests."

Guilt sparked in Dominic's chest at the thought that he might have inadvertently put Artemis in an awkward situation that had somehow spiraled into something much worse. "Perhaps," he agreed. He'd certainly noticed Miss Sharp's not-so-subtle digs at his fiancée this morning. "But I think there's only one way to find out for sure. My dearest daughter, when you see Miss Sharp, would you mind sending her to the library? I think it's about time we had a frank conversation about what she may or may not know about Lydia Lovelace."

After Celeste quit the library, Dominic repaired to his desk and picked up *Lady Violetta and the Vengeful Vampyre*. To think that all this time, Artemis had been hiding the fact she was a Gothic romance author from him.

She must have feared that he would think less of her, perhaps even be angry with her. Or worse, that he'd refuse to provide the funding for her academic college because she wrote books containing salacious content. While Celeste's disclosure had certainly been a surprise, he couldn't say he was overly shocked. It would explain why Artemis had a penchant for using phrases peculiar to her own books as curses. And why she was such a staunch defender of the genre she loved so much.

Once upon a time, he would have been unhappy with Artemis for keeping such a secret from him, but now…now he was just ashamed that she hadn't felt he was on her side. That she couldn't see that he cared about her enough or could confide in him.

It wouldn't be long before he remedied that situation. It was about time Artemis knew exactly how he felt about her.

But first things first. He opened Lady Violetta's story and

began to read, properly, as Celeste had asked him to. By the end of the first chapter, he was thoroughly engrossed and barely noticed when the coffee he'd rung for earlier arrived. He was just beginning the third intriguing chapter when there was another interruption. A timid rap on the library door heralded the arrival of Miss Sharp.

With a reluctant sigh, he closed Artemis's book and eyed his fiancée's apparent rival as she entered the room. "Miss Sharp," he said, beckoning her closer to the desk. "There's a matter of some import that I'd like to discuss with you."

"Oh… Yes of course, Your Grace," she said, her manner grave yet as timid as a schoolgirl's as she approached. "I hope everything is all right…"

"Not really," he said with an exaggerated sigh. "As you know, I'm more than a bit disgruntled to learn that my fiancée isn't here. I can't help dwelling on the fact that she quit Town so suddenly and with barely a word to anyone. It's disappointing indeed." He drummed his fingers on the cover of *Lady Violetta and the Vengeful Vampyre*. "It's almost as though she *had* to leave…" He paused and aimed a narrow-eyed look at the governess. "You wouldn't happen to know anything about that, would you, Miss Sharp? Because when you said you didn't want to make an unwarranted accusation, I did wonder if you had any pertinent intelligence that could shed some light on the matter…"

A flaming-red blush crawled up the governess's neck to her face, setting her whole countenance ablaze. "I…ah…no. No, I wouldn't, Your Grace," she said. "I mean, I was worried that Lady Celeste had been reading your fiancée's books in secret…which is why I decided to hide them. But other than that, I really haven't heard a thing. Well, apart from what Nurse

Quincey told me about Miss Jones's pressing need to visit her sister. And of course it was quite wrong of me to speculate that it had something to do with that horrid newspaper article in the *London Tatler*. I really do want to reassure you again that I'm not one to listen to gossip. Or spread it."

Little liar, thought Dominic. While he was tempted to challenge her outright and ask if she preferred to listen at keyholes so she could glean her gossip firsthand, he decided to try a different, more subtle tack. He'd rather Miss Sharp disclose what she'd done to make Artemis leave instead of forcing an admission from her. It was time to drop a few innuendo-laden bread crumbs himself.

"Hmmm. I suppose it's all for the best, really," said Dominic, "that Miss Jones is away at present. Putting aside all questions of taste, I'll admit I've had some doubts for a little while… about certain things…" He sighed heavily and flipped through the pages of Artemis's book. "You think you know someone, and before too long she shows her true colors, revealing the sad fact that she's not as honest, trustworthy, and dependable as you thought. When I heard about this Lydia Lovelace business in connection with my fiancée…" He affected another sigh and shook his head, letting the silence extend.

As Dominic expected, Miss Sharp's expression shifted from the realms of "concerned" into a look that was practically alight with eagerness, perhaps even bordering on bloodthirsty glee. "Oh, Your Grace, I'm so, so relieved to hear that you *are* aware of the situation after all. It has been *such* a weight on my mind, knowing Miss Jones is actually that awful author Lydia Lovelace. I wasn't sure what to do when I first learned the terrible truth, but when it was clear that Miss Jones was continuing to corrupt Lady Celeste's mind with her abominable books and outlandish, bordering on outrageous ideas, I simply had to act. And it didn't take much, you'll be relieved to hear." Her mouth curved into a smug, superior smile. "Just the mere hint of exposing her shocking secret to Lady Northam and to the newspapers was enough to send her packing. I'm afraid your assessment of your fiancée's character is correct. She truly isn't honest, trustworthy, or dependable."

Dominic cocked a sardonic brow. "Actually, that particular comment was about *you*, Miss Sharp. It seems you've misread the situation entirely. And it disappoints me—nay, it angers me—to hear you proudly profess that you would stoop so low as to quite blithely threaten the woman that I love. The woman that I'm going to marry."

"Oh... But...I... That's not..." the governess began, hands fluttering wildly about her like a pair of mad butterflies, but Dominic cut her off.

"I do not want to hear your attempts to justify your actions, Miss Sharp. Suffice it to say, it is not your place to cast aspersions on my fiancée's character or to take matters into your own hands. And in a malicious, underhanded manner that does you no credit. What sort of person threatens to blackmail someone else? You know that's a crime, don't you, Miss Sharp?"

"But...I thought..." Miss Sharp lifted her chin. Her bottom lip trembled, but only for a moment before she mastered her emotions and said, "I was only trying to protect your daughter, Your Grace. I believed that your opinion was similar to mine when it came to Lydia Lovelace's books. That you agreed with me that they were harmful and that Lady Celeste shouldn't read such rubbish. How was I to know that you no longer subscribed to that view? I was motivated to safeguard my charge from harm, nothing more."

"Well, it seems that my views were wrong, Miss Sharp. My daughter has since convinced me to try Miss Lovelace's—or should I say Miss Jones's?—books"—he raised *Lady Violetta and the Vengeful Vampyre* in the air by way of demonstration— "and so far, what I've read is well plotted, beautifully written, and thoroughly captivating. Yes, there are some scenes that describe romantic trysts, but they are not as graphic as I initially thought. I'm certain Chapman and Hall would not deign to publish my fiancée's novels if they were *that* vulgar and offensive.

"And while I do appreciate that you were trying to protect Celeste, your methods were entirely objectionable. I'm sad to say, your character, which I once believed to be above reproach, is wanting. You lack integrity, compassion, and discretion. And because of that, I'm afraid that I can no longer employ you as my daughter's governess."

Although it took some effort, Dominic pushed himself to his feet. "My sister, Lady Northam, will see to it that you find another situation. And if you even think of breathing a word about my fiancée's pseudonym to another living soul"—he eyed the governess through slitted lids—"I'll have you charged with blackmail, and you can be damn certain that you'll never find employment with another peer's family ever again. Who would want to hire a governess who cannot be trusted to keep confidences? But would instead wield them as a weapon?"

"Oh…Oh, Your Grace… I would never…" Miss Sharp had begun to wring her hands. Desperation and tears filled her eyes. "I promise you that I won't say a thing. To anyone. Ever. I give you my word."

"Under the circumstances, your word will not be enough. After such a betrayal, you no longer have one iota of my trust,

Miss Sharp. I'll have Morton draw up a contract—a confidentiality agreement so to speak—which I'll have you sign before
you leave. I expect you to be packed and gone from here by the
end of the day. Which I'll warrant is more time than you gave
Miss Jones when you threatened her. Now you may go." He
nodded toward the door. "I have much to do."

"Yes, Your Grace. I wish you well, Your Grace." The apparently chastened governess dipped into a curtsy and then she
hurried from the room. After the door closed behind her,
Dominic was certain he heard a choked sob or two, but he
had little sympathy for the perfidious, far too holier-than-thou
woman.

He rang for Morton, and after instructing him what to put
in Miss Sharp's contract—the man possessed a law degree from
Cambridge and had once practiced as a solicitor—Dominic
settled into his favorite chair by the fireside and began to read
Artemis's book again. He probably should return to bed, but
damn it, he needed to do something to keep his mind busy
while he waited to hear back from his fiancée.

And Celeste had been right. The writing was exceptional. It
was the sort of book that was impossible to put down.

Chapter Thirty-Three

ARTEMIS STOOD ON THE PLATFORM OF PANGBOURNE Station, her hands trembling as she accepted a telegram from the lad at the telegraph office.

A telegram from Dominic.

And then after she'd read it, all she could do was clutch the piece of paper to her chest. Even though the weather had turned inclement and rain bucketed down beyond the portico where she sheltered, her heart beat a joyous rhythm. *He's all right. He's all right. He's all right. He's all right.*

Brushing away the tears distorting her vision, she perused her fiancé's words once again to make sure she wasn't dreaming.

> *My beloved A.,*
>
> *Good news! My fever broke late last night. On the mend & I remember everything! By the time you receive this, Det. L. will have arrested Lord G. I hope all is well with you & your family. I count the hours until I can see you again.*
>
> Yours utterly & completely,
D.

Not only was Dominic safe and sound, and all but professing that he loved her, but Gascoyne would no longer pose a threat to him or anyone else.

Artemis glanced at the clock suspended above the stationmaster's office. It was almost a quarter to ten. She estimated she had just enough time to dash off a quick reply to Dominic to let him know she was on her way back to Dartmoor House and to compose a message for Aunt Roberta's coachman to take back to Highfield Hall. Phoebe deserved to know about Gascoyne's downfall. While the viscount's arrest for the attempted murder of Dominic couldn't repair the damage he'd done to Phoebe's reputation and her heart, at least her sister would know fate was meting out some sort of punishment to the man who'd deliberately used her to further his own sick ends.

Artemis pushed Dominic's telegram into her pocket, and after hefting her overstuffed carpetbag into her hand, she hurried over to the telegraph office.

> *My darling D.,*
>
> *I'm overjoyed to hear that you are recovering & that G. will be brought to justice. About to catch the 10 a.m. train to Paddington from Pangbourne. Will be at your side before noon.*
>
> > *Yours entirely & unreservedly,*
> > *A.*

She hesitated, and the clerk behind the counter raised an eyebrow. "Is that all, miss?" he asked.

Artemis frowned. Should she broach the potentially volatile

topic of her alter ego and Miss Sharp's ultimatum? It was clear Dominic didn't know anything about that particular matter yet. Her joy might be short lived if he rejected her for her lack of honesty and the fact she was Lydia Lovelace.

But she didn't have time to worry about that now. In less than two hours, she would be with Dominic, and they could sort everything out face-to-face.

For better or for worse.

Pushing aside her apprehension, Artemis smiled at the clerk. "Yes, that's all. Thank you."

She paid the fee to send the telegram and just as she'd fare-welled Aunt Roberta's coachman, the train to London pulled into the station.

I'm coming, Dominic, she whispered to herself as she claimed a well-padded seat in one of the first-class carriages. *I just pray that you can forgive me for not being honest with you about who I really am.*

———

The morning had turned dark—rain poured down in buckets in Belgrave Square—and Dominic glanced at the longcase clock for what seemed like the thousandth time. It was well after half-past ten. His telegram to Artemis had been sent hours ago, and there was apparently a telegraph office at Pangbourne Station, a mere two miles from Highfield Hall, so surely Artemis would have received it by now. Perhaps he should send another, informing her that Miss Rosalind Sharp had been given her marching orders and there was nothing to fear. That Artemis's secret was safe. That he loved her unconditionally. If only he was strong enough to jump on a bloody train so he could tell her in person—

His frustrated thoughts were interrupted by another knock at the door. It was Morton, ushering in a rather damp-looking Detective Lawrence at long last.

"Your Grace, my sincerest apologies for the delay in reporting back to you," began the tall, barrel-chested detective, his expression as somber as a mortician's. Indeed, the man appeared almost nervous as he shifted his weight from one foot to the other and gripped his dripping beaver hat in his hands. "But there's been an unforeseen development in the case."

"Oh, yes?" Dominic put down Artemis's book and frowned. Apprehension gnawed at his belly. "What's happened?"

Detective Lawrence's Adam's apple bobbed above his starched collar. "I don't want to alarm you, but at 3:00 a.m. when we attempted to bring Gascoyne into custody at one of his clubs—the Firebrand, in fact—he gave us the slip. Through a secret passage in the club's cellar that we knew nothing about."

"So he's currently at large," said Dominic grimly.

"I'm afraid so, Your Grace. But I have men watching his usual haunts, his town house, all of the train stations, and the main roads in and out of London. There are also several officers watching both Dartmoor House and Northam House as we speak. Considering Gascoyne has considerable assets in America, I suspect he will try to flee the country via one of the ports rather than come after you or anyone you care about. But I thought it prudent to err on the side of caution. I agree with you that the man is unpredictable with a vicious streak."

Bloody hell. Dominic dragged a hand down his face. A breath-stealing combination of anger and alarm gripped his gut. If Gascoyne tried to enter his home or Edward and Horatia's, he'd rip the mongrel apart with his bare hands, wounded shoulder or not.

Thank God Artemis was in Berkshire.

Although she might very well be en route to Paddington Station if she *had* received his telegram in time and had decided to return. He glanced at the clock again. It was almost a quarter to eleven. Morton had informed him earlier that the first train from Pangbourne Station to London departed at ten o'clock, and the journey took precisely one hour and fifteen minutes. In half an hour, Artemis might be stepping off the train at Paddington.

And Gascoyne was out there somewhere. Perhaps he was even at Paddington Station right at this moment, trying to slip onto a train heading to Bristol where the head office of Gibbs's Shipping, his late wife's company, was located.

Jesus Christ and all his saints...

Dominic hauled himself to his feet. "Are you sure you have enough men out there keeping a watch on Paddington Station, Detective Lawrence? Because my fiancée might be arriving on a train—"

There was another knock at the door, and Morton admitted a footman bearing a folded piece of paper.

A telegram. From Artemis.

As Dominic eagerly scanned the message, joy warred with acute trepidation. When his gaze snagged on the last few words, his heart clenched.

Yours entirely & unreservedly,

A.

If anything happened to Artemis...

"Morton, get my greatcoat and hail a hackney. I'm going to Paddington. Artemis is arriving in thirty minutes."

"No need for the hackney, Your Grace," said Lawrence. "I have a carriage waiting outside. I know the weather is abysmal, but if the traffic isn't too bad, we should be there in fifteen."

"Good," said Dominic. "There's no time to waste."

Chapter Thirty-Four

ARTEMIS HOISTED HER CARPETBAG IN ONE GLOVED HAND and lifted her skirts with the other as she alighted from the train and wrestled her way through the bustling throng on Paddington Station's Platform One. At least on this occasion, she didn't have to worry about her traveling trunks going astray. In her haste to return to London, she'd packed a minimal amount of clothing and personal items.

A wry smile tugged at the corner of her mouth. The weight of her carpetbag seemed to belie that fact. And as usual, she'd neglected to bring an umbrella. To make matters worse, she'd chosen to wear a completely impractical walking gown of Sèvre's blue sateen with a profusion of frothy white lace spilling from the sleeves. Her largely ornamental straw bonnet adorned with deep-blue satin ribbon and white feathers was perched at a precarious angle on top of her simply styled curls. For once, it seemed her feminine vanity had reared its head because she'd wanted to look pretty for Dominic.

Overhead, rain hammered down on the station's wrought-iron and glass roof. She'd be soaked within the space of five seconds when she emerged onto the street and tried to hail a hackney cab.

She *almost* laughed then. So much for looking pretty. Although, it wasn't as though Dominic hadn't seen her soaking wet before. Not that her appearance would matter one jot if he couldn't forgive her for her duplicity.

Surely, he'll understand, she told herself for the hundredth time as she put her head down and stepped into the pouring rain. Dominic was a reasonable man. A progressive thinker. He wasn't puritanical or a stickler for the rules. Certainly not when he was with her. When he was truly being himself.

In any event, she supposed she would soon find out how far his open-mindedness extended.

Up ahead through the sheets of rain and shifting forest of umbrellas, she could see quite a few hackney cabs clustered at the curb. Hopefully, at least one of them was free. Picking up her skirts, she sidestepped an enormous puddle and then her shoulder collided with a wall of muscle cloaked in damp black wool.

A hand shot out and gripped her upper arm with such brutal force, Artemis gasped.

"Well, well, well," said a low voice dripping with derision close to her ear. "Fancy meeting you here, Miss Artemis Jones."

The traffic was worse than bad. It was abominable.

Detective Lawrence's coach had crawled from one impossible snarl to the next through the teeming streets of London. If Dominic possessed the stamina, he would have jumped out and run the remaining distance to Paddington Station.

By the time they'd turned the corner from Gloucester Terrace into Praed Street, then inched toward the Great Western Royal Hotel and the station's entrance at the pace of a hobbled snail, Dominic was champing at the bit with frustration. According to his pocket watch, it was already twenty minutes past eleven. "This rain is making it impossible to see a God damn thing," he growled, rubbing at the befogged window with his coat sleeve. "Artemis is out there somewhere. And bloody Gascoyne could be too."

"Agreed, Your Grace. But rest assured, I have men everywhere," said Detective Lawrence. "The next train to Bristol departs at half-past eleven. If Lord Gascoyne is anywhere about, we'll nab him even before he reaches the platform."

"Yes, but what if he's turned up his collar and he's hiding beneath a hat and umbrella?" challenged Dominic. "Do all of your officers know exactly what he looks like?"

"Most of them have been given a detailed description and have seen a rough sketch," said Lawrence. "Only three have met him in the flesh."

"Christ," muttered Dominic. He rapped on the carriage roof, and before it had even stopped, he was throwing open the door and leaping out into the deluge.

Screw Gascoyne. As long as Artemis was safe, the dog could go to the devil.

Ignoring the throb of his shoulder and the thundering of his heart, Dominic charged through the rain toward the station's entrance.

There. Up ahead in the far distance… Was that Artemis?

Dominic caught a flash of auburn hair that beckoned to him like a flame through the scudding rain and chaotic flow of pedestrians. With no umbrella to speak of and a ridiculously small bonnet that offered little in the way of protection, the woman's red locks, although darkened by the rain, still stood out.

It *was* Artemis. Dominic would recognize her anywhere.

He increased his pace, not caring who he bumped into and pushed past in his haste to reach her side.

And then his heart all but slammed to a stop when he saw

that Artemis—it *was* her—had crashed into another pedestrian by a glut of hackney cabs near the curb. A tall man with an umbrella. He'd apparently seized her by the upper arm and was now bending low to speak in her ear.

Gascoyne.

Bloody blazing blistering bollocks.

———

"Lord Gascoyne," breathed Artemis. Fear clamped her chest in a vise as she stared up into the viscount's sneering face. "You're... you're not..." Somehow, she tamped down the terror ricocheting through her veins and marshaled her thoughts. "You're supposed to be in police custody."

He smirked. "Well clearly, I'm not."

Anger blazed through Artemis, and she jerked her arm in an attempt to free herself from his bruising grip. "Let me go," she hissed, blasting him with the full force of her she-devil glare. "Leave me be or I'll scream blue murder."

"I don't think so, my dear," he said. "You're my insurance policy. You're coming with me to Bristol."

"What? Are you planning to skewer with me with the tip of your umbrella?" she snapped back, struggling against his hold again. "I'm not budging, you idiotic arse. I won't be your damn hostage. You can go to Hades."

A muscle in Gascoyne's jaw flickered, and his eyes gleamed with a strange, feral light. In the next second, his umbrella fell to the ground, and he was reaching into his greatcoat pocket. The uncompromising muzzle of a pistol pressed against her side.

Oh no. Artemis froze.

"Perhaps this"—Gascoyne jabbed her with the pistol again—"will change your mind, Miss Jones." A wolfish grin that was more of a snarl curled his lips. "Unless you want to feel a bullet ripping through your chest cavity and shredding your lungs and heart to pieces, I suggest you start walking."

"Not bloody likely," Artemis muttered. Whether it was her instinct to survive or utter stupidity, she couldn't be sure, but with all of her might, she swung her free arm, and her carpetbag collected Gascoyne in the ribs. Hard.

The viscount emitted an *oof*, stumbled on the slick cobblestones, and then in the next instant, he was being tackled. Thrown to the ground by another assailant. A man.

Dominic!

Artemis cried out as the sharp crack of a pistol shot rang out. All around her, chaos erupted. Men shouted. Women screamed.

But Artemis was barely aware of any of it. All she could see was Dominic.

Dominic's prone form on top of Gascoyne.

Her heart stumbled. Her jagged breath sawed in and out. Time seemed to fracture and still.

And then Dominic rolled to the side and, with a deep groan, hauled himself to his knees. Beneath the folds of his greatcoat, Artemis could see that his arm was in a sling, but otherwise he seemed to be all right.

"Dominic! Oh, thank God." She dropped to her knees beside him, and as the man she loved beyond all understanding lashed her body to his with his good arm, her gaze fell on Gascoyne.

The viscount was dead. His sightless eyes were open, staring up into the leaden sky as the drumming rain continued to fall. A dark, bloodred stain bloomed across the front of his pale-gray waistcoat.

"Don't look, my love," murmured Dominic against her sodden hair. "Don't look."

"I won't." Artemis reached up and gently caught her fiancé's beloved face with one gloved hand. "All I see is you, Dominic." She swallowed. Licked her lips and at last found the courage to utter the three words she'd been dying to say to him for so very long. "I love you."

His beautiful, chiseled mouth tilted into a soft smile. "I know. Entirely and unreservedly?"

"Utterly and completely," she whispered. "I'm yours forever. If you'll still have me." Drawing a shaky breath, she locked her gaze with his. "But there's something I need to tell you."

Dominic's lips parted as though he were about to respond, but then a dark, towering shadow loomed over them.

"I'm sorry to interrupt you two lovebirds, but I've got a crime scene to sort out," said Detective Lawrence. "And Your Grace, you might want to get out of the rain before you catch cold. You're not going to succumb to another bloody fever on my watch."

"Nor mine," said Artemis.

"Good. You can take my coach back to Belgrave Square," the detective continued as Dominic climbed to his feet with Artemis's help. "I witnessed everything that happened, and Gascoyne has no one to blame but himself for his demise. Your formal statements can wait until later."

Chapter Thirty-Five

ONCE THEY WERE SETTLED INSIDE DETECTIVE LAWRENCE'S carriage and it had moved off, Dominic gathered Artemis into his arms. He buried his face in her hair. Inhaled her heavenly scent.

When he'd seen Gascoyne trying to haul her off, when he'd caught a glimpse of a pistol pressed into her ribs, he'd seen red.

Christ, if anything had happened to her...

But it hadn't and she was here. Soaked to the skin but otherwise whole and unharmed.

And she loved him.

She loves me... This beautiful, brave, fiercely intelligent woman loves me.

And she deserved to know that he loved her too.

He gently brushed a dripping lock of hair away from her cheek and tucked it behind the shell of her ear. "Artemis..."

She stiffened in his arms. "Oh, drat and Dicken's dingleberries," she muttered, raising her head. "I've left my carpetbag behind. We have to go back. At once."

Dominic gave a disgruntled grunt as he adjusted his position on the hard seat. "Don't worry. I'll buy you another and replace everything that's in it." Egads. Why was it so bloody difficult to tell this woman that he loved her?

But Artemis gave an emphatic shake of her head. "You can't. Not everything. You see, there's a...a special notebook inside. One that I regard as irreplaceable. I simply can't lose it."

Ah… Dominic caught her chin between gentle fingers as understanding dawned. "Would that notebook happen to contain your next manuscript, Miss Lovelace?" he asked softly. "*Lady Mirabella and the Midnight Monk?*"

She gasped and her eyes widened. But before she could respond, he'd knocked on the carriage roof and ordered the driver to stop. "Don't worry, I'll be back with your carpetbag and your manuscript in a jiffy," he said as he threw open the door.

"No, Dominic. Wait. I'll go," she said, grasping his coat sleeve, attempting to stay him. "You shouldn't be out in the rain."

But it was too late. He'd already climbed out and was retracing his steps. His shoulder might be throbbing like hell and he might feel like he was seventy-eight, not thirty-eight—but he would get Artemis's manuscript back if it was the last thing he did.

When he returned a few minutes later, bag in hand, Artemis cried, "Oh, thank heavens."

"One of Detective Lawrence's officers was looking after it," said Dominic as he joined Artemis in the cab again, depositing the sodden bag beside her. He frowned with concern as she began to fumble with the buckle. "I hope your notebook is all right."

"So do I." The clasp came undone, and within a fraction of a second, she'd pulled a book bound in red leather from a tangle of linen. "It's fine," she murmured as she quickly flipped through the pages. Then she looked up. Confusion clouded her eyes as she searched his gaze. "How…how did you know? About any of this? About who I really am?"

Dominic smiled. "I'm a duke. I'm all powerful and all knowing."

As he expected, Artemis rallied. "Balderdash," she said with a small snort of laughter, then gave him a gentle poke in the chest. "Out with it. Confess."

He laughed too. "I will. I will. But here in the back of this rather uncomfortable and none-too-clean"—he wrinkled his nose—"police carriage, I'm only prepared to give you an abridged explanation."

Artemis's fulsome bottom lip dipped into an exaggerated pout. "Very well. At least tell me how long you've known that I'm Lydia Lovelace."

"Only since this morning. And I *do* know everything." He gentled his tone as he continued, "I know what that two-faced, far-too-priggish governess did to you. That she coerced you into leaving me by threatening to expose your secret."

"Oh…" Artemis paled. "I see…" She sighed, the sound infinitely sad. Remorse filled her eyes as she said, "I didn't want to go, Dominic. More than anything, I wanted to stay with you, but I was so terrified. If Miss Sharp had gone to the newspapers, my dreams of starting a college would have been destroyed. But then…" Her gaze firmed and she lifted her chin a fraction. "This morning I realized something. Something profoundly import-ant. I decided that I didn't care if Miss High-and-Mighty Sharp ruined my reputation beyond repair. I *had* to return. Indeed, I was waiting for the train at Pangbourne Station even before I received your telegram telling me that your fever had broken. I had to be with you because you, my darling Dominic, mean more to me than anything else in this world.

"Of course," she added, "part of me was filled with dread at just the thought of having to tell you that I'm Lydia Lovelace. I was worried that you too would condemn me for the books that I write and agree that I'm not fit to open a school."

"Oh, my darling. My love—" Dominic began to gather her close to kiss her doubts away, but Artemis wriggled back.

"But wait, that's not all I have to confess." She faced him, her expression still grave. "Not only did I conceal the fact that I'm an author you disdain, but I also supplied Celeste with copies of my books. Behind your back."

He smiled gently and stroked her cheek with the back of his fingers. "I know that too. Celeste told me."

"And you're not angry with me? Or with her?"

Dominic offered her a reassuring smile. "To be perfectly honest, I *was* taken aback. At least at first. But no, I'm not angry. Not with either of you. Far from it." His smile turned wry. "Almost dying does tend to give one a different outlook on life. And I do understand why you hid your writing career from me. Because of my concerns about Celeste, I *had* been quite disparaging about your alter ego's books. But it seems my contempt was entirely unwarranted. Arrogant ass that I am, I scoffed because I was ignorant. However"—he gave her a slow grin—"I hope you'll be pleased to learn that at Celeste's urging, I've started to read *Lady Violetta and the Vengeful Vampyre*, and I'm utterly addicted. Celeste was right. You are supremely talented, my lovely Artemis. And I can't wait to continue reading your book as soon as I get the chance."

"Oh…" Artemis's cheeks had turned a delightful shade of pink. "You really think I'm talented?"

"Very much so. You'll also be pleased to know that Miss Rosalind Sharp has been dismissed, effective immediately. When she proudly declared that she'd forced you to leave, I sacked her on the spot. And, before you begin to fret that she'll go to the newspapers, she won't. She's going to sign a legally binding confidentiality agreement in exchange for my silence about her misconduct. So you have nothing to fear, my love. Not anymore."

"I simply don't have enough words to thank you," Artemis whispered. "You've done so much for me. Avenged my sister. Saved my life." She raised her notebook. "My manuscript. My reputation. Yet when you needed me"—shame weighted her words—"I left you. I shouldn't have."

"You have nothing to feel guilty about, Artemis. I remember you. At my side. Taking care of me. Whispering that you loved me. That our engagement was real and that you wanted to marry me. The things that you said gave me such hope."

"I meant it," she said softly. "Every single word."

"And I…" Dominic drew a deep breath. "I love you too, Artemis Jones. My heart, such as it is, is yours and yours alone. And even if you tell me that you don't want children, or if fate decrees that we cannot—whatever the reason—I want you to know that it doesn't matter. *You* are enough for me. You are *everything* to me. I only need you."

"Oh, Dominic." Artemis cradled his jaw with trembling fingers. "When we were at Ashburn Abbey, I realized that I *do* want to have a child with you. I know, deep in my heart, that if we are so blessed, it would bring me such joy."

He swallowed. "You do? Truly?"

"Yes." She smiled, her beautiful brown eyes shimmering with tears. "I do. Because I trust you. And I trust in the idea of 'us.' For the very first time in my life, I believe that happily-ever-afters are not only found at the end of a book. They *are* real."

"Artemis…" A great wave of emotion rushing through him, Dominic shifted his head and kissed her palm. His voice was low and raw as he at last told her all of the things that had been brimming inside him for so long. "My love, if you only knew the depth of my feeling for you. You are my lifeblood. The reason my heart beats. You are the light that warms my very soul and I cannot live without you. Tell me again that you love me." Dominic slid a hand into the wet, tangled curls at Artemis's nape. Rested his forehead against hers. "Tell me that you're mine."

"I love you. I'm yours," she whispered. "Forever and always."

Dominic wasn't sure who initiated the kiss first, but in the end, it didn't matter. His mouth found Artemis's, and his heart rejoiced at the feel of her lush, lithe body in his arms, the way her fingers curled into his damp hair, the press of her sweet lips against his, the supple stroke of her tongue. The delicious taste and scent of her. The little moan she made in her throat.

If he could capture this perfect moment and store it in a bottle, it would be all he'd ever need to sustain him until the end of his days.

When they at last drew apart, both breathless and disheveled and grinning like besotted fools, it was to discover that they'd arrived at Dartmoor House.

"Shall we go inside, my beautiful wife-to-be?" asked Dominic.

"We shall," agreed Artemis. "And I don't care who is about, or what anyone thinks, but I'm ordering a hot bath for both of us and then locking the door."

Dominic flashed her a deliberately wicked smile. "I concur. And afterward, when I retire to my bed to rest and recuperate, you can show me the inspiration for some of your books' saucier scenes."

"There's actually a bath scene in *Lady Mirabella and the Midnight Monk*," Artemis murmured as they ascended the stairs to the front door. "You can help me get the choreography right. If your titanic truncheon is up to it…"

"Oh, don't worry, my love. It's only my left shoulder that's temporarily out of commission. I'll be quite happy to demonstrate that everything else is in perfect working order."

And that's exactly what he did.

Epilogue

Somewhere in London. Several weeks later…

"WHAT ARE YOU UP TO, DOMINIC? I CAN'T SEE A BLASTED thing." The blindfold Artemis's new husband had fashioned from a black silk scarf had turned the bright, late spring day into night.

"If I tell you, it won't be a surprise, love," he said with a soft chuckle. "Trust me, I won't let you trip or fall. Just do as I say and follow my lead."

"Very well," Artemis grumbled as Dominic steered her along a cobbled pavement to heavens knew where. With one of his large hands at the small of her back and the other at her elbow, she trusted she was safe and wasn't in any imminent danger of stumbling and twisting her ankle or, worse, breaking her neck.

Hopefully, whatever Dominic had in mind wouldn't take too long. She had things to do, such as finishing all of her packing for their honeymoon. Just two days ago, she'd married Dominic by special license. It had been a quiet but joyous wedding ceremony at nearby St. Paul's Church at Knightsbridge, followed by an intimate reception at Dartmoor House. Both events were attended by only a handful of close family members and friends, including dear Lucy and Jane. However, Artemis and Dominic were lingering in London for a few more days because they were both obliged to complete a few essential duties before quitting Town for a Grand Tour of France, Switzerland, and Italy.

Indeed, this morning, Dominic had already conferred with various business colleagues and then they'd squeezed in a quick trip to the offices of Chapman and Hall just off the Strand so that Artemis could deliver the completed manuscript of *Lady Mirabella and the Midnight Monk* to her editor.

This mysterious excursion was apparently just a quick detour on the way home to Dartmoor House.

Deep down, Artemis was nothing but intrigued, even if she was a *teensy* bit piqued about being kept in the dark, both figuratively and literally.

They halted and Dominic prompted her to lift her skirts. "We've a short flight of stairs to scale and then we're almost there," he said.

Artemis did as he bade and then she heard the sound of a key turning in a lock. The soft creak of a door as it swung open. Dominic gently urged her to take a few more steps forward, the door snicked shut, and then he murmured, "Are you ready?"

She nodded, suddenly breathless with excitement. "Yes."

The blindfold loosened, then fell away, and Artemis found that she was in a large entry hall with a checkered floor of black and white marble; a vaulted ceiling with a glass dome skylight that let in a soft pool of sunlight; and an elegant, divided staircase of oak with a wrought-iron railing that swept up to a grand gallery. There were no furnishings to speak of, and the sound of Artemis's boot heels echoed throughout the brightly lit chamber as she turned around, taking everything in.

Curiosity curling through her, she said, "It's a vacant town house."

"It's more than that," said Dominic with a smile. "It's *your* town house, if you want it. And you can turn it into a ladies' academic college if you think it will suit."

Artemis's jaw dropped open. "You're not serious."

He grinned. "I'm perfectly serious. We had an agreement, Artemis. You helped me repair my relationship with Celeste ten times over, and now I'm helping you to realize your dream of opening your college. And to that end"—he reached inside his coat pocket and withdrew a slip of paper—"I also have a cheque made out to Artemis Winters, the Duchess of Dartmoor, in the amount of twenty thousand pounds. Of course, if it's not enough, I'm happy to provide you with whatever additional funds you require until you have everything that you need. And that includes any ongoing costs such as staff wages."

"Oh, Dominic." Artemis crossed the floor and took the cheque from him with shaking fingers. "I'm speechless. I never expected…" Her words trailed off as her voice cracked. "You are the most wonderful, remarkable man and I'm so grateful I bumped into you that day in the rain outside Paddington Station."

"We, my beautiful, clever wife, were meant to be," said Dominic, slipping his hands about her waist and drawing her near. "Fate has decreed it."

"I think you're right." Artemis smiled up at her handsome, generous husband. "And to acknowledge all that you've done for me, and to celebrate our union, I've decided this school will be called Dartmoor Ladies' College."

Dominic's gaze grew serious. "Are you certain? It is your brilliant idea. Your venture."

"I've never been more certain of anything. We've wedded our futures together, and your name is now mine too. Dartmoor Ladies' College it shall be."

Dominic tilted her chin up and kissed her gently. "I am honored indeed, Your Grace. You know, you don't have to say yes to these particular premises though. We can search elsewhere."

"Well, I *would* like to have a look around first to see what the rest of the rooms are like."

"Of course. A Grand Tour is in order."

A set of double doors opened onto a spacious chamber that appeared to be a disused library. Several denuded bookcases lined the wood-paneled walls, and at one end of the room stood a sizable oak desk that had apparently been left behind.

"What do you think of this piece, Your Grace?" asked Artemis as she sauntered over to the desk and then ran a gloved fingertip over the slightly dusty leather blotter.

She glanced back at her husband, who was watching her intently with a certain heated gleam in his eye. A look that made her insides melt with liquid longing.

"It's yours. If you want it," he said, his mouth tilting into a thoroughly enticing smile. Arms crossed, he was leaning a shoulder nonchalantly against the doorframe. Almost a month had passed since he'd been shot, and just looking at him now, it was difficult for Artemis to fathom that he'd hovered on the brink of life and death.

The mere thought of almost losing him made her want to celebrate every moment of their lives together even more. And of course, she couldn't wait to start a family with Dominic. Suddenly, such a petty task as packing didn't seem to matter.

"Hmmm… I'm not sure…" She released an exaggerated sigh and tugged off her gloves with calculated slowness. After placing them on the blotter, she then leaned suggestively over the edge of the desk. "Perhaps you could help me to test how sturdy it is, Your Grace," she said over her shoulder, her voice a low, provocative purr.

Her invitation to make love couldn't have been more blatant, and within moments, Dominic had crossed the room to join her.

"God, how I love you, Artemis," he groaned against her ear before turning her and effortlessly lifting her onto the desk. His kiss was slow and imbued with such lingering reverence that Artemis thought her heart might burst from the sheer, transcendent joy flowing through it. A child would be a blessing, but the gift of them, together and whole and happy, was more than enough too. Whatever the future held, they would both embrace it, because they had each other.

Keep reading for an excerpt of the
next in the Byronic Book Club series

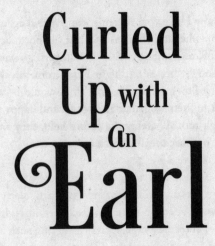

Curled
Up with
an
Earl

Chapter One

Hampstead Heath
Summer 1858

AT THE AGE OF EIGHT-AND-TWENTY, MISS LUCY BERTRAM could easily, perhaps even quite confidently, define the sort of person she was: thoughtful, analytical, observant, practical, diligent, imaginative, kind.

Also, most unfortunately, quivering-like-a-barely-set-blancmange nervous around strangers—particularly members of the opposite sex who were prospective suitors. Indeed, the mere idea of entering a high society gathering such as a ball or a soiree—even a dinner party—where countless sets of eyes were bound to settle upon her, was enough to make her feel positively faint with terror or cast up her accounts. Possibly both.

Although, at this present moment, Lucy was completely alone in a deserted rural laneway—unless one counted her family's ancient pony, Juniper, as company—so she wasn't nervous *precisely*. However, she could certainly own to feeling more than a little anxious and a great deal flummoxed. And while her powers of observation still appeared to be intact, her practical streak had all but deserted her. Because she simply had no clue how to go about dislodging the mired back wheel of her gig from a muddy ditch. At all.

As if that wasn't bad enough, there was a summer storm grumbling on the horizon. The roiling bank of dark-as-a-bruise clouds that had been brewing over London since mid-day was drawing ever closer, and the ominous low rumbles of thunder were making poor Juniper stamp and snort and twitch.

Of course, when Lucy had set out from her home, Fleetwood Hall, less than an hour ago to run a few errands in the nearby hamlet of Heathwick Green, she *had* noticed clouds amassing above Hampstead Heath, along with an unmistakable heavy sultriness in the air. It was the sort of sticky humidity that promised a downpour. But she'd dismissed any niggling concerns because Heathwick Green was so close to home, and it wasn't as though she hadn't made this trip with Juniper a thousand times over. And while the lane was muddy from a heavy rain shower earlier in the day, for the most part, it wasn't particularly boggy or hazardous.

However, what Lucy *hadn't* counted on was the enormous brown hare that had decided to dart from the prickly briar hedge, straight across Juniper's path. The hare's lightning speed and proximity had startled the usually unflappable pony and sent him off course toward the verge where the drainage was poor, and now they were well and truly stuck. No matter how much Lucy attempted to coax Juniper forward with gentle flicks of the reins and encouraging words, the gig hadn't budged more than an inch.

Fudge and fiddlesticks and fiddle-dee-dee. Huffing out an exasperated sigh, Lucy resigned herself to the fact she was going to get dirty and probably drenched to the bone as she gathered up her wide crinoline skirts of faded blue muslin and climbed down from the gig. As her kid leather boots sank into a patch of sucking mud, she winced. To say that her maid, Dotty, would not be happy would be an understatement.

Lucy wasn't particularly happy either, not when she glanced under the gig and spotted the extent of the problem—or should she say the depth of it? The ditch was a veritable quagmire and there was no doubt in her mind that Juniper wouldn't have the strength to pull the vehicle free. It was rather a shame that "brute strength" wasn't one of her own defining attributes because then she might be able to give Juniper a helping hand with a bit of a heave-ho from the rear.

On the positive side, Fleetwood Hall wasn't that far away. If she unstrapped Juniper and led him home—there was no way Lucy could ride bareback in her present attire—they'd be there within twenty minutes, and they *might* escape the approaching tempest. But that would also mean she'd have to abandon the gig, and while she liked to think that no one would make off with it, someone might.

That eventuality would be nothing short of a disaster. Her father, Sir Oswald, could ill afford such a loss at this point in time. They were already down to a skeleton staff at Fleetwood Hall, and as it was, Lucy was constantly battling to make ends meet with the limited household budget her father had allocated. The loss of the gig simply couldn't be borne. Not by her father, or herself. The little two-seater carriage meant that she could go wherever she liked, whenever she liked...even if that was just to Heathwick Green or to the village of Hampstead to run errands. Or most importantly, to the train station so she could travel to London to meet with her friends and fellow Byronic Book Club members, Jane Delaney and Artemis Winters, the newly wedded Duchess of Dartmoor.

Or to search for her brother.

Monty... It had been over four months since her older brother had fought with Father and had then disappeared into the night with a valise and without a word since. Lucy missed him desperately and because she was certain he didn't have any independent source of income, she was worried sick about how he'd been faring. Every time the post arrived, she prayed there'd be a letter from him—even if it was just a short note—reassuring her that he was all right. But since April, she'd heard nothing. And Father would not be drawn on the subject either—about whether he'd heard from Monty or what had led to their estrangement. But then, it wasn't unusual for her father to be uncommunicative, even grumpy of late. As soon as Lucy got back to Fleetwood, she would check the small bundle of mail she'd picked up from Heathwick Green's posting inn, The Wick and Whistle, to see if Monty had written to her. Just like she always did.

But first she had to get home.

Lucy impatiently pushed an errant lock of hair off her sticky cheek and glanced up and down Fleetwood Lane to see if anyone was headed her way—someone who might be able to render assistance. But the thoroughfare was deserted. Which wasn't all that surprising; no doubt other folk in the vicinity had already hurried home because of the impending storm.

As though the elements had heard her thoughts and wished to mock her for her hubris, the thunderclouds emitted a low warning growl and a sharp breeze caught at Lucy's bonnet and gown. Even the sun had now retreated.

There was nothing for it. She would have to free Juniper and take her chances that no one would steal the gig.

With another sigh, Lucy lifted up her skirts as best she could and gingerly picked her way through the treacherously slippery sludge to Juniper. The gray pony tossed his head and snorted as if to say, "Now hurry up. I don't have all day," and Lucy laughed.

"I'll have you free in a jiffy, my dear old boy," she said as she tugged off her gloves, tossed them onto the worn leather seat of the gig, then began to unharness the pony from the traces. There were umpteen straps and buckles but since her father had laid off Fleetwood Hall's groom several months ago, Lucy often helped the young stable boy, Freddy, with Juniper, so she knew what she was doing.

She'd just started to loosen the pony's breast-collar when there was an almighty clap of thunder and lightning flashed. A flock of jackdaws sheltering in a nearby oak tree shot into the air, squawking and shrieking, Juniper whinnied and shied... and in the very next moment, Lucy felt like she was skating on ice. Her feet went out from under her, and she fell backward, plopping unceremoniously onto her derriere with bone-jarring impact. Mud squelched between her fingers and oozed around her stocking-clad ankles and this time she couldn't stop herself from cursing aloud.

"Barnaby Rudge and buckets of fudge," she grumbled. Could this day get any worse?

It seemed it could because a shadow that was darker than the encroaching storm fell across her. Looking up, Lucy couldn't suppress a startled gasp. A ruggedly handsome man was staring down at her, his towering, broad-shouldered frame silhouetted against the mass of roiling black clouds behind him. For one wild moment she fancied that one of the ancient gods of the sky like Thor or Jupiter had descended from the heavens. If the stranger had been brandishing a thunderbolt or two instead of a carpetbag, she wouldn't have been the least surprised.

His cobalt-blue eyes were almost hidden by a tousled sweep of sable-brown hair. Save for the flicker of a dimple in one lean cheek and the twitch of amusement at the corner of his wide mouth, he'd be forbidding if not altogether intimidating. He seemed like the sort of man who could fell a man with one well-aimed punch. Or help to liberate a gig from a ditch.

He was certainly the type of man who could set someone like her to the blush. Especially when he doffed his wide-brimmed felt hat and drawled in a deeply rumbling Scots brogue, "Can I help, you, lass? You look like you're in a wee bit o' trouble."

"I…" Lucy's whole face felt as though it was burning. Her mouth had gone dry, and her stomach was a mass of knots. "Yes. Yes, thank you," she managed at last with a feeble smile.

"You're no' hurt, are you?" he asked as he put down the sizeable carpetbag and then extended one large bare hand toward her. His knuckles were scarred and scraped, his palms calloused—not the hands of a gentleman by any means.

Gentleman or not, Lucy couldn't very well refuse his offer to help. And despite his looming bulk, at this particular juncture, she couldn't see any reason *not* to trust him. His demeanor was pleasant enough.

Lucy wiped her mucky palm upon her skirts before she placed her hand in his. "My pride might be a little dented, but that's all," she muttered in answer to his question as she clambered to her feet. Although, if truth be told, she was a little winded and her tailbone might be a tad bruised. Not that she'd admit any of that to the stranger. Instead, she murmured an embarrassed, "Thank you."

Casting her gaze downward, she rubbed her hand upon her gown again and tried not to notice the snug fit of the stranger's buff breeches and top boots—the way the fabric and leather seemed to be molded to his muscular thighs and calves. She certainly couldn't bring herself to meet the man's curious eyes. Indeed, she couldn't bear to think what he thought of her at this present moment. If one looked up "mortified" in any dictionary, "Miss Lucinda Bertram" would be a fitting definition.

"It's no' a problem," he said, pulling a kerchief from the breast pocket of his dark green jacket. "Although, I'd be lying if I didna admit I'm more than a wee bit curious about what happened here…"

Lucy gratefully accepted the pristine square of linen and cleaned her fingers. "An unexpected series of mishaps I'm afraid," she began, then proceeded to describe in a great rush how the gig had become mired and what led to her fall. "If it hadn't been for that darned hare. The way that it shot out of nowhere without warning… Rather like a skittish March hare I suppose. We get a lot of them on the heath… Only it isn't March of course…" Oh dear, she was blathering on like *she* was utterly harebrained. It was something she did when she was anxious. She drew a deep breath in an attempt to halt her runaway tongue and to give her a moment to order her tumbling thoughts. "At any rate, unless I can free the gig, I'll have to leave it here. It truly is stuck."

The Scot grunted as he took back the soiled kerchief and wiped his own hand. "Aye. I can see that." A wry smile pulled at the corner of his mouth. "But no' for much longer."

Relief surged but ingrained politeness made Lucy say, "If you're sure it's not too much trouble…"

"Of course it's no', lass. Ye dinna want to get caught in the storm do you?" At that very moment, thunder boomed above them and the trees and briar hedge shivered and shook as a gust of icy wind tore past, chasing away any lingering sultriness in the air. It wouldn't be long before the downpour hit.

"Well, no…" Lucy conceded.

"Good." The stranger moved close to Juniper and began

to reharness the pony with an efficiency that was impressive. "I'm glad we agree. If you wouldna mind hopping back in your seat…"

Lucy frowned. "You can't mean to free the gig while I'm sitting in it. I'll just add unnecessary weight."

He glanced over his shoulder, openly smirking. "A slip of a lass like you? I dinna think so. Although…" He shucked off his jacket and tossed it, along with his hat, onto the gig's seat as though he were claiming a spot. "If you could persuade yer pony to put a *wee* bit more effort in while I'm pushing from behind, it would be greatly appreciated."

A splinter of irritation pricked. "The wheel *is* quite bogged," said Lucy, suddenly feeling the need to defend her pony. "And Juniper isn't as young and sprightly as he used to be. Are you sure you can manage this? I'd be happy to hold onto Juniper's bridle and coax him forward while you push."

"And risk having you get trampled on or run over if you lose yer footing again?" The Scot began to unfasten his cuffs and roll up the sleeves of his cambric shirt, exposing corded forearms that were strangely transfixing. "No' a chance. Trust me, pushing the gig while you are in it willna be a problem," he said. "So you'd best stop your havering and hop in before *I* pick you up and put you in."

What? Lucy's mouth dropped open. *What a managing, over-bearing, rude-word-that-rhymes-with-farce.*

Of course, she was grateful for the stranger's intervention, but she wouldn't be ordered about or manhandled like a sack of potatoes…even if it *might* be quite true that she could very well slip over again. However, before Lucy could formulate any sort of response—unlike her dear friend Artemis, witty retorts were not her forte—a raindrop, cold and heavy, plopped onto the tip of her nose. This was followed by a barrage of more icy raindrops, so rather than argue, Lucy swallowed her chagrin, hiked up her skirts, and scrambled into her seat.

As she took up the reins, the Scotsman rounded the back of the gig, and at his signal she urged Juniper forward with a few encouraging clicks of her tongue and a gentle snap of the reins. Within moments, the vehicle lurched forward and they were free of the mud. But not free of the rain.

It was now coming down in sheets and the wind had grown wilder, ripping at Lucy's bonnet with angry, icy fingers. If she didn't make haste, the gig would surely get washed away. Thunder cracked and lightning briefly illuminated the air. And then the Scotsman, carpetbag in hand, leaped into the gig beside her.

"Weel, what are you waiting for, lass?" he demanded over the roar of the storm. "I dinna ken where you are headed, but I'd suggest you get us out of this infernal weather before we drown or get struck by a bolt from above."

Despite his high-handedness, Lucy couldn't really quibble with the man's logic—he *had* gone out of his way to help her and she couldn't begrudge him a safe place to shelter—so she snapped the reins again and Juniper took off at a spanking clip. No doubt the pony wished to be home too.

Within the space of five minutes, they were turning the corner into the beech-lined lane leading to Fleetwood Hall. The Scotsman gave a low whistle as they passed between the estate's grand iron gates and followed the gravel-lined drive toward the three-story, white-washed manor house. "You live here?" he asked as he raked a dripping curtain of dark hair away from his brow and his gaze wandered over the building's ivy-clad façade.

Even though she was soaked to the skin, filthy, and shivering, Lucy couldn't hide her own slightly smug smirk. "Yes," she said as she directed Juniper around the back of the house toward the stables. "I do. Welcome to Fleetwood Hall. I'm sure my father, Sir Oswald Bertram, would like to meet you...Mister..."

"William Armstrong," he said and Lucy had to press her lips together to suppress a laugh. "Mr. Armstrong... How apt," she said before she could stop herself.

William Armstrong slid her a sideways glance from beneath the dark sweep of his spiky, rain-wet lashes. Lashes that Lucy would kill for. "You wouldna be laughing at my name now, would you, Miss Bertram?" he asked, wry amusement lacing his tone. "It is Miss Bertram, I presume?"

"I... Yes. It is. Lucinda Bertram." Despite the cold air, Lucy felt her cheeks grow warm. It seemed she had indeed teased the braw Scotsman.

How entirely singular. It was not like her at all. Miss Lucy Bertram didn't tease or flirt with gentlemen, especially not handsome-as-Heathcliff strangers with rough hands, granite-hewn jaws, sharply-cut cheekbones, and shoulders wide enough to fill a doorway. She usually turned bright red and stumbled over her words and retreated into her shell, much like a Galápagos tortoise. It was almost as though the raging storm had unleashed a reckless, more brazen streak inside her. One that she'd hitherto been unaware of.

How...novel.

They'd reached the stables and Lucy drew the gig to a halt in the yard beneath a slate-tiled portico. The cobblestones were awash and the rain still teemed down in buckets, but at least they were now out of the worst of the weather. The stable lad materialized from the shadows of the stalls and Lucy tossed the reins to him. "Make sure Juniper gets a nice rubdown, Freddy," she called down to the lanky youth, who'd already begun to release Juniper from the traces. "And an apple with his oats when he's cooled down. It's been a rather wild afternoon and he deserves a treat."

Freddy bobbed his head. "Yes, miss." He darted a curious glance at Mr. Armstrong but didn't say anything as the Scotsman leapt down from his seat and rounded the gig to Lucy's side.

Before she could finish gathering up her sodden skirts in preparation to alight, the Scot grasped her about the waist. "Here, let me give you a complete demonstration that I do indeed, live up to my name, Miss Bertram. Just so you dinna have any doubt."

Oh... Doubt was the farthest thing from Lucy's mind as she was lifted down from the gig as though she weighed nothing at all. As her feet met the slick cobblestones, she found herself looking up into William Armstrong's harshly handsome face. Somehow, her hands had landed upon the man's rock-hard chest—a chest that was clad in nothing but soaking wet, practically transparent linen.

Even more disconcerting was the fact that she could feel the Scot's touch as it lingered about her waist. The pressure of his fingers and the warmth of his palms seemed to penetrate her muslin gown, boned corset, and shift, heating her flesh beneath. The scent of rain, leather, and shaving soap—pleasantly astringent with notes of musk and spice—teased her senses. With his deep blue gaze, the way it held hers before dipping to her mouth... Every part of Lucy seemed to tighten yet soften at the same time. Goosebumps of awareness spread over her skin and her breath quickened as something hot and dark and thrilling unfurled inside her. Even the air around her and Mr. Armstrong seemed to crackle with expectation.

As Lucy's gaze brazenly lingered on the Scotsman's face, she was suddenly overwhelmed by the strangest sense that she'd met him before. That he was somehow familiar. But for the life of her, she couldn't quite place him.

Although, perhaps she'd once met him in a dream. Or in a book...

When her nose wasn't buried in a scientific journal or she wasn't gardening or peering through a microscope at a sample, she was invariably reading a Gothic romance novel. Yes, her fertile imagination had simply cast William Armstrong as the "brooding hero" in the unfolding drama of "getting caught in a late summer storm."

Thunder growled and lightning flickered and the strange spell enveloping Lucy was instantly broken. Mr. Armstrong seemed to wake up as well, as he dropped his hands and stepped back. "You should go inside, Miss Bertram," he said gruffly, nodding toward Fleetwood Hall. "Before you catch cold." His gaze had become shuttered. Remote. Perhaps even a little forbidding.

"Yes..." Lucy wiped the rain from her eyes, suddenly feeling chilled to the bone and oddly disappointed. But he was right. She should return to the house. She was cold and wet and grubby and it wasn't as though she hadn't a thousand things to do. Her father's latest journal article for the Linnean Society on strychnine trees endemic to Ceylon wouldn't get written by itself.

Nevertheless, decorum decreed that she couldn't just leave Mr. Armstrong here in the stables. She summoned a smile that she hoped would pass for inviting rather than uncertain. "You must accompany me. I can at least offer you a cup of tea and a slice of cake to say thank you for your help. And I'm sure you'd like to dry off." Goodness, he so needed to dry off and don some more clothing because the way the man's shirt clung to every hard plane and contour of his well-muscled upper body...it was most distracting. Lucy swallowed and, with an effort dragged her attention back to the Scotsman's face. "I'm sure my father will want to thank you as well, Mr. Armstrong."

But the Scot shook his head. "No. That willna be necessary. At least no' for now. I'll stay here and help Freddy with Juniper and the gig."

Help Freddy? Lucy's astonishment must have shown on her face because Mr. Armstrong cocked an eyebrow, before he executed a perfect bow. "Your father has recently hired me, Miss Bertram. I'm Fleetwood Hall's new groom and coachman. I'm to start today."

"Oh...I..." Lucy blinked. Why hadn't her father said anything? But then, this wouldn't be the first time he hadn't shared his plans with her. Time and again she'd been the last to know what was going on.

Mr. Armstrong must have mistaken her surprise for disbelief as he said, "I have a letter from Fleetwood's steward, Mr. Gilchrist, confirming my appointment to the position in my coat. And my references are in my carpetbag. I can fetch them if you'd like."

"No...no you don't need to do that, Mr. Armstrong. But I'll let my father and Mr. Gilchrist know that you are here. And please, do pop into the house for that tea and cake. Or perhaps you'd like something more substantial? Mrs. Gilchrist—she's our cook—will be more than happy to put something together for you. Some soup or a sandwich? I know there's some left over roast beef and Mrs. Gilchrist makes the most excellent mustard pickles. There might even be a pork pie in the larder.

And a barrel of small beer. We get it from The Wick and Whistle Inn at Heathwick Green. I don't drink it myself—I'm partial to tea and on special occasions, a sip of elderberry wine or sherry—but I know my father likes to have a glass or two after a hard ride…"

Oh, figgy jam and spotted dick. Lucy bit her lip to curb her babbling. The idea of seeing William Armstrong every single day was too much. She couldn't quite decide if her heart was tripping with nervous dread or excitement.

At any rate, Mr. Armstrong tilted his head in acknowledgement of her panicked outpouring. "All of that sounds verra satisfactory, Miss Bertram. As soon as I'm done here in the stables, I'll make myself presentable and put in an appearance." Then he turned his attention to Freddy and Juniper. Lucy was clearly dismissed.

Ha! To describe William Armstrong as high-handed would be an understatement. Lucy retrieved her basket and shopping parcels from the storage box at the back of the gig, then rushed across the stable yard toward Fleetwood Hall's rear entrance that led to the kitchen. As she paused in the open doorway, unlacing her mud encrusted boots, she glanced back toward the stables, and had the oddest sensation that Mr. Armstrong was watching her with his dark-as-a-midnight-sky eyes.

Surely not, thought Lucy. It was more likely the case that he was laughing as he recalled the moment he came upon her. A baronet's daughter, wallowing in the mud.

Oh, how lowering. Of course, she suspected the groom would never mention the incident again, but that hardly signified. Whenever she saw him, whenever she needed the gig or decided to go riding and he accompanied her—Father would insist that he did—she would know he'd be thinking about it.

Not only that, she'd also be forever thinking of the moment she'd foolishly imagined Mr. Armstrong might kiss her.

Lucy emitted a disgruntled sigh and firmly shut the door on the rain and her ridiculous fancies. She was the spinsterish daughter of a practically impoverished, somewhat eccentric baronet. She'd be more likely to achieve the impossible and gain entry to a university to study the botanical sciences and be accepted as a member of the male-dominated Linnean Society than wed any man, let alone someone like him.

The opinion of the mercurial Scots groom—*a servant*, she reminded herself, *that you met only half an hour ago*—shouldn't matter one iota. So, why oh why was a tiny part of her tempted to ask Dotty to press her best pink silk gown and dress her hair in ringlets and dig out her rose-scented perfume like she was some silly young debutante out to impress a gentleman at a ball?

Author's Note

To my dear readers, I just wanted to let you all know that I've taken a little bit of artistic license to tell my story.

Firstly, Heathwick Green is my own invention. It's very loosely based on the hamlet of Hatch's or Hatchett's Bottom in Hampstead Heath.

I also mention a scientific society—the London Botanical Society—which, from what I can fathom, existed from 1836 to 1856. It eventually became the Botanical Society of the British Isles and is presently known as the Botanical Society of Britain and Ireland. My story is set in 1858, so I'll readily confess that I've played with history by suggesting one of my characters—Miss Lucy Bertram—is still a member of the original Society, even though it seems to have been dissolved in 1856. However, it is quite true that the London Botanical Society did admit women as members.

Acknowledgments

To the fabulous Christa Désir, my editor at Sourcebooks Casablanca, thank you from the bottom of my heart for believing in my story. Your editorial input has been invaluable, and I will always be grateful for your insight and support.

A huge thank-you must also go to the entire Sourcebooks Casablanca team who've worked so hard to make this book the very best it can be.

As always, thank you to Jessica Alvarez, my wonderful agent, for all that you do. It's truly appreciated.

Last but not least, I must express my boundless gratitude to my family—my amazing husband and our two beautiful daughters. Thank you for supporting me every step of the way. I love you all so very much. (And to Richard, special thanks to you for the gift of "Lucifer's love truncheon." You never fail to make me smile.)

About the Author

Amy Rose Bennett is an Australian author who has a passion for penning emotion-packed historical romances. Of course, her strong-willed heroines and rakish heroes always find their happily ever after.

A former speech pathologist, Amy is happily married to her very own romantic hero and has two lovely, very accomplished adult daughters. When she's not creating stories, Amy loves to cook up a storm in the kitchen, lose herself in a good book or a witty rom-com, and when she can afford it, travel to all the places she writes about.